THE HISTORY
OF THE WORLD
BEGINS IN ICE

Praise for Kate Elliot's The History of the World Begins in Ice

"My kind of fantasy—grabbing a handful of genres, mashing them together like playdoh, then unfolding them into something genuinely fun. Fresh worldbuilding: check. Protagonist who feels real but extraordinary: check. Hot romance: check. Reimagines the global power balance if myths were real and the Black Death was just a leeeetle deathier — what, you didn't want that? Well, now you do."
— N.K. JEMISIN, author of The Broken Earth Trilogy

"*The History of the World Begins in Ice* is a delightful collection of stories from the brilliantly conceived universe of the Spiritwalker Trilogy. It also includes intriguing short essays about the characters and the world itself, complete with good, readable maps and some nifty illustrations. Highly recommended."
— KATHARINE KERR, the Deverry series and *Polar City Blues*

"I loved the world of the Spiritwalker Trilogy! Elliott's writing is original and fabulously imaginative, epic in scope, while never losing sight of the intense personal story of the characters."
— MARTHA WELLS, author of The Murderbot Diaries

"Such a richly textured book. So many different perspectives, so much lore, and the tour de force is that the stories stand alone but are all part of an ongoing tapestry. And craft essays too!"
— ALIETTE DE BODARD, author of *Navigational Entanglements*

"Brilliantly faceted, perfectly carved — Kate Elliott's boundless imagination is a jewel. A sparkling collection from a generous and incisive writer."
— C. J. LAVIGNE, author of *In Veritas*

THE HISTORY OF THE WORLD BEGINS IN ICE

STORIES AND ESSAYS FROM THE WORLD OF COLD MAGIC

KATE ELLIOTT

FAIRWOOD PRESS
Bonney Lake, WA

THE HISTORY OF THE WORLD BEGINS IN ICE
A Fairwood Press Book
November 2024

First Edition

Fairwood Press
21528 104th Street Court East
Bonney Lake, WA   98391
www.fairwoodpress.com

Cover art © 2024 by Tom Canty

Frontispiece © 2024 by Jody Lee

Color fold-out insert © 2013 by Julie Dillon

Interior story art © 2024 by Julie Dillon, Kelsey Liggett,
Todd Lockwood, Nilah Magruder, Lee Moyer, John Picacio, Jemma
Salume, C.N. Rowen Shiotsuki, Charles Tan, and Wendy Xu

Maps © Jeffrey L. Ward
Chapbook cover illustration © 2024 by Allaine B. Leoncio
Chapbook interior illustration © 2024 by Jody Lee

Cover and book design by Patrick Swenson

ISBN: 978-1-958880-19-7 (trade)
ISBN13: 978-1-958880-18-0 (limited)

Fairwood Press Trade Edition: November 2024
Printed in the United States of America

*To the many readers who, over the years, let me know
what they love in my writing, and thus keep me
determined to continue down my creative path.
This collection truly is for all of you.*

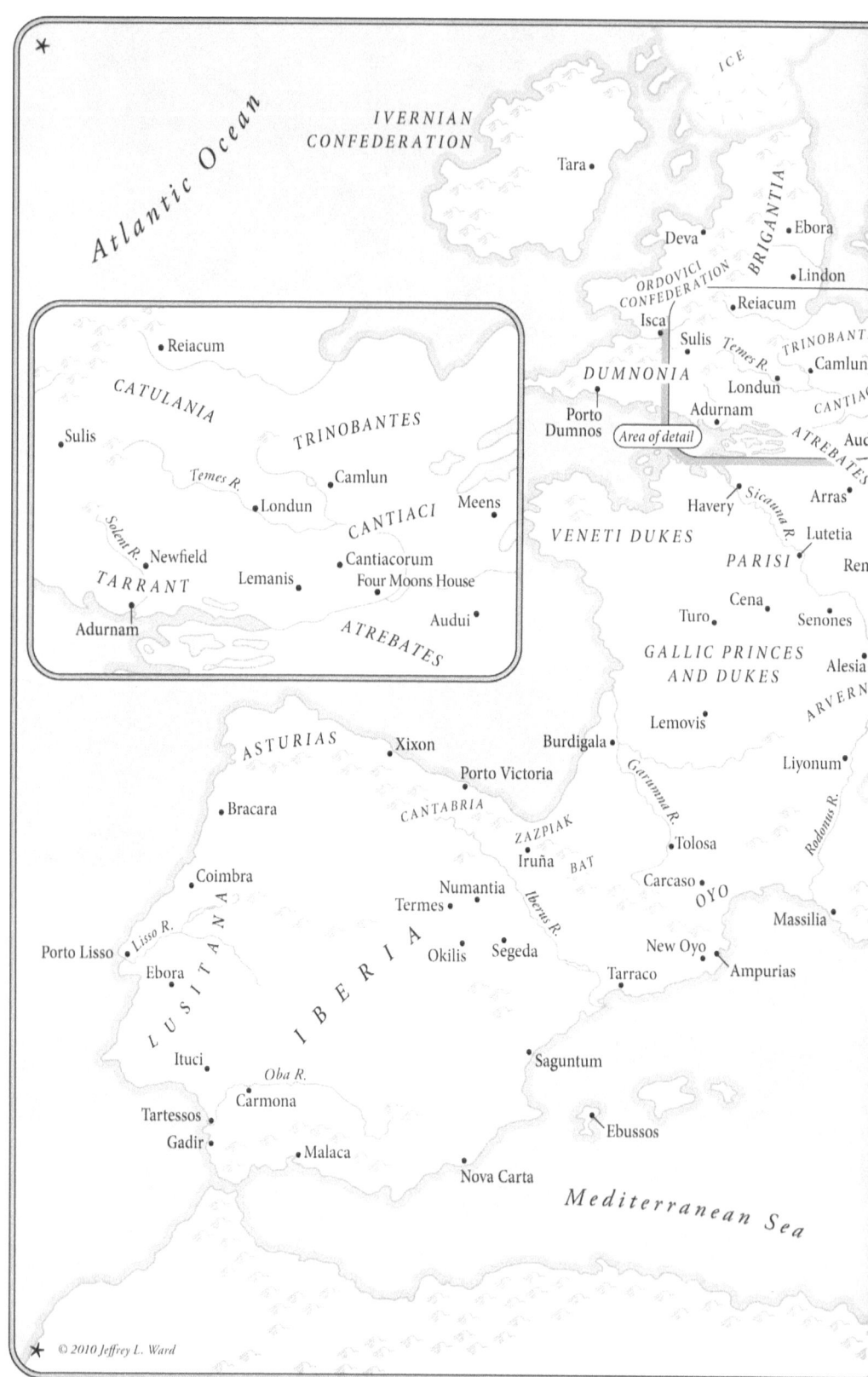

© 2010 Jeffrey L. Ward

Boreal Ice Sea

ICE

Baltic Ice Sea

BALT
NOMADS

Crescent
House

Carn

Cimbri

NEURI

BELGAE

Boreal R.

Tretchtum

Sala

Noviomagus

Anvers

Kumbi

Colonia

WAGADOU
FEDERATION

Rhenus R.

Trevorum

New Gao

Maiacum

Argentum

Raurica

HELVITIA

ICE

Mediolanum

Zena

Nikaia

Asa

EMPIRE OF ROME

Alalia

Rome

Tharros

Neapolis

Motya

Qart Hadast

New Jenne

Vistula R.

Zavist

TENE DUKEDOMS

Ister R.

Bruna

Vendunia

Grad

Emona

Tergeste

Salona

Europa

*

1837 (Augustan Year)

LUSATIA
PRINCIPALITIES

PANNONIA

Buda

EMPIRE OF THE AVAR

ILLYRIAN
PRINCES

Skodra

Dyrres

EMPIRE OF ROME

ICE

ICE

ICE

T R O L L   C O U N T R Y

KLAMATH

Spirit R.

Great R.

Flat R.

Whistler

Bah-kho-je

Cahoki

CHUMASH

DINÉTAH

Hopi

Taotho

Cemetery

INOKA

Zuni

T'iis R.

K'owi'n

Acoma

Miami

To'ono O'dahm

CONFEDERATION

OF THE PEOPLES

C O M A N C H E R I A

Chikasha

Great R.

Suma

Choctaw

Big R.

Syrakousai

PURÉPECHA

Aztlan

KINGDOM

Canpech

Tho

Tzintzuntzan

Tlaxcalla

New Gao

Tetzcoco

M A Y A

Tilantongo

M I X T E C

Noh Peten

Tehuantepec

CITY

STATES

ICE

ICE

TROLL COUNTRY

HAUDENOSAUNEE

OyoR.

Adananv

Savana R.

TSA-LA-GI

1838 (Augustan Year)

THREE
NATIONS
ALLIANCE

Muscogee

ESCAMPAHA

Calusa

BAHAMA

Stapaha

SIBATEO

Atlantic Ocean

YUMA

Habana

HABAKOA

YABAKE

KAYKO

CUBA

TAINO   KINGDOM

Coba

INAWA

KISKEYA

BORIKEN

Chactemáal

Sharagua

EXPEDITION

Tibes

SHAIMACCA

THE   ANTILLES

EYERI

Atasiay

KALIPHUNA

CHIBCHA KINGDOM

TULE

ICE

ICE

ICE

Contents

Foreword

PEOPLE (ESPECIALLY INTERVIEWERS) SOMETIMES ASK ME, "WHICH IS your favorite of the books you've written?" to which I always reply, "That's like asking which of my three children is my favorite."

It is honestly true that I don't have a favorite novel out of all those I have written so far. Each book has something about it I treasure, perhaps an element or scene or interaction that I think works brilliantly in context, or a character whose nuances I feel I captured exactly the way I wanted to, or a vibe I really like, or a sentence I adore, or a perfect plot twist, or even just a writing craft problem that I worked hard to solve.

There is so much I love about the Spiritwalker books and stories. The characters, of course, who walk through their world with all their flaws that I worked so hard to make believable and compelling, whether the reader loves the characters or, in some cases, very much does not. The world, with its late-18th-and-early-19th-century overtones, imbued (I hope) with a strong sense of a fantastical alternate-historical path and the vivid sights, textures, smells, tastes, and rhythms of this made-up world.

Perhaps most of all, I love the tone of the Spiritwalker universe. The novel trilogy is funny in a way I hadn't thought I could manage in my writing, not up until I wrote them. That's because Cat is funny, and the novels are all told in her voice. Once I let go and let her voice speak through me, I not only had the easiest time writing her story, but it was just such a delight to write.

The one thing I will say about this trilogy—and this universe—is that for reasons I can't explain or even fathom (except possibly that I have needed to tell some of its stories from points of view that aren't Cat), I have written more short fiction set in this universe than in any of my other universes. For that matter, I believe I have written as many Spiritwalker-universe short stories as I have written non-Spiritwalker-universe short stories, in total. The world and its dynamics still ring through me.

All the stories stand alone. Most were written with the expectation that readers would be unfamiliar with Cold Magic. A few will have greater resonance if the reader has read the trilogy, but their plot, characters, and narrative purpose work as complete stories in and of themselves.

A quick note about the chronology of the short fiction included in this collection:

"The River-Born Child" takes place about twenty years before *Cold Magic*.

Both "Bloom" and "A Compendium of Architecture and the Science of Building" take place about eight years before *Cold Magic* and are set in time about nine months apart from each other.

"The Beatriceid" takes place at some point in the year before *Cold Magic* begins.

"To Be a Man" takes place in the same time frame as the closing chapters of *Cold Magic*. In Chapter 28, when Bee and Cat realize they are essentially prisoners in the Barry household, Rory offers to turn into a saber-toothed cat as a distraction so they can escape. They, of course, get out of the house and continue their adventures. After the confrontation at the factory, and while being escorted home, Cat overhears two soldiers talking about a saber-toothed cat that got into the prince's menagerie. "To Be a Man" follows from there. In the last chapter of *Cold Magic*, Rory shows up (after his adventures) while Cat and Bee are crossing the city at night.

"The Secret Journal of Beatrice Hassi Barahal" is meant to represent Bee's account of what transpired during the three novels, with her sketches.

"The Courtship" follows on directly from the end of *Cold Steel*.

"'I Am a Handsome Man,'" said Apollo Crow" and "A Lesson to You Young Ones" both take place a year or two after the end of *Cold Steel*. The events in "Finding the Doctor" happen some months or a year or so onward from there.

"When I Grow Up" takes place about thirteen years after "Finding the Doctor," a rare case in which there is a clear chronological marker available through the ages of the older children.

One of the great pleasures of bringing this edition into the world was commissioning art by so many excellent artists. I utterly love their different visions and am so grateful they agreed to share in this project. From the original Julie Dillon illustrations for "The Secret Journal," back in 2013, to the illustrations drawn specifically for this collection, I am delighted, thrilled, and dazzled by their artistic brilliance.

Last of all, and always, you readers have been so incredibly kind, enthusiastic, and supportive of this world and these characters. I could not do this without you.

THE
STORIES

The River-Born Child

art by Todd Lockwood

T HE PEOPLE WHO RESCUED THE BOY FROM THE RIVER AND TOOK HIM IN weren't unkind. They gave him a name, Kemal. They fed him the same as their four children. They never burdened him with more than his fair share of the chores. The father built a rope bed for him with a straw-stuffed mattress that kept him off the floor, although he was never cold enough, even in winter, to need a blanket.

From the money she earned selling eggs, the mother paid the small fee for him to go to the village school, where he sat alone on a bench against the drafty back wall and learned his letters and numbers like the other children. In fact, the egg business thrived after the day they shepherded him from the icy riverbank into their farmstead. As soon as he came to live in the household, they never lost another chicken. All manner of predators stayed away because, as the schoolmaster finally informed him eleven months later, even wild beasts understood that the river-born were cursed.

"Cursed?" he asked that day, a quiet autumn afternoon when the other children had already left for home. The people who raised him refused to hear such profane talk in their pious house. "What kind of cursed am I?"

The schoolmaster was an exhausted-looking man who tolerated Kemal staying after the end of school and plying him with endless questions because the boy was his best student. Indeed, he was a veritable maw of curiosity, always eating until he had intellectually chewed through all the books in the schoolhouse and the schoolmaster's private library of twenty precious volumes besides.

"You were never a baby, cherished and suckled like ordinary children. You walked out of the river on two legs, looking like a well-grown twelve-year-old. Just by looking at you, everyone can tell you are a river-born child, not a real child. All color was drained from you by the watery womb."

Kemal considered his pale-milk hands, folded on the table beside the schoolmaster's brown ones. The man wore spectacles. Through these, he examined Kemal with the sort of normal-brown eyes that Kemal saw all around him in the faces of ordinary people, not like his own ice eyes. The schoolmaster's hair was black like everyone else's, not white.

"I don't remember anything before I saw my father and mother." He broke off.

"They are not your father and mother."

"I know." His shoulders slumped. They told him so time and again, and yet his first memory was of slithering out of the river and seeing the people and thinking: *This is who I am. They are here so I can follow them. They are my fathers.*

The moment the thought had taken hold, a strange feeling had twisted through him, all the way down to his bones. After that, he stood up on two legs, and they told him he was a boy and should come with them. They took him to their house, where they gave him clothes to cover his naked body. Afterward, they explained, when he got confused, that they were not both fathers but a father and a mother. That two of his four brothers were actually sisters, girls, which he kept forgetting because, deep in his mind, he had a vague memory of being surrounded by male siblings like himself, all swimming like mad to get to the surface before they drowned.

"Kemal!" The schoolmaster leaned forward as if he'd seen a glint of gold he could pluck from a buried vein. "Have you remembered something? Some recollection from the river?"

"No." At home, they taught him never to speak of his hazy memories of the river, so he tried to forget, but that just meant his thoughts drifted relentlessly back to the river, time and again. Yet when he wandered along the bank, he saw nothing in the water to remind him of his emergence. Only fish and bugs swam there as the current swept restlessly on.

There was no one else like him. Probably he just dreamed of male siblings like him so he would feel less alone.

"Do you ever think of running away?" asked the schoolmaster one day. He was idly flipping through the pages of the journal he kept in a language Kemal could not read. It was the one thing the man refused to teach him. "Find a life where you might become a scholar? Perhaps learn some other useful profession? You're intelligent. You have a seeking mind, Kemal."

"Where would I go? How would I eat? Who would take me in? People fear me because I am a monster. It's dangerous for me out there. They tell me so all the time."

The schoolmaster picked up a stylus and spun it through his fingers. "If I gave you a map, told you what backwoods paths to shadow, would you walk to an academy that might take you in? It's the place where I studied. The Minister of Students there had high hopes for me. Alas, I did so poorly on the imperial exams that I was assigned a placement in this cursedly forsaken village. Still, she liked me. If I wrote a letter of introduction, she might be persuaded to take you in."

"What if the minister rejects me? What then?"

The schoolmaster's frown was all the answer Kemal needed.

"It sounds like everything I could dream of," he said, "but I don't want to die. So I better stay here where I'm safe."

Footsteps thudded on the schoolroom porch. The door opened and the mother entered, twisting the ends of her shawl in her hands.

"Kemal? Ah! Here you are. I couldn't find you."

He rose as a sign of respect for his elders, as he'd been taught.

The schoolmaster also stood as a *rattle-tat-tat* rumbled faintly in the distance.

"Are they here? Come early? They don't usually reach us for another ten days." For once, the schoolmaster's voice had a sharp edge to it instead of its usual enervated tone. "I suppose you must have sent word to the market town."

"We obey the law," she agreed curtly. "We only waited this long to send a report because an extra pair of hands were so useful in our fields this year. Not to mention the chickens! No one can fault us for that!"

"And so harvest is come and gone. When the imperial troop reached the market town and read the report, they'll have made haste to come to our unimportant little village first in this region, won't they?"

When the schoolmaster met her gaze, she looked away as if she were ashamed.

Kemal didn't know what to think about this baffling exchange. But as the rattle-tat-tat grew in volume, its stirring *rum-put-a-pum-drum-drum* made Kemal stand straighter, wishing he could dash outside to look.

"Are the imperial tax collectors here already, come to take the yearly tithe?" he asked excitedly. "I hear they look very grand in their uniforms. Will there be a feast, and cider, and cake? Just as my siblings tell me?"

"They aren't your brothers and sisters," the mother said with such force that he took a step away from her and bent his head to show his obedience.

"My apologies. I did not mean to speak out of turn."

"How can you be so cruel?" demanded the schoolmaster. "If only—"

"You don't have two sons who need to raise a bride-price if they want to marry," she snapped. "You don't have two girls to educate and clothe. You are paid a stipend from the emperor's purse while we struggle to pay the tax set on us by the imperial tax collectors. When a windfall drops at your feet, you, too, would pick it up. Kemal, come with me."

As she strode out the door, not looking back, Kemal paused to give a shy smile to the schoolmaster, who looked wearier than ever. "Will there be cider?" he asked. "That's my favorite."

"I'm sure there will be cider." The schoolmaster grimaced as he spoke, then dabbed at an eye as if grit had gotten into it. "We pretend to virtue and honor at the same time as our guts churn through and make excrement of all that tastes sweet and good."

"What does that mean?" Kemal whispered, shocked, for no crude talk was allowed in the household of the father and the mother.

"Kemal!" the mother called from outside.

He walked to the door.

"Kemal," said the schoolmaster softly. "Whatever they tell you, remember: You are not a monster. You are no different from any child, and more inquisitive and intelligent than most."

"Do you really think so?" Kemal could not restrain a grin, even though the father and the mother told him that smiling was indecent and shameful. "I have worked very hard to be a good and obedient student."

The schoolmaster's face crinkled up in a way Kemal did not quite understand. The man waved a hand and said brusquely, "You must go. The rest of us shall remain here in this benighted backwater, as we deserve for our cowardice."

Kemal hesitated, wondering if it would be impolite to express his opinion, a form of speech much discouraged at home. But the urge got the better of him. He blurted out, "You are a good teacher," and hurried out lest he discover he should have kept silent and not broken the rules.

Rules were the hardest thing to learn because they often made no sense and were rarely written down. Sometimes people would say one thing but do another. Each new interaction was a process of learning because subtleties and nuances varied between people and could even change with the same person across days and weeks. The mother might pat him approvingly on the shoulder one day, when he reported he had gotten all of his grammar questions correct at the school, and send him to stand on the stool in the corner the next week for the same thing, on the charge of braggadocio.

As if she could hear him thinking, the mother beckoned. "Hurry along, Kemal. Don't lag behind for thinking too much."

He rushed to catch up. She strode along in the brisk way of a person with too much to do and not enough daylight to do it in. He paced her past the temple where the road branched into two and onward along the riverfront. A bend in the road opened up onto a vista of vegetable gardens and the familiar two-story front of the house with its overhanging balcony and stone footing.

Twelve horses waited on the road outside, ridden by soldiers in dashing red-and-black uniforms with braided gold trim. Two officers wearing the same uniform, with dazzling gold tassels at the shoulders, stood on the porch talking to the father. The siblings crowded the open door, staring, seeing Kemal and the mother, way up the road, before the others did.

The wind picked up at his back, a merry breeze as astonished and ex-hilarated as he was to see noble horses and imperial soldiers in this humble village, at their very house.

The horses' ears flattened, and their nostrils flared. Tails raised, several tried to run, only to be pulled up sharply, while others turned in a nervous circle as their riders held them on a tight rein.

The officers looked upwind just as the mother grabbed Kemal's shoulder.

"Stop here," she said.

"What are the horses afraid of?"

Her hand tightened on his shoulder, so he stood as still as he could. The officers stepped down from the porch and, with the father walking three steps behind them, marched in their direction. The officer with a beard had a hand on his sword hilt. The other officer had no beard and, instead, the swell of a bosom beneath his uniform, which possibly meant he was a female like the mother and the sisters, but on the other hand, he was dressed like the bearded officer except for the mage-mark on his collar: a circle split into silver and gold for ice and fire.

By now, all but two of the horses had been calmed, while the two still-panicked ones were ridden into the lee of a windbreak of poplar trees planted beyond the garden.

The officers halted a body's length from the mother. At first, Kemal thought they were showing her respect, but then the beardless one drew a stiff whip from his belt and held it out to point at Kemal.

"This is the river-born monster?" the beardless officer asked, looking not at Kemal but at the mother. "I've never heard tell that they walk on two legs and look like people."

"I am not a monster," Kemal muttered with a spurt of rebellion, thinking of the schoolmaster's words. "I am a boy."

Both officers startled. The bearded one skipped back a step, eyes wide.

The beardless one lifted the whip as if thinking he must strike with it. "Or talk!"

The mother said, "Kemal, be silent. It is rude to speak to exalted imperial officers if they have not given you permission."

"It speaks," repeated the bearded officer. "I've never heard of their kind doing that before! Much less looking so much like a child. Can it manage other simple tasks as well?"

Kemal wanted to tell the man that he was a boy so, of course, he could manage simple tasks, and conjugate all his verbs correctly, as well as iden-tify all of the provinces of the Empire of the Avar, recite the Five Founding Decrees of the Empire, and solve elementary equations and write geometric proofs. But the mother's hand on his shoulder weighed heavily, so he kept his mouth closed. But he seethed.

The calmed horses became agitated again, clipping up their legs, shaking their heads as they pulled on their bridles.

"We have let the child live in our house, among our own children," said the mother.

"Isn't that dangerous? To keep it in the house?" asked the bearded officer.

The beardless one lowered his whip, his gaze on Kemal so uncomfortably probing that it made him want to shift around like the anxious horses. He kept still by reciting, soundlessly and only in his mind, the eleven precepts of a virtuous society: Obedience, Submission, Diligence. . . .

The mother's answer interrupted his thoughts. "If you give him firm, clear orders and do nothing that startles or agitates him, you will find him meek and obedient, hardworking, and quick to learn. Have you any other questions, Your Honor?"

"The report at Market Town says you found him last winter, eleven months ago. Why did you not send a message at once?"

"Winter makes the roads impassable, Your Honor. Likewise, the imperial edicts tell us to look for river-born beasts, rare animals who lack all color. No one said anything about children. At first we thought he was an abandoned child. But later we realized he is not what we expected."

When she spoke these words, she exuded a strange scent he did not understand.

The beardless officer did not seem to notice. He exchanged a glance with the bearded one, and shrugged. "Very well. We are as surprised as you are. But we will take him."

At once, she snapped back, "The reward money for the delivery of a river-born beast to imperial agents is set by law. If you wish to include the clothes on his back, there will be an additional charge for the items, which we will have to replace."

The officers looked at each other.

With a crooked smile that made Kemal think the man half-angry and half-amused, the bearded officer said, "Very well. We will take him, clothes and all, since we have nothing to fit. You drive a hard bargain, mistress. Yet this is such an unexpected windfall, I cannot complain."

"Just as we said ourselves, Your Honor. We will take the money in coin or in kind, not in writ, if you please. And a sealed and signed acknowledgement of the exchange, so there can be no doubt later of how we came into the reward money."

How badly Kemal wanted to speak, to figure out what was going on. But the mother had told him to be silent, so he waited until the officers walked away toward the horse troop to confer. Yet still, the mother and the father remained on the road, not taking him back to the house where the siblings waited. The two sisters and the two brothers were staring so hard that he thought their eyes might fall out, even though he knew eyes could not literally fall out. It was just a turn of phrase.

Even so, even trying to be good, he felt an unpleasant pain in his chest and the sting of tears in his eyes. Pressed beyond bearing by the anguish of not knowing, he said, "What is happening?"

The mother and the father exchanged a look like night and day conspiring to make twilight.

The mother said, "The emperor wishes to meet you, Kemal. These officers of the imperial guard have come to take you to see him."

A flare of excitement burst, then pinched down as the pain grew sharper. "But I will come back here afterward, won't I?"

"If the emperor allows it, of course," said the mother.

That was when he understood, for the first time, the lie in her voice. It rubbed against his flesh like sandpaper; it smelled like the char of ash; it tasted both bitter and sweet on his tongue, for lies have a smell and a taste that cannot be consumed without gagging.

He thought of what the schoolmaster had said, but it was too late to run back to the school now and ask for the map and the letter. The emperor wanted him. No one could thwart the emperor's will.

"Why do they think I might be dangerous?" he asked instead.

"Usually the river-born are beasts, predatory animals like to wolves and eagles and horrible bears and monsters, but you are shaped like a child."

"Am I not a boy?" He rubbed at his stinging eyes, for tears were cause for scoldings in the house. Children yielded to punishment with acceptance and, if they obeyed, they were never punished. He had learned this lesson so quickly that sometimes, when they thought he wasn't listening, the mother and the father admonished the other children to be more like him in dutifulness and docility, and he soaked up their secondhand praise like sunshine after weeks of cloudy days.

"You are shaped like a boy, but you are river-born," said the mother. "For that reason, you are going on a grand trip to see the emperor. Keep your face and hands clean and your clothes tidy. Do not speak unless spoken to, and do as you are told."

"Unless you are asked to perform a criminal act," said the father. "You are not a thief or a murderer, nor are you to be abused."

"Hush! What nonsense!" she spat at the father. This small tempest made Kemal quiver, for in the normal course of life, the two of them never disagreed. "These are the emperor's own guard. They are not criminals."

The father muttered words under his breath that sounded remarkably like, "That's what we tell ourselves." But no one in the village ever criticized the emperor, so Kemal decided he had misheard.

"It's better this way," said the mother.

The officers returned with a heavy pouch, which they handed over to the mother.

The beardless officer turned to Kemal and held out a coil of rope with a loop at one end.

"Hold onto this rope. That way we won't lose you. You'll have to walk behind the horses until they become accustomed to your smell. After that, we will let you ride. You're small enough to double up with one of the soldiers."

Kemal looked at the mother and the father for permission. The mother's face was stony, like she got when there wasn't any more bread and the children were still hungry.

The father said gruffly, "Go on. You belong to the emperor now."

He belonged to the emperor now.

The troop set out at once. The horses ambled along all afternoon, at a pace that was easy to keep up with as he trotted along behind. His new companions glanced back to check on his progress, but no one spoke to him. At the end of the day, they halted and set up a little encampment with sentries to patrol the perimeter, although he could have told them that no creatures except small animals and flitting birds wandered anywhere close by. The soldiers pitched lean-tos, canvas to protect against rain, should any come over the night, although Kemal could have told them that none would, for rain's scent always swept before it, and the wind remained dry. Servants set up the officers' tents: two smaller, separate sleeping tents and one larger tent, in which a table and chairs were unfolded.

The beardless officer created the most astonishing magic, which Kemal had only seen once before when a troupe of traveling theatrical players had stopped for a single night at the village. The officer shaped a gauzy glow into a sphere of cold light and settled it into a little wire basket placed on the table. After washing in a basin, the officers went in to eat their meal by this magic-born light. The tent curtains remained closed so no one could look inside. Servants brought food in and took out the empty platters.

Kemal was given an old saddle blanket to sit on at the edge of the campfire circle, surrounded by dashing cavalrymen. His share of rations was the same as theirs, only less because he was a boy and not an adult. As the men chatted cheerfully among themselves about such delicate topics as one man's sore foot and another's tale of being cheated at dice, Kemal decided the injunction not to speak without permission surely referred only to the officers.

At a pause in the conversation, he asked, "Do you belong to the emperor too?"

The startled soldiers exclaimed aloud, staring.

"It speaks!" cried one, whose uniform's gold braid had three stripes, not just one.

"Am I not allowed to speak?" he asked anxiously. How he wanted them to like him the way the schoolteacher did! Or if that wasn't possible, to tolerate him as the family did.

The men looked at each other in the way people did when they speak with their eyes, which meant they knew they were thinking the same thing, even if Kemal was too ignorant to understand what that message was.

Three Stripes nodded to the others, then said, "Do you have a name?"

"Yes. My name is Kemal. Do you have a name? May I ask what it is?

The man snorted, and the others chuckled. "You may call me Sergeant. That's for my three stripes. Two stripes is Corporal. Single stripes are Trooper."

"Do all single stripes have the same name? I don't know any other one named Kemal in my village."

"That's because there is no one else like you in your village. Anyway, you won't be going back there."

"I won't?" This answer worried him. "The mother said I would return home if the emperor allows it."

The sergeant whistled, low and long. "A clever woman with her words. So you shall, Kemal. She is exactly right. You will return home if the emperor allows it."

"Poor kid," one of the troopers muttered under his breath, thinking Kemal could not hear him.

Another scoffed, "Don't be fooled by how he looks and that soft voice. He's a monster, a worm, they say, maggot-pale like that, even if he looks and sounds like a boy."

"I am not a worm." No one had ever called him a worm before. A powerfully disobedient urge to defend himself rose as heat in his belly. The mother was not here to scold him, so he spoke: "That is a very rude to thing to say, Trooper. Is courtesy not among the Eleven Precepts of a virtuous society?"

The men laughed, elbowing each other. He wasn't sure what to make of their laughter, what it meant. No one laughed at the house of the mother and the father; laughter was considered frivolous.

"I am a boy," he added, feeling he must hammer in this point lest they question him again. "I went to school with the other children."

"Went to school, did you? Learn anything there? Can you recite the Eleven Precepts?"

Kemal could tell the sergeant didn't believe he really knew them. However, after he had successfully listed them, in order, the sergeant looked delighted, as at a jolly game of *Chase Me Round The Corner* or *Cat In Ribbons*. He went on, testing Kemal with elementary tasks. Addition and subtraction. The daily prayer for the health of the emperor, (long may he reign without trouble from the ill winds of the spirit world and its yearly tithe). The Twelve Holy Deeds of the blessed warrior Marwas and his mage wife Tulwasa, who sacrificed themselves in order to save the life of the first emperor from the Wild Hunt and, in doing so, laid the foundation for the military and the mage wings of the imperial army.

The fire flickered. Its flames fluttered out until all that remained was embers. A cough broke into their merriment, a chilly presence that smelled of ice and winter. The beardless officer stood before them.

"What is this clamor, Sergeant? I hope you are not mistreating our prize."

The troopers jumped to their feet, so Kemal got up too.

"Not at all, Captain. He is a veritable treasure-house of knowledge. I wish my children paid such attention to their lessons!"

Everyone laughed except the beardless officer, who eyed Kemal up and down before replying to the sergeant. "Keep your voices down. Who knows what wolves prowl, seeking to dine on our feast. It's good fortune for our unit to be the ones to bring him to court. We'll be richly rewarded. But others will covet what we hold. Don't forget it. Now, troopers, we leave at dawn. He'll have to ride with one of you, so sort it out. Make sure he has a cloak with a hood to conceal his hair and face."

"Yes, Captain."

The officer walked away to one of the sleeping tents. The fire took heart in his absence, and flames licked eagerly back up the unconsumed wood.

"It's always us, isn't it?" said one of the troopers, the original scoffer. "We're the ones who have to wade through the mud. Meanwhile, the horses get skittish around the creature. Easy to say, when it's not your mount what has to endure his presence."

The sergeant snapped his fingers as others muttered in agreement. "Hush, you blunt swords. I'll take the boy, since the rest of you apparently aren't good enough riders. Chorki, give him your spare cloak. You don't need two."

The scoffer's complexion darkened as he huffed like a bellows. "But my mother gave me that when—"

"Did you hear me the first time?"

"Yes, Sergeant."

"You can have it back after."

"Like I'd touch it again. It'll have to be burned." Trooper Chorki shook his head as he rummaged in his saddle bags. He handed over a homespun-wool cloak with a hood.

"Please accept my thanks, Trooper Chorki," Kemal said. "This is very good work, well-woven and evenly hemmed, just like the cloaks the mother weaves for her sons—her children, I mean. She has daughters too. I didn't really need one, otherwise I am sure she would have made one for me, too."

Chorki's wide eyes and open mouth gave him a surprised look, which he shared with his comrades. "'Well-woven and evenly hemmed!' Just when I think I've seen and heard everything."

Another trooper jeered, "You haven't even seen your own—"

"Ratshit, shut your cursed mouth!" barked the sergeant.

Kemal jumped, not accustomed to coarse tones and insults shared between companions.

The troopers made haste to roll out their bedrolls beneath their canvas lean-tos. The sergeant tied Kemal's rope to a stake with a complicated knot and warned the sentries to keep an eye on him lest he think to run home in the middle of the night. Kemal wanted to tell him that he would never disobey, especially not the emperor's order, but everyone was turning in for the night, or at least those that weren't on guard.

No one suggested he join the troopers beneath the shelter of their lean-tos, so he lay down between the row of little tents. There was a kind of camaraderie that went along with lying on a saddle blanket and cloak and drifting drowsily amid a crowd of nearby bodies. Sleep overtook him, dragged him down into dreams of swimming within a press of slippery shapes, ever upward, toward a glimmer of undulating light—almost there—and breaking the surface of the water to find himself staring upward at an unknown, bearded face.

"Up! Up!" ordered the sergeant, poking him with a staff. "I've untied the rope. Do your business quick, in the grass. It's time to go."

Up he got and did his business as the troopers briskly readied their gear and horses to depart. The sergeant's horse was a battle-trained gelding, so the sergeant informed him, able to endure the roar of battle, the howl of wolves, and the smell of blood. Even so, the animal shifted restlessly as Kemal approached, tossing its head and kicking once, forcing him to dodge. The sergeant gave him a carrot to offer to the horse. This gift appeased the gelding, who allowed the sergeant to swing Kemal on behind him.

"Hold on, and don't fall off, for we have a long way to ride and no time to waste picking you up off the ground. Do you hear me?"

"Yes, sir."

The troop departed in a rumble of hooves, their crisscross banner flying proudly upon a friendly wind. Kemal had never ridden a horse before, and he didn't much like it. Horses had a scent that made him lick his lips hungrily, although he'd never eaten horse meat. The only flesh the mother and the father served at table was fowl and fish, from chickens they kept and fish caught from the nearby river. The same river he'd come from. But he wasn't a fish. Was he? Yet who were the others he dreamt of? The crowding bodies? The slippery shapes? His brothers?

No, not his brothers. He wasn't a fish, nor a beast, nor a monster. He was a boy.

The soldiers rode with concentration, intent on their goal. The journey quickly took on a routine. Every time they reached the outer fields of a village, Kemal had to cloak his head. They would ride to the village headman's house, where their horses would be watered and fed a bit of grain, though not much. While this was going on, the officers would present an accounts book for the headman to examine. According to what was written in the book alongside the village's name, the headman would hand over a bag of tax money to the officers. This payment of would then be recorded in the book. In every village, they were also given bread, cheese, vegetables, porridge, fruit, sausage, and other food and drink. The unit never had to forage for or feed itself. The empire's people fed them, and they collected the annual tax to take to the palace, everything written and double-checked in the accounts book.

The weather remained dry; 'kindling weather,' the father called it, while the schoolmaster called it 'drought.' The officers were eager to get to the palace, so they did not linger, not even at towns with spacious lodgings or villages with sheltering barns. Camping was good enough for experienced campaigners, a steady routine of set-up at twilight, after which the soldiers would eat and perhaps sing. Increasingly, they quizzed Kemal, entertained by his ability to answer without hesitation. Who wrote *The Cabinet of Good Governance*, and what are its eight chapters? Who was the third emperor, and in what year was His Peerless Refulgence taken by the Wild Hunt on the Night of Masks? In what fabled city did the famous 'dawn battle between mages and dragons' take place?

After some evenings, the officers took notice of the lively assembly. They, too, became intrigued by the stolid patience with which Kemal correctly answered almost every question put to him. But after all, had he not read all of the books on the schoolmaster's shelf?

Because the officers had been educated in the same manner as the schoolmaster, their questions grew increasingly arcane: What are the two kinds of mages? Into which sea does the Darlas River run, and what manner of sea serpent may you catch there? How do you measure the longitude of a star? Can you recite from memory the one-hundred stanza poem written by Jhogo Len the Bright Voice about the dawn battle between mages and dragons, after which dragons came no more into the Empire of the Avar, accepting their defeat?

Kemal said, "The mother said that to recite all one hundred stanzas is to preen with unseemly pride. Only a court-wreathed poet is allowed to speak the consecrated words. She forbade me from speaking it aloud."

The beardless mage exchanged a mysterious glance with the bearded officer before addressing Kemal. "I give you leave to speak the story aloud. Tomorrow will be a long day, dawn to dusk across the Salt Barrens. Let us enjoy a good story tonight to give us heart for the dust to come. To remind ourselves of the purpose for which we serve, the life of the emperor and the stability of the empire."

Kemal had only read the poem twice, stirred by its vivid images and the terrible death of the third emperor, who was also a mage. Even such a lofty highborn person, surrounded by an army and magnificent palace walls, could not turn away the shadowy Wild Hunt when it came calling for its yearly tithe on the Night of Masks. After the second time he read the poem to himself, the schoolmaster gently informed him that the mother had demanded he lock it away from Kemal, who had been overheard retelling its most exciting passages to the siblings when they were meant to be about their chores.

But he needed only to rummage down into what he thought of as his mind's storehouse, where everything he read resided in its own distinct cubbyhole. He fetched out the poem, let the memory settle onto his tongue, and began to speak the beloved words of the second-most-important dynastic poem in the empire.

This is the story as it was told to me. Let no one speak these words otherwise, but that they speak them as I, the Bright Voice, spoke them first, according to the truth of the matter as it resides between heaven and earth.

Let it be known.

The first Avar emperor was a mage, but the second emperor was not. Because of this, a conflict developed between two factions within the imperial dynasty: those who thought a refulgent emperor must be a mage and those who thought an emperor ought not to be a mage.

In those days, dragons out of the east occasionally traveled through the vast central plains of the world, on their way to and fro, visiting distant relations. There were not so many dragons in the world, even then. Indeed, they were mysterious and kept their business to themselves, but they were also powerful and deadly when they chose to bestir themselves.

Their presence in a land could be both a curse and a blessing. A curse, should they grow hungry for too many sheep or become desirous of interfering with the deeds and activities of humankind, especially mages, whose magic they did not like, for reasons no one knew. A blessing, as the saying goes, that *where dragon-kin bide, the Wild Hunt does not ride.*

Whether out of a desire to cause trouble for the newly founded empire or because they wished to diminish the influence of mages, some among the dragons threw their support behind the faction that supported the emperor who was not a mage. The conflict erupted into outright civil war, which culminated in the spectacular dawn battle fought across the canals and walls of the old imperial city of Golden Mansion. In the end, the reckless magic wielded by mages and dragons combined to flatten the glorious city into wreck and ruin. But the mages prevailed.

Their leader, a prince among mages, drove all dragons thereafter from any lands under the control of the Empire of the Avar and established a magically sealed border, beyond which no dragon was allowed to pass, (although the poet was not specific about the means by which this ban was enforced). Then the prince took the throne as the third emperor. He proclaimed that thereafter, every emperor must be a mage, according to the will of heaven and earth. The fate of the second emperor, who had not been a mage, remained unknown, but he was never again seen beneath the light of the sun.

The third emperor was a keen and canny sovereign, wise to the ways of the world, clever at negotiating, harsh toward enemies, and gracious toward friends. The empire grew swiftly beneath the hooves of his mighty armies, who wielded sword and mage-craft in the service of the emperor. East and west, the empire expanded inexorably, pushing against the countries and tribal nations along its borders, swallowing what it could and trampling or burning what it did not desire for its own.

In the end, the dragons took their revenge for their banishment merely by doing nothing. For with their absence in imperial lands, it transpired that one year, the Wild Hunt rode into the empire on the Night of Masks and took as their yearly tithe the third emperor, whose magic tasted more sweet than honey to their ravenous maws.

After this, the fourth emperor, too, was taken on the Night of Masks, after a mere six years of rule. And after this, the fifth emperor carefully read the learned notes left behind by the first emperor. Within this careful calligraphy, the fifth emperor discovered a secret, and on this secret, built a new ceremony atop the Night of Masks. Thereafter, no emperor was taken by the Wild Hunt.

Kemal was never sure if the poem was meant as a triumphant celebration of victory—mages defeating dragons—or a cautionary tale about getting what you wished for without undertaking to fully examine the possible consequences. When he had asked the schoolteacher, the man had sighed and told him he was just a boy and thus had much more to learn. That he had the makings of a scholar, if only the mother and the father would allow him to learn all that he was capable of.

Now, Kemal thought, perhaps the emperor would allow it!

"That's quite a victory tale," said the bearded officer, nodding approvingly after Kemal had finished. "Don't you agree, Reva?"

The beardless officer shook his head. "I've never thought so. But I'm impressed by the recitation, Kemal." He took his time studying Kemal, then said, "Your paleness is a sign that you must be taken to the palace, but sometimes a baby is simply born with little color. That's an entirely different thing. Just as horses have coats of different colors, so do people. Are you sure you're truly a river-born beast? Not just a very pale boy?"

"The mother and the father told me I came from the river."

"What do you recall?"

He shook his head stubbornly. Of course, it was wrong not to be agreeable and obedient, but he could not bear to reveal his disquieting dreams. What would they think of him then? Still, the fact remained that he had come from the river, so all he could say was, "I am a boy, not a monster."

"Ah, well," said the mage. With that, everyone except the sentries went to their bedrolls.

The ride across the Salt Barrens had a hot, harsh feel, even though summer was past and autumn's days grew shorter. The ground had been baked to a hard pan long ago. No villages, ponds, or wells offered respite all the long and weary day. The receding green plains were soon lost beneath the western horizon behind them, after which there was nothing to see except a grim spine of mountainous spurs to the north, like a monstrous dragon turned to stone. Indeed, in the schoolmaster's storehouse of old stories, there was one about a dragon that had been turned to stone to become this very chain of mountains. However, the schoolmaster had told Kemal that it was unlikely any creature could be that large, so probably the story was just a poetical way of describing the empire's antipathy to dragons and how these most powerfully magical of creatures had been fenced out, never more to walk in lands controlled by the Avar. No, the schoolmaster had gone on to explain; he didn't know how it was accomplished either, not being a mage.

Just before dusk, they reached an oasis in the midst of the flat landscape: trees, gardens, brick houses surrounding a miraculous well, and a brackish pond of a peculiar greenish color at the northern boundary of the fields. The shadowy mountains loomed beyond, more than a day's ride to the north.

The community had seen the soldiers approaching, alerted by the dust kicked up by the horses, as well as by the frantic barking of the village dogs. Thus, a delegation awaited them, men in long tunics and sandaled feet flanked by women whose hair was concealed beneath brightly colored scarves instead of the hats worn by women in Kemal's village. The dogs whined, tails tucked and ears down, and kept their distance as the troop arrived and the officers dismounted. The soldiers glanced sharply at Kemal, as if the dogs' suspicion was his fault.

"Your Excellencies!" An elder shuffled forward, bowing the four times mandated by the Twenty-Two Stations of Courtesy for civilians receiving imperial dignitaries.

"We are not excellencies, just captains," said the bearded officer with a gruff, annoyed look. He was a person of meticulous grooming, but after the day's ride, his uniform bore unsightly smears of dust, and his face and beard were caked with grit. "We seek water and feed for our mounts, and food for ourselves. I must suppose there is not spare water for washing, so I will not impose that duty upon you. We will keep separate from your people, according to the law. We'll be on our way at dawn for the second part of our crossing."

"You are all that is most pious and deserving." The elder kept bobbing. "I pray you, in the name of the Peerless Refulgent Emperor, hear my words. One of the women has somewhat to show you that she caught not ten nights ago, at the full moon, in the pond. Of interest to the palace, according to the law. With a price attached."

"What matters it to us what was caught in a pond? We seek only the river-born."

"Ah." The elder bobbed yet more. "For you see, our pond is fed by an underground river that flows down from the mountains."

A river-born beast!

Every soldier turned to look at Kemal, where he sat uneasily behind the sergeant.

"I'll be damned," muttered the sergeant. "What a rare chance! We are either twice blessed or twice cursed."

The mage officer said, "Kemal, you must come with us."

The sergeant swung him down and handed the rope's loop over to the officers. Kemal walked a respectful three steps behind the officers, with the rope looped up in his hands so it didn't drag on the ground.

The elder led them through the dusty village, past the well, the gardens, an empty corral, and a strip of weed-infested gravel. All along the processional way, dogs trailed at a distance. Lean and scruffy, they growled but never came close. The village folk stood in silence by their houses as they stared and stared and stared. At him. Maybe at the officers. He hoped at the officers.

Beyond the gravel strip rose a brick wall, and within this enclosure, a wire cage, and inside this cage, a pale dog.

Only it was not a dog, not once you saw it up close. It had the look of a dog, as if created by an artist who had never seen a dog but, rather, had a dog described to them by another person, who had also never seen a dog. Slope-browed, toothy-muzzled, rat-tailed, with a moon-white coat as patchy as a scuffed rug, and a strangely uneven back, as if it had started to grow a crest along its spine but hadn't gotten further than lumpy spurs. Seeing the village elder and the officers, it growled, though it was more of a gurgle, not the sort of sound any true animal makes.

All at once, it raised its head, whipping it side to side as it tried to get a look at something out of its sight. A ripple ran across its skin as if something within churned in a whirlpool of emotion. It yipped anxiously. It whined, sniffing the air. It had smelled him. It had smelled Kemal.

A pressure leaned in, as of a presence pushing against the skin of Kemal's mind, the part of him that remembered the river: a slippery nudge, a word-less question, a gasp of hope. Fear pounced and devoured him whole. He did not even know what he was afraid of, but a powerful urge to remain hidden from the creature struck him hot and then cold. He stayed carefully out of sight, behind the others, easy enough for a boy to do, who is smaller than the big adults.

"Here is the monster," said the elder. "There is a reward, is there not? I will accept it on behalf of the woman who found him."

"I'll be cursed as a sand louse," remarked the bearded officer. "What a windfall. The river-born are rare as pearls in the grass to begin with. And I'm cursed sure no unit has ever brought in two river-born in the same year."

The beardless officer made the sign to avert the evil eye. "Enough, Meghur, don't tease, lest ill fortune perks up her ears and sidles over to smother us. Are we sure it's not just a deformed dog? I've seen all kinds of things in these backwater villages. They say animals who lick too much salt give birth to misshapen get."

"One way to find out."

The bearded officer approached the cage, a hand extended as one would to an ordinary dog so it could make the person's acquaintance through smell. Not that dogs ever allowed Kemal to get close, but he watched other people play with and pat dogs. He sometimes forgot it was impious to wish for some-thing you oughtn't to have and wished that he might play with and pat dogs too. Though, perhaps not this dog.

The creature went wild, lunging toward the officer, grappling with the bars of its cage as it tried to gnaw through the iron. Its gurgling grew sharper, angry. It gaped its jaw wide open and huffed hotly, as if exhaled breath could damage its hated foe. For hate it did, if the fury of its reaction was anything to judge by.

The officer took a step back with a frown that made Kemal's insides cringe. "How are we to transport this thing? Kemal, come here."

For the first time in his life, he did not move when he was told. "I don't want to."

The officer's normally benign expression vanished into a blizzard of annoyance. "I did not ask what you want. Come here!"

The beardless officer took a step to accompany him forward, but the bearded one snapped, "No. Let him come on his own. We have indulged him enough, treating him as a boy."

"I am a boy!" cried Kemal.

"You are not a boy. Now do as I say. Come here!"

With what hunched shame did he creep forward. Every person there watched him, and the elder and his people even took several steps away. The pale creature grew quiet. It also backed away as he approached, tail down. But as the wind shifted, and he got closer, it flattened itself to the ground and wriggled forward to the bars, making an odd piping sound like a choked whistle. The noises fell upon Kemal's body as speech might, and this much of it he understood: fear, loneliness, despair . . . and yet a slithery hope of recognition, like the sight of the mother and the father's house at twilight, Kemal walking home from the fields. A lamp burning in the window.

"Like calls to like," said the bearded officer.

At the sound of the man's voice, the creature leaped backward, spitting and snarling once again. Its terror worked hard in Kemal's heart. It pained him to feel it, for the creature had done nothing wrong except emerge from the water, all alone. He set a hand on a bar. The creature stopped yelping and shoved its muzzle against his skin.

Slippery bodies undulating upward, intertwined as they struggled toward the light.

"No," he said aloud, hand clenching the bar. "I am a boy."

The creature sighed, relaxing as it pressed closer against the bars as if to warm itself against him. *Brothers.*

But it was a monster. Mute. Malformed. An animal.

They could not be brothers.

"It will slow us down, but that makes the most sense," said the beardless officer.

What would slow them down? He had lost track of the conversation. He had time only to be startled as the cage door was opened and—with no warning—a push from behind shoved him inside—beside the monster. He couldn't even stand up; he had to crouch, settling to his knees. It was humiliating.

"I've been obedient," he cried. "I haven't caused any trouble."

"Meghur, are you sure about this?" protested the beardless officer. "It seems cruel. He's just a boy."

"He's not a boy, Reva. You're as bad as the troopers, ensorcelled by his soft voice and modest ways. That's how monsters get you. They charm their victims first, then kill and eat them."

The bearded officer's voice had the same cold certainty as the mother's. Had the mother never liked him at all? Had she always thought him a monster? Had he only believed that if he worked harder and was more obedient that she would warm to him, soften, even rest an approving hand on his shoulder as she sometimes did with the brothers and the sisters?

The creature nuzzled him, so content with his presence that when the villagers brought a wagon and hoisted the cage into the wagon's bed, it neither snapped nor snarled. No one else talked to Kemal after that. The officers went off to find a bed and a meal. Two troopers came to stand guard over the cage, including Chorki, but the young trooper would not speak to him anymore. Would not look at him. Kemal might as well have vanished.

Later, the bearded officer brought an empty bucket, a mug of well water, and a bowl of scraps, the sort one would feed to a dog. This was Kemal's supper, although he shared it with the creature, for he could not bear to treat it with cruelty. A monster it might be, but that did not mean it did not wish for a touch of kindness, which it made clear in how it stuck to Kemal's side, warm and steadfast. The night passed slowly, for he was too anxious to sleep as the late moon rose and the stars walked their precession around the sky. As the schoolteacher had taught him: the great world is a vast sphere and, as it slowly turns, the sky seems to move, although it is the world that is turning.

Dizzying, when one thought of it.

Slippery.

Seated cross-legged, leaning against the bars, he dozed at last with the creature stretched alongside his leg. In his dreams, he chipped his way out of a gleaming eggshell using only a long tooth. He rolled and wiggled toward the irresistible smell of water. Through water, he fell between worlds, out of a gauzy existence where nothing held a permanent shape, rising up through the river to breach the surface and thrash his way to the other world with its solid shore. What he was when he rolled up upon the rocky shoreline, he did not know, but then he saw them, he saw the boys, and thus he was to be a boy. That was what his body told him.

Become the thing you see that has the power to move and act, to blend in. That is how to live.

He woke with a start at dawn. The troopers brought two village horses to pull the wagon containing the cage he shared with the creature.

"Sergeant? Corporal? Trooper?"

They would not look at him. They did not speak to him. He was in the cage now, with the monster. That made him a monster too. Even the beardless officer no longer spoke to him. Only the bearded officer brought him scraps of food every evening, took the waste bucket away for another to empty and wash out, then brought it back.

Days passed as they traveled east through open countryside on well-traveled paths past villages and occasional towns and, now and again, encampments of round tents nestled amid herds of sheep and horses.

All this landscape was new to Kemal. Curious and enthralled, he reveled to see it, recognizing places on the maps he had studied with the schoolmaster. Yet it was so lonely in the cage, except for the creature, who was content merely to have a companion, to not be alone in the world. But Kemal had no companion, although he did not scorn the creature. It was just a dog, of a kind. Maybe he was just a boy, of a kind.

No. He was a boy. He had to be a boy.

For the first time, he wondered why he was being sent to the palace. Why did the emperor want him if everyone else considered him a monster? But he no longer had anyone to ask who would answer.

Thus, after many days of travel across quiet grassland and past tree-studded rivers, they came to the emperor's palace. The imperial residence appeared first as a tower on the horizon, then grew to become a city split into two parts. On one side rose buildings made in the usual way with sod and brick. On the other side rose grand tents larger than any village house, woven in reds and greens and yellows and blues. Bright banners flew from their peaks. The troop rode along a wide dirt avenue into the center of the city, past a bustling marketplace, crowded inns and smelly stables, noisy workshops and stalls where street food was for sale, flooding Kemal with a hundred appetizing scents.

Amidst this hustle and bustle, though, it was the cage on the wagon that attracted the most attention. Soon, a parade of curious onlookers tromped along behind the troop, singing a song Kemal had never heard before, in a dialect whose words he couldn't quite understand. Something about the emperor's life and the blessed sacrifice gifted to the empire by the great heaven god, who loved the people—and the emperor most of all.

Despite this clamor, the stolid troopers ignored the shouted questions from the crowds. They even raised their whips to warn off people trying to push forward to get a closer look. Kemal did not know what to do beyond curling up with his arms tight around himself and the dog-creature huddled against his knees in fright, growling low in its throat. He didn't want it there, the way it leaned on him, the way he had been trapped in with it. He wanted to look at the city, to drink in these strange and marvelous sights, but the coarse and mocking shouts felt like a thousand cuts welting his skin. The animal shuddered, and he rested a hand on its head until it calmed.

At last, they reached a palisade that stood the height of two men, a thick wall built of sod. A closed gate opened to admit them. Beyond the gate lay an open area like the village square back home. An officer with a white beard and a grave expression came forward to interrogate the officers. This man did not approach the cage himself, but he looked Kemal's way three times, and each time, his frown grew darker, and his bushy eyebrows drew lower in a most alarming fashion. Kemal wanted to speak, but he did not have permission, so he said nothing. The dog-creature licked his arm.

After a long wait, a new individual appeared: a beardless man wearing a long robe woven in a bold pattern of blue and yellow and a tall hat decorated with shiny beads and silver ribbon. The mother would not have approved of this garb, but she was pious, and pious people did not wear garish colors and immodest hats, or so she often said of some of the other mothers in the village.

A pouch of coins changed hands, passing from the garish individual to the bearded officer. The sergeant, the trooper Chorki, and the beardless officer cast one last glance toward Kemal, but they departed without a single word, not even a nod of acknowledgement. They rode back out through the gate, leaving him seated in the cage with the creature, who was all that he had left. It nestled closer as if it felt the curl and tangle of an ill wind rising. He scratched its neck. It settled again and purred with a low rumble.

The horses were unhitched, and the wagon was pulled instead by great-thewed servants, down a lane created by fabric walls so high, they blocked his view. So deep did they travel into the midst of the tent city that he no longer had any idea where they were. He smelled meat cooking, oil burning, sweat and perfume, people and animals. He heard voices talking in a diction unlike that of the village, more like that of the schoolmaster, languid and precise. A song drifted across the air, with a haunting melancholy that twisted right down into his heart. He had used to sit at the back, when the family sang pious prayers in the evening. Hearing her children's voices lifted in pleasing harmony was the only time the mother ever smiled.

He wanted to go home.

After some time, the servants halted at a gate decorated with an image of a recurve bow, the symbol of the empire. Kemal had never been allowed to touch weapons, or even handle a knife. However, the schoolmaster had showed the boy his own bow, for, according to the law, every child in the empire learned to use a bow. Every child except Kemal, he thought sourly as guards opened the gate to allow the wagon to pass through.

Through the gap, he glimpsed a huge scaffolding that rose into the sky like a towering, long-necked beast, strange to his eyes, for he had only ever known the stout buildings of the village. Before he could make sense of it, a servant came running with a shout. The wagon halted. A blanket was thrown over the cage, blocking his view. Now, when the wagon moved forward, he no longer had any idea where they were going or what was around them. The vehicle took several sharp turns before coming to a stop. The big cage was jostled, then dragged to the edge of the wagon's bed. A person called out orders. An object bumped against the cloth. The pale dog whimpered and jumped into Kemal's arms.

The cage door was opened from the outside, but when he peered through, he saw the opening led into an even smaller cage, so he didn't move. The hafts of spears began to poke through the bars, catching in the cloth and prodding him from all sides, urging him toward the door. He had no choice but to clamber through, the pale dog still shivering in his arms. Once through, he stood in a tall cylinder of a cage that reminded him of a birdcage he had seen in the office of the mayor of the village. In this cage had lived a bedraggled nightingale, trapped for its song.

His new cage was covered by canvas, even along the bottom. He didn't understand this until, with the squeak of a pulley, the cage began to rise up off the ground, creaking upward. How high, he did not know. As it swayed back and forth, he clung to its bars, dizzy with confusion.

Eventually, the cage stopped rising. It swung sideways and jolted to rest on a hard surface. People chattered around him. A bowl of scraps was shoved past the bars, through a slit in the canvas. A trough attached low along the cage was filled with water from a long-necked vessel, thence withdrawn. After this, the voices receded, descending. All he had left was the cage and the pale dog, who whined, turned two circles, and lay down.

The touch of sun on cloth faded. Wind stirred the fabric. Although he tugged at the covering, the canvas had been fixed to the cage in a manner he could not shift. Even the slit was fastened from the outside.

He was so tired. He curled up in a ball with his companion—not his brother, not that—and slept fitfully off and on through a breeze-troubled night.

Dawn came with a blurt of horns and a rousing *rum-pum-a-tum-a-tat-tum* of drums.

There was nowhere to piss but in the empty scrap bowl or the water trough, so he and the pale dog pissed in the bowl rather than foul the water.

It struck him then that the pale dog had some manner of intelligence, for it had begun to copy him in the matter of elimination and tidiness, rather than to just piss on the ground as animals did. What did that make the river-born beast? Not a boy. Perhaps not a dog.

Voices approached, accompanied by the sound of feet thumping on stairs. The pale dog rose to its feet, legs stiff. Kemal stood too.

"Are you sure, Your Refulgence?" someone asked. "No need for you to bestir yourself to this inspection. Another can do it."

"Are you trying to hide something?" The voice held a tone rubbed raw with impatience. "It has never happened in the history of my honored predecessors that two river-born were brought in during the same year. The most we have ever had is one. This is a sure sign of heaven's favor."

"Surely it is as you say, Your Refulgence!"

"Yet are they real or are they fake, like the one brought in last year?"

"Fake?"

"Oh, of course, you weren't here, Matun, were you? Did you not hear of the scandal? My cousin was in charge of offerings last year and assured me the river-born beast brought in to stand as surety for me—*me!*—was a true specimen. But I am not a fool, although you all think me young and untried. I sent one of those visiting scholars from the University of New Jenne to inspect the beast, for they are all eager to poke and prod the river-born, if they can find them, and usually they can't. It turns out an enterprising scoundrel had used chalk to mimic the effect."

"Chalk!" The answer had a choked anxiety.

"I had the creature put down, for it was a sorry thing, underfed and sickly. And for his trouble, I had my cousin placed in the cage on the Night of Masks, in place of the river-born. It was he who stood in this place when the Wild Hunt arrived at midnight. I can only assume they liked the taste of his magic. So, do you wish again to say that I do not need to inspect the beast whose existence protects me from being gobbled up by the Hunt?"

In a flat tone, the other person replied, "Of course not, Your Refulgence. My most abject apologies."

"Do not underestimate me, Matun. Captain, go ahead."

The canvas was peeled back to reveal six hazy shapes. The pale dog's ears and spiny crest flattened, its tail tucked between its spindly legs, growl barely audible. Kemal blinked until his eyes adjusted to the early morning light.

The first thing he noticed was that the cage sat upon a platform set high up on a tall wooden scaffolding. From up here, the shape of the tent city looked like a great spiral with a single wide avenue cutting through it from its exterior walls, straight to the base of the scaffolding.

The second thing he noticed was the six people staring at him in shocked silence. Four wore military uniforms like those of the troopers, only theirs were adorned with elaborate silver braids and feathery crests sprouting from their shoulder epaulets.

"But this is a boy," cried the youngest, all astonishment. He was dressed in a silk tunic and matching trousers, both embroidered with gold thread. A circlet hammered out of gold nestled atop his black-haired head. He smelled as if he had just stepped away from a burning hearth; there were embers on his breath. His hands were sheathed in gloves. If one looked closely, sparks flashed in his eyes. "Ah! There is the river-born beast, at its feet. Is there some reason a boy was brought all this way, with the monster?"

"They are both river-born," said the person beside him. He was a beardless man, but after a moment, Kemal identified her as stout, healthy woman like the mother, which made him want to trust her. But she smelled of winter. She was a cold mage, as the beardless officer had been. There was hesitation in her voice when she added, "So the report states."

"Can that be true?" the young man demanded of her. "He looks like a boy."

"I am a boy," said Kemal desperately. "I am not a beast or a monster."

The young man startled, taking a step back, and cried, "By heaven's high harness, it speaks! This *must* be a boy. The beasts have never been known to speak. Here, boy, stick your arm out so Matun may touch it."

The mage winced. "Must I?"

"Of course you must. That pallor could be chalk! Do it!"

All here obeyed the young man. Kemal could see that much. Since he wanted to show he was an obedient and intelligent boy, he said, "Your Refulgence, you must be the emperor. I am your obedient servant."

"If you are, then you will give me your arm!"

Kemal pushed an arm between the bars, although it went no further than the elbow, for the bars were purposely set close together to prevent any slender creature from slipping through.

Matun grimaced.

"Go on!" The emperor's brow grew cloudy. A breath of heat rolled from him, for he had magic too. He was a fire mage, if the schoolmaster's teaching was correct, and it always had been, in Kemal's experience.

The cold mage drew an embroidered handkerchief from a sleeve and, with a wrinkled nose, dabbed at the back of Kemal's hand softly, then rubbed harder, then harder still. "No. Nothing. This is his natural coloring. He is one of the beasts."

"Such coloring means nothing," insisted the emperor. "There are a few white-haired, milk-skinned people born here and there in the empire every few years. My uncle took such a one to be one of his lesser wives. He thought her coloring a novelty. In the nations in the far west, there live many people with straw-colored hair and maggot-pale skin."

"The westerners are not so pale as this, and many are quite dark, like those New Jenne scholars whom you relied on. Regardless, Your Refulgence, I have read the affidavit from the villagers who saw him walk out of the river with their own eyes."

"What if they were lying to get the reward money?"

"Then they possess arts of disguise beyond my understanding. But we will find out for certain at the Night of Masks."

The emperor's mouth twitched in a way that made Matun take a step away from him. "You would like that, would you not? Being the only other adult member of the family with the mage gift. Making you next in line, should the Hunt take me because you mistook the matter."

Take him where, Kemal wanted to ask, but he said nothing. The pale dog hid behind him, a soft gurgling growl rumbling so quietly the people didn't notice as they poked and prodded at each other with hostile expressions.

"No, of course not. I am your humble servant, Your Refulgence. My branch of the family is but a minor lineage. You know that."

"Of course I know that. Therefore, I have an easy solution. You shall wait here on the Night of Masks, beside the cage. Let the Hunt take the river-born, as it wishes, although the dog seems a weak thing, not worthy of interest. If the Hunt does not wish, or the boy is just a boy, then you shall stand surety for the empire, shall you not? But, of course, if you are correct, you shall have nothing to fear. The Hunt never gathers a mage if a river-born beast is available, even one so weak as the dog. Our mage power is tasty to them, but not as attractive as the taste of the river-born."

Matun's smile had a sickly quaver. "Of course, that is my duty, Your Refulgence. I will stand surety, as you command. But let us not leave the matter to chance. Let us send an imperial messenger to Buda or New Jenne, requesting that a scholarly delegation be sent to examine this prodigy, a thing never before seen: a river-born child."

The emperor laughed, but he didn't sound happy. "Thought better of leaving the Night of Masks to chance, have you? Or offering yourself out of loyalty and love for me, your emperor?"

"I merely recalled that you and I have often discussed what exactly these river-born beasts might be. Why does the Wild Hunt take them, and if not them, then why a mage of the imperial bloodline? And why not every year but only some years, and not others? Wouldn't it benefit us to know? Have I not suggested you establish a university here in your own city? Then we could have our own scholars to consult on these matters. Your uncle himself spoke of establishing such a university."

"My uncle is dead, and I am not my uncle. He was too interested in the doings of the westerners and forgot that we are a people of the grasslands, archers and riders, not farmers with dirt on their hands, not scholars who never breathe fresh air, only the mildew of books."

"Of course, Your Refulgence." Matun sighed.

The emperor shaded a hand to look eastward over the spiral layout of the city, toward the rising sun. "Captain, let us go. Which horse am I riding today?"

"But Your Refulgence," cried Kemal, "may I not go home now that you have seen me? The mother said I could come back home if you allowed it."

Everyone jumped.

After a moment, having calmed himself, the emperor turned to Matun. "It's incredible that the creature appears in the guise of a child. The beast's ability to speak and parrot words is uncanny. Troubling! It might be a form of cunning magic, meant to charm and endanger us. Even more troubling, it might be a sign of an unknown change in the warp and weft of the worlds."

"Maybe the scholars of New Jenne know something of it," said Matun with a flicker of expression that made Kemal uneasy. "We know so little, Your Refulgence. We know that on the Night of Masks, the Wild Hunt rides. That they hunger for magical things. Mages, in particular. Mage-born emperors are even better, redolent with the scent of both magic and the power of commanding armies and territories. But if a river-born beast is presented to the Hunt, as if on a platter at a feast, then they will take it instead and leave the empire in peace until the next time they ride this way. Has it always been this way in these lands? No. It seems to have begun during the reign of the third emperor, after the dragons left. Why are things as they are? How can we know if we do not investigate? Is there any way to halt these incursions? To truly fence ourselves away from the depredations of the Wild Hunt?"

The emperor frowned. His eyes had a smoky, churning gleam. "Very well. Send for the scholars. Maybe they can figure out what this strange creature portends."

He turned away and, with the soldiers, descended the stairs. The cold mage studied Kemal with a frown like the one the mother got on her face when she was trying to decide whether to add a bit of sawdust to the last of the flour to make the bread go further.

"If I cannot go home yet, I would like to attend a university," said Kemal, with reckless fervor, thinking of the schoolmaster, his shelf of books, and his suggestion that Kemal steal away to the school where the schoolmaster had received his own education.

"By the High Heavens! I have never seen or heard the like! 'Attend a university!'" Matun muttered the words to herself.

"If you are going to leave me here, might I at least have a book to read?" Kemal asked politely. He hated the way she examined him as if he were an insect, something to be squashed. He hated that she would leave him all alone but for the pale dog that was not his brother, not his like. Not his anything.

"What need have you for a book?" she asked.

"I like books!"

"You can't read," she said.

"I can read," he cried indignantly. "I have read all the books on the schoolmaster's shelf. More than once. I know them all by heart. I recited the entire one-hundred stanza poem written by Jhogo Len the Bright Voice about the dawn battle between mages and dragons for the troop that brought me here. Why can't I go home?!"

"Incredible! The New Jenne people will be enthralled by this mimicry of speech. Then they'll help me. I know it."

She, too, left, turning her back on him.

The emperor did not mean to allow him to go home.

For the first time, Kemal walked through all the final conversations he'd had with everyone who he'd left and been left by since the troops came for him. A yearly tithe. The schoolmaster suggesting he run away.

You belong to the emperor now.

The mother and the father had known all along what happened to the river-born. They had known all along that the emperor sought ones like Kemal to stand as surety on the Night of Masks, because the Wild Hunt would take the soul and body of a river-born beast before it would take a mage-born emperor. They had known all along that he was not coming back. That the emperor would never allow it, ever.

He sank down to his knees, head bowed. The pain in his heart squeezed until he thought he would choke on it. The pale dog shoved its scruffy head against his belly. For a long time, they sat in silence together, not moving.

For a long time, for days and days and days, Kemal and the pale dog huddled in the cage atop the scaffolding. It wasn't the wind or rain or cold that bothered him. It was the truth that hurt.

Now that he understood, he could chain together the pieces all by himself. The city of tents was a spiral: hard to enter, hard to escape, like a maze built to keep out spirit creatures unaccustomed to the mortal world of physical objects, as the schoolmaster had once said. The straight avenue through it would be opened on the Night of Masks for the Wild Hunt to approach. Although Kemal did not know where the Wild Hunt came from or where it went when it departed, he did know that the Hunt belonged to the spirit world, which some called "the ever-shifting land beyond the river."

He also now suspected that his dream-memories had been telling him all along that he had come from the spirit world too. He had walked out of the river. He hadn't been born like ordinary people, real people, real children.

He thought of the slippery shapes, the undulating light. Breaking the surface.

"I am a boy," he said to the sky.

The sky said nothing. The dog nestled closer. The days passed.

Caretakers brought food and water, took away waste. They brought him a blanket and a cloak, not that he really needed them. Yet, although he asked more than once, no one brought him a book. No one spoke to him, nor did they answer when he spoke, which the mother and the father would have said was discourteous, but perhaps the rules were different in the emperor's palace, or perhaps the rules were only different for talking to river-born. Now and again, he heard people discussing by what mystery he was able to mimic speech and whether the scholars would be able to figure it out once they got here. Once, he thought he saw the sergeant and Trooper Chorki at the base of the scaffolding, staring up at him, but maybe he was just hoping it was them, and really it was some other pair of curious soldiers.

One morning, in the teeth of a brisk wind, servants brought figures woven of straw and wreaths wound out of dried flowers and began hanging them around the scaffolding. Along the straight avenue, masks were hung from every pole, their hollow eyes positioned to gaze down the avenue toward whatever would be riding through the spiral city and to the skeletal tower at its center. All were painted as death's heads: skulls of foxes, bulls, wolves, horses, and human folk with empty eye sockets and swirling patterns drawn onto their cheeks.

Back in the village, people put up similar decorations on the morning of the Eve of Masks, which, at sunset, became the Night of Masks. Masks and wreaths and straw guardians were talismans and amulets that shielded against the Wild Hunt as it pursued souls on the deadliest night of the year, the night when the mortal world and the spirit world drifted so close together that the Hunt could cross over and, for one night, ride as a swirling shadow through the lands.

People in the village feared the ill fortune following along as the Hunt passed. A shadowy glance might fall upon an unwary person peeking out a window, thus marking that person for bad luck in the coming year. A shadowy hand might brush the head of a hapless onlooker, its touch the harbinger of death at some point in the months before the year cycled around and the Hunt descended again.

But the schoolmaster had told Kemal that the Wild Hunt cared nothing for most mortal souls. For its yearly tithe from the mortal world, it sought a single soul, brimful of magic, whether a cold mage or a fire mage. That was why the early emperors had died. But the schoolmaster never told Kemal how the later emperors had stopped the Hunt from taking their lives, however sweet and powerful their magic might be.

Now he knew. They offered up a river-born beast instead. Him, or the pale dog, or both together, perhaps, for they were each small, slight creatures, scarcely worthy of a second glance. Yet he had no magic, and if the pale dog did, he saw no sign of it.

Why would the Wild Hunt crave a weak, little beast over a mighty emperor-mage?

The scholars came that afternoon.

In the morning, Kemal heard the commotion of their arrival, a hum of bustling noise from the direction of the largest of the huge, round tents that comprised the emperor's palace. Many banners flew there, brisk and bright in the wind. For a while, the city grew quiet. Kemal stood clutching the bars, too anxious to sit. The dog wound around his legs, whining softly.

At length, a procession appeared in the open ground surrounding the scaffolding's stairs. Imperial guards marched at the front, followed by the emperor, who appeared rather short amid the foreigners. For foreigners they had to be: The tallest had straw-colored hair and skin as light as milk! Another had skin as dark as soot, although his hair was silver-colored.

Kemal had read the schoolmaster's geography book and recalled all of it. Thus he wondered, might the milk-skinned person be of Celtic ancestry and the soot-skinned person of Mande? These two peoples had joined forces several hundred years before to cast a net of rulership over the western territories, their principalities and mage Houses working in concert. Each with their own patch of ground to tend, as farmers would say, and all the villagers in the empire were farmers, even if the emperor and his guards and kinfolk never farmed but rode and herded and fought and conquered instead, as their ancestors before them had done. The schoolmaster was also one of the imperial kindred, though of a far lesser rank.

Whereas Kemal looked like the villagers, only he was colorless, with white hair, ice eyes, and skin so pale his veins showed through, while they had black hair, brown eyes, and complexions neither milk-pale nor soot-black. Did he only look like he was trying to resemble a villager, when he was really something else? As the pale dog didn't really quite look like a dog?

The group reached the base of the scaffolding and started up the stairs.

Kemal shifted back and forth, staggeringly nervous as the footsteps grew closer. What would they think of him? Would they believe he could speak? Would the emperor punish him, if he talked without being given permission? After so many days alone with only the pale dog, he wasn't sure if he had any courage or heart left. Even so, curiosity tugged at him as he waited.

Two soldiers appeared with their sabers drawn. The emperor followed, wearing his gold circlet and gold-threaded garments. His expression as he inspected the cage reminded Kemal of a village mother showing off a new hat. Following after him came the scholars. The two foreigners were built like the father, while the third scholar, built like the mother, looked like she might have grown up in a village. They chattered in a language he did not understand, looking him over like a marvel set upon a shelf to admire.

The silver-haired scholar had the seamed, solemn face of an elder but the regal stance of a person who never doubts he is in charge. Which was odd, because the emperor was there, and yet the old man somehow felt more solid and powerful. His presence made Kemal feel strangely tongue-tied, words rubbed away. What if he spoke, and the old scholar ignored him, or mocked him, or declared he was only imitating sounds? The thought of such a comment coming from the scholar became unbearable, a harsh pain in his chest. As the man studied Kemal and the pale dog with a frown on his distinguished face, even the pale dog flattened itself onto the floor of the cage, ears down, as if feared nothing more than to be dismissed as unworthy by this flood of scholarly discussion.

The emperor tapped a booted foot several times in restless succession to get their attention. "Matun sent for you because she believes you may have some wisdom with respect to this peculiar apparition. Not the beast, I mean. The boy. Have you?"

The mother-scholar bowed in acknowledgement and replied in the same language. "Your Refulgence, we are astounded. There are no records in our annals of such an event."

The elder's gaze flickered as if a window onto a burning-emerald flame had been opened and then closed. Probably it was just the angle of the sun.

The mother-scholar went on. "It certainly looks like a boy in every way, Your Refulgence. Are you sure it is one of the river-born?"

"We have an affidavit from the people who saw it walk out of a river. It was not born to anyone from the village where it was detained, and its complexion is real, not chalk."

"Humans without color in their complexion are called albinos, Your Refulgence," said the straw-haired man. Although he was very light-skinned, he had a rosy, sun-kissed blush to his cheeks, and his hair had the subtle shades of a wheat field, lightened but not lacking in color. "But what do you think, Prince Napata?"

The emperor's gaze fixed on the old man. "A Kushite scholar, are you not, Prince Napata?"

"I am so," the old man agreed. "From an ancient lineage, as you surmise. I have long had an interest in these so-called river-born. Thus have I traveled through many lands, seeking information about them."

"What have you concluded?" the emperor demanded.

The old man took a step closer to the cage. The pale dog whimpered, and its tail thumped twice. Was the smoke that stung Kemal's eyes coming from the hundreds of hearth fires that warmed the city?

"The river-born emerge from rivers at wildly erratic intervals that are tied to the phases of the moon. In their naked state, they usually appear in a form like to scaly eels. Thus, the appellation of water worms, which they are sometimes called. But after taking many testimonies from eyewitnesses and people who have spoken to eyewitnesses, we may conclude that when a river-born creature breaks the surface and touches the shore, one of two things will most commonly happen: it will be eaten by a predator, or it will alter its appearance by changing shape to mimic the first animal it sees."

But he had seen people first, Kemal thought. The children, and the mother and the father. But mostly the children. He had seen them, and his body had changed to match them.

The old man was going on. "This shape-changing out of its scaly eel form into an animal offers some protective benefit, for the nearest animals will then not immediately see it as prey."

"Except the river-born have no color. That is how we recognize them," objected the emperor. "All this, we here in the empire understand already. What use is the university to me, therefore, if it cannot tell me anything I and my forebears do not already know?"

The old man continued. "Do you not wonder why the Wild Hunt will always slake its hunger on one of the river-born, however humble that beast may be, no more prepossessing than this pale dog, rather than an appetizing emperor with mage gifts and the power to make war upon his enemies?"

The emperor frowned. "My forebears wrote about this question, it is true. They had no definitive answer for it. But it doesn't matter, not as long as the Wild Hunt takes them if they are offered. That is why we have kept up the custom of bringing river-born to this place for the Night of Masks. Thus, the empire remains strong and stable. That is why we no longer need fear the Wild Hunt."

"Is that so?" asked the old prince.

He paused, letting the question sink in. He had a regal way about him that stood in contrast to the emperor, in all his power. Kemal could not help but notice that he alone did not call the emperor by his title, as if the old man held equal status. And maybe he did, for the Empire of Kush was the oldest and most venerable of all civilizations. According to the schoolmaster, it was the first stone upon which all the great works of humankind were laid.

"What do you mean?" demanded the emperor.

"If you did not fear the Wild Hunt, then you would not have erected this giant scaffolding. You would not line the avenue with protective masks and talismanic wreaths. You would not cage such humble creatures, this pale dog and this pale boy, so the hunt would take them instead of—as you must certainly fear—instead of them taking you."

With a ragged inhale and a flash of anger, the emperor gestured toward the sky. "I did not agree to your visit so that I might be insulted! Tell me, is the boy river-born?"

The other two scholars launched into a soothing babble of apologies. The old prince smiled, but a tremulous emotion quivered in Kemal's heart at the subtle angle of this smile. Somehow, he thought the smile was for him, but how could that be? *Why* would that be? He was nothing to these scholars, just a creature to study.

Yet while the others were placating the young emperor, the old prince bent forward as if to examine the platform's floor. As he was doing so, he slipped a pouch from his loose sleeves and set it quietly on the planks. While the others were busy kowtowing in response to the emperor's proudly sulking rejoinders, Prince Napata stood back up and used his foot to nudge the pouch through the food slot and into the cage.

"What do you think, Prince?" asked the straw-haired man, for the ongoing discussion had hit a fence with the emperor's sullen silence.

"I am reminded of the words of a poet," the old man remarked. "Death is certain even if one merely waits on the shore, watching the current glide past, out of reach of its opaque waters. Waiting without purpose is also a form of death. Life happens when a brave soul dives into the river without knowing what lies beneath."

"What is that meant to signify?" the emperor retorted, as prickly as a thorn bush.

The old man turned his back on the cage. For the first time, Kemal realized that the old prince was merely pretending that the cage—and its occupants—meant nothing to him, even though they did. He was concealing, if not outright *lying*, about his true feelings. Perhaps even lying about his knowledge to the emperor himself. But wasn't lying bad, according to the mother?

But hadn't the mother lied to him all along? Hadn't she always intended to send him to the emperor, knowing that death awaited him at the palace?

The old scholar's tone had a snap to it when he responded, like the strike of a sharp stick. "Why, surely you comprehend the poem's meaning. You did not wait for your predecessor to pass out of the mortal world, did you not? You took action to assure that you became the next emperor. Some blood was spilled, or so goes the account that came to the university. Am I mistaken?"

The emperor stiffened in outrage, chin lifted, nostrils flaring. "I took that which was promised to me on the basis of my august lineage, my martial victories, and my mage-craft," he retorted in a stinging tone. "Do you intend to insinuate that I have no rightful claim?"

He sounded peevish to Kemal's ears, which struck the boy as strange, for what had an emperor to prove to mere scholars or even a mere foreign prince?

"I speak as a scholar. That is all."

"That is never all." The emperor's annoyance snapped, and a hot gust engulfed the area, reminding everyone that he was a dangerous fire mage. "I am done here. And so are you. This audience is over. You and your people will depart at dawn. And never again set foot in my empire."

He stamped down the stairs, followed by his guards. The mother-shaped scholar hastened after, tendering a cascade of apologies as turgid as spring mud. Prince Napata clasped his hands behind his back, serenely surveying the view from the scaffolding as if the spiral sprawl of tents and the cold, clear sky conveyed a pleasing message to him.

Meanwhile, the one named Matun spoke to the straw-haired scholar in a hushed undertone that Kemal nevertheless overheard. "What of the assurances you made? What help can you and your Tene dukes offer me to rectify the injustice done to my branch of the imperial lineage? I am the rightful heir!"

"Not here," the straw-haired man muttered with a twisted frown directed toward the other remaining scholar. He gave a curt bow, of a sort, to the old man. "Prince Napata, if you will, I would not leave you to descend last."

"Would you not?" remarked the old man with a raised eyebrow. "Then I shall go, shall I not? And hope that the words I have not spoken will yet be heard."

"You speak in the form of riddles, then, for that is the way of the Kushites," said Matun, with a nervous smile.

The old man glanced toward the cage, catching Kemal's eye yet looking away before the others noticed. "So we are told."

Leaning on the railing, Prince Napata began the laborious descent, his limbs stiff with age and his balance chancy. Yet his gaze flashed upward one last time with a spark of warning— or encouragement.

As soon as the heads of all three were out of sight, Kemal grabbed the pouch and carefully opened it. The inside dazzled: tiny mirror shards strung on supple wire and laced with heavy wool thread—and a lot of it. But when he shook them out, the threads and the wire knotted together in a tangled heap. The pale dog jumped back anxiously, then, after a glance to see that Kemal wasn't afraid of it, crept forward to sniff at the nearest twist of wire.

With shaking hands, Kemal spread the mess of sharp shards out and delicately worked to pull them apart. He could tell what it was, even in this jumble: it was a net. But what good was a net of mirror and wire to him?

By now, he was sickeningly aware that with each breath he took, the sun sank lower and lower toward the horizon. Toward the Night of Masks and the Wild Hunt's ride.

Still, he had nothing else to do. No one hope to grasp. It took such a long time to take apart the stubborn knots. More than once, he pricked his fingers and had to lick a spot of blood off the digit. At intervals, the pale dog nudged his arm, or licked his sleeve, as if in encouragement.

Below, servants paced the length of the avenue. They sprinkled salt at the threshold of each gateway that led into their tent compounds. They set up tripods with lamps at the base of the pillars that lined the avenue and lit wicks one by one. Each lamp gave a soft, golden glow to the mask or wreath affixed to each of the pillars, to its grimacing skull face or its circle of withered, purple stone-heal flowers.

The final afterglow of the sun faded. There was no moon, and although the stars shone, a gauzy mist veiled their bright presence. All that was left was a lightless city, huddling unseen in darkness, and a column of eerily glowing mask-faces, frozen in anger or in fear, receding into the gloom.

The scent of burning sage and rosemary tickled Kemal's nose. The pale dog sneezed. The air grew grimly cold as the evening wore away toward midnight. Not a sound could be heard; all the world hushed, even the wind.

At length, exhausted, he finished his work. He commanded the pale dog to lie down and draped the smaller mirror net over it, tucking the edges carefully around so that no stray paw or its long tail peeped out. He wasn't sure what else to do, whether the net was meant to be thrown or used to protect himself and the dog, but he had to do something and he had to trust someone, and the old man was all that was left to him. Maybe the mirrors would shine like a beacon and draw the Wild Hunt to them all the faster, but if so, he was already doomed. He had to try.

A breath of wind curled down from on high. A faint, bell-like tone vibrated against his skin. A slow drum beat rolled as of thunder grumbling . . . or maybe it was the grind of unearthly wheels against the grime and grit of the mortal world: a coach rumbling closer.

An unseen hound barked excitedly, answered by a faraway chorus of yipping and howling.

A hollow in the sky lightened, swirling.

Something was about to appear.

Trembling, fumbling, Kemal tried to sling the other net around himself in the manner of a hooded cloak, but it got caught on his elbow and most of it clattered to the floor of the cage.

Footfalls tapped on the stairs. He grabbed for the net, dragging it toward him, thinking to hide it behind his body in case it was a guard, wanting to curl it around him for protection in case it was the Wild Hunt— and then a person climbed the last steps and halted on the platform.

A tall figure faced him, heat boiling off their shadowed form.

Yet . . . everyone knew the Wild Hunt was as cold as death, so who was this standing there so close beside him?

Kemal could not see the person's face, but all at once, he knew it was the old man, knew it by the smoky, sun-drenched smell, by a tug in his heart, by the whine of greeting the pale dog gave. The pale dog recognized him. Trusted him.

"Best get that on over you," said the old man. So it was for protection; Kemal felt a spark of pride for his own instinct. "And why did you not speak earlier? I was told you can speak."

"It was forbidden," said Kemal, then thought it prudent to courteously add, "Prince Napata. Your Highness."

"Incredible."

"What is incredible?" He was getting a little tired of everyone assuming he couldn't speak.

"That you appear to me as a boy."

"I am a boy!"

"You are not a boy."

"I am a boy! I am called Kemal. Why do you insult me?"

"You are not a boy, Kemal. But we have no time for this. I gave you the mirror net lest I was unable to get away from the palace. But the emperor disinvited me from the evening's feast. He continues to be offended by my truthful words. A good thing too. He made it easy for me to depart the main compound by the servant's entrance and walk here."

"What do you want?" Kemal asked. "Why did you come back?"

"Why, I came for you! For you and your brother."

"It is not my brother! It is a dog!"

An offended growl answered him, and he flushed, and said to the pale dog, "I'm sorry. I didn't mean to insult you."

The prince smiled slightly, and rubbed the dog under its muzzle. "It is not a dog, Kemal, not any more than you are a boy. Regardless, 'brother' is a figure of speech. He is not an actual nest-brother, I mean to say, but a brother as in a recognition of a relationship in kind."

A loud, excited yipping rent the quiet night, interrupting the old man. The color of the air abruptly changed to a sickly hue. The Wild Hunt had arrived.

A horrible apparition glided along the avenue. A coach-and-four raced in and out of the ovals of lamplight, flashing into view and then vanishing. As the coach passed each pillar, the protective mask or talismanic wreath attached to it crackled over with a rime of ice and burst into a spray of shards.

The coach was black, driven by a white-haired, stocky coachman who seemed the most solid thing about the conveyance. The coats of the horses were by turns bone-white and as red as though they were sweating blood. A footman in the shape of a person with wings held on to the rear, feathers rippling. Although the coach's windows were open, they were as opaque as if opening into nothingness. There was no one inside, or there was everything inside. Accompanying the coach came beasts, racing: fanged hounds with tongues lolling, smoothly running leopards, winding snakes and panting wolves, silent owls and keening hawks.

Kemal's gaze snapped back to the old man as an agonizing fear overtook him. "Are you the Master of the Wild Hunt?"

A smile cracked that old face to reveal something deeper, older, and more formidable within. "I assure you, I am not."

The pale dog nudged the prince's leg, as if to show it did not fear him.

"Come now," said the prince more sternly, "let us get the net over our bodies. It will be easier if the Wild Hunt turns away than if we have an altercation."

"But I'm locked in here, and you're out there."

The old man set a hand on the cage door with its heavy iron lock. A flash as bright as a blacksmith's forge blinded Kemal briefly. The pale dog leaped back against the cage bars as a loud snap shuddered through the air. The broken lock dropped to the platform as the old man flung open the cage door and stepped inside. He grabbed the net and, with a graceful spin and flare, tented the mirror shards over himself and Kemal. Before it quite settled, Kemal hastily bent to keep one edge lifted with an arm so the pale dog could creep in and curl around their feet. Then he dropped it and straightened to press against the prince's side.

"No matter what you see or hear, remain silent."

Kemal nodded, too frightened to speak.

They waited as the coach rolled nearer and nearer still. The howling and baying and yelping and snarling and growling and hissing and cackling and keening grew louder and louder and louder until Kemal thought it would pound his flesh and bones into dust. Yet the presence of the old prince comforted him, like the solidity of a stone in shifting sands, like the warmth of a hearth on a cold night, like a shelter set against surging winds, like the schoolmaster's kindness in teaching him purely for the love of teaching and the desire to see a child learn while not asking anything in return.

The old man remained beside him even as the coach's wheels left the ground and it flew up to the height of the platform. The horses and vehicle loomed large and then larger, until they filled half the sky, impossibly huge, the black coach a maw so wide, it could swallow the tower, the avenue, the tents, the city, the whole world. For the coach was death personified, was it not? And this was the mortal world.

The old man put an arm around Kemal, who was shaking with terror. "There, there," he murmured, and glanced down at the pale dog pressed against his boots. The mirrors winked and shuddered beneath the turbulence created by the hunting beasts screeching and howling all around. The wind was a whipping gale seeking its prey.

In the window of the monstrous coach appeared the face of a young-looking man with blazing eyes and a cruel smile. Yet he blinked in surprise as he looked toward them. He rubbed at his eyes as if they hurt. When he spoke, his voice was both hot and cold, both buttery-smooth and edged as with the sharpest knives.

"Where, where are the whispery worms? The rich, ripe maggots? The exquisitely enticing hatchlings? Come out. I can smell you. Come out. Come out."

His gaze did not fix on the mirror net but kept looking all around it, as if his eyes could not fasten on the shards' shimmering gleams. The coach circled the tower once, twice, and a third time, questing, seeking. Then, without warning, it turned aside, rising higher and ever higher as if mounting a spiral path on into the heavens, until it became a moon, a star, a dot of light. Until it vanished.

The night fell calm.

All wind ceased.

Lamps puffed out as if snuffed by one long, blown breath.

The Wild Hunt was gone.

Kemal feared to move in case that ravening pack of beasts and the deadly coach and the direful threat of the man with the cruel smile were waiting to pounce the instant he revealed himself.

Nothing happened, and nothing stirred. A gentle breeze returned, as on any ordinary night. The old man calmly lifted the net off them all. With no concern for the sharp edges, he neatly folded both nets up and slipped them back into the pouch. The pale dog licked the old man's hand, and he patted it with an absent smile, which is when Kemal realized he could see the old man because the scholar's body was limned with a tracery of fiery-gold light. Not cold magic, with its icy-white glow. Yet not fire magic either, with its crackle of barely tamped-down flame, which few humans could fully control before the fire burst out of them and consumed them whole in an obliterating blaze.

His magic was something else. Something unknown. Something unspeakably old and strong.

"As I suspected," the old man remarked with some amusement, "the emperor is not so powerful a mage as he believes himself to be. The Master of the Wild Hunt came for you and your brother. Now, thwarted, he has departed to pursue a sweeter magical scent elsewhere in this benighted mortal world. Thus we, too, may safely depart before the emperor gets wind of this night's events."

"Depart?" Kemal asked. "You and me and the . . . the dog, I mean. I never gave it a name, but I guess it deserves a name, too."

"All in time. Now, shall we go down?" The old man tucked the pouch back up his sleeve. He spoke as if they had just finished a lazy summer picnic on the bank of the river. "I have arranged for my carriage to be brought round to the palace gate. That is not so far a walk, after which we will ride in some comfort, I hope. It is too far to walk to New Jenne, for two young ones such as the pair of you. I am so glad to have found you in time."

The pale dog stuck to the old man's heels, so Kemal followed as well, ever obedient, stumping down the stairs as he tried to make sense of everything that had happened. *Found you in time* was too much to take in, so he asked the question that most concerned him: "To New Jenne? To the university?"

"Yes."

Kemal swallowed his excitement. Trepidatiously, he ventured, "May I study at the university?"

"Is that what you wish?" The prince's tone did not change; it held no scorn, no challenge. It was just a question, strange as that seemed.

"Yes! The schoolmaster said I was his best pupil. I like to learn. More than anything."

The flavor of the air changed, as with a pleasing waft of flowery aroma. "Well, then, my young pup. So you shall."

He did not like being called a pup—like to the pale dog, once again—but he knew better than to protest. Still, his annoyance at the comparison made him think of home. "But what about the mother and the father? Are you not going to take me back to them?"

"To the people who sold you to the emperor? No, Kemal, you are not meant for that life. Shall it trouble you, though, to come with me and not go back there?"

"I don't know," he admitted, because *there* was all he had ever known until this journey. Yet only the prince had protected him, and the pale dog. No one else had. And the pale dog had trusted the prince upon first meeting in the same way it had trusted Kemal.

"We shall take these stages slowly, lad. You are an unusual case, it's true. In time, you will learn what home is."

They reached the bottom of the tower. Without hesitation, the old man headed down the center of the unlit avenue, toward the distant sod wall that surrounded the tent city. His step was spry, and with each stride, he seemed to grow less aged, less wrinkled, as if, at the tail end of the Night of Masks, a mask of his own was slipping off, one that no one else had known he had been wearing. The pale dog lashed its tail eagerly as it trotted alongside, pleased at its freedom. Kemal hurried to keep up, for he was still a boy, after all, not a full-grown adult like the tall, wiry scholar who was also the prince of an ancient lineage. Or so everyone called him.

"How many days does it take to get there?" Kemal asked, turning over in his head the maps he had traced with the schoolmaster at his elbow. "New Jenne is part of the Wagadou Federation. We must travel through Pannonia, and then the Tene Dukedoms, first. Or there might be a more northerly route through the Lusatia Principalities. But it might be very cold there by now."

"You have studied your geography, I see," said the scholar approvingly. "We shall take the route into Pannonia. That route allows us to leave the empire as quickly as possible, although it will take us longer to reach New Jenne via Buda."

"Buda! There is a university there too! Founded in 1635, by—" He broke off as the prince raised a hand to call for silence.

The prince halted. The pale dog halted. Kemal halted. The ground spoke grumblingly beneath the soles of their feet: horses. Kemal turned to look back toward the tower and saw, beyond it, lanterns held high and burning brightly amid a squad of horsemen riding inexorably toward them.

"I had hoped to avoid this," the scholar sighed resignedly. He set a hand on Kemal's shoulder and, with a slight pressure, moved the boy to stand behind him. "The emperor is cannier than I supposed. He's realized you weren't taken by the Hunt, and that he wasn't either. He's come to see."

"But—"

"You are safe with me, Kemal."

The words were spoken so simply, but Kemal felt them in his flesh, in his bones, in his heart, in something deeper still, like a slippery memory of water. Head high and ragged ears erect, the pale dog, too, did not waver from the old man's side as the horsemen arrived.

The young emperor rode at the front, clad in a brilliant surcoat, armed with a saber and with a bow. Hot anger burned on his brow. His eyes raged as he spoke in a fury. "A thief in the night! You dishonor your guest rights, old man."

"Turn aside now, young one." The scholar's voice was calm but firm. "This confrontation need not happen."

"Indeed, it need not. Give me back that which is mine, and I will allow you to leave. This is my only offer."

"Neither of these two are yours. They belong only to themselves."

"So be it." The emperor raised his bow, arrow nocked. With a word, he called flame to the iron arrowpoint. To his soldiers, he commanded, "Shoot the dog first."

He loosed his burning arrow.

An undulation of intense heat sucked away the cold night air as into a vast, shimmering furnace. The old man's form dissolved into a twisting funnel of shadow and light, which spun outward to grow larger, and larger yet, until a huge, winged beast, gleaming with copper-colored scales, blocked the avenue. With a hiss, the creature incinerated the flying arrows, scattering all into ashes. It spread its wings and—with one wing flap and one hot, heavy huff—sent the horses tumbling backward. Riders fell to the ground. Horses staggered to their feet and bolted in stark fear, back the way they had come, for not even all their battle training could make them stand against this.

A dragon.

A dragon!

It was as tall as a house, outstretched wings wider than the road, claws as long as swords, eyes blazing as if made of burning emeralds. Half the soldiers turned tail and ran after the horses, while the other half stood their ground as the emperor lurched back to his feet. The young man—descendant of those who had driven dragons from this very land, sealed the borders against their kind—stared as the dragon opened its great prickly snout to display sharp, white teeth. He raised both hands as if to call down his fire magic. But in a flash, he was blown backward by a blast like furnace heat.

The dragon's voice rumbled with the crackling power of a thousand surging bonfires. "Not as strong as you believe yourself to be, are you, young one? You are not worth my time, not any more than you were worth the trouble of the Master of the Wild Hunt, who has ridden on to seek a more powerful life to take as the mortal world's yearly tithe. Now, let me be clear. Your borders are no longer closed to us. If you ever again offer up any of the river-born on the Night of Masks, one of us will come. You do not want that. Begone, and trouble me no longer."

With a huff, the dragon spat sparks over the huddle of soldiers. Even the young emperor, proud and blustering as he was, took a step back, then

another, then another, backing away without ever turning his back on the towering dragon.

A bump against his leg caused Kemal to look down. He jumped out of sheer startled shock. There, nudging him, was not the pale dog but a spindly little dragonet, copperish in color, no larger than the pale dog had been, but now appearing as an imperfectly tiny copy of the great dragon. As if, seeing the old man change, the pale dog, too, had remembered how to become. Had remembered the lesson of their emergence from the water, upon laying eyes on the most powerful thing they first saw. Or maybe Kemal had had it wrong all along. Maybe the river-born were simply dragons trying to become dragons and didn't yet know how or who or what a dragon was. Perhaps because they'd been scattered out of their nest, away from those who would care for them and show them the way.

At length, the emperor and his people retreated so far into the darkness that the dragon furled its wings and, with a faintly thunderous clap, swirled once, swiftly, and became the old man once again. His seamed face bore just as serious an expression as ever, though maybe even rather more displeased.

Then he looked down to see the little dragonet. He smiled delightedly. "Ah! My little one, you have come home."

It fluttered eagerly but could not yet fly.

He said, "Can you change back into the dog? It would be best for our journey. When we are safe, we shall commence your learning. Just think on how you were before. Let your body pattern into that shape."

The dragonet bobbed its head. The air shimmered, the copper smeared, and the pale dog returned, only this time with a darker and more coppery coat and a more dragonish canine muzzle.

"Very good," he said approvingly. Then he turned to Kemal. "You did not change when I changed. That's how it usually goes, the first time. It's instinctual."

"I am a boy," insisted Kemal, but now he wondered. Was he a boy? What was a boy? Who was he? Could it be he was really . . . a dragon?

Surely not. Yet why else had the elder come all this way to save him?

"We must hasten before that reckless sprout brings an entire division of horsemen, because then, alas, it will get messy. I would rather you not have to witness that at your tender age."

He started walking. Kemal and the pale dog trotted alongside. It took a little while to get to the sod wall and its gate. Here, a carriage waited with a coachman, a footman, and six horses; this was a vehicle meant for speed. The servants greeted the old man by his title and opened the carriage door so he could climb in. If the presence of the dog and the boy startled them, they said nothing.

Comfortably padded seats awaited them inside. Kemal sat beside the old man, and the dog jumped up on the opposite bench with new confidence, tongue lolling in a canine smile.

Prince Napata rapped on the carriage wall. The vehicle began moving, picking up speed. At first, he kept a window open so he could keep watch back the way they'd come. When at last they passed under the city's outermost wall and rolled onward into the countryside, he sat back. He regarded Kemal with those fiery eyes.

"Felt you no tug? No whirlpool in your bones? No urge to become what I am? What we all are?"

"No," said Kemal softly. He wasn't sure whether to be relieved or to weep. Mostly, he feared the old man would not want him if he was not—could not be—what the scholar had come all this way to rescue. Better to make a clean break of it now, if he was going to be rejected. "I am a boy. That's what they kept telling me."

"Ah. That's what you became to survive."

"What if . . ." He shifted anxiously. "What if I can't become a dragon, like you say I am? What if I am just a boy, after all? What if I can't change?"

"It would be unusual, it's true." The old man paused, closely studying Kemal's expression with a tender concern no person had ever shown toward him before, not even the schoolmaster. After a moment, he patted the child's shoulder reassuringly and with his most kindly smile. "And it doesn't matter. You have time to discover what path you will walk, whatever that path may prove to be. What matters is that you and your brother are under my care now. You are safe with me."

As the carriage journeyed through the night, Kemal did not feel sleepy. Questions crowded into his mind, one after the next, until the most pressing one finally burst out of him.

"Do you know the story of the dawn battle between the mages and the dragons? The one that destroyed the city of Golden Mansion?"

"I confess, I do not."

"The chronicles say that afterward, the mages drove the dragons out of the empire, and that is why there are no dragons in the empire."

The old man chuckled. "Is that what they say? Well, there are other accounts that have more of the truth in them."

"Ones I can read? In New Jenne?"

"Ah. Well. There has been a change of plans. Unfortunately, I had to reveal what I am in front of the emperor and his soldiers. News will get around, so we can't return to New Jenne. We'll travel farther west, maybe as far as the ocean. We'll make a new nest for ourselves in a new city, where we aren't known. There are a number of respectable towns and cities to choose from, with academies and universities appropriate for a bright child, who is interested in the world, to learn all he wants to learn. Does that appeal to you?"

The dog thumped its tail. Maybe it had been able to change itself into a dragon, but it still couldn't talk or read or write, Kemal thought smugly. That was something only he, the river-born child, could do.

"Yes!" He could not stifle an excited smile. "More than anything, I want to learn."

The old man—the dragon—smiled warmly back at him. "Then so you shall."

Bloom

art by Nilah Magruder

W HAT WAS A RESPECTABLE MAGISTER, WHO HAD SERVED AUTUMN House for all his adult life, to do? The mansa called Titus to his study and gave him the order direct.

"Titus, I wish you to take my cousin's granddaughter, Serena, with you."

Of course, he could not object straight-out. "As it is said, the comfort of a woman is in her home."

The mansa had looked old to Titus's eyes when Titus had come to the mage House as a fifteen-year-old. Now, thirty-two years later, the mansa looked positively decrepit, a shell of a man with wrinkled skin and age-whitened hair. Yet those keen eyes did pin a man, as if he were an insect on display in a museum of curiosities.

"It is the elder's place to show the paths to the young. You are our House's most experienced and powerful diviner. Thus, you must train her in her calling, now that it has so unexpectedly bloomed."

The compliment lessened the sting a trifle, but the command still chafed. "It cannot be appropriate for me to travel with an unmarried girl who is not my daughter."

"Have you traveled recently with your daughters?" the mansa asked drily.

Titus folded his hands tightly together, searching for a reply, but his thoughts tangled with a pressure in his chest, and he could not answer.

The mansa sighed and patiently went on. "Serena is young, yes, but a woman, not a girl. She was married."

"That is right! I recall it now." He was grateful for the change of subject. "She was married out to Twelve Horns House and sent back in disgrace."

"In fact, she returned of her own choice."

"Imprudence is the mark of a fickle woman! I have two diviners I am already training. The presence of a girl would disturb our travels and, no doubt, result in their being too distracted to learn."

"Since you feel your apprentices are not man enough to control themselves, I will send along my sister Kankou and one of her women as chaperones. As for Serena, I have good reason to believe she will not be careless or flighty."

"She will become sickly and cause a disaster. You know how girls are. Obviously, she already has shown herself to be disobedient and selfish. Anyway, if she has the true diviner's gift—which one must doubt because it is a rare calling—then she can confine it to the nursery and the schoolroom, as women properly do."

"The flower cannot bloom without sunlight. She needs experience out in the world. You know we sail in desperate straits and are sinking. We are among the least of the mage Houses. Our lineage is weak. In the schoolroom, we have only two budding mages, neither of whom can do more than quench a candle's flame."

"I have done my duty in this regard!"

"I do not fault you, Titus. We all regret your son's passing."

Even after eight years, the hideous memory rose: his bright, clever, robust son lying wasted and feverish as pus-filled blisters crowded the lad's skin and his lungs slowly failed. But he had taught himself not to move or speak until the feelings subsided.

The mansa had a quill pen on his desk, which he picked up, examined with exaggerated care, and with the faintest tilt of a frown, set back in its carved-ivory holder. He cleared his throat. "For myself, Titus, I am grateful for your daughters, who have been good friends to my grandchildren."

The mansa paused. Since there was no reason to comment on the frivolous dealings of girls, Titus merely nodded.

The mansa sighed again and went on. "We have neither wealth nor prestige with which to interest the other mage Houses to make alliances with us. We need fresh blood. I believe Serena may be able to find new mages at the earliest unfurling of their first bloom."

Titus respected his elders, but this was too much. "Do you not trust me to serve our House, after all my years of loyalty?"

"I do trust you, Titus. But neither of your current apprentices seem to show much promise in finding newly bloomed cold mages before the diviners of richer Houses sense them and swoop down to snatch them from us."

Since this was manifestly true, Titus said nothing.

"Who will follow you as diviner for our House when you are too old to travel? Answer me that."

Since there was no answer, Titus said nothing.

"I am not asking, Titus. You will take her along. That is all."

Since the death of his son, he had spent as little time as possible in the wing of the House where women walked freely and spoke as much as they wished. So on the day of departure, he had no idea which of the callow girls Serena might be, as a flood of chattering, excited females surged into the outer courtyard to see her off.

Of course, his daughters walked among them, laughing in the capricious manner of heedless girls. Fabia was a tall, lanky eighteen-year-old, and Cassia, at thirteen, seemed to be more filled out every month. When they saw him standing by the carriage, their smiles flattened. Fabia took hold of her younger sister's hand. With wary gazes, they approached, halting at a respectful distance.

"Honored Father, may you have a peaceful and successful journey," said Fabia in a toneless voice.

Cassia leaned against her sister and murmured the same words, but with eyes lowered rather than with Fabia's impudent stare.

"Is all well with you, Daughters?" Titus replied in the same formal way.

"Of course, all is well, Honored Father." Fabia's gaze flickered sideways as if she meant to say something more and then restrained herself. "And with you? Is all well with you?"

He said what was proper in reply. Every time he looked at them, he thought of how the evil sickness that had killed the boy had caught the girls first. Their pock-marked faces were a visible reminder of what they had survived and what he had lost.

Cassia tugged on her sister's arm. "Here is Serena," she said in a low voice, as if the appearance of this distraction was a relief.

There the young woman came, accompanied by the terrifying Kankou. To his disgust, Serena was no awkward, gap-toothed heifer but a young woman of perhaps twenty years of age, in the full bloom of fresh beauty. Indeed, had any Europan painter been asked to illustrate the epitome of youthful, womanly beauty, the artist would have chosen her as the subject, for she was everything most pleasing in a woman. She had strong shoulders and an ample posterior. Her complexion was suitably black and flawless, her lips full of promise, her gaze as serene as her name. She wore modern dress, it was true, the skirt fitted over her full hips, and her waist emphasized by the tight cut of her fashionable jacket. He could not approve of such frivolity. What would these women do next? Expose their thighs?

But she had tied her headwrap in a complicated structure of knots that made him think of difficult questions that could be puzzled over for hours, and she greeted him with scrupulous respect and a generous smile. The women and girls embraced and kissed Serena with enthusiasm before singing her, Kankou, and Kankou's woman, Leontia, into the carriage. His apprentices, Anwell and Bala, wore glowers as they followed. Titus made his farewells to the assembly and allowed the coachman to help him in.

*

By the second week of their travels, he had become so accustomed to Serena's accommodating presence that he was shocked beyond measure when she spoke, one chilly morning, without him addressing her first.

"Magister, I beg your pardon, but I wonder if we might turn north."

They had reached the Rhenus River and were waiting for the ferry at the front of a line of vehicles. The sound of the streaming river had led Titus's thoughts into a bittersweet memory of how he and his son had used to play chess in the fountain garden, with its constant gurgle of falling water. So it was with a tincture of asperity that he opened his mouth to dismiss her comment as the frivolous nonsense it was. But another voice broke in first.

"Magister, we just came through that region and divined nothing," said Anwell, casting a hostile glance toward the girl.

Bala added, "It's probably just overexcitement and a desire for attention."

"Why does the jack bray its foolishness before the elder speaks?" Titus snapped.

As irritated as he had been at having her foisted on him, still, he did not like to allow young men to believe they could be disrespectful whenever they wished. First, they would start with this girl, who treated them with a reserved politeness that did not at all encourage their efforts to impress her, and next, they would think it bold and manly to show insolence to their elders.

"Why north?" he asked her, hoping to use this as a teaching experience. "We traveled that route three days ago."

"I am not an experienced diviner, Magister, but I sensed . . . something unusual."

"Give me a moment."

He shot a quelling glance at the young men, then shut his eyes and plunged his awareness into what his teacher had called "the loom of nyama."

A warp and weft of energy undergirded the world, weaving into and through everything that existed. These energies could be transformed but never created or destroyed, and from them, all actions and reactions arose. As a diviner, Titus could spill like a fish through these dense waters and, in them, discern, like silvery fish in the sea, the life force of human souls. Cold mages had the ability to manipulate the ebb and flow of these energies. A trained mage radiated a pattern of light, which was impossible to describe even to another diviner, for each diviner had to learn to understand how to perceive and negotiate the loom in their own way.

Deep in the ocean of ceaselessly moving energy, a bud of light might suddenly flare with a raw, unformed glamour: This was the mark of a person whose magic had burst into flower. Mostly these blooms were youths coming into their adolescence, although occasionally an older person, who had lived for decades in quiescence, would wake up to find themselves able to handle the threads of nyama, also called energy or power.

In a mage House, of course, such people were immediately sent for training, a process that took many years. But not only the House-born had cold magic. Nyama flowed everywhere through the world. Thus, anywhere and at any time, a person might all-unwittingly bloom. Such House-less people were fair game to whoever found them first. By this means—recruiting new potential mages—a small mage clan like Autumn House could restore its withering fortunes.

Swimming in his mind, through the nearby shoals and bays of these intangible waters, he sought a flare of light but found nothing. Emerging, he turned his head to look at the girl with what he intended to be a kindly nod.

"You have mistaken the matter. There is no bloom."

She spoke in her composed voice. "I sensed it first as a pressure against my heart. It's not a bright light, but as if a struggling flame is concealed beneath a gauze wrap."

Her description was so oddly specific that he cast back into the waters, just to see if he could discover what she meant, or else prove her wrong. Perhaps because divining came so easily to him, he might have missed a glimmer the girl had spotted instead. Maybe she was mistaken, but maybe she had looked harder because she was anxious to be accepted and had thus acted with particular vigilance.

When Titus was young, he'd experimented with different ways of sensing discrete signatures of magic within the great wash of energy, but the old diviner who had taught him had ridiculed as "womanly" any method but that of diviner's sight. Titus retained a vague memory of letting touch guide him. Just as she had suggested.

And there it was: a breath of substance, like an exhalation along his skin. In the diviner's trance, he flowed northward, letting the faint pressure lead his path until he passed a point, and the pressure of exhalation shifted to the other side of his arm. He came around to find himself in a hollow of glowing energy, an area where many living beings clustered. A town.

He saw the incipient bloom as if it were a candle glimpsed behind a translucent window shade. No! There were two candles there, one a bit brighter, but the second rising behind it. The intensity of the light was building imperceptibly, noticeable only because the gauzy covering seemed to be slowly dissolving in two spots.

He opened his eyes with a surprised gasp. All heads turned toward him.

"If I do not mistake what I have just divined, there are two young mages on the cusp of blooming."

Quite unlike her usual subdued and compliant manner, Serena broke in eagerly. "Two! I thought the fainter light was a mirror effect. But I haven't your experience in divining, Magister. Two at once in the same household is unusual, is it not?"

"It is rare, and usually means twins." He preened a little, glad to still be worth something alongside these fresh sprouts. "The gauzy shield that hides them means that possibly no other mage House is yet aware of them. We must reach the family before they fully burst into their power. Before another diviner with more to offer can find them."

He rapped on the small window that opened onto the driver's bench. When it scraped open, he said, "Morcant, take us out of line for the ferry. Take the River Road toward Venta Erkunos."

He was surprised at the certainty he felt. This was the right choice. One, he had to admit, in all fairness, that he wouldn't have noticed, if not for the girl.

By late afternoon, they reached the bustling market town.

"Our first concern is to track down and negotiate with the family," he said to his three apprentices. "To that end, we will split up for faster searching."

"As soon as I have secured rooms for the night," said Kankou, in the tone that assured no one would argue with her, and, of course, he would never have done so regardless.

Cold magic was anathema to fire. Thus, when traveling, cold mages stayed at inns built with a hypocaust. Any large town and ferry crossing boasted such an establishment. Even if no mages had ever slept there, the chance that they *might* someday meant the inn could advertise itself as of the highest quality of establishment, worthy of mages and princes alike.

An innkeeper greeted them at the gate, hands clasped, demeanor welcoming. A youth brought them water to drink in welcome, offering the refreshment to them in order of age, beginning with Kankou.

"Maestra, we are honored by your presence. Magister, please be welcome. Of course, we can arrange chambers." The innkeeper examined the women and the men as if trying to sort out their relationships. "How many chambers will you need?"

"One for Magister Titus and one for Magister Serena and Leontia and myself to share," Kankou said imperiously, then paused. She studied Anwell and Bala through narrowed eyes, although by no other means did she express disapproval. After a moment, she nodded to Titus, inviting his input.

He saw an opportunity to let Anwell and Bala know, without directly scolding them, that they had overstepped in their treatment of Serena. "The rest will sleep in whatever accommodations you provide for those who attend us."

"Of course, Magister," said the innkeeper, all pleasantry, as he ignored the shocked expressions of the young men when they realized they were being sent to sleep with the servants.

Kankou gave Titus a curt nod of approval, fortunately brief, since he preferred to avoid her notice altogether. She turned to the innkeeper. "We will retire to our chambers now, if you will be so kind."

"My apologies, Maestra. Another group has just left unexpectedly, so it will take the housekeeper a short interval to make sure a proper set of rooms is readied for mages of your importance. If you will allow me, we have a private parlor where you may wait in comfort with food and drink. This way."

Another group has just left unexpectedly. Titus chewed over these words as he followed the innkeeper to the parlor. Had they arrived too late? Had a diviner snatched the prize out from under his nose again?

The parlor was appointed with couches and tables, but it was not, in fact, private, if by private one meant for their party alone, as would have been appropriate for a magister of his standing, traveling with a venerable maestra, who was sister to a mansa. As Titus entered, he was appalled to see an expensively dressed man already seated at one of the tables, sipping at a cup of tea with an expression of discontent. The man wore a starched boubou of an exemplary gray-blue color. The cloth rustled as he stood to acknowledge their entry.

"Peace to you, Magister," said the stranger. "Does the afternoon find you at peace?"

"I have peace, thanks to the mother who raised me. And you . . . ?" Titus hesitated. Sending out tendrils of magic, he found himself in the presence of another cold mage, this one with the latticework aura of a diviner like himself, not just some mage House steward traveling about the business of his mansa. His worst fears founded! But he kept his voice level as he continued the polite greeting. "Does the afternoon find you at peace, Magister? And your mother and father and the people of your household? I hope they are at peace."

"There is no trouble. And your family also, may the Lord of All shower his mercy upon the world. I am Belenus Cissé, son of . . ."

He faltered, seeing the women as they crossed the threshold. His mouth, so round with pleasantries, turned shockingly flat and hard, and his eyes flared.

"Serena! I am thunderstruck that you have the audacity to show your face in public after what transpired. And yet, why would it surprise me? The world already knows you as shameless!"

The hostility of the comment, baldly spoken without any softening allusion, took Titus aback. People halted in the entryway, whispering as they tried to catch a glimpse of the altercation. Anwell and Bala smirked, as if they thought it the best joke of the trip to see the girl demeaned before witnesses. The innkeeper blanched as he looked from one mage to the other.

Kankou watched in stony silence. Of course, she expected him to solve this, but the situation had burst so unexpectedly into his face that he was left struggling for words.

Into the silence left by his shock, Serena's voice lifted, mild and humble, in the manner befitting women, and yet not at all quailing. "If the monkey can't reach the fruit, he says it is rotten."

Titus turned to see Serena regarding the man, her countenance so serene that he struggled with delight at her composure and a little residual disgust that she remained so calm while he had not been up to the task of defending the honor of their House.

Her gaze shifted to him, and she blinked twice.

"Magister, Aunt Kankou and I will modestly retire to be about our business. I am sure you and the Cissé from Twelve Horns House will be busy about your drink and dinner for *some time*. As it is said, let a man not hurry about his supper or his conversation."

Of course, Belenus Cissé was here on the same trail they were. But the man's grimace lacked any of the triumphant glory a diviner naturally felt when he had fished a freshly bloomed mage from the ocean of power. That meant he either hadn't found the pair yet or hadn't yet convinced them to bind their fortunes to Twelve Horns House. As much as it grated, Titus was the only one who could keep him busy while the others went looking.

"Yes, I will certainly take my fill," Titus agreed.

As soon as the door was shut to leave the two men alone, Belenus sat heavily, breathing hard.

"Are you . . . ?" He seemed unable to speak the next word, as if he feared Titus was Serena's new husband rather than her teacher.

As if any man would want that kind of trouble in his life! His marriage had foundered in indifference even before the death of their son had sundered their lives.

"I am the senior diviner of Autumn House. I am traveling with my three apprentices—Anwell, Bala, and the young woman." He made no mention of Kankou; if the man couldn't divine her exalted status as the mansa's sister and chief administrator of Autumn House, then that was his problem.

"Forgive my bluntness." The man gestured for Titus to join him at the table. "I was taken by surprise to meet her here, so far from either of our Houses."

"Indeed, it is far. I hope you have had a peaceful journey, Magister."

The other man opened his lips to reply but closed them when the innkeeper appeared with a fresh pot of tea and a tray of dates, sesame-honey bars, and soft, hot buns made of sweetened yam flour. In silence, the innkeeper poured, lingering too long as if waiting for them to begin talking, and finally took away the cold teapot that had already been on the table. As soon as the door closed, the flood started.

"How can I have peace when I have been treated with such disrespect by that perfidious, ungrateful woman?"

"You are the husband? I did not know. I was traveling at the time."

"I asked for nothing that any man does not expect: an obedient, modest wife to bear me children and concern herself with my comfort. I see she has gotten her way."

"A woman's mind goes no farther than the tip of her breast."

"Quite true. Quite true! She was obedient enough when she came to me, and quite without any pretensions to divination. But then she began to speak of dreams and the touch of feathery petals on her face, as if these ridiculous fantasies are the same as a man's clear vision of magic blooming."

"No man can understand a woman."

"Indeed. Indeed! Worst, the women of my House indulged her. Her pretty manners deceived them into thinking her honest and compliant, when all along she was hiding the terrible truth."

"The hidden rot will soon break the branch."

Belenus was no longer listening. Like floodwaters, he would run until the rains of his grievance stopped pouring. "You know, you people are not a prestigious mage House. It was as good a marriage alliance as a girl like her could expect. But she thought she was too good for me, when I am a respectable diviner, having made a name for myself by finding three powerful young mages in the city of Havery before anyone else discovered the children. There was something wrong with her all along. Dry soil will sprout no growth."

Titus winced, but the other man didn't notice. He just kept going.

"What use is a barren woman? A woman gives birth to a mage. She does not become one, whatever she may say. And that isn't all that happened . . ."

Titus was already regretting being trapped at the table. Abruptly, he realized Serena had known the man would spout endlessly in defense of his sour tale and tarnished pride. So he spoke a trite phrase of interest or a query whenever the man paused long enough to draw breathe. It was always enough to keep the man going.

The portrait Belenus painted of Serena was not a flattering one.

Outside, the shadows grew long as the sun sank into the west.

The innkeeper appeared. "Magister Titus, your chamber is ready. You may take supper as soon as you wish, or after dark, if that is more to your preference. We are fortunate to have a mage in town, a person with a humble gift, who comes at dusk to light cressets with cold fire, for your convenience."

"You will join me for supper, of course," said Belenus.

"Of course," said Titus politely. "Let me wash off the dust of the journey."

"Yes, yes. In fact, I have some business to attend to before supper. I should have done it earlier, but then you came and have talked so much that I forgot my purpose here." He called for a servant and hurried out of the inn.

Titus considered hurrying after him, but Serena had had such a sense of surety about her that he decided to seek her out instead.

The innkeeper led him to the back part of the inn, with its three corridors letting onto guest rooms: one passage for men, one for women, and one for families. As he glanced down the women's passage, a door opened, and Serena came out, wearing a different jacket than she'd had on earlier and a freshly tied headwrap. She looked lovely and unflustered.

Titus halted in consternation as she walked up to him, smiling that same serene smile, which suddenly exasperated him.

"Did I endure that man's petulant grumbling merely to discover you have spent your time grooming yourself in your room?"

She looked at the innkeeper, then back at him, and said, "Perhaps, Uncle, you will accompany me to the temple. As a stranger in this town, I do not feel comfortable making my offering alone."

Titus was so astounded by this odd statement—all this time, she had made only the ordinary offerings at altars within the inns in which they stayed—that the innkeeper beat him to a reply.

"Magister, please allow me to engage a guide to assist you in sightseeing. May I particularly recommend the architecture of our temple dedicated to Jupiter Taranis, which is famous throughout the region for its surviving Roman portico and ingenious wheel design?"

Serena smiled and smiled, and finally, Titus remembered the way his son and littler daughters had used to signal to each other with silent smiles before they got up to mischief.

"My thanks, but we shall just take a family stroll," he said, falling in with Serena's fiction about kinship.

The innkeeper withdrew.

Serena walked briskly to the back of the building and led him out through a delivery passageway that led past the inn's kitchen and stable yard and into an alley.

"We have them," she said in a low voice as he hastened to keep up, and something of the sweet nature of mischief entered his heart. His own pulse pounded harder with anticipation. A long time ago, watching his children about their lively frolics, he might even have laughed.

At the corner, she glanced furtively both ways, then pressed a hand to

Titus's arm to stop him from stepping out onto the street. He peeked out past the corner of the inn to see Belenus Cissé, flanked by a brace of servants and striding into the fading afternoon glow. Serena said nothing, nor did her expression give away her thoughts or indeed any tremor of dismay at having run into the man she had once called husband and afterward discarded.

"This way," she said.

Rather than running after the other diviner, she led him right across the street, into a humble votive temple with a sagging gate. The temple's sad little courtyard was populated by two hens and a badger in a cage. A faded mural depicted a crowned woman riding a lion as she hurled a thunderbolt. A priestess wearing the crown of Celestial Juno waited on a cramped portico. The flame of the lamp by the door wavered and went out as the two mages approached.

She greeted Serena with a genuine smile that turned to a cautious stare as she greeted Titus. "Magister. May it be well with you under the crown of the holy queen of the heavens."

"This is my teacher and elder, as I told you," Serena reassured her. "Titus Kanté of Autumn House."

He and the priestess exchanged polite greetings, and afterward the priestess said, "In here, Magister."

Titus hadn't developed the powerful cold magic that characterized the great mages of the mage Houses in Europa. He hadn't the reach to kill an entire hearth's fire just by walking through the door, not as any mansa did. He could not paint illusions out of moisture in the air, nor had he ever shown enough strength to be allowed to learn the perilous secrets of forging cold steel. He could not kill the combustion of an entire factory just by walking past the steam engines that powered it.

Divination was a subtler form of the same magic, present only in a few. It was necessary to the survival of the mage Houses but, despite that, wasn't praised and lionized in the same way. Diviners did not rise to become mansa of their House.

But even he, subtle and small as his magic was, could quench a candle flame. Even he could pull a thread of cold fire out of the spirit world, form it into a ball, and use it to light his way. He was about to do so when he realized the chamber, whose door the priestess blocked, was already aglow with a chilly, white light. Neither Anwell nor Bala had enough control to shape cold fire. Perhaps Serena did, and had hidden this ability from him all this time. For as much as he had disliked Belenus Cissé, some parts of the man's sordid tale had resonated with Titus in suggesting Serena was a secretive, calculating opportunist, who wore her beautiful face as a mask to take advantage of innocent, well-meaning men.

The first thing he noticed about the chamber was its modest furnishings: a plain wooden table, two benches, and a sideboard laden with a pitcher and the sort of lopsided cups that a potter sells for cheap because they've been made by an apprentice. Kankou sat at the table beside an elderly priestess, wrapped in shawls against the cold.

An exhausted-looking woman faced Kankou and the priestess. A toddler shivered on her lap. She had the white skin of Celtic ancestry, marked with early wrinkles, but it was the burn mark across the right side of her face that really stood out. Perhaps she had been pretty once; now it was all Titus could do not to wince at the unsightly scar, and that only because his mother had taught him better than to embarrass a person in public with such a reaction.

Behind her stood identical twin boys of perhaps thirteen years of age, a common age for magic to bloom. The sphere of cold fire hovered between them. Diviners could trace the threads of magic that wove through people, and to Titus's fascination, the sphere was attached to both of the boys, as if they had figured out together how to create it. As if it arose from them working together.

Another sullen youth leaned against the wall, arms crossed, a threadbare coat pulled tightly around his shoulders. He resembled the twins and, like all the children, had brown skin and curly, black hair. Boys this age always reminded Titus of his son, except that his son had never frowned; he hadn't been made for frowns.

As Titus entered, Kankou rose. The exhausted woman rose. Even the sullen youth pushed away from the wall to stand. Only the priestess remained seated with the privilege of age, one age-palsied hand grasping a cane.

Titus greeted the elderly priestess first, as was fitting in a holy temple.

"Maestra Selva," said Kankou to the mother, "this is Magister Titus Kanté, of whom I have spoken."

"Magister," the woman said, before lapsing into the silence of the overwhelmed.

The toddler struggled in her arms, starting to whimper, and the sullen youth slouched over to take the child from her, thank goodness.

Titus opened his hands. "My greetings to you, Maestra. To have twins who bloom at the same time and work together, as these two do, is a rare thing."

The twins glanced at each other with shared surprise.

"I told you he would divine your connection," said Serena warmly, and they smiled at her as if they already trusted her. Belenus had talked about her wily ways, how she had turned the women of Twelve Horns House against him.

"Such a gift is a rare thing," agreed Kankou, "which is why, Magister, we will be taking Maestra Selva and her four children to become dependents of Autumn House."

Soft-hearted, impractical women!

"It is not our usual arrangement," he said, trying to figure out a way to disagree with Kankou without saying so outright, in front of others, which would cause him no end of trouble now and later, once they returned to the house. "I, too, began life outside a mage House. I was discovered by a diviner from Autumn House, where I now reside. My people were given generous compensation in exchange for my leaving home to join the House. I did not bring my family with me."

In a burst of Celtic emotion, the woman rushed out from behind the table to grasp his hands in a shockingly familiar manner. Hers had the thick calluses of a person who has worked at rough labor. "That is why I'm here. When the other diviners came to the clan's gate this week, they offered compensation to the head of the household for my children. But I won't let them be handed away! They and their brothers are all I have left of my beloved husband."

She sobbed. The older son hunched his shoulders. The twins clasped hands, and the globe of cold fire brightened in a most astonishing way, which made Titus forget about everything except the chance of watching such a rare conjoined magic grow and flourish.

"Maestra Selva is a widow," Kankou explained, and since Kankou was herself a widow, Titus felt there was nothing more that needed to be said.

But, of course, people always had to say more, telling him stories he didn't care to hear or droning on about the grief he must feel when he just wanted people to leave him alone.

"My people are miners, the least of folk, hauling rocks out of the mines," said Selva. Her speech had the untutored and unwashed accent of country people. "I fell in love with the young blacksmith who had been brought into our local forge. My family washed their hands of me, saying I ought not to set my sights above my place in life. When my husband took me back to his clan, his people scorned me for my laborer's hands and low birth. Of course, blacksmith clans marry among themselves. I never asked to fall in love with him and aim so high. It just happened. My husband did not reject me, despite their disapproval. He protected us when he was alive. But after the accident—"

She touched the burn scar on her face. The twins stared at the floor. The sullen youth pressed a kiss to the head of the toddler, with a gentle affection that tugged at Titus's heart.

". . . After that, his family have treated us as little better than servants. Now they plan to enrich the household treasure with the compensation they will receive for children I gave birth to!"

"It would be best for everyone if Maestra Selva and her children join Autumn House," said Kankou, in a tone he knew better than to argue with. "The twins will feel more comfortable if their mother is with them and they know she is safe."

"But—"

"Her elder boy has great promise as a musician. He makes the djembe speak."

The sullen youth's gaze flicked up, and his slumped back straightened to a performer's swagger as Serena smiled encouragingly at him.

Kankou went on. "Blacksmith clans have been handling nyama for longer than cold mages have existed, as we both know."

"Fire mages!" he said scornfully. "Quick to burn out, dangerous to all around them."

"And yet, here, a blacksmith and his country wife have sired two budding cold mages."

"Maestra Kankou and dear Serena have treated me as a sister and offered us a home," said Selva. "Please do not cast me aside, Magister. My husband's people tried to send me home, but my family don't want me back, and I can't leave my children. They're all I have."

So be it, Titus thought. Let the women sort out the strain of extra mouths to feed and bodies to clothe; that was their prerogative and responsibility in the House. It would be a triumph to bring home these twins and present them to the mansa, who had, anyway, an elder brother's favoritism toward his younger sister Kankou, for they shared the same mother of blessed memory.

"It will be well," he said. After a moment's consideration, he added a nod for Serena. "It was well done, Serena."

Serena flushed, pressing a hand to her chest as she swallowed and murmured, "You honor me, Magister. It is all due to your generously agreeing to teach me."

Kankou's stern expression softened. "I will arrange for a second carriage to convey the family. Selva and her children will be staying with us in the inn tonight."

He only then noticed how shabbily Selva and her children were dressed, their clothes much mended and made of coarse wool rather than the fine damask one would expect of a prosperous blacksmith clan. The older boy wore the trousers and jacket of the working class rather than the proper robes that any respectable young fellow would wear when not at work. They didn't even have a trunk for their possessions, only a single tattered bag and an old but well-cared-for drum. The toddler clutched a cloth doll missing one of its button eyes. Poor relations, indeed. No wonder the woman wanted to escape.

"The only question, Titus," Kankou went on, "is whether you wish to continue to travel for a few more days, seeing that Imbolc falls tomorrow."

The four cross-quarter days were always the most fruitful time for magic to bloom in a person because the veil between the mortal world and the spirit world pulled thinnest on those days. Of course, no mage rode abroad on Hallows Eve, the most dangerous time of year, but Titus and other diviners usually made their tours around Imbolc, Beltane, and Lughnasad. Too often, he came home empty-handed: mages were rare, and even when he found one, richer Houses could offer better compensation.

But not today.

"I think we may all safely return together knowing we have done our best for Autumn House," he said. And that was that.

He arranged for a tray to be brought to his chamber so he could eat without encountering Belenus Cissé. But late that night, he was woken by a hammering on his door. When he opened it, Cissé shouted drunken obscenities at him and punched him in the nose, so hard that blood flowed. Only the prompt intervention of Titus's manservant Orosios, prevented Cissé from beating him with a stick. Cissé was escorted away, his curses ending in a predictable bout of loud vomiting and querulous whining.

The horrified innkeeper arrived with fulsome apologies.

The pain wasn't so bad—Titus had suffered worse as a youth prone to fistfights—but he accepted a compress soaked in witch hazel and retired to gloat in his victory. His nose was bruised and swollen, but the ache gave him perspective. It reminded him that the mansa would be pleased, and he, Titus Kanté, would be feted and praised by the other men.

So it was that the next day, they once more approached the ferry across the Rhenus River. Their two carriages advanced along the main street, through the town that had grown up around the ferry, with inns, food stalls, a wheelwright and a tailor, and a forge set far enough away from the approach that passing cold mages would not quench its furnaces.

The ferrymaster escorted them past the rest of the line to a place at the front, where they waited for the ferry to return from the far shore. This time when Titus closed his eyes, he allowed himself to recall one particular twilight afternoon, when he and his son had been playing chess in the fountain garden, tiny Cassia dozing on his lap, and Fabia leaning on her older brother's shoulder and singing some childish melody. The boy had gotten up to light a lamp at the far corner of the garden—too far away for Titus to quench it by proximity—but it wouldn't light; the lad couldn't make a flame. He had bloomed, just as Titus—and everyone else in Autumn House—had hoped.

What a moment that had been. But it wasn't the magic Titus recalled. It was the way his son had made a celebration of everything, however small or large, by including everyone around him.

Bestirred by a melancholy wisdom, and mindful of Serena's tactful praise of his teaching, he addressed Anwell and Bala. The young men were sitting on the facing bench, wearing identical churlish frowns.

"Patience is also a lesson. As it is said, the flowering tree will bear fruit."

The surly set of their lips suggested stubborn natures that did not want to learn. Maybe Titus wasn't the right teacher for them. They might do better being married out to another mage House.

"Perhaps there is something you wish to say to me," he said, stricken by an inexplicable desire to hear their opinions. "We are the three of us men, alone in this carriage for the first time on this journey. You may speak freely."

They glanced at each other.

At length, Bala muttered, "Magister, you favor her because of her beautiful face."

The accusation irritated him, but he kept his voice even. "Manners and modesty are a woman's beauty. Furthermore, it is due to her vigilance that we found the twins, when the three of us would have gone on. Can you say otherwise?"

"One deed doesn't build a name," murmured Anwell peevishly.

Titus said nothing, sensing the two young men were about to break and spill. The silence stretched out, leavened by the sound of the river streaming past and the creak of wagons and cracks of laughter among people waiting for the ferry. He'd learned as a child that by holding his tongue, he could remain impervious while others spoke. In this way, he was able to enjoy his own thoughts as chatter flowed around him. But sometimes, as now, he was required to listen, however annoying the words were bound to be.

"She's proud," Bala spat out. "You forget we sat in the schoolroom with her. She ignored us, thought she was too good for the likes of us, even though she had no magic. Everyone seems to forget she didn't bloom until she went away to marry."

"Yes, and what happened there?" Anwell added. "The husband she discarded was certainly angry about it, as we saw. She was happy at first to marry into a better house than ours, wasn't she? And then she was too good for him after her magic bloomed, and so she came back to us instead, didn't she? We're just warning you, Magister. She'll walk over your body to a higher branch if you're not careful."

"She didn't even get pregnant," added Bala unkindly.

Titus opened his mouth, although whether to remonstrate or agree, he was not sure.

A nearby shout startled him. The reverberation of the voice had scarcely died away when it was followed by a hammering on the side of their carriage that shook the entire vehicle.

"Open up! Coachman, open this door!"

The door was flung open from the outside to reveal Morcant. The coachman's sun-reddened face was further flushed by a grimace of anxiety.

"Magister—" he began, before being rudely shoved to one side by an armed man wearing a tabard marked with the oak tree of Venta Erkunos, the town they had so recently left.

"I am a magister of Autumn House," said Titus, staring down the armed man, who was, after all, merely a retainer who served a local prince. "Why do you trouble me with this disturbance?"

The armed man stepped away to reveal a constable, whose cap bore the oak sigil as well.

The constable spoke. "I seek a woman named Selva, who has stolen four children who belong to the Camara clan of Venta Erkunos."

Camara was a common name for blacksmiths. This charge was so serious that Titus gestured to Morcant to set down the steps. He descended as into the face of a storm. For there, at a prudent remove, stood a pair of blacksmiths and a vigorous old woman, whose hands bore the calluses of a master potter. The sting of their fire magic pressed against Titus's reservoir of cold, a wash of barely contained heat.

Titus had come from a family of respectable farmers, for whom proper manners and public constraint was how one behaved. As a boy, he had both marveled at and been a little afraid of the flamboyant behavior of the local blacksmith, who made a performance of the work he did, singing as he worked, or commenting upon the flight of birds. Everyone feared the destructive power of fire, but the young Titus had admired how the blacksmith wielded power without the least appearance of apprehension. Fire mages always lived a breath of control away from dying in flames. Maestra Selva's dead husband and the burn scar on her face was proof of that.

Of course, people bored of waiting in line for the ferry had gathered to stare at the members of a blacksmith clan confronting a mage House's carriage. But they all kept their distance.

The presence of the constable meant no one exchanged a proper greeting. This was a matter of law, so it was the constable who spoke. "Four Moons House has already given compensation to the Camara clan for the reception of two children, identified as cold mages, into the household of Four Moons House. I have been called into service by three elders of the Camara clan, including the mother of the children's father. Do you deny you have the children with you?"

Titus prized his honesty, but a wily thought teased him now: What if he let them look inside his carriage to see only Anwell and Bala? What if they could get away with the twins by pretending the second carriage wasn't theirs?

He could not stomach the lie.

He tried a different argument. "Has the children's mother no say in this transaction? Was her permission obtained?"

The elder blacksmith replied in the reasonable tone of a calm soul who prefers to work things out.

"You ask the question the wrong way around, Magister. Our son's children may not be stolen from his family without our permission. We did not give it. The woman has no legal status to act on behalf of underage children who are residents of my household. We negotiated with Four Moons House before you arrived."

A sudden wailing, like that of grief, broke out from the other carriage. Its door opened, and Kankou descended with her usual imperturbable dignity. The constable took a step back, out of respect, as she crossed to stand beside Titus. Even the blacksmiths acknowledged her arrival, as a worthy elder and distinguished woman.

In a low voice, she said to Titus, "We cannot make an enemy of the mansa of Four Moons House. He can destroy Autumn House if we anger him."

"I thought the matter was taken care of and all negotiations proper and closed," he said in as even a tone as he could manage. All the attention focused on him by so many strangers roused in him an enraged sense of humiliation. "I had no idea there was a prior claim beyond the attempts of Belenus Cissé. If I had known . . ."

Hearing his voice start to rise, he closed his mouth.

"I confess, I have erred." Kankou spoke as if the stares and devastating blunder did not trouble her at all! "Maestra Selva misrepresented her situation. Serena's kind heart did the rest."

Of course this trouble was the fault of the young woman! He had known all along it would be a mistake to bring her. And yet, even still, Kankou—and thus by extension, the mansa of Autumn House—defended the girl!

The sobbing Selva was helped out of the second carriage by her elder son. She swooned when she saw the elders.

"I will accompany the twins to Four Moons House myself," the potter said. "The other two will return home with my brother. As for you, Selva, you may take yourself off, as you so clearly wish to do, if these mages will have you, which I doubt. For you have proven yourself disloyal, on top of everything else."

The youth dropped to his knees, a hand pressed to his heart. "Please, Mamamuso, do not send our mother away from us, her children."

The elder blacksmith said, magnanimously, "Selva may return to the household. She is still nursing the baby, after all."

To which the potter replied, "But we will have no more of this foolery from the likes of you, Selva." She herded the stricken twins to a waiting carriage.

The toddler was taken by the elder blacksmith—held tenderly, Titus was relieved to see—and Selva roused enough to stagger after the baby, leaving her elder son to carry the worn bag and the precious drum. Thus were they enfolded back into her deceased husband's clan.

The blacksmiths took their leave in the rudest manner imaginable, as if Titus and his people were nothing more than common folk, who could be passed on the roadside without a glance or greeting. It was getting dark, and as if in direct insult, they lit torches that Titus's frail cold magic wasn't strong enough to quench. He wished his anger could douse every hearth fire in the ferry crossing.

"It's so sad," whispered Serena to Kankou. "She was desperate to escape. They haven't been kind to her."

"Sentimental women!" Titus muttered.

A man trotted up, wearing the chain of the ferryman's assistant. "Magister, my apologies, but the ferry has halted for the day. There will be no crossing on Imbolc, so you'll have to take the first crossing in the morning of the day after tomorrow."

A headache of pure thwarted rage assaulted Titus, causing stars to burst in his eyes. His manservant Orosios hurried over to him, aware of the signs, and soon Titus sat in a comfortable chair in the parlor of an inn, sipping at a tisane of feverfew. A bowl of hot water scented with drops of lavender oil sat at his elbow, so he could inhale its soothing properties.

He had hoped that the women would show him enough respect to allow him the parlor to himself. But although Kankou had banished Anwell and Bala, she and Serena sat side by side on a couch, chatting companionably, as if Serena's rash decision hadn't brought disaster down upon his reputation. Kankou carried a bag of beads with her, and she was threading a bracelet as Serena embroidered the neckline of a shirt.

"What should I have done differently, Aunt?" Serena's voice never trembled, nor did she weep. She was simply too self-possessed for Titus to believe in her naïve protestations. "Her tale reminded me, in some parts, of my own."

"It is a hard thing," agreed Kankou. "I do not like to leave women in such situations, nor should we ever turn our backs if we can do something. But I fear it was a misstep. Your kind heart overwhelmed my prudence. Although, I do not blame you for it, after what you went through."

"Will Four Moons House seek revenge on us, if the blacksmiths tell them what happened?" the girl asked. "Might they come here to accuse us or charge us with a crime? I studied the maps carefully before we left, and many of the villages south and west of this crossing owe clientage to Four Moons House."

"That is true," replied Kankou. "Their main estate is not so far from here, not that we of Autumn House have ever been invited to visit such a grand establishment."

"Could we send a letter to their mansa with our regrets for causing an incident?"

"No, indeed, we could not!" Titus interposed, setting down his cup. "A man of his status, reputation, and power could ruin us with a few words. It's better if we not remind him or anyone at Four Moons House of this debacle."

"As I was about to say," Kankou continued, with a stark glance whose disapproval caused him to close his hands into fists, "we are beneath the notice of such a princely mage House. I doubt the blacksmiths will mention the matter to them because this little misadventure reflects poorly on them as well. That their precious son fell in love with an uneducated rock hauler's daughter, for one, and that she outwitted them enough to almost escape. Imagine if they had to tell the mansa of Four Moons House that they had lost their own children and didn't know where they had gone."

She chuckled. A smile chased across Serena's face.

Titus decided he was not hungry enough to eat supper with women who could find humor in a man's dishonor, so he went to bed and suffered through a dream-plagued night.

He came downstairs the next morning, feeling slightly better, only to find Serena and Kankou in the parlor before him.

"May I pour you tea, Uncle?" Serena said. "I am sorry for what happened. I have ordered the porridge that you like for breakfast."

Women's smiles did soften a man, especially a man who was both hungry and thirsty. A server arrived just then, with bowls of steaming hot rice and millet porridge covered in milk and garnished with crushed peanuts and sugar. His headache had vanished, although the throb of anger remained, but he could wait to discuss the whole sorry episode until they returned home and brought the matter before their mansa. Anwell and Bala hurried in and sat down to eat.

That's when it happened. A force slammed into him. He was buffeted by a magical storm like pounding hail brought down atop alarming gusts of wind. The deluge deafened and blinded him for several breaths, then cut off so abruptly that the first thing he wondered was if he had been taken by apoplexy.

Slowly, he realized the normal sounds of life—the rumble of wagons on the road, a barking dog at the inn gate, and footsteps along the corridor— went on as usual. Except for a cry from the far corner of the inn. The furnace room that heated the hypocaust system.

"The fire has gone out!"

"What was that?" asked Bala, looking both startled and delighted.

Anwell said, daringly, "Was that a bloom? I felt it!"

"That was surely too powerful to be the first bloom of a budding mage," retorted Bala, giving Serena an accusatory look. "I hope some powerful cold mage hasn't come to punish us."

Serena looked at Titus. "What do you think, Magister? It was so strong, I'm not sure where it came from. It feels as if it came from everywhere."

He sent his divination along the path of its residue, a trail that led back through the town and out into the countryside, amid the sparks and tendrils of animals and plants. "The residue is fading fast but is still visible to my divining eye. It leads into the countryside."

Kankou frowned. "As Serena mentioned last night, some of the villages hereabouts live in clientage to Four Moons House and thus would be beholden to a master too powerful for us to gainsay. Under the circumstances, perhaps it is wisest simply to move on."

Serena stood with head tilted, as if she was listening to the invisible threads of nyama. "The bloom was very strong, Aunt."

"It was," Titus agreed. Now that the stunning assault had waned, he could measure how startling it truly was. The chance to redeem this terrible journey made him bold—and reckless. Yet he chose his words carefully. "Surely there can be no harm if Serena and I investigate such an astonishing incident. It would be a shame merely to travel on as if nothing had happened."

Kankou nodded with understanding. "You are correct, Titus. You and Serena should go. I am too old for a breakneck journey across rough paths, so I will stay here with Anwell and Bala to look after me."

The young men's expressions became almost comically outraged, but, of course, they could not protest what Kankou decreed.

She went on without acknowledging their distress. "Morcant will drive you. Take your manservant, in case you run into any trouble. Orosio has got a strong arm. Leontia will act as Serena's chaperone." A sly smile peeped out, suggesting all the mysteries of the women's wing, to which men had only limited access. "She has a strong arm too."

Soon, the five of them were trundling south on a rutted wagon track. Titus's manservant sat outside on the driver's bench with Morcant, and the two women were seated inside, facing Titus. Serena braced on the bench, seeming about to break into speech each time they were jostled and jarred. Each time the girl opened her mouth, Leontia would press a gloved hand to the young woman's skirt, right at her knee, some women's communication that men were not meant to fathom.

A particularly hard jolt broke Serena's resolve.

"Did Belenus Cissé tell you his story to try to make you dislike me?" she asked, so bluntly that Titus was appalled.

"Men will speak when women are not present," he said, repressively.

"Serena, do not taste the sauce when it is still boiling," said Leontia, warningly, although in a far more lenient voice than Titus would have used.

The girl sat back with a tense mouth and a proud lift of her chin.

In this uncomfortable silence, they went on for some time. Finally, the carriage halted. Morcant opened the door onto a landscape of broken woodland.

"Magister, we can go no farther. One of the horses can be ridden, if it pleases you."

"We'll walk. It's not far."

He and Serena set out.

"I smell smoke. And pine!" Serena said, inhaling enthusiastically. Her earlier indignation seemed to slough off. She had a healthy stride and a vigorous appreciation of the country air.

"Find the tendrils of magic, which you should still be able to sense. Follow them as you follow the trail of smoke."

He hung back, letting her take the lead, and only gestured in the correct direction when she hesitated. As they trudged through the winter-whitened grasses, he realized that both magic and smoke led toward the same place: a hollow marked by the presence of a holy oak tree. Beneath its mighty branches, two men tended a campfire. The firepit held ash and charred logs, as if it had been burning all night and gone out recently. The eldest of the men was attempting to nurse a flame with new kindling, without any luck.

A deer whose internal organs had been removed was hanging from one of the branches. Beyond the canopy, another four men were field dressing two more deer. These were country men, dressed in wool tunics hung with charms and painted with the symbols used by hunters to protect themselves in the wild.

Serena reached out and grasped Titus's hand, squeezing so tightly, he would have protested if this simple expression of trust and kinship had not shocked him into silence.

"Look," she whispered, pointing toward the hanging deer with her chin. "Magister, I mistook it for a tundra antelope, but it has a third horn. That is no creature of mortal earth, is it?"

He pulled out of her grip and walked forward to see better. The two deer having their organs removed appeared in all ways to be ordinary animals. But the other animal's third horn was knit out of the silvery glamor of magic.

The hunters straightened up from their task. The eldest gestured to the others to stay where they were and came forward to greet them. He wore his hair in many braids, each end tied off with a tiny amulet. His weathered face was enlivened by a steady gaze. Of all people, hunters had the least to fear from mages. People had hunted in the interstices between the mortal and spirit worlds long before cold mages had learned to pull tendrils of cold magic out of the spirit world and use it for their own ends in the mortal world.

"Peace to you, Magister," the man said. "Does the day find you at peace?"

As Titus greeted him in the same manner, Serena took several steps to the right, surveying the land beyond the oak's canopy. The hunters watched her with respect and did not move.

"Magister, look there," she said, tone so sharply edged that it grabbed his attention instantly.

On the opposite side of the tree and the fire, beyond the oak's canopy, a youth was standing with a knife in one hand and, in the other, a dead grouse dangling from a leather cord. He had turned to stare at them; a bold lad indeed.

Titus's first thought was at how fickle girls were: The youth was unusually good-looking, with an almost uncanny perfection of features. He looked a few years younger than Serena, perhaps sixteen, no longer a boy, but not quite yet a man. In a few years' time, women—and men who were inclined that way—would no doubt be beating a path to his door. How shallow of Serena to have noticed a handsome face while ignoring the others.

Then he thought of his own son, who had been this age when he'd died, and the shadow cut straight through his heart.

Serena tilted her head to one side and blinked twice. At first, he thought she mocked his grief, but she was just signaling.

The elder hunter had ceased speaking. None of the party looked toward the lad. It was as if they were pretending the boy didn't exist, in the hope Titus and Serena would not see him. Maybe they hadn't felt the magic, or perhaps they feared what would happen next.

Titus let his awareness reach the boy. To his surprise, he hit what in the mortal world would have felt like a pane of glass. The bloom of magic had exploded outward and then retreated hard, pulled as into a shell. Seeing that they were looking, the youth at once fixed his gaze on the grouse, although nothing about the set of his shoulders made him seem the humble villager he surely was.

"Who is that boy?" Titus asked, loud enough that his voice carried beneath the cold weight of the afternoon's cloudless sky.

"He is just a boy," said the elder.

"We are diviners. We sensed a bloom of cold magic."

The lad took several steps farther away from the fire. At once, a wavering flame caught its courage and licked up a dry stick of kindling.

"Our fire did go out at a gust of wind," said the elder, "but as you see, Magister, it is burning. There is nothing here for you."

Serena caught Titus's eye and shook her head. "The boy is a cold mage," she said softly. "I think he knows but does not want to know, and thus is desperately trying to build a shield around himself. You feel that shield, too, do you not?"

Titus thought of the intangible surface, like an invisible pane of glass. "I do. It's highly unusual for an untrained mage to be able to instinctively construct such a barrier."

The elder nodded to his companions, and they went back to work, all except for the lad, who continued to watch.

"We are villagers in clientage to Four Moons House, Magister," said the elder, "out hunting for meat to feed our families through the end of winter scarcity. That is all."

"That is not all," said Titus, disliking the man's evasiveness. "The bloom of a new cold mage may surge and ebb over several days, or weeks, or even months when it first flowers. And today is Imbolc, an auspicious time for mage-craft and the first hint of spring."

Serena was still looking toward the youth. She said in a clear, warm tone, directing her words toward the lad, "A cold mage has the right to choose their own path. Even if those around them tell them they must obey."

"Furthermore," added Titus, "I am within my rights to make an offer to the boy's clan, by virtue of having reached him first."

The boy said, "I'm a hunter. That's all. Whatever else you might think isn't about me."

"Enough, Andevai," said the elder. He again addressed Titus. "As I said, there is nothing for you here, Magister. Please—"

He broke off. They all heard the sound of riders. The hunters set down their knives as six horsemen emerged from the trees. Serena retreated to stand beside Titus. She self-consciously straightened her headwrap before clasping her hands at her waist with womanly modesty.

Four of the men were soldiers who wore indigo tabards. Titus himself never traveled with soldiers. He trusted in his status as a diviner to protect him, and anyway, Autumn House could not afford the expense. But when he turned his attention to the other two arrivals, expecting to see diviners like himself, come to compete over the lad, he realized his mistake. Only then did he notice the markings on the soldiers' tabards. They wore House livery with four moons: crescent, quarter, gibbous, and full.

"Serena," he said softly, in warning, but it was too late. The danger had crashed down on top of them.

The tall, heavily built man who dismounted from a big bay gelding was no diviner. A few years younger than Titus, he was a man in the full power of his maturity, and an intense aura of magic radiated from him—not visually, of course, but perfectly tangible to any diviner. He wore a knee-length jacket of indigo, of the finest cut and cloth, a garment the mansa of Autumn House could never afford, and certainly not as casual wear for an afternoon ride. His face was as black as Titus's own, although this man had coarse, tightly curled, dark-red hair, a reminder that the ancestors of the mage Houses came from both the Afric south and the Celtic north.

That he was accompanied by an elderly djeli—what those of Celtic ancestry might call a bard—affirmed his identity. This intimidating personage could be none other than the feared and formidable mansa of Four Moons House, a man to whom princes gave way. When the budding fire went out as if sucked clean away, the potency of his cold magic was confirmed.

The mansa's gaze swept the scene. He paused on Serena with a widening of eyes that then narrowed appreciatively, but politely looked away to continue his scrutiny of the hunters. By the way his gaze skimmed disinterestedly over the lad standing out in the grass, Titus could tell the mansa was no diviner; he had not identified the boy as the source of the bloom. This prize might be salvaged yet, just by keeping his mouth shut and his demeanor cool.

"Mansa," said the elder hunter, going down on one knee beside the dead fire.

"We are looking for a freshly bloomed cold mage. Have you any knowledge of it?"

The elder shook his head. "I am a hunter, mansa, and a farmer, and a council member of your village of Haranwy. Mage matters lie not within my purview."

Meanwhile, the djeli had walked over to the animal hanging from the tree and was examining the creature with the greatest interest. Like mages and hunters, a djeli could see what was invisible to the eyes of those who had no direct access to nyama, but he was not a diviner either, and might overlook the boy.

"Who are these people?" the mansa asked the hunter, indicating Titus and Serena.

"Mansa, I am Titus Kanté of Autumn House."

"I don't know the name. One of the lesser Houses, I assume."

"We are among the least," agreed Titus, not without a sardonic twist to his tone.

Serena's lips quivered, and she offered Titus an appreciative side-eye and a tiny nod of support.

The mansa saw her do it, and he made a slight grunt like a repressed chuckle.

"Our estate lies near the city of Anvers," Titus added with more tartness than he intended. Serena touched her elbow to his arm to remind him of her presence. "Ah! And this is my apprentice, Magister Serena."

Mage House women did not bow to men—it was beneath their dignity—but she spoke in her warm voice. "Your Excellency, we are a small House with a proud lineage, descended from the Empire of Mali, just like you."

"A remarkable assertion," said the mansa, in the defensively amused tone middle-aged men often used when faced with a young woman who carried both beauty and intelligence with confidence. "But it is true that in some manner, we mages are all cousins. To that end, I would invite you—" Now he was careful to address Titus. "—to join me for supper. We have a special meal prepared in honor of Imbolc."

Titus hesitated. He wanted the mansa to leave. Yet such an invitation, from one of the most prestigious and powerful mage Houses in Europa, was an opportunity that his own mansa of Autumn House would tell him to accept. He had to balance the chance to snap up the boy against the incredible favor being shown to him, a connection that might be nurtured in the future.

So far, the day had remained clear and bright, with not too much wind, but now a breeze stirred and brought with it a swirl of snowflakes as clouds moved in. Or maybe the sudden rise of wind came from the mansa, for the most powerful cold mages could draw down cold fronts and even shift the air in the heavens to daunt those who thought to challenge them.

"As well, it is wiser to avoid travel on Imbolc, a day on which the weather is notoriously changeable," the mansa added with a heavenward glance as a cloud skimmed over the sun. Titus could not help but wonder if the man was altering the weather to suit his own purposes. "With that in mind, I invite you to spend the night at Four Moons House, which lies nearby. It grows dark early. If you are lodging at the ferry crossing, you may find it difficult to return there by nightfall. I must assume you find yourself here on the same errand as I am on myself."

"We stopped here to ask directions," Titus said. "But if I may speak so boldly, Your Excellency, I admit I am surprised to see you, since you are no diviner."

"Our diviner is traveling elsewhere. Even we who are not diviners felt that wash of magic. It is gone now."

"A curious incident," said the djeli, stepping back from the animal. "But it may be explained by this creature. Some villagers are known to retain the secrets of hunting in the spirit world on the cross-quarter days, when the veil between the worlds grows thin. It may be that some magic leaked out of the spirit world when they returned."

"Could that be?" the mansa asked the elder hunter.

"The secret is not mine to share," said the hunter in answer.

The mansa accepted this statement without argument. Mages held that certain aspects of mage-craft were too dangerous and potent to be revealed to those who were not mages, so they could scarcely demand answers from hunters who had their own private knowledge.

"Aunt Kankou will never forgive us if we don't take the mansa up on this astounding invitation," Serena whispered in Titus's ear. "The boy will go home. Notice how neatly his village elder revealed the village's name in our hearing. He intended that information for us. We can find the boy later."

So it was that the mansa gave his horse into the care of his soldiers and graciously accompanied them in the carriage. He treated Leontia with careful respect, and for her part, the usually easygoing woman was too daunted by his presence to speak a word.

But like all great princes, the mansa had an ease of manner that encouraged Titus to converse while never becoming too familiar. He asked about the history of Autumn House and how it was established in the city of Anvers. Titus gave rote answers, not wanting to reveal too much of the household's dismaying situation. Truth to tell, he was also fretting over the village boy, his chance to snatch a victory out of the defeat he'd suffered in losing the twins. It was Serena who quietly saved the day with a series of charming anecdotes, dating from the time of her great-grandparents.

"—and when my great-grandmother challenged the prince's bard to a duel of wits, it turned out his blade was not as sharp as his boasts implied. After that, the prince dismissed the bard and married my great-grandmother, who, as I have mentioned, was by that time a widow, and free to marry as she pleased. A number of her relatives left Five Mirrors House in Lutetia and joined her in Anvers. There, they formed their own small but independent House."

"Ah, so your people are descended from Five Mirrors House," said the mansa.

"For some, that prestigious connection will be seen as Autumn House's chief claim."

"But not for you?" he asked, with a bit too teasing of a smile for Titus's liking.

"A wise woman knows her own mind."

"And a wise man listens," the mansa replied.

Her gaze flashed to meet his, and for an instant, Titus was sure it was the powerful mansa who blushed, not the calm young woman.

"I respect my great-grandmother for choosing the more difficult path," said Serena. "But tell me, Your Excellency, I was surprised to hear you refer to a single diviner. Has Four Moons House only the one?"

He shifted on the bench beside Titus as if the question made him uneasy, not that Titus could imagine anything making a man of his stature uneasy. But evidently, Serena's presence made the man loquacious. "It is an odd happenstance that Four Moons House has produced so few diviners in recent generations that my sister is the only one left to us. My aunt arranged my second marriage because the woman was a diviner, but alas, she has left the mortal world."

Titus murmured the proper sentiments and condolences.

After echoing them, Serena asked, "And your first wife? She is not a diviner?"

"No, she is a daughter of Two Shells House."

"Oh!" said Serena, looking ingeniously impressed, and indeed, to be allied with one of the two first mage Houses settled in Europa was impressive. "They are in Gadir."

"Yes. She is not herself a mage, but she is the daughter of mages. My grandmother of blessed memory arranged the matter when I was eighteen. At that time, my great-uncle was mansa, and it was by no means yet determined that I would become mansa after him."

"The strength of a mage House rests on the heads of its elders and the legs of its children," said Titus, because Serena was certainly speaking too much.

"That is true," agreed the mansa, without looking away from Serena. "Two Shells House certainly has produced potent cold mages in its time, but my grandmother arranged the match for the trade opportunities it provided us. In fact, my first wife is fruitfully engaged in commerce. She travels frequently and lives most of the year in Gadir, among her own people."

Serena glanced at Titus and blinked twice, as she had done before, a signal that meant "trust me." More fool he was, to ever have trusted her. For her perfidious nature slithered into view at that very moment, as her beautiful lips parted to reveal the full foul deception of her nature.

"So, Your Excellency, your House's lack of diviners explains why you did not notice the bloom among the hunters."

Under any other circumstances, the mansa's startlement would have been amusing. He was not a man to be easily surprised or overset. "What bloom?"

"The youth standing out in the grass. A handsome boy. He held a grouse, as if he'd been sent out there to clean it, but in truth, he was staying as far away from the fire as possible."

"But the fire was burning when we arrived," objected the mansa.

Titus felt his mouth working soundlessly, and it took all his will to clamp his lips down over the curse he wanted to throw at her for betraying her own House in this unfathomable and unforgivable manner.

"As Magister Titus has so wisely taught me, the bloom of a new cold mage may surge and ebb over several days, or weeks, or even months when it first flowers," she said with that same limpid gaze that apparently really did conceal a rotten heart. "But I will tell you this, Your Excellency: my divining tells me he will be a powerful cold mage, more powerful than any of us may even understand."

"He's a village boy," the mansa scoffed. "His people live in clientage to my house. They are little better than slaves. People with such a low ancestry may learn to create cold fire to light rooms, but they do not become potent cold mages."

Even in the face of the mansa's disbelief, Serena's expression did not change. "You will see that I am right."

"Will I?" he said, and it was impossible not to hear the flirtatious tone animating the words.

Titus fumed, but he could say nothing, although he wanted to.

The wheels of the carriage hit gravel, and the mansa added, "We have reached Four Moons House. Please, be welcome."

The mansa himself helped Leontia and then Serena down the steps, his hand lingering too long on Serena's gloved fingers. Another carriage sat by the portico steps, attended by constables wearing the oak sigil of Venta Erkunos. In the grand entryway, two thin children sat huddled on a stone bench off to one side, waiting opposite the closed door of what was likely a formal audience hall; Titus heard voices from behind the door, where people were having some sort of conference. Seeing Serena, the twins leaped up and rushed over to her as if she were their long-lost cousin.

"Magister Serena!"

She allowed them to hug her, for it was clear they were distraught.

"Who are these?" the mansa demanded, eyeing their rough clothing with distaste.

"They are two fine young cold mages, freshly bloomed, and unique in their ability to twine their magic together," said Serena, giving each child a pat on the head.

"And how do they know you, Magister?" he asked her.

"With your permission, Your Excellency, I shall tell you the tale over supper."

"I anticipate the story with the greatest delight," said the mansa.

A stately woman descended to greet him, and Titus was disgusted to see that Serena quickly won over this dignified elder as well. Had the girl no shame at all, charming her way into their hospitality?

After they had washed up, he tried to pull her aside, but she merely said, in the most high-handed way possible, "Uncle, please trust me."

"How can I trust you? You gave up the secret of the boy, our best hope! And for what?"

He broke off as the realization hit him.

"Foul, perfidious girl! Is this the wiles you spun before, when you angled for a match with Twelve Horns House? I will tell the mansa the truth of your disgraceful and shameless behavior when you were there! Then he won't be taken in by your beautiful face. Bala and Anwell warned me."

Serena's mouth trembled. "What is the truth, Magister? Do you know it?"

"Belenus Cissé told me everything."

"Did he tell you that he drank too much and was often impotent? That he was so angry when my magic bloomed that he beat me until I miscarried?"

The statement took him aback. Yet the prospect of returning empty-handed to Autumn House prodded him into intemperate speech. "What did you do to deserve such discipline?"

"I did nothing except refuse to remain with a cruel husband. I knew people would talk, that they would criticize me, but no woman deserves such treatment. So, I asked several of the most respectable women in Twelve Horns House to write letters on my behalf, in secret. Why do you think they did so? Because they knew what kind of man Belenus is. Their support, and that of Aunt Kankou and the elder women of Autumn House, is how I convinced our mansa to allow me to return. Tell our host whatever you wish, Magister. I am not ashamed, and I will not be shamed for leaving a man who abused me."

Her fury was a blast of wind to which Titus had no answer.

She bristled at his silence, then added defensively, "Would you have acted thus to your wife?"

"Of course not! I am not—" He broke off. An unwanted memory of his son, as a baby, flashed into his mind: a darling infant, full of smiles for his doting father.

"You are not a selfish man with a brutal temper, as Belenus Cissé is."

"How can you know that?" he retorted, swamped by an incredible surge of indignation at the entire appalling turn the exchange had taken.

"Because I knew your son. We were children together in the schoolroom."

Her words stunned him more than any slap to the face. Of course, she had known him. The many children of Autumn House grew up together, a life of shared community, one Titus had often felt uncomfortable with, having grown up in more solitude.

"He was a considerate boy with a kind word for everyone. You can be sure, we girls all knew it—and knew that such sweetness in a boy would have been mocked or even beaten out of such a child by a harsh sire, one who cared only about the appearance of strength and manly fortitude. He often said people thought you were standoffish, but that it was only because you were reserved and a little shy. He called you the best of fathers."

Titus blinked rapidly to try and halt an upwelling of tears. His limbs were frozen, and he could not speak to stop her as she went on with a relentless lack of pity.

"He was so protective of his little sisters. That is how he got sick, isn't it? When they came down with the smallpox, he climbed in through a window of their quarantine chamber to tend to them."

"We tried to keep him out," he whispered. "But the girls were so sick, and they would only settle when he was beside them. He was always strong and healthy, so in the end, we let him stay because he was so patient with them. So good. And they recovered."

Serena said nothing, just stood there with quiet calm.

At last, he gasped out, "I should have forbidden it. I should have locked him up to keep him away from them."

"Maybe he saved their lives," said Serena. "How can you know, Magister? You chose the path of compassion for your children's fear and pain."

He could say nothing, think nothing, feel nothing.

She took his hands as a daughter might and looked into his eyes as no one had in such a long time. "It's how I have known I can trust you. Please know, Magister, that you can trust me as well."

Her sympathy overwhelmed him. It infuriated him that he had exposed himself to her so baldly, that she now held the deepest secrets of his grief as a hostage to her plans.

Yet it was the memory of his dead son that kept him silent throughout the supper, during which Serena regaled the table with a slyly entertaining and pleasingly self-deprecating story of how she had entirely mistaken the matter of the twins in Venta. Embroidered into her tale was also a cunning plea to treat the children well, to think of the circumstances in which the twins had grown and how they might miss their mother and worry about her.

"For children, like plants, grow best when they have both water and sunlight," she finished with her usual poise.

Her earlier blast of anger had been swallowed up into the shield of her serenity. Her composure defeated him. It defeated the powerful mansa and his table of peers, who melted before her perfect manners and lovely smile. Worst of all, Titus suspected she was right about the youth they had stumbled across in the countryside, a lad who was even now being collected and brought to Four Moons House, as the mansa mentioned offhandedly during supper.

Another promising boy lost because he hadn't acted when he should.

*

And thus, they came home.

"I fear you are sickening, Titus," said Kankou as their carriage rolled at last, some days later, into Anvers. "Are you sure you are feeling well? For you have not spoken ten words since your triumph at Four Moons House."

"My triumph?" he muttered peevishly, then hated himself for sounding like Anwell and Bala.

"You can be sure I will tell my brother the whole."

He could not tell if the words were a threat or a promise.

Indeed, when they arrived at the ramshackle gates of Autumn House, he was not even allowed to wash and change his clothing. The moment Kankou had finished speaking to her brother, Titus was summoned into the mansa's study, with its threadbare couch and an old desk whose broken right-front leg had been repaired with leather cord and twine. The old man was spinning illusions out of the air, as mages like him could do, a skill Titus had never grown into despite all his studying and practice.

The mansa had created an architectural study like a toy model formed completely of light. He was examining a collection of buildings from all angles, a remarkable feat of shifting perspective that humbled Titus every time he saw the mansa do it. Of course he was proud of his own divining skill. But as a boy, when he'd bloomed and been brought to the House, he had hoped for more.

After a moment, Titus realized he was looking at an image of a restored and expanded Autumn House, with a second wing built on, new stables, and a larger schoolroom.

Seeing Titus, the mansa smiled. He looked ten years younger.

"Our fortunes have turned, and it is all due to you, Titus!"

"To me?"

"Kankou has relayed to me a letter from the mansa of Four Moons House, penned by his own hand. You may imagine my surprise that such a prestigious House should take an interest in our humble lineage. Something about a village boy in clientage to their House, whom you tracked down and wanted to steal?"

Titus said nothing, and fortunately, the mansa chuckled as if it were the greatest joke imaginable and went on.

"But it turns out the letter is to open negotiations for a marriage. With Serena."

"Serena? They want Serena to marry an untutored, lowborn village boy?"

"Ha! What a fine dry sense of humor you have, Titus. The mansa himself wishes to marry Serena. Such a man may please himself when it comes to a third wife. It seems he means to do so with our Serena. I cannot decide whether to be displeased with you, Titus, or glad."

"Displeased with me?" He still felt confused, adrift on a river carrying him into unknown lands.

"I believe Serena will become a powerful diviner. Now we will lose her to Four Moons House. But all is not lost. The mansa tips his hand by describing her too complimentarily. So I will drive a hard bargain. I will demand several young mages from his House in exchange for her going there."

"Ask for the twins," Titus said at once. "I suppose you might see if you can get their mother and brothers as well, for the twins will thrive with their family about them, and the older brother can make the djembe speak."

"I am sure I have no idea what you are talking about, but it sounds sensible. With such a prestigious alliance, I can also ask for Four Moons' help in arranging other marriage alliances. Also, Serena will not forget her home, and she will not forget our wives and daughters who aided her when she needed their aid. She's a good, loyal, and exceedingly clever young woman. She will continue to help us from her new place in the world. So, Titus, while I knew you would train her well, for you are a careful teacher and an excellent diviner in all ways, you have outdone yourself in this matter. We will hold a special feast in your honor, in the men's hall."

Stunned by these accolades, Titus went to his suite as in a daze, but the empty rooms troubled him. Orosios was busy unpacking, and for once, Titus did not want to be alone. He wandered to the garden with its sparse winter foliage and, at length, found himself at the corner where stood the gate to the women's wing. Where his wife kept her suite of rooms. Where his daughters were growing up.

Of all people, it was Serena who caught him lurking, for he had not quite enough nerve to go in at such an unexpected time. She was giggling amid a cluster of girls and young women, but the instant she saw him, she broke away and strode over.

"Uncle!" She took his hands in hers, smiling, and it was impossible not to respond to that smile with a softened heart and a sense that anything might happen. "I knew you would trust me, Uncle. And I thank you for it. You'll see. This will change the fortunes of Autumn House."

"And your own fortunes." His tone sounded accusatorial to his own ears, and yet her smile widened as if he had praised her.

"He is a fine man and the most impressive cold mage I have ever encountered, is he not?" She spoke with all the starry glamor of a woman dazzled by masculine power and status.

"He is indeed," he replied, since it was true, and truth mattered to him.

"Here!" She released his hands and turned him to face the crowd of girls and young women who had been congratulating her. "Here are your daughters, come to greet you."

It was a lie but so beautifully spoken that he took a step forward as the others cleared thoughtfully away to leave the three of them alone. Fabia and Cassia greeted him with their usual formal manners and wary gazes, the scars on their faces the visible reminder of what he had lost. And, to be fair, of what their mother had lost. The older brother who had loved them, and whom they had loved, whom they had also lost, and whose name no one would ever speak again.

It was so cold in the winter garden. Cassia shivered beneath her cloak.

Fabia suddenly said, in a harsh voice that reminded him of his own, "Did you hear? Is that why you came to see us, when otherwise you ignore us except at our monthly dinner?"

"Of course I heard about Magister Serena's possible betrothal. I was there, after all."

"Of course other people's business is all you would think about. So you don't yet know that Cassia bloomed while you were out hunting for something better?" Cassia poked her sister anxiously, and Fabia's brilliant, wild expression closed up. "My apologies, Honored Father. I spoke out of turn."

But the words hung in the air regardless, bright and hard, able to be examined from so many different angles. Titus grasped for the simplest one first.

"You are a cold mage, Cassia?" he asked, thinking of the wonderful, beautiful day her brother had bloomed.

Her brother had always been able to make little Cassia chortle, but since his death, she had become a grave, serious girl. She folded her hands at her waist and nodded solemnly. A terrible thought rose unbidden from the barren fields of Titus's heart.

He thought: I would like my daughters to smile when they see me.

He searched through the rugged terrain that had allowed him to keep his dignity for all these years. Swallowing, he finally found a phrase to speak, the words he would have said to any chance-met person out on his journeys when he sought fresh blooms.

"Can you show me?"

She glanced at Fabia for permission. Her sister made a face of disdain but said, in a tone of deepest affection, "Yes, go ahead, Cassie. You may as well shock him, too, you secretive goose. Hiding it from us until you'd mastered the trick!"

The girl held out her hands, palms up. In her low voice, she said, "I see it in my mind, as if there is a tiny opening into the spirit world in the center of each palm. Then, if I reach in, I can pull out a thread."

She touched the tips of the fingers of her right hand to the center of her left palm and, turning the right palm up, drew three woolly threads of shining magic, as if from out of her palm. After deftly curling the threads into a sphere, she compressed them into a ball of cold fire, the size of her small fist. It was a tremulous act of magic, though, and faded two breaths later.

The sight was like a fist to his belly. Titus could not speak.

Fabia said, "I told you he wouldn't be interested."

"No! Quite the opposite!" he cried. "It's a rare gift for a newly bloomed mage to create cold fire before they master the ability to quench a candle's flame."

"It just takes concentration," said Cassia.

"Can you show me again?"

Fabia's eyebrows shot up.

But Cassia smiled. Like her magic, the smile was tremulous, ready to fade, but pride held it fast. "I can do it again. I've done it fifty times—"

"At least one hundred," muttered Fabia, with a crooked grin that reminded him of happier days, when the world was still full of promise. But Fabia's joy was all for Cassia. When she looked at her father, her face closed again, as a flower against the dark.

He said, hoarsely, thinking of the blacksmith's boy who made the djembe speak, a boy who might be looking to get married to a compatible partner when he came to Autumn House, "Do you still sing so sweetly, Fabia? You were always singing, from the moment you had words."

"She never stops," said Cassia, with the eagerness of a girl who wants her sister to be praised. "She's singing festival songs tonight, at the masquerade. Because she's so good."

"Hush," Fabia hissed. "He's not coming. He never does."

It had been easier to keep them at a distance, like being safely wrapped in gauze. But the journey had rended something in him, not shattered but rather torn to let through a glimpse of light. Through such subtle rips in the veil separating the worlds, a cold mage could reach from the bleak realities of the mortal world and into the infinitely shifting energies of the linked cosmos. Titus recalled the day he himself had bloomed, the way the world had cracked around him, leaving him feeling breathless with excitement but also terrified at the wisp of smoke dissolving above the quenched candle's flame. If he wanted to embrace the power, he had to reach out his hand and his heart.

"I would like to come, if you want me there."

Cassia stared in honest shock, a hand pressed to her chest. Then she looked at her sister to gauge her reaction. Fabia examined her father through the shield of distrust he had earned.

"Why?" she demanded. "Why do you want to come, and why should we want you?"

Cassia gasped.

But it was indifference that was barren. Fabia's anger was water and sunlight.

"I shouldn't have turned my back on you," he said slowly, unfurling the words with care. "You girls never deserved that, and I regret it."

"We miss him too!" Fabia snapped. She grasped Cassia's hand defiantly, lifted her chin, and, in a caustic tone, said, "I guess if you wanted to come, we can't stop you." Her gaze dipped down to the ground as she struggled with her modesty . . . and lost. She added, with the tiniest smug smile of satisfaction, "I'm singing three songs."

"Three!" he exclaimed. "That is an honor, indeed, Fabia."

She crossed her arms. But she didn't move away.

They stood in that pause between one transformation and the next, where sunset turns into night, and night into dawn.

Cassia glanced at her sister, then extended a brave, hopeful hand toward her father. Titus stepped forward and grasped it.

A Compendium of Architecture and the Science of the Building

art by Wendy Xu

B Y THE TIME HE RETURNED HOME AFTER ALL HIS YEARS OF WAN-dering, Magnus Diarisso had come to prefer a fire burning on cold days rather than the elaborate hypocaust system that heated the mage House. The sound of wood settling, sparks popping, and ashes sighing helped him relax.

He told his nephew, the mansa, the powerful cold mage who was head of Four Moons House, that he did not want to live in the main house with its comings and goings and the children's chatter and the inevitable intrigues and gossip. He wanted space to think, to at long last write the compendium of architecture whose composition he had had to delay, time and again. After all, this, too, was part of a life's work: to pass on what you knew to those who would come after you, to keep the chain of knowledge intact from one generation into the next.

A modest suite of rooms was built to his specifications alongside the carpentry barn: a small bedchamber and a spacious study where he could do architect's work and receive visitors, now that he was too old to comfortably travel. From this haven, he supervised the four carpenters and the occasional village men brought in for larger projects.

What he liked best was waking up at dawn in complete isolation.

So the incident came as an unpleasant shock that chilly winter morning.

As usual, he had risen and stoked both circulating stoves in the barn. He was standing at a window in his study, looking over a beautifully fresh blanket of untouched snow, when the fire in the study's stove went out, and he was slammed to his knees. Iron groaned, under strain, and coals snapped from red to white, their heat sucked out. He braced himself on his hands. For one breath, taken in and held, he was sure the roof was about to crash down on top of him.

But the rafters held. The iron stove did not shatter. The trees in the orchard did not even sway—for there was not a breath of wind, nothing but his pounding heart and relieved exhale as he calmed himself.

Something had happened in the main house. Magnus was cursed-sure he wanted nothing to do with whatever cold magic had slipped its leash and choked out fires five-hundred paces away from the palatial building where the mages and household members lived. Probably his nephew, the mansa, had felt obliged to school the adolescent lads in the boys' dormitory. Even out here, he'd heard that this current cohort was a lot of trouble, with more wrangling and fistfights than the schoolmasters knew what to do with. Lord of All! In his day, the elder women of the House shut down such nonsense immediately; no young fellow wanted to be brought before the women's council until it was time for them to arrange a marriage for him.

With a smile, amused at his own discomfort, he creaked up to his feet with a wince and probed at his abused knees to make sure there was no lasting damage. Then he dusted off his hands and returned to his fire-building, starting over again with the stoves at either end of the big open space of the barn, where most of the work was done. He liked to have the space warm by the time the men came in. The courtesy pleased him, and they were certainly grateful.

He returned to the study, got the fire going again where he'd been cooking millet in milk for his breakfast porridge. A kettle of water heated for his morning tea. He set out his plate and knife, poured boiling water in and out of the teapot, and put the tea on to steep. Shelled peanuts garnished the porridge, alongside three dabs of butter. As the butter melted, he prepared two slices of day-old bread—one buttered and smeared with honey, and the other buttered and laden with cheese—and arranged them on a plate, which he set down at a three-fingers' gap beside the bowl of porridge. By the time this exacting ritual was complete, the tea was ready. He poured a thimbleful of piping hot tea at the little altar to the ancestors and cut a sliver of bread and cheese likewise, with a dollop of the thick porridge. The prayers came easily, for he had said them every day of his life.

The window on this side looked onto the southeast corner of the east wing of the main house. To Magnus's surprise, several men surged out to trample around into the orchard before vanishing, as on the hunt for a missing lapdog. What a pleasant thing it was, not to have to be involved!

The fire in the stove huffed and went out.

Was there to be no rest from these magical intrusions?

Again, he rose and went into the carpentry barn. It was impossible to eat in peace if he knew the circulating stoves weren't burning. But as he entered the vast, cold space beneath the lofty rafters, a sound brushed at his hearing. He cocked his head to gauge what direction it came from, amid the shadowed corners and unfinished projects, and slowly worked his way toward the stacks of fragrant lumber stored in orderly ranks.

A person was sitting half-hidden in the shadows, pressed in between two tall stacks of lumber. He was sobbing and trying to choke it down. A moment's study told Magnus this was a lad at that difficult age, when he is no longer really a child but also not yet a man.

Magnus coughed, and the lad looked up in surprise.

What rage and humiliation seared from his eyes!

They stared at each other. After a moment, remembering the respect due to age, the boy dropped his gaze.

He said nothing, nor did he shift from his hiding place. Rather, he seemed frozen, stunned. He had bruises on his face and down both arms, rings of bruising like hands had been holding him. His face was smeary with tears and snot. Reflexively, perhaps realizing that someone was now looking at him, the boy wiped his face with the back of a hand, then winced, for even that movement hurt him.

Magnus cleared his throat with another mild cough. "Now that you are here, I need help. We're preparing rough boards to become finished planks for furniture. Do you, by any chance, know how to saw?"

He'd been making conversation in an easy voice as a way of introducing a calming tone into the air between them. To his amazement, the lad nodded, though with the wary caution of a person who has been expecting to defend himself against a vicious attack.

"Good, then I shan't have to teach you the basics," Magnus replied in that same clement tone. "There is a basin with water where you may wash before you begin. Aprons hang from those hooks. You may take any one of them. If you are cold, I can find a wool tunic for you."

"I am not cold," said the lad, in a harsh and clipped voice, then visibly checked himself and added in softer but just as precise speech, "I am not cold, Uncle, but my thanks for the courtesy."

"Well, then, pick out your tools."

Magnus chose five rough boards and took them over to a worktable to measure and mark where he wanted them cut. The youth rose stiffly. His chest was allover bruises, still blooming, and he had blood on his right shoulder blade from a pair of deep welts. His knuckles were blood-streaked. He walked stiffly too. That had been some kind of fight. Or worse. Likely shockingly worse, if he was any judge.

Magnus had seen seventy-one winters pass, and in that time, he had measured and marked a great deal of the world. By the evidence of those broken sobs, now stifled, the boy would welcome no mention of whatever circumstances had driven him to seek the shelter of the barn. Lads were fiercely and fragilely proud; he had been so himself at that age.

Magnus's lack of magic meant he could never hope to be anything but the son who would never measure up to his own esteemed father, a man so magically gifted, he had been able to forge cold steel. Pride had driven Magnus to study at university, to get away from the family, and architecture had caught his interest. Pride had kept him away, had kept him traveling from city to city and estate to estate, where he was, of course, received as an exalted son of Four Moons House and, of course, as a highly trained and exceedingly desired architect. A man could leave a physical mark on the world with his architect's skill.

The lad took one of the leather aprons and chose both a crosscut and a ripsaw before going over to the worktable.

Magnus moved away to a different worktable, where he was indulging his recent interest in designing a portable desk with hidden drawers and writing surfaces that must all fold precisely into place. He angled himself so he could observe the lad without it being obvious he was watching.

The youth had worked a saw before. He had an apprentice's skill; he knew enough to look over the marked line to orient himself, as well as to check for knots. Besides that, he was careful and steady with the saw. He worked like a lad who had been allowed around men of skill, to be trained to follow them in time. As he worked, he relaxed enough to sing softly. At once, part of the mystery clicked into place for Magnus. The lad lost his meticulous diction and sang with the rustic accent common to villagers, providing his own call-and-response.

Where had he come from?

When Magnus tried to relight the fires in the barn, they would not burn.

So, here was part of the answer. A bruised and battered youth had fled to the carpentry barn after some kind of altercation or assault, in which he had suffered a humiliating degree of harm. Most strangely, he was a cold mage—young and untrained, yes, but unusually powerful, as evidenced by the dead fires.

Magnus went back to his bedchamber to fetch one of his worn and faded tunics. As he was crossing back through his study, he saw, through the window, the four carpenters approaching the barn. The four regular carpenters were yardmen who lived in the lane of cottages just past the orchard. According to the complex hierarchy of House lands, they stood above village men. This meant they were allowed into the main house for work projects under Magnus's supervision, while village men brought to help at the carpentry, when he needed extra hands, were never allowed into the main house at all.

He went out through the visitor's door in the study to intercept them before they could enter the barn.

"Was there some business at the house this morning?" he asked the eldest.

The men shrugged, and the eldest said, "Fires went out in all our cottages. That's all we know, Maester."

"The fires are all dead here in the barn, so you may as well go home and see if your wives have better luck kindling your own stoves." They chuckled at the innuendo. "No need to come back until tomorrow. Go on."

They thanked him. He was known as a fair if exacting taskmaster, one who would be lenient with respect to side business, so long as you gave him solid work.

As soon as they were gone, he went back in and took the old tunic to the lad.

"To work here, you must be dressed properly. You may wear this for now."

The lad took the garment with the obedience Magnus now recognized as village manners, more formal and hidebound than a prince's hall. "Thank you, Uncle. I am almost done here."

"Do you know how to flatten a reference surface?"

The lad glanced toward the rack of planes, then at the rough boards. "I have done it."

"You may continue with that and prepare all five boards."

"Yes, Uncle."

Magnus latched the doors of the barn from the inside and returned to his study. Out of curiosity, he tried to relight the fire, and this time, it caught, which likely meant the lad was now calm enough that his cold magic wasn't radiating unmanageably. Magnus ate his porridge and poured himself a fresh cup of hot tea, then opened his workbook to where he had left off yesterday. Early on in his life, he had written a treatise on arches, before he'd become so much in demand that there had been no time to write. For years, as an architect in charge of countless projects, he'd been forced to manage the trouble and disorderliness of others, a task he had never relished. Now, in this peaceful study, he had embarked on his final project, the organized accumulation of his hard-earned knowledge: *A Compendium of Architecture and the Science of Building*.

As expected, there came another interruption. Two of Magnus's great-nephews came to the door and stamped about impatiently until he let them in. Like him, they had no magic, so the fire did not go out.

"Uncle, we are wondering if you have seen a boy," said the first one. "Not our age cohort but younger, sixteen."

Magnus remained standing, therefore they also remained standing. "Tell the mansa I wish to speak to him."

They had the brusque manners of young men accustomed to having other people jump out of their way. "He is very busy, Uncle. There has been trouble in the schoolroom."

The second one broke in. "It wasn't in the schoolroom. It was in the boys' hall, just at dawn."

The first gave a sniggering laugh of the sort Magnus truly detested, for it lingered in his ears as mockery of another's pain. "Finally put that jumped-up peddler's bastard in his place in a way he'll never forget. But now he's vanished."

"I do not wish to be troubled by your gossip. Tell the mansa that he wishes to speak to me. You may go."

Even they heard the chill in his voice and recalled, at last, that he was an elder, and their great-uncle besides, not some hired hand. With fulsome apologies, they hurried out.

Magnus went back into the barn with the bread, honey, and cheese.

The lad was wearing the tunic but was still barefoot, although the lack of shoes didn't seem to bother him. He had taken the chance of being alone in the barn to wash his face thoroughly, all traces of blood scrubbed away.

Magnus set the tray on a side table and beckoned the boy over, indicating a bench. "What is your given name, lad? I'd like to have something to call you."

After a fraught hesitation, during which Magnus wondered if the boy would bolt and run, he said very softly, "Andevai."

"You will eat something, Andevai. Then you may continue your work."

Obediently—unlike those two overindulged young fellows!—the lad sat gingerly and, after a wince and a shift to put more of his weight on his left thigh, dug in. Magnus went to the worktable, looked over the boards, and came back to sit on the bench. He settled into silence, leaving an opening for the lad to speak; it was his experience that if you did not fill the space between two people with your own words and just remained patient, then after a while, they would feel driven to fill that empty space themselves.

The lad finished his meal thoroughly, in the manner of a person who hasn't always been sure he would get enough to eat on any given day. The silence drew out a little longer, but silence had never been troublesome for Magnus.

At last, the boy straightened his shoulders, gathering his courage, and spoke. "Uncle, it's hard to get a consistent flatness. And I keep getting a valley down the middle of the board. And the edges are tearing out. How can I do it better?"

Magnus nodded, careful not to smile. The question pleased him, yet he sensed the admission of ignorance was a delicate display of trust, and therefore had to be handled with care. "Would you like to learn to make boards that can be used for the best quality of furniture? The carpenters here are allowed to sell furniture on the side, those that they've made in their free time."

"I want to do things properly—and well. Why do a thing at all if you cannot do it properly? If you do not do it to the best you are able?"

Ah.

"Millet does not become beer the day it is soaked. Let me show you."

They went to the worktable. As a House-born and highly sought-after architect, he had not often worked near apprentices, although he had allowed aspiring architects to work alongside him from time to time, if they had good manners or, on two notable occasions, when they were young women who no other master architect would mentor. But he had long observed the maesters among his stoneworkers and carpenters and their ways of dealing with the people they supervised. He had seen who produced the best and most reliable workers and those who ruined the youth who came to learn from them. Magnus's style was patience and a great deal of standing back to see how the apprentice coped.

The lad was a quick study, and remarkably diligent, maybe a little too fixated on a perfection whose reach was beyond the skills he had at present. Most amazingly, he was willing to repeat and repeat without any trace of frustration, just an intense focus on the task.

After they worked on two planks together, Magnus left him to work on the others alone and returned to his study.

Just in time, as it happened, for as he put a log into the stove, the hotly glowing coals were sucked straight to cold ash. The heavy footsteps of an impatient man thumped on his porch. Magnus opened the door to admit his nephew, the mansa of Four Moons House. Such a position among princely families generally went to the eldest son of the lineage, but among mage Houses was always and only held by the most powerful male cold mage.

It had started to snow. The mansa swept off his hat and politely shook it over the grass before coming inside.

He was a big man, full of himself, aware of his grandeur, and yet for all that, a responsible steward of the huge household over which he presided.

"I am having a deal of trouble and many demands on my time, Uncle. But out of respect for your age, I am come."

"Tell me about this boy."

The mansa had been holding his hat, clearly eager to get the conversation over and done with so he could return to the main house. With a sharp intake of breath, he set the hat right on Magnus's desk, on top of his precious notebooks and precise technical drawings. "What do you know about the boy?"

"I know he is in my barn planing a board right now." Magnus controlled a frown as he swept up the hat and hung it from one of the hooks set into the wall by the entryway. Then he checked the papers. Only a few drops of moisture had stained the notebook at the top of the stack. "He has what I would call village manners, which are, I might add, better than the manners I've just been treated to by a pair of House-born young men. What are their names? Must I take the matter of their disrespect to the women's council?"

Naturally, the mansa was thrown off by this demand. Great princes always were, when called to account by people they'd forgotten had the right to reprimand them.

Magnus used the mansa's silence to continue in his quietly inexorable way, which he had honed to great effect while dealing with patrons and clients who complained when their fanciful dreams weren't structurally or aesthetically possible.

"The boy has been beaten, and I suspect worse has been done to him besides. After some consideration, I believe he must be the person whose cold magic killed all of my fires at dawn, despite the distance between the house and this barn. Such a strong pulse of cold magic suggests . . ." He watched his nephew's expression twist into a grimace of distaste. "I am not sure what it suggests. Perhaps you can enlighten me, nephew."

"Now and again, a desperate person may wield a strength they cannot normally possess. An aberration if you will. He is a troublemaker."

"Is he?"

"He is disrespectful."

"I find that difficult to believe. Has he shown disrespect to you, nephew?"

"To *me*? Of course not. To the other boys of his cohort, however . . ."

"What manner of respect is he expected to show to them? Are they not age-mates and fellow cold-mages-in-training?"

"They are his betters."

"His *betters*?" Slowly, the mystery unfurled itself into the light, for Magnus was quite sure the other boys of the cohort hadn't the magical strength to extinguish fires in such a wide radius, not even in the throes of anger and humiliated pride. He'd have heard of such a House-born prodigy, if so, for everyone would have been boasting of it incessantly.

The mansa sighed with a great heave of his shoulders, as if to remind Magnus that this entire conversation was a drain on his valuable time. "He is a village boy, as you must have already seen for yourself. The descendent of people our ancestors rescued and generously brought with us to a new homeland. His grandmother was brought up to the house to work in the kitchens. That's part of the service the village owes us, as you know. She got pregnant by a clerk, no one of importance."

"A man with no magic, is that what you are saying?" Magnus asked with an ironic twist to his lips.

The mansa did not notice, so intent was he on his grievances. "She was sent back down to the village for being uncooperative, ungrateful, and difficult. The son she bore—his father—never showed the least sign of cold magic. And why should he have? In two hundred years, no person out of the village of Haranwy has managed any more magic than to shape cold fire to light our homes and inns. They are slaves, incapable of the full power of cold magic."

"Yet not incapable, as we have seen today."

But the mansa had already gone on, his tone heavy with an unpleasant tincture of disgust.

"That isn't even the worst of it. At least the villagers who are bound to our House are respectable folk, who have a place in the world. His mother hasn't even a lineage or a village. She was born in a cart. A peddler's daughter. Imagine! Such depth of magic cannot possibly reside in a person of such low birth. The incident cannot have been but a momentary burst of anger."

Magnus put a hard rein on his temper, but the anger leaked out in the cold snap of his tone. "What do you mean to do with a person of such low birth, then?"

"He must return to the schoolroom and learn enough to serve us, according to his place in the world."

"And the other boys of his cohort? The ones who mistreated him in such a vile way? Do you mean to allow these boys to continue with such outrageous behavior, to pretend it didn't happen? An evil secret is like fresh meat. When it rots, it smells." He meant to pause, to offer a space for the mansa to reply, but realized he didn't want to hear whatever his nephew had to say. "I will personally take the matter to the women's council, and you will recall that when I returned home, it was agreed I would not have to be involved in the day-to-day running of the House, so I would have the freedom to work on my compendium. That's how strongly I feel about looking the other way in cases of this nature."

A glimmer of shame creased the mansa's brow. "It is true the boys went too far."

"Saying 'I am sorry' does not heal the dog's bite."

"It won't happen again!"

"I will make sure of it. Because what if you are wrong, nephew? Such treatment is unacceptable, whoever the child. But what if he is as powerful as it seems? What then?"

The mansa crossed his arms, shielding himself against a question he did not like and an answer he could not quite bring himself to contemplate.

"Can you deny that it is within the bounds of possibility, however unlikely you think it?"

That frown surely terrified many, but Magnus merely waited it out.

"I cannot deny it. Even though I am sure you are wrong, Uncle."

"Consider the matter carefully as you proceed. That is my advice. Now you may go. I know you have many demands on your valuable time."

Finally, the mansa remembered the manners his mother had taught him. He dropped his gaze respectfully. "I hear what you are saying. As for the boys' hall, the women's council will have the final say on the matter. They have already made *quite* clear to me this morning that they are not pleased the situation was allowed to go so far. I have had an earful."

Magnus would have clucked sympathetically under other circumstances, having himself had to sit through more than one scolding by the women's council at other mage Houses, where he had been engaged on building projects, although, mercifully, it had never been his behavior being censured. He could not bring himself to feel sympathy now, however, and perhaps his stolid silence prodded his nephew to continue more graciously.

"And may I add, Uncle, if I have not said so recently, that it gladdens me you have come home to us. It was the great wish of my heart that you would find a way to return, knowing of the welcome we would give you. I hope you may find peace and harmony here with your kinfolk, after all your years of wandering."

Softened, Magnus granted him a nod. "So I hope as well, nephew. Your words are well-spoken. I have felt welcome. And my odd habits of solitude have been kindly tolerated, though they may seem strange to many."

"We are each as we are." With this tendentious proverb to restore his confidence in his own supreme wisdom, the mansa took his leave.

Magnus waited until he could get the fire going again, then went back into the barn.

The lad noticed him coming at once and eagerly showed him his work, which he was not yet finished with because he had been working in the methodical way of a person who wants to get it right more than he wants to get it over and done with. They discussed what he'd been doing and some alternate techniques, until the lad abruptly stepped sharply back from the worktable as if it had bitten him.

"I want to learn, but probably I cannot," he said, looking wistfully around the quiet, cold peace of the carpentry barn.

"Why would that be?"

"They will make me go back to the schoolroom." He shuddered.

"Do you not want to go back to the schoolroom?"

He inhaled, as if wishing to fill himself with the pleasant smell of sawdust and cut wood for courage. In a trembling voice, meant to sound strong, he said, "I have to go back."

"Why is that?"

"Because I am a cold mage."

"Not every cold mage need do more than learn the basics. There are humbler roles that cold mages of lesser reach can fill. Shaping cold fire to light rooms, for example . . ." He trailed off as he realized the boy was not listening. He had a faraway look in his dark eyes, thoughts building an unseen edifice.

"I am going to be better than all the rest of them," the lad muttered.

The words displeased Magnus. "Are you? Is that your sole aim? To be better than them?"

His gaze flashed up. For an instant, his fierceness shone with the power of a restless, inquisitive, intelligent, proud, and ambitious mind, unconcealed by any veil of false humility worn as protection. Then he shuttered himself and looked down. "You know who I am, don't you, Uncle?" he said to the floor.

"I do, if by that you mean you are the boy who put out all the fires this morning. The village boy whose magic bloomed nine months ago, and who has done nothing but battle with the other lads in his age cohort for the nine months he has been up at the House. But who you actually are, I do not know. So let me ask again. Is your sole aim in learning cold magic to be better than the rest?"

The lad's hesitation stretched long and longer still. Magnus imagined a wrestling match, but he could not yet be sure with what opponent the youth was wrestling. At length, the boy spoke, measuring his words with the precision of a person who has learned to watch what he says, lest he be punished for the truth.

"I was angry when my magic bloomed. It was the last thing I wanted. But now that I have felt the reach of magic in my heart, I know it is what I am meant to be. I am a cold mage, so I am going to learn everything they can teach me about cold magic. I am going to learn how to do it properly, without fault, until I do it perfectly. Will I best them? Yes, I will, and you can be sure they will know it. That I will rub it in their faces every day. But if you tore me away from here and locked me in a solitary tower, I would still learn everything, without fault, until I did it perfectly."

The architect considered the unformed youth before him. A boy becomes a man through a process of building the framework that undergirds him. This foundation makes him strong enough to withstand the storms of life that will inevitably come. It was so easy to go wrong at this stage. To not shore up the foundation adequately. To burden the structure with too much ornament. To ignore basic soundness in favor of demanding something your own prejudices make you think will serve you better.

This boy could go very wrong, very quickly, and was like to do so if left solely in the hands of Magnus's nephew, sad to say. The mansa was a powerful man, who walked athwart the world with easy privilege. He had already decided who he needed the boy to be and therefore what his prospects were.

Yet when a troubled, angry, upset boy asked only one question, and that question was how to do something better than he was already doing it, simply because he wanted to do it right, then it was time to take a closer look.

Magnus gave a gentle cough, more to work up his own nerve than to alert the boy that he was about to speak. "Andevai, you could continue to work with me and still attend your lessons in the schoolroom."

The boy's chin came up as he blinked. "How could that happen, Uncle? They won't allow it."

"Do you know who I am?" he asked, aware of how his humble workaday clothing must appear to a village boy, whose chief knowledge of the noble scions of the mage Houses was likely the fine garments, polished speech, and accomplished arrogance of the people raised beneath its magnificent roof.

"You are an elder, Uncle. Also, a carpenter."

Magnus smiled. "I am a man who can tell the mansa that you will work with me as often as you are free to do so, and to make sure you are given the freedom to work here without any slight coming to your studies. The only answer I need from you is if this is a situation you are interested in."

"To come here, when I am not in the schoolroom?"

"Yes. Whenever you wish. Under my supervision."

The lad rested a hand on one of the boards he had just planed, running his fingers through the curled-up shavings.

"Yes," he whispered with desperate hopefulness, then rubbed again at his face as if afraid he was crying. "I would like that, if it is possible. If it can be done with no harm coming to my studies."

"Come with me now, and I will sort it all out. I cannot stop up the other lads' mouths, but I suspect you have a sharp enough tongue hidden behind your polite manners that you can defend yourself with words as long as they are not allowed to touch you. We will go speak to my sister."

"Your sister, Uncle?"

"Yes. She is head of the women's council, and a powerful cold mage in her own right."

"Maester!" His eyes went wide, and he took a step back, as if he expected to be slapped. "My lord. I did not know. How should I address you?"

"I prefer Uncle. Are you ready? It won't be easy, but if you are determined and willing to work hard, the journey will be worth it."

No hesitation this time. "I am ready."

So, after all, later in the day, when it had all been sorted out with far too much discussion for his liking, Magnus finally sat alone at his desk, where he considered his *Compendium* and the many pages he had yet to write. He had believed the compendium would be his last edifice, but it was not a building at all, he now realized; it was the memoriam of his life and work to share with others whom he would never meet.

He contemplated his precious solitude and all the things he had returned home to avoid.

With a faint, wry smile, he took out a new notebook, wrote the boy's name on the first page, and, on the second, recorded the work with the boards and what tasks ought to come next, the first glimmerings of an architectural plan.

The Beatriceid

art by Julie Dillon

BOOK I

1 There was an ancient village called Adurnam,
   Founded by the Celts of Tarrant fame.
   Along the sea, they plied their leather boats
   And fished and farmed and lived in amity,
   If amity is one raid every year.

6 Then came across the sea, on winds of change,
   The bold Kena'ani, wise merchants all.
   Made famous by their victory at Zama,
   They sought out harbors new, and tin and wool,
   And on this shore they landed. Very soon,
   They drafted trade agreements and built homes.
   With vigor, the town grew into a port
   Whose gleaming wharves and bustling markets swelled
   Into the jewel and heart of western trade,
   Where every ship flown north, a cargo lades.

15 Adurnam's fame grew great. The Romans came.
   Cloaked in fog and lies, as is their wont.
   Their stadia and roads blighted the earth,
   Until the Celtic tribes, having enough,
   Shook free the heavy yoke of Roman rule.
   Before the warlike Celts, the empire fled
   To take its refuge in Latium walls
   And slake its thirst for gold in minor wars.

23 But left behind, Rome's footprints hammer deep,
   Whose boots must trample down Truth's fragile keep.
   Who will stem the tide of Roman lies?
   What voice lays fortunate claim to verity?

BOOK II

27 Thus Blessed Tanit turns her kindly eye
       To seek her faithful daughters in the crowd
       Of pupils who arrive on morning's blush
       Into the hall of the Academy,
       That court of learning where the young
       Can measure out the workings of the world
       And scope the orbits of the moon and sun,
       The cunning nature hidden within beasts,
       Deeds of man and woman, keenly sung.
       All this, and cautious speculation, too,
       Into the secret lore of mages cold
       And blacksmiths' fire. So do the gods o'erlook,
       From vasty heights, our tiny little world.

40 Thus they come, in twos and fours and tens,
       Pupils from the fashionable homes
       Of the city's highest-ranking clans,
       With lineages and language as diverse
       As these waters on whose shores we live:
       Celt and Mande, Rome, Iberia,
       Kena'ani and Kush, Oyo, Avar.
       All who can afford it send their youth
       To take their places in the lecture halls
       And rooms where knowledge rains upon their heads.

50 There sit the richest girls, the Roman snobs,
       Who laugh and tell the tales that they believe
       Will earn for them attention from young men,
       Whose clans and looks agreeably contend
       For princely favor or a wealthy bride.

55 Chief among them, Pulcheria. Long
       The acknowledged leader of the set.
       She smiles and blushes, falsely, and begins.

58 "I sing of arms—that's swords, not arms and legs—
       And Aeneas, who did brave the salty sea.
       The salty sea, I say, but not the rivers,
       Because rivers, as we know, do have no salt."

62 Her friends assay a laugh, applaud her wit,
　　All while sidelong-eyeing fine young men.
　　They simper and display their fashionable hair
　　With knots and bows a-flutter, dazzling bright,
　　This style the newest vogue in these dull halls,
　　And woe betide those girls who, due to lack
　　Of coin or conformable hair, cannot so style
　　Themselves in current mode. These sit alone.

70 As on the chamber's poorest bench, there sits
　　A quiet, cat-like girl, Kena'ani.
　　She reads a book. But words scald ears, and thus,
　　She lifts her head to better hear the tale.

74 "Fugitive, the bold Aeneas fled
　　The burning pyre of Troy with all his men.
　　For years, the pitiless sea was all they knew,
　　As angry Juno's hate hounded them far
　　And wide, with waves and gulls their only friends,
　　And not one shore to welcome them to home.
　　It was so hard to found the race of Rome."

81 So mutters quiet Cat, "Not hard enough."

82 But Roman ears are quick to catch a slight.
　　Pulcheria turns her head to glare,
　　By which her profile shows to best effect
　　And decorative bows and knots to sway.
　　The young men look, and smile, and thus become
　　The audience she all along has craved.
　　So, on she speaks.

　　　　　　"Yet dutiful Aeneas
　　Will in nowise despair. He leads his men.
　　Across tumultuous seas, they come to land.
　　Spy glassy bay and black-browed cliffs. Not sure
　　If this land will grant haven to the lost,
　　To those who wander far with pious hope
　　And seeking answer to what will soon become
　　A fateful question, on the deck, he stands.
　　His men await his word. But still he stands,
　　Uneasily athwart the ship's proud head—"

98 She breaks off as new smiles crease the lips
   Of those she hopes will most admire her tale.

100 So speaks the quiet Cat: "Folk call them prows
    Or stems, as those who ply the seas must know.
    To be uneasy athwart the ship's proud head?
    That doth portend a different apprehension."

104 The haughty Roman girl lifts up her chin,
    Her eyes ablaze with anger so astounded
    that at first, she merely huffs. Her friends,
    Their mouths do shield with hands. She burns,
    Sensing the mortifying beat of mocking words.
    A clamor in her head shrieks, "Vengeance mine!"
    And yet her cunning guards intemperate speech.

111 "What mewling do I hear?" she says. "My friends
    And my companions, have your ears been soiled
    By lowly merchant's wares that are mere dirt,
    Not the gold of civilized discourse?
    Who even speaks aloud of things best left
    To silence and respectful curtains drawn?
    No mention would an honorable soul
    Make of that which well-bred folk do leave
    Behind closed doors. But how can we expect
    A crass Phoenician to abide by rules
    That their untidy mercenary minds
    Cannot sell and make a profit on?
    Give her a coin—and let her close her mouth."

124 She reaches for her purse. She finds a coin.
    "One as or two?" she asks with vicious smile,
    And flips a coin across the gap between,
    Meaning for the flashing copper coin
    To strike her hated foe right in the face.

129 But angry cats are quick. Thus, with a snatch,
    Swift Cat captures the coin out of the air
    And throws it back, both accurate and strong,
    Like any Argive spear was flung at Troy.
    The as hits true. It strikes her Roman nose,

And Pulcheria shrieks.
                The young men laugh.

135 "You! You! You! You!" she screams! "You! You! You! You!"
      She shakes a fist.
                "Don't hurt yourself," Cat drawls.

 137 "You crawling vermin! Baby-slaughtering tribe!
      You might as well go prostitute yourself
      At Tanit's temple gate. But what is this?
      Oh dear!" She gives vent to pretended gasps
      Of sad regret. "I should never have said,
      For we all know that every Phoenician girl
      Already has."

              This slur, or indeed the one
144 Against the Blessed Tanit, overwhelms
      Young Catherine's tenuous calm, admittedly
      A trait whose scant reserves she's now drained dry.

147 To the attack, she springs. She jumps upon
      The bench, and thence upon the table too.
      From the schoolroom's dimly lit back wall,
      She bounds, so light of foot that it may seem
      A certain feline grace does drive her feet,
      As from table to next table she does leap.
      With a cry, the Roman girl draws back,
      Behind the quivering bodies of her friends,
      A shield wall of silk, expensive gowns
      And all the bows and ribbons in their hair
      Like banners fluttering in a storm-swept air.

158 "Will no one guard me from this cruel assault?
      This unharmonious brute? Immodest girl!
      How dare you strike at me? For am I not
      A modest picture of chaste piety? While you!
      You! You! Are nothing but an unbecoming beast!"

163 Too late, Cat finds herself caught in that place
      She likes the least: The censure of all eyes.
      Hard to fade from notice when she stands

Atop a table shaking with righteous rage.
She's trapped by her own nature. What to do?

168 "Apologize at once!" cries Pulcheria,
Who, like a jackal, senses lowering doom
And means to gnaw this flesh and bone until
The last worn tatters of repute are dead.
Dead. Dead. Dead. Dead. The battle lost.

173 Cat knows not what to do. Her pride rebels
From speaking even one soft, humbled word.
Yet all have seen her act in such a way
That Pulcheria's sneers are long forgot,
Her crime of grossly unbecoming slurs
Does fade compared to Cat's rash, rough assault.

179 "Bow down and beg forgiveness. You! Bow down!"
The Roman girl awaits her foe's defeat.

181 All wait. All stare. Cat trembles. What to do?
The room grows hushed.
                              And yet, the gods can hear.
The Blessed Tanit guides her favored daughters
And shelters them in times of storm and stress.
A sound! A foot does fall before the door.
The threshold shakes!
                              Bold Beatrice arrives!
Her beauty is her sword, her gleaming eye,
Her gaze, a spear to part the seas of doubt.
All those her eye surveys take swift steps back
As if to get some distance from her scorn.

191 "What's this?" she asks. "What have I missed today,
That drives my dearest cousin to stand atop
A table as if the seas are soon to rise?
Is this some Roman custom of debate?
Perhaps a means by which some stand below
While others must, of course, be stood above?
Who then shall rise, and who perforce shall fall?
Who must command, and who, in truth, bow down?"

199 "The girl did cast a coin against my face."

200 "You threw it first!" cries Cat, then silent falls,
    As Beatrice does raise a pretty hand,
    Whose graceful wave the young men do approve.

203 "Oh, la! Such goings on! What started this?"
    She asks.

                        And Pulcheria does reply,
205 "I merely told the true tale of Aeneas."

206 "Oh, that! I know it well. Shall I proceed?"

207 A blink is all it takes. Cat knows the plan.

208 Into the room, bold Beatrice does sail,
    And every eye does capture her fine form,
    Her sterling intellect and majesty,
    Like that of Didos, queens of Qart Hadast,
    Who led their people far across the seas
    To found a prosperous city, rich and strong.

214 "To Qart Hadast, he came," says Beatrice,
    "Aeneas, fled from Troy and tempest-tossed,
    His ships and men and household gods he brought
    To Libya's fertile shores, where he sought peace.
    Son of Venus! A manly man, it's true!
    How fortunate to wash upon these shores,
    Where nectar flowed in honey, and cattle grazed,
    And every shrine and temple rich with gifts,
    In honor of the well-belovéd gods—"

223 "Who feast on infant blood!"

                        "You tell a lie!
224 But let that pass, for my tale's not yet done."

  225 So Beatrice takes center stage and smiles,
    And all who look upon her must forget
    That Cat, who was just now upon the table,

Has vanished. She is gone. She can't be seen.
Bold Beatrice speaks on.

                       "So gather folk
230 Who happily will feast the weary men.
The Dido welcomes wanderers brave and true
And, likewise, all with thrilling tales to tell.
And, in all honesty, her eye is caught
By the particular beauty of the man
Who calls himself Aeneas and their lord.
His raven hair, his brilliant eyes, his smile,
His sculpted shoulders, shown to best effect,
His arms, his legs . . . Enough! 'Tell us your tale,'
The Dido says with generosity,
As servants bring a feast munificent
And cups that never once fall scant of wine.
Tongue loosened, he does speak, at length, of deeds
And fights and storms and suffering and pain.
Oh, what a man he is! to suffer angst
That no mere woman dares hope to comprehend.
Always polite, the Dido nods and smiles,
And smiles and nods as he goes on and on,
Sure of acclaim, for every man's account
Has great import, as we all know is true."

250 The young men, list'ning, pause. One nods and grins.
The rest do hesitate, for they're not sure
If nods and smiles do signify assent,
Or possibly some other hidden view.

254 "Of course, it's true!" cries Pulcheria, quick
To grab advantage while her foe is quiet.
"What noble man! What brave audacity!
No common man could soldier ever on,
His shoulders heavily burdened by his woes."

259 "And handsome shoulders too!" says Beatrice,
"Or so the Dido thought as she grew bored
And gave her mind free rein to walk amid
The more enlightening groves of learnéd thought:
The means by which a scholar calculates
Precise circumference of our great, green Earth,

The equinox recession, how to plumb
The ocean's vasty depths. The winds! The stars!
The gods are kind! For all their cruelty,
They still have given beauty to the world,
Which humans can extol and praise and seek.
These thoughts did cause a smile to tease the queen's
Becoming lips. A spark shone in her eyes,
Which he mistook for admiration's blush.
Thus kindled, in his heart and loins, a lust
To fondle her with his ideas—and love.
What woman could resist? So ran his thoughts,
While she considered altitudes and math.

277 'Too terrible, the pain I now recount!'
His cry did echo in the marble hall.
'And yet the gods did favor me, it's true,
Which I shall now relate . . . in chapter two.'

281 'We shall go for a hunt!' she intervened.
'And the next verses leave for later on.
We'll rest this night and then ride out at dawn
Among a mighty crowd, and with my hounds,
Shall race the stags and lions to their end!
Such sport shall entertain us, shall it not?'

287 He says, 'Your word is law, oh mighty queen,'
Meaning the words to have a second sense
That he supposes will engage her heart.
Escorted to his room, he lies abed,
Where flames of love do flood and drown him whole.
Again, again, again, he thinks of her:
'She looked at me with soft, forgiving eyes!
I am thick in her heart. She will recline
Amid my strong embrace. She'll marry me!
The land she rules, her breasts, her Venus mound,
All this shall welcome my supremacy.'
It's hard to sleep, so very swelled is he."

BOOK III

299 While Beatrice holds forth, a shadow hunts
   Through the academy, seeking its prey.
   'Tis in the kitchen Cat finds what she seeks,
   Though no one working there can see her pass.
   A jar of honey, borrowed. That is all.
   Wrapped in shadow, she returns posthaste,
   Into the schoolroom creeps unseen,
   Where none do know she's missing—nor returned.
   None but Beatrice, and she'll not tell.
   Their plan relies on secrecy, it's true,
   And none more secret than a cat who can
   Conceal herself in plain sight, and a bee
   Whose buzzing will attract every last eye
   And keep the audience all well-entranced.
   So Beatrice continues. She speaks on:

BOOK IV

315 "Thus dawn's sweet light does bring the hounds to bay.
   The hunters take their places. She appears,
   More beautiful than gold, and strong as iron.
   A purple cloak does hang down from her shoulders.
   Her quiver has an ornament of gold.
   Her hair falls careless, free, and unadorned,
   For no adornment outshines majesty.

322 Aeneas, too, looks splendid. She admires
   His flowing hair, his graceful poise, his lips.
   And so they reach the hills where stags do run.
   The chase begins, and yet the gods step in."

326 She takes a breath. And all her listeners brace
   For the words that all must know come next:

328 **"A dreadful storm! Hail! Wind! The thunder rolls.
   Lightning scatters horses!"**

Her loud voice
Does make all listeners jump, surprised,
And then giggle with laughter at their fright.
So none, not Pulcheria, not her friends,
Note the shade that slips and slides among them.

334 Beatrice resumes.

"Queen and lord
Take refuge in a cave. They are alone.
He means to speak at length, with honeyed words.
She chooses the more interesting act,
Engages him in pleasure and delight.
For her, an afternoon's sweet dalliance,
But in his mind, they're married. It is love!
Love and conquest's all the same to him.
He tries his best to please her, and he does.

343 Then, when the storm is over, they depart.
They hunt. They feast. The days pass in abandon.

345 He corners her one night and, fierce, he speaks:
'Oh, glorious queen! Yield to my yearning heart!
Let us join our selves, our hearts, our souls,
Our kingdoms!'

'What kingdom have you?' she asks.

'The one that we will share! You and I,
Together we will rule in harmony.
Where is my crown, my dearest love, my sweet?'

352 '*Your* crown? Crown you?' she says. 'I need no king.
I've ruled alone for years. My people thrive.
If our arrangement does not satisfy,
Then you may sail along to other shores,
And I will kiss you for a last goodbye.'

357 What madness clutches her, he cannot tell.
But clearly, she has lost all of her mind,
Such as it is, for how can she refuse?

All know that women crave a man's firm hand.
These thoughts do rage as anger in his heart.
He stalks the streets at night. He mutters threats.
Among his men, he whispers mutinous words.
He sings of arms. He tries to raise revolt,
And thus he is arrested. Put to death.
A foreigner whose treason comes to naught."

BOOK V

367 "That's not the tale!" cries Pulcheria, stung.
    "'Twas Dido fell in love and died, not him!"
    She stomps her foot. She huffs. She shakes her head.
    The bows and ribbons that ornament her hair
    Do flutter as she draws all eyes to her.
    She will defeat her Phoenician foe! She will!
    The girl may be pretty, it is true,
    But she is poor, and everyone must know
    That riches and high status win the war.

376 "Then do go on," bold Beatrice implores,
    "Please, let us hear the story as you know it.
    For I am sure that these young men do hope
    To hear the dulcet tones of your pure voice
    Raised in praise of Roman history,
    That tale much told. Your diligence, I'm sure,
    Is like unto the ants, for ants are wise:
    They fill their larder as you store up words—"

384 "May I go on?" snaps Pulcheria.

                                          "Please!"

    And Beatrice does step back from the fray
    To give the Roman girl the space she needs
    And all attention. Thus plays out the plan.

388 "Of arms, I sing!" she cries. "Of swords and spears.
    Of that harsh battle, Aeneas's sad fate.
    When his ships came to Qart Hadast, it's true,
    He was engaged to tell the tale. 'Please do!'

The queen whose name was Dido did beseech,
For she was struck by his manly physique.
And thus she sat, enthralled, as he did speak
In manly tones, and manly words, and these
Sharp mem'ries of Troy's fall, he bravely shared,
While queen and countrymen, aghast, did stare:
'So in the ruined city, we did fight!
The enemy did trample in our halls!
Our temples burned! Our gates thrown to the ground!
Our women lost. Our sons and pride cast down!'"

402 She flinches. Twitches. Flicks a crawling ant
From her fine skin, her peerless, milk-washed arm.
She shakes her head.

                  Bold Beatrice exclaims,
"Is something wrong?"

                      "No. No! I shall go on.
His tale he told, a tale—" Another flinch.
Her fingers pinch an ant. "A tale told well—!
What are these creatures crawling up on me?
Get off! Get off!"

                 Now all can see a swarm,
An enterprising trail. Industrious ants!
Up, up, they climb! Up legs, up arms, up necks,
And suddenly chaste Pulcheria shrieks,
"Off! Off! Foul ants! They're everywhere!"
                       Her friends
Likewise, do find themselves with skin and hair
Beset with ants, a mob of ants intent
Upon the bows and ribbons in their hair.
They brush, they rub, they hop, they skip, they bow,
Bent almost double, best to scrub their hair,
To wipe the ants away. And when they touch
Their hands to bows and ribbons, they do find
The silk and satin sticky, sweet, and moist,
All covered o'er with honey. Thus, the ants
Have come en masse to feast.

Everyone laughs.

424 They pluck the bows and ribbons from their locks
    And fling them to the floor with cries and groans.
    "What plague is this?! What infestation crawls?!"
    And last do they run, weeping, from the room.

    BOOK VI

428 Bold Beatrice sits down. And Cat does too.
    The young men shift, the women glance around.
    Oh, silence! No one knows quite what to do.

431 "A tale told well, twice told's a tale indeed!
    I'm sure on this, we can all well agree."
    Says Beatrice, commanding their regard.
    "Of arms, I sing, of ships, and of a queen,
    The famous Didos of a mighty land.
    If you tempt their wrath, they will requite
    Lies and blows tenfold and bring down blight.
    So, let this be a lesson. Listen well.
    Toy not with us. All enmity, let go.
    We smile upon our friends and smite our foes.
    To what divinity do we give thanks?
    To Blessed Tanit, she who grants her strength,
    Protection, favor, shelter, all of this,
444 Unto her daughters, and to us, her kiss."

To Be a Man
A Roderic Barr Adventure

art by Charles Tan

I T MIGHT HAVE BEEN THE DOG, OR IT MIGHT HAVE BEEN THE WOMAN. HE wasn't sure.

When he had prowled into the garden from the enclosed parkland beyond, the little pug dog had been yapping in a skull-rattling fashion. His first instinct was to shut it up. He'd also wanted to cleanse his palate of those tickling feathers from the peahen he'd had so much fun chasing down in the parkland. So, he'd bounded after the dog, snapped it up, and shaken it. The dog was small and fatty and sour-smelling, but at least it didn't have feathers.

Then a woman's voice tensely said, "Blessed Venus! Step back out of sight, Felicia. A slow step. Don't startle it. Just back away, and it will eat that hells-cursed pug and not you."

"But do you see what it is, Ami?"

"Yes, I see what it is. It is a very large and very hungry saber-toothed cat."

He raised his head just as the dog weakly wriggled, its blood dribbling down his dagger-like incisors.

"It's so beautiful."

A woman stood on marble steps lined by troughs of prickly winter shrubs that were dusted by snow. She was anything but prickly. She was delectably plump. She was wearing indoor clothes, with a bodice laced tightly over a full bosom and white petticoats pulled up to keep their hems out of the snow. Her ankles were so shapely, he wasn't sure whether he wanted to gnaw on them or lick them.

The pug gave a last little farting gasp.

Her ankles, or the pungent scent. Hard to say which triggered the sudden flowing river of change that cut through his lean cat's body like the tide of a dream, changing him from one creature into another. He shivered out of the skin of the cat—in which he'd been born and in which he lived in his natural home in the spirit world—and slipped into the skin of the man's body he wore here in the Deathlands.

Which meant he found himself sitting on his bare ass in cold, slimy snow.

He spat out a foul-tasting, hairy mouthful of bloody skin. The pug plopped limply across his lap like an incongruous set of lumpy drawers.

Scraps of the clothing he had been wearing when he'd changed earlier, from man into cat, shed onto the ground around him with a smattering of pats and thuds. A torn hank of boot leather caught between his toes. His long black hair—and the dead dog—were his only covering.

How on earth did creatures survive in this blistering cold?

"Oh! My!"

He looked up to see the woman, the one the other had called Ami, venture onto the steps. She was tall, strong like a whip, much darker in skin than the first, and with a magnificent cloud of black hair surrounding her head. She also had a metal stick in her hand, which she held as if she knew how to whack with it. She halted beside the paler, plumper one called Felicia. Together, they stared at him.

"Yes, that was my thought too," said Felicia. "He's gorgeous."

He wiped his blood-smeared mouth with the back of a hand before smiling at them, for he was sure his half sister Cat would have told him to use proper manners. "I have no clothes. They came off. My apologies."

The two women looked at each other. The wordless interchange reminded him of Catherine and her spoiled and irritating cousin Beatrice (no actual relation to him, he was glad to know!). Cat and Bee spoke a great deal without saying anything. Sometimes they did it when they rattled on with words to addle their listeners into thinking they hadn't even a pair of half thoughts to rub together into one. Other times, they displayed the uncanny ability to look at each other and come to an unspoken agreement.

"And I'm cold," he added, aggrieved the two women hadn't already noticed that he *would* be cold because he had no garments. Cat would have noticed. "I'm very, very cold. And I'd like to wash out my mouth. I didn't mean to bite the pug," he added, for it abruptly occurred to him that the rules were different here, and he could not just take what he wanted. "Perhaps it was a favorite of someone. However unlikely that may seem."

"That nasty little beast!" said Felicia, taking another step down as she looked him over. "It pisses on the couches and bites us as it wishes, and we are the ones who get slapped for it by the mistress."

Rory considered the dead dog. "My apologies, then, if there will be trouble for you because of what I did." He grasped it by the scruff and hoisted it with a sigh. "It is an unsightly creature. But I suppose it's dead now and can't be living again."

Ami gasped. "Blessed Mother, Felicia! Don't go any closer! You don't know what manner of creature he is. He could be anything, prowling about on Solstice Night!"

Felicia reached the base of the steps and halted on a strip of pavement swept free of snow. "What's your name?" she asked boldly. "How could you be a saber-toothed cat one moment and a . . . man the next?"

The tall one gave a snorting sort of sound like a choked-off laugh. She strode down the steps in an arrestingly commanding fashion, a woman who knew how to take charge. Halting beside Felicia, she brandished the metal stick, which he finally recognized as an implement with which you could poke fires.

"What is your name? Are you a cold mage? I don't think so, for I never heard that cold mages could change shape. It's only creatures from the spirit world who can change."

Still holding the pug, he stood. Their gazes took in the lines of his body, and then they looked at each other again, and Felicia's brow raised in a deliciously charming way.

"Roderic Barr, at your service," he said, offering a smile to sweeten the introduction, "but you may call me Rory. That's my pet name. What shall I do with the dog? How can I help you? I wouldn't want you to be punished for me biting it. That doesn't seem fair."

"Little enough about life is fair," said the tall one, but Rory noted how she nudged Felicia with her hip, as if reminding her to not say anything. "How did you get in the garden?"

"There was a tree and a wall and another tree, easy to leap and climb if you know trees. Where I come from, I'm used to trees and walls. I'm very agile."

"I don't doubt that," murmured Felicia with a sensuous upward curve of her rich red lips.

"Hush," said the tall one. "Don't even think it, Fee. He's some kind of spirit man. My grandmother would tell you such creatures cross over from the spirit world to seduce women."

"And then?" asked Felicia. "What happens then?"

"Then everyone is pleased," said Rory. "Is there something wrong with that?"

A bell rang, shaken impatiently. Ami and Felicia winced.

"Where is my Coco?" cried a booming female voice from within. "Where is my little chub'ums? He'll take his death if you force him outdoors to do his widdle business! Really! Why you cannot let him do his business under your cots as he likes to do, for it's safest and warmest there on these cold winter nights . . . Girls? Girls? Where have those lazy sluts gone?"

"Hide!" said Felicia. "Behind the troughs."

"What about—?" He shook the limp body with a hand, rather as he had earlier shaken its living self in his jaws.

"Hurry!" Ami leaped down to grab him by an elbow and drag him to the prickly shrubs.

He'd grown up in a pride of saber-toothed cats ruled by his mother's implacable will, so he simply never argued with females. With the oozing pug still in hand, he dashed behind the shrubs and crouched. The stone was like ice against his bare feet. The needles scratched him most painfully. But when a woman dressed in a robe of flowing gold swept out onto the patio at the top of the steps, bellowing about her chub'ums and her ungrateful servants, she did not see him. Another small dog was tucked in the angle of one of her arms. This one appeared even more foul-tempered and unpleasant than the corpse he held.

"Where is he?" she demanded.

For a moment, he thought she *had* seen him, but then he realized her only thought was for the missing dog.

"We just saw him run inside through the parlor curtains, Your Highness," said Ami, with a smile so false it would have curdled milk.

"My poor frightened Coco! You chased him! You heartless beasts!" The Highness happened to be standing closest to plump Felicia. She slapped her. The pug on her arm snapped at Felicia, too, teeth catching on her sleeve. Felicia took a step back, but the Highness grasped her sleeve and wrenched her back toward the growling dog. "Don't try to run away from your crime!"

A snarl escaped Rory, and he shifted forward to his toes. He would have leaped up to pounce on her, but Ami pounded the metal poker into the stone, once, in what he took as a warning to stay put. The pug began to huff out a wheezy cascade of barks. Its beady, black eyes were fixed on the shrubbery, for it had clearly smelled Rory or the blood of its missing companion.

"We have not seen him, Your Highness," repeated Ami with a false smile.

Yes, yes, obviously they were lying to protect themselves; he could understand that. But that awful woman wasn't being fair to them at all. Yet by the flash of Ami's gaze toward the shrubbery, as if fearful he might spring out, he knew he had to stay hidden.

Felicia raised a hand to the red stain on her cheek. She spoke in a voice as smooth as cream. "Your bath is ready, mistress. We were just coming to tell you when we discovered that Coco had to do his business. Ami will be glad to take His Highness the Exalted Ramses inside, for the cold air has startled and discomforted him. I will escort you into your bath."

"How can you think *I* can think of even having a bath at a time like this, with my little chub'ums so scared and likely shivering and cowering with fear! You are heartless and devoid of feeling, but no doubt you cannot help it, being a bastard's bastard child. Only my devotion to your grandmother keeps you in my service."

"I cannot express my gratitude, Your Highness."

"Of course you cannot! It is inexpressible, what I have sacrificed for you!" She lifted a hand to the heavens as if exhorting some personage who lived in the clouds. The gold bracelets on her arms jangled as they slipped to her elbows. The pug in her arms nipped at the bracelets, clearly as ill-tempered as the Highness and, fortunately, just as distractible. "But the gods lay their claim on us to be generous. That is our princely lot in life."

The speech exhausted her reserves. She swayed as her lips pinched together, as if to trap all the things she did not want to lose. She had an otherwise pleasant face, though soured by the expression of a person accustomed to slapping all underlings who did not accede quickly enough to her demands.

"I shall faint!" she decreed with the certainty of an oracle.

Felicia dabbed the woman's forehead with a scrap of fine linen, carefully avoiding the pug as it struggled to shift close enough to fasten its teeth around her fingers. "Take my arm, Your Highness. I shall help you inside and to your couch."

"How can you think I would abandon my sweetling so?! It is your flawed nature that twists your heart so cruelly. You must find Coco and bring him to me! I must lie down." She snorted out a copious sob, a sound similar to the honking of the big, wild cows he and his mother's pride of saber-toothed cats sometimes hunted. "I haven't even the strength to feed poor Exalted Ramses his supper. You can see he is starving! But I do not doubt that you care nothing for his suffering!"

"Let me assist you into your chambers, Your Highness," said Ami.

"Aurea!" the Highness bellowed.

A moment later, a girl not yet full-grown scurried out onto the porch. She had the look of a mouse, sure it is about to be gulped down, and she cringed as she made a clumsy curtsy.

The two serving women, again, exchanged glances.

"I can help you in, Your Highness," repeated Ami. "Let me take the Exalted Ramses."

The Highness shoved the growling pug into young Aurea's arms. It bit, mouth fixing over the girl's scarred fingers as its growl rose in pitch to a shrill frenzy.

The girl shrieked.

The Highness slapped her. "How dare you abuse Ramses so?!"

With a practiced swish of her sleeve, Ami got cloth in the way of the pug's next snap as she snatched the dog from the girl's arms. The beast squirmed impotently as Ami swept inside without a word, fabric muzzling its head.

"Come here, Aurea!" commanded the Highness, holding out an arm. Blood dripping from her bitten finger, the girl scuttled under the out-swept arm, with its jangling bracelets. She physically sank as the Highness settled her weight on her, but as the Highness moaned, the girl staggered inside with her. A curtain swished down behind them.

Wind rattled through the branches. A crow swooped overhead as if to investigate the altercation. Ami returned, without the pug, shaking out a damp spot on her sleeve and carrying a shawl.

"I put him in in his bed and took away the stairs so he can't get down," she said. "How I hate that foul, stinking beast. He peed on my arm!"

Felicia hastily shut the glass-paned doors.

"The way she torments that child by pretending to favor her makes me want to smash her head in," added Ami with a flourish of the poker.

"That's a stabbing weapon, so it wouldn't do well for smashing," Rory said. "Can I stand up now? My right leg is falling asleep, and my feet are cold."

"You can't stand up until we're sure she won't come back. Put this on." She tossed the shawl over the shrubbery.

"Cat would make sure I had shoes," he muttered as he tugged the shawl around his shoulders.

Heartlessly, Ami turned away from the bushes to confront her companion. "We must do something, or she'll kill poor Aurea. The girl has become nothing but bones and skin. And for her to prate on about her devotion to your grandmother, Fee! That nasty bitch bought your family's debt purely to hold it over a woman who was prettier than she was when they were young. Not that your sweet old grandma would have ever shoved it in her face back in those days."

"You don't know my sweet old grandmother very well, do you?" Felicia's smile, as sumptuous as gravy, distracted Rory from his cold feet. He licked his lips, wishing he could be licking hers instead. "They still hate each other. Every morning when I wake up, I think of why I'm stuck here for seven years, and I know that every time Her Royal Bitch sees me, she has to remember my gorgeous granddam. Let her stew in her own juices until she dries up! Rory? You can come out now."

Ami's hard glare softened as Rory cautiously rose to his feet. He held out the pug.

"What in the hells are we going to do with the cursed dog?" Ami muttered.

"Bury it?" Felicia studied the limp canine with a frown.

Ami shook her head. "The gardeners will find it. You know how the prince hates anything disturbed, except what he has given permission for. This time of year, any digging will be quite obvious, even if we try to hide it behind the shrubbery."

"Throw the corpse in the privy?"

"She'll have it raked. You know she will. One of the stablehands will be made to do it."

"What will happen to you if the Highness finds the dead dog?" Rory asked.

Felicia blanched, her magnificent bosom quivering.

Ami shrugged. "Fee will be whipped. So will Aurea, just for the pleasure the old cow gets in knowing she can command it."

"Whipped!" If he could have laid his ears back, he would have. "Will you be whipped too?"

"No. I'll be sent home in disgrace. She dares not lay a hand on me, for my family is too important. But one of my poor cousins will be sent to take my place. I don't mind serving the bitch. Keeps me free from a marriage I don't want. You must be freezing. We've got to sneak you inside."

He was shivering, but his honor was on the line: He had created the problem that would cause them to be harmed. So it was up to him to solve it.

"I could eat the dog," he said.

Ami looked thoughtful. "The whole body?"

"Not the bones and skin. But the insides, anyway."

Felicia was clearly a tenderer soul. She pressed a hand to her mouth. "How could you do that? Wouldn't it be nasty?"

"I would have to change back. Then I could eat it. You'd have less to get rid of."

"Are you experienced at that sort of thing?" demanded Ami.

He considered the pug with a frown. "I've never eaten this sort of creature exactly . . ." Ami's eyebrows had drawn down, so he paused.

"Changing back and forth at your own will, I mean," she said.

"It's something I didn't know I could do until recently," he temporized, for he wasn't sure how much he ought to tell them. But he liked the way they were looking at him, with hopeful, interested expressions. A man who did a good deed to make up for his bad deed would surely be rewarded. He might even hint at the sort of reward he would like most. "You would have to help me. You'd have to be very brave. I would have to become a cat and eat as much of the dog as I can. Then you'd have to persuade me back, to remind me how much I would rather be a man than a cat."

"You wouldn't just eat us?" Ami asked, but she was biting her lower lip as she considered.

He smiled, flashing a glance at Felicia. "Not in that way, anyway."

Felicia gave a most gratifying gasp and blushed bright red.

The music of Ami's answering laugh was so seductive that his man-part stirred alarmingly, even in this tremendous cold.

"Oh!" said Felicia. "My!"

"You think we might coax you back from cat to man?" murmured Ami.

"I think you've already had your answer," he said, not bothering to hide because—even though Cat would likely have told him it was very rude to stand naked in public in such a state—his two new friends were not troubled by it. "But my feet are very cold. Could we make a decision quickly?"

The two women looked at each other. If his feet hadn't been *quite* so cold, he would have enjoyed the way their expressions spoke instead of words. Ami's lips quirked up in a half smile as her eyebrows rose, as if with a question. Felicia's mouth parted as she exhaled, and she ran white teeth over her lower lip, in a way that made Rory want to nibble that luscious mouth right there.

"All right," said Ami, turning back to him with the poker slightly raised and slightly trembling, rather as he was. "We'll do it."

He set down the pug on the stone. Hands at his side, he considered his man-body and the memory of his cat-body and how the two things were the same body, but different in texture and movement. Deep inside himself there flowed a current like the stream of a river. He let his awareness sink into the current; he dropped into the flow where his cat-body waited, ready to pour back into his flesh. He let the cat out and put the man in the river.

He changed.

A shiver flew through him. His body curled forward as it bristled with fur and claws and teeth. He huffed out a breath and brushed his whiskers along the pug's body. It smelled better than he had been thinking it smelled. Lots of nourishing fat! But not much time!

He pinned the body with a paw and carefully opened up the belly with a sideways tear. Blood oozed. He licked it up and pulled out flesh and liver and the fatty heart, leaving aside the intestines, working around the bones and spine. It was a pleasant morsel, coming after the less-appetizing pea-hen, which had been scrawny and dry. Sour blood and bits and scraps of fat and liver dribbled from his mouth. He settled onto his haunches and began cleaning himself. Then felt the sting of cold snow on his hindquarters and wondered if there might be a more sheltered place to settle down.

Suddenly, two larger morsels slipped in on either side of him. He sniffed. They smelled very tasty, in a way he could not quite identify. He didn't want to devour them, precisely; he wasn't hungry, or at least, not in that way. A hand brushed his neck, then kneaded down the line of his spine. He rumbled, then began to purr.

"He's so tame," whispered the plumper one to the more muscled one.

The muscled one with the cloud of hair bent so close, her breath misted along his muzzle and caressed his nose. The tips of her hair mingled with his whiskers, making him shiver with delight. "I don't think he's as tame as all that. If he would just change back into a man, we could find out."

A man? What was a man? A man was shaped something like them, wasn't it? Upright, a fast runner, but with flesh that was not very appetizing, when it came down to it. He could be a man if he could just remember the way the river flowed and dive into it, even though water was not really to his liking. But their thighs brushing against his flanks made him think a swim might be worth it. Their hands petted him, and their voices murmured with crooning promises.

Anyway, he liked this new skill that was a sort of freedom. As a cub, he had learned to hunt. Hunting made him useful and gave him pleasure. Not being trapped in a single form gave him a weapon the poor creatures here in the Deathlands did not have, for they were confined into one form from birth until death. All they could do was grow and die.

He twisted his thoughts inward and plunged into the current. The flow poured around him and through him and into him, and he made his thoughts take a man's form. The change shuddered through him, and he became a man.

"That wasn't too hard!" he said, rather delighted at himself for managing it so easily.

Think of what Cat would say! She would praise him, wouldn't she? He was less sure of his mother's opinion, as she was always apt to give him a long, reproachful look when he attempted to impress her, as if to say, 'Why are you bothering me with these trivialities?' He frowned. An unpleasant taste rimed his lips, and his paws—his hands—were streaked with blood and other more unsavory substances. He was sitting right by the ripped-apart carcass of what had once been a small, fat, squashed-face dog. The intestines simply reeked, for although he had been careful not to puncture them, they had spilled anyway, and the dog had voided in its last moments. His bare feet slipped in the mess.

He wrinkled up his nose, lifted a hand to his lips, and licked at it, but in man-form the taste of blood made him gag.

"Hurry," said Ami briskly, throwing the long shawl around him. "We have to get you inside before anyone sees you. But the dog . . ."

Felicia reached under her own skirts and pulled off her drawers. "I'll wrap it up in these until we figure out how to hide the rest. The laundresses will just think I'm having my bleeding."

He sniffed. "You aren't bleeding, though. You're not even in your fertile passage. Won't people know it for a lie if you say the blood is yours?"

She flushed. "How can you tell?"

"Can't people smell here?" he asked, astonished.

"That's very rude, to talk about people smelling," said Ami in a kindly way meant, he supposed, to gently correct him. "But what did you mean, that she's not in her fertile passage?"

Standing, he bent closer, pulling back his lips and brushing his cheek alongside Ami's. She was attracted to him, that was obvious by her smell. "You're not fertile at the moment either," he said.

She drew back so sharply, he thought he might have offended her, but when he examined her wide eyes and lifted chin, he thought, instead, that she was merely startled.

"Did you want to be bred?" he asked. "If you're not fertile, I can't manage any breeding."

"No, no, all the better," she said with an arched eyebrow and a quizzical smile as she studied him. "Women would pay a lot to a man who could tell when they weren't fertile. Especially one as attractive as you are."

He almost said, *"Am I?"* but decided that, since he knew he was, and since he knew they thought he was, it might be unseemly to say so. So he merely smiled; to acknowledge that they all were happy was true.

Her smile sharpened, lips twitching up. "But I warn you, you're a bit forward to say so, so bluntly, to two women you barely know."

He coughed out a curt laugh. "Now you're just teasing me. I can tell what your body is saying. But my apologies if I'm not to say so. I haven't quite figured that out yet. My sister Cat is always correcting me. I have a lot to learn. As long as we don't get caught with the corpse." He broke off to turn in the direction of voices sounding from inside.

He stepped back behind the row of potted shrubs as Fee bent to roll up the bloody skin and bones in her spotless white linen. The voices moved on, footsteps tap-tapping on wood flooring. No one came outside into the cold after all, like sensible people remaining indoors where there was warmth.

He was starting to shiver again. Out of the darkness, a voice called out a bellowing "Halloo" and was echoed by a second, then a third, from farther out. A light swayed on the distant wall: a lantern being carried.

"Bright Venus," said Fee, "you're cold, you poor naked man. We've got a hot bath that the princess has rejected. Do you think we can sneak him in? She went to lie down, and she'll want freshly heated water when she wakes."

Ami pushed a hand over her hair, a gesture that looked habitual. "If we're discovered with a man in the women's quarters, we will certainly both be turned out bare-ass naked in the snow. The sensible thing to do would be to have him turn into a cat and jump back out over the wall."

"Darling," said Fee in a coaxing voice, like a child begging for one more piece of cake, "you can hear that the watch is changing, so he can't go right now in any case, lest the soldiers spot him. Anyway, there's no telling if he can get back out the way he came in. Let's get him clean and sort it out after."

"I like to be clean," said Rory, with what he hoped was a grateful smile that wasn't too begging nor too eager. "It's especially nice when others lick me."

The two women exchanged a glance, fraught with an emotion he felt as a hand caressing his skin. His body reacted predictably, even though his feet were terribly, terribly cold.

"After heating and hauling that bathwater," added Felicia suddenly, "I should hate to see it go to waste."

"Yes," said Ami decisively, and to his surprise, both she and Fee giggled in a girlish way that made his loins grow hotter and his ears burn as with whispered promises.

"I'll carry the dog," he added, thinking it a polite gesture that they might appreciate. "I'm already bloody."

He picked up the flaccid leavings. Fluids mottled the linen. Ami swept the stone with a branch broken off from an evergreen shrub, then wiped up the last of the spume with her sleeve. Rory followed Felicia inside, as quiet as if he were stalking unsuspecting prey. In a way, he was.

Inside and up the steps, the floor was remarkably warm, oozing pleasure into the soles of his feet.

"Ahh, it's so much better to be inside than outside!" He brushed a shoulder along Fee's.

The touch brought her to a halt, and she looked at him sidelong in a marvelously delicious way. Fee blushed and chewed on her lower lip as if she were chewing on him. He sniffed. Dog scent drenched the chambers. Streaks of dried urine stained chair legs, table legs, and the lowest span of the brightly painted wallpaper, where the dogs had marked where they wished. Their dribblings spotted the fine carpets like a series of tiny ponds, long since dried into rancid swales. The Highness's fraught moans echoed through the linked chambers like labored grunts. Her bedchamber lay to the left, through a series of closed doors. In the opposite direction, Rory smelled blessedly hot water.

Fee's hand brushed his elbow. She pulled it back nervously, then with a delightfully skittish grin, let her wonderfully plump fingers tickle on his forearm. His hair tingled at the touch, and she inhaled in a way that made him quite amorously inclined.

"Come with me," she whispered.

He dipped his head down to brush his cheek against her soft one. "I'd like that."

She let go of him so fast that he thought he had offended her. Yet with a teasing backward glance and a provocative swish of her lushly rounded hips, she hurried off toward the bathing chamber.

From behind a curtained alcove, a dog whined with thwarted anger. Rory pulled the curtain back and glanced into the chamber beyond: a spacious room furnished with gold-painted wallpaper and two gilded beds covered with dog hair. In the dimness, the noble Ramses huffed indignantly. Ami had indeed deposited Ramses on his bed and pulled away the steps, so the ungainly creature could not descend unless it leaped. Rory was pretty sure it was too fat to leap and, in any case, too accustomed to its privileges to make the attempt.

Cornered and trapped, the little thing growled shrilly at him, quivering all over.

Ami slipped up beside Rory and slapped him on the ass.

"If he starts barking, we're all in," said Ami. With her free hand, she tossed a hank of bread that landed neatly, right in front of Ramses. His growls turned into slobbering as he set to gnawing on the crust with the sort of gluttonous lack of fastidiousness common to dogs. Meanwhile, Ami's fingers strayed along the curve of Rory's ass before darting up to grasp his elbow. "Come along, Rory."

He followed obediently through a set of linked sitting chambers, lit by handsome gold lamps molded in the shapes of overly fed hounds, so unlike the lean, cruel beasts he knew in the spirit world that, at first, he thought they were meant to be cows. Behind a pair of carved doors lay a small stone room painted with a mural of cavorting mermaids and dolphins engaged in unexpectedly acrobatic water games. The room was fitted out with a large brass tub brimful with hot water. Six full buckets and two large brass pitchers, suitable for pouring, sat on a stone bench alongside. There was also a rack to hang a robe or dress or other clothing, and a closed wardrobe. At a side table with a basin, he washed the blood off his hands.

"These aren't the real baths," said Fee, who was waiting beside the tub with her gaze fixed shyly on the floor. "The maidservants wash here. But the Highness likes us to bathe her here. She likes to pretend she's a lowly servant, cavorting among her friends."

"You just bet she does," remarked Ami. "Since the prince never touches her, we're the only ones, except her hired lovers, from whom she ever gets a stroke. We do it to keep her temper under control. If she weren't such a misbegotten tyrant, I would almost feel sorry for her. But she is, so I don't."

She began to strip off her clothes.

"Ami!" breathed Fee, turning pink.

"You know what I think of her!"

Fee gestured to the now mostly naked Ami. "Not that. Your clothes . . ."

"Oh! Well! He can't be expected to wash himself after everything he's gone through, can he?"

"He can't!" agreed Rory. "After everything he's gone through? Certainly not! What do I do with—?" He held up the damp cloth that veiled the remains of the oozing corpse. He was so distracted by Ami's long, dark limbs and firm breasts that he took a step back and set the dead dog beside the door, to one side, before turning back to the women with his slyest smile. The shawl slipped off his body. "Where do I get in?"

"Do you say such things for their double meaning or are you just that charming?" asked Ami with a laugh.

"I like to let people wonder how tame I am. Until I eat them up."

"You are the worst flirt I've ever met," said Ami appreciatively, as she slipped out of her drawers.

Such soft, pleasing undergarments they were too. He took them from her before she could drape them over the bench and held them over his hips.

"Do you think they would fit? My sister says I'm not to wear women's undergarments because I'm male, but I think that's not fair. What do you think?"

Ami was as bold as Fee was shy. She pressed herself against him, naked chest to naked chest, and looked him right in the eye, for she was quite tall. She spanned his hips with strong hands. "I think they would fit you, but you'll look oh-so-much-better handsomely clad in a dash jacket and well-fitting trousers, don't you think?"

"Whatever you think is what I think," he murmured into her ear, and then he nibbled at the lobe.

She had such an air of command that the way her breathing grew unsteady made him most pleasantly excited.

She steered him toward the tub. "Now you've gotten me dirty, too, you wicked beast. We'll have to both go in the tub. Darling Fee, what are you waiting for? I know you've seen naked men before. And Bright Venus knows we've been in that tub together before."

His ass came into contact with the tub.

"In you go," said Ami, wrapping an arm around him and tipping him backward.

He grasped her just as tightly, and together, they fell in with a huge splash that soaked the front of Fee's gown. The wet fabric clung to her generous curves and displayed the rounded curve of her breasts and her erect nipples in a most marvelous way.

"Now I'm wet," said Fee, in a tone whose astonishment made Ami laugh.

"Milady Aminata?" a mouse-like, girlish voice murmured from outside the closed doors. "Milady Felicia? I don't— I mustn't— I'm sorry—"

"Angry Jupiter," muttered Ami, sitting up in the bath and pushing Rory behind her. He found that he could curl his naked body around hers in a very amorous way and keep his head hidden by pressing kisses between her shoulder blades. "What is it—ah! Mmm. What is it, Aurea? Aren't you attending Her Highness?"

"She sent me to look for Coco," came the plaintive voice. "The mistress is wanting him."

"Is she up?"

"No, she is sleeping."

"Well, then, child, we'll sort it out later. We're just warming up in here. We were so cold from searching outside that I thought our toes would—stop that!—freeze off. You had best go to the kitchens and try the yam pudding, to make sure it is fit for when Her Highness wakes up. And the biscuits and the rabbit, too, for you know how Her Highness likes her food just so. Make sure you try everything, and not just a spoonful, either, enough so you— ah!—so you can make sure it will be to her liking. Go on. She won't wake for another hour."

"But I can't. Her Highness ordered me to look for Coco."

"Felicia and I will look for him, I promise you. As for the other, I command you, for I am senior to you, so you must obey me."

"But I'm not allowed—"

"I'll obey you," murmured Rory at the same time, exploring the part of Ami that rested under the water.

"Ah! Stop that, you beast!"

The little voice quavered. "Milady, did I displease you?"

"Yes! You displease me by not eating enough to keep up your strength and feed your appetite. I have changed my mind. You must eat two bowls of yam pudding first, at my order, and then try all the other foods. Is that clear, Aurea?"

"Two bowls?"

Rory discovered how well his two hands could fondle Ami's two breasts. Her head sagged back against his, her hair caressing his two lips.

Fee had been standing mute and damp, looking from tub to door and back to tub. "Yes, you must eat two bowls of yam pudding for supper every night, Aurea," she said with unexpected decisiveness. "Besides the rest of your meal. That is an order. Go right away, so you can eat as much as you wish while the Highness sleeps. And then take a nap until we call for you. Go!"

The scuttling footfalls of the girl faded.

"You're feeling frisky," said Rory with a laugh.

"So I am," Felicia said as she stripped off her gown and gathered up a thick bar of soap and a sachet of herbs and leaned over the tub.

So she was, and Ami too. They frisked quite delightfully and energetically, in a way that splashed a great deal of water over the floor. Eventually, they ended up on the floor, on a pile of lovely, thick towels. They took their time, indeed, they did.

But, really, considered in the greater scheme of things, it was all over far too quickly. Rory was granted the merest scant interval of lying, spent and satisfied, with a woman on each side, nestled cooingly against him, before a high, light bell sounded.

Ami sat up. "Curse the old bitch with boils and an itching arse."

A great deal of shouting and bellowing rose from the princess's rooms. A birdlike scratch scraped the door.

"Lady Aminata. Lady Felicia. Her Highness is awake and looking for you. She's rousted the gardeners to search the grounds. I didn't tell her yet where you were, but . . . ."

The one truly impressive thing about the Highness was her voice. "Aurea! Where is that useless bit? Why is she not here by my bedside?"

Although Rory could tell she was nowhere near, her shout carried marvelously, like warning of a distant storm that would break over them at any moment.

Ami went to the door and cracked it open. "Aurea. Go tell Her Highness we're outdoors, looking still. That will give us time to make sure she doesn't find us here. Hurry."

The girl scuttled off as Ami closed the door and turned to regard, first, her naked companions and then the messy linen that wrapped the remains of darling Coco. "We have to get you out of here," she said to Rory. "The problem is that men are not allowed in this wing. The moment you're seen, they'll know something is up."

"Will you be punished?" he asked.

Her frown had a grim cast that chased all thoughts of dalliance out of his mind. His lazy languor burned off at the thought of these delectable females being punished, especially because he would have been responsible, and they left to accept the blame. His mother always told him that if there was anything she hated, it was males who let the women do all the work. "I would rather give myself up to spare you that. If I become a cat again and run back through the garden, they'll never know you were involved."

"The soldiers will shoot you!" exclaimed Ami, with a look of real alarm.

Fee planted a firm kiss on Rory's lips, but then rose. "I know exactly what to do."

She flung open the wardrobe and rummaged around until she found what she wanted. "Here." She dropped men's trousers, shift, waistcoat, and a sober-green dash jacket onto Rory's lap. "Get into these."

"But Fee—?" Ami's protest died as Fee tossed a clean gown at her and shook out a second dress, one cut to fit Fee's more generous figure.

"He's got no beard. We'll dress him in a gown, veil his face in a shawl, and tell the guards at the gate that he's my cousin, come to visit me for the day and leaving now for home. His hair is long and beautiful enough to be a woman's. Once he's outside, he can take off the gown and go about as a man, although it will be cold without a coat."

"My sister will find me a coat," he said, much taken with this idea as he swiped Ami's drawers from the bench and pulled them on, covering them quickly with the trousers so she wouldn't notice and thus object to his stealing them. So soft!

"You're brilliant, Fee!" breathed Ami in a voice so tender and admiring that he paused while buttoning up the front flap of the trousers. They were gazing at each other as if they wanted nothing more than to lick each other, and he abruptly felt that, while this had been a pleasing dessert for them, he wasn't truly necessary to their repast.

After all, he was leaving, wasn't he? He had to return to his family, and they naturally would make their own little pride in the territory where they roamed. A sigh escaped him, nonetheless.

"Dearest Rory!" said Fee at once, rushing over to him. "You're so honorable and good."

"Am I?" he asked, not to demand their agreement but because he wanted to be honorable and good. That was what males were meant to be, wasn't it?

"You are," she assured him. "Let me help you with those buttons."

Ami dressed also. "I still don't know what we're going to do with darling Coco," she said as they all finished dressing and the women helped sort out his gown so the drape and flow did not reveal the men's clothing beneath.

"I have an idea," said Rory as they wrapped the shawl around his head in way that made him seem a modest woman, one who did not wish to be stared at on the street. "A very cunning and devious idea. But you can't know, and you mustn't watch. Wait here."

"You can't let anyone see you!"

"There's no one outside right now. The Highness is wailing in her bedchamber, and the servants are either waiting on her or shivering about out in the cold." He gave them his sternest look, the one he reserved for moments of extreme danger or when he really had to convince his mother not to swat him after he had played a trick on his spoiled and obnoxious little sister—the other one, not Cat. To his surprise, they opened the door enough for him to slip through. He picked up the stinking remains and sneaked out.

Stealthy as only a cat can be, he sought the den of the foul beast, behind the curtained alcove.

Then he returned to the women.

"It's taken care of," he said with a smile. "Trust me."

The voice shook the walls. "Where are those sluts? Where is my darling Coco?"

"Hurry." Ami dragged him out of the bath chamber and along a servants' narrow hall, by the light of the lamp Fee carried. A pair of lamps marked a door barred from the inside. Ami pulled open a square viewing hole and peered out.

"Who's out there? Ah, Captain Gaius, it's you. Open up. Lady Felicia's cousin has to get home. She was visiting, but Her Royal Highness is in a pet."

The soldier standing guard laughed. "Are you telling me that's something new today? I reckon I'm glad I'm out here and you're in there tending to her fits and starts. Stand back, girls."

Ami slid shut the viewing hole and then gave Rory a sound kiss. On the other side, the guard fiddled to unlock a mechanism, for, evidently, the door was barred on both sides. Fee unbarred the door. As it swung in, the captain raised his lamp to take a good look at them, with a proprietary air that made Rory want to claw him. But he knew better than to pick a fight and draw attention. So he smiled winningly instead. The man was rather good-looking, with the bluff, muscular build of a fellow who spends a lot of time wrestling and running and hacking at helpless objects. His broad hands looked as if they might be very adept at squeezing and kneading. His gaze was certainly probing.

"Who is this lovely? I've not seen her before, and I know all you girls by sight and by that lovely sway of your ass, Lady Felicia."

Lady Felicia was not, perhaps, as enamored of Captain Gaius as Rory thought he himself could be, given the chance.

"This is Rory," she said in a cool voice, far removed from her passionate utterances not long ago. "She's not a servingwoman to the princess, Captain, so you must show her respect."

Ami added, "She's really a saber-toothed cat dressed in a man's skin and wearing a woman's clothes."

"I have very nice man's skin," said Rory helpfully. "Do you want to see it?"

Captain Gaius laughed, slapped Rory on the ass in a most gratifying way, and then, unfortunately, stepped back. "You women and your jests. Go on. There's a commotion brewing, for I heard the wall captain call up half the men. If the old bitch finds me chatting up you lot, she'll have my balls. Get out of here."

A male voice shouted for the captain. With a frown, he signaled to them to stay put as he stepped away around a corner and into a guardhouse. Across the courtyard, a closed gate in a high wall promised access to the city beyond.

"I can't believe you told the truth, Ami," said Felicia under her breath. She was still holding Rory's hand, and with obvious reluctance, she released him. "About Rory, I mean."

"The benefit of telling the truth is that so few people believe you. You must go, Rory. Though I'm sorry to lose you so soon after finding you."

"All will be well," he assured them. "The Highness will never suspect you."

At that moment, out of the depths of the princess's wing, a mighty shriek cleft the night like the anguished howl of a wounded monster.

"My chub'ums! My Coco! Aieeee! Ramses! *How could you?!*"

Rory smiled smugly, imaging how sour Ramses must look with his nose smeared in blood and his paws dabbling in the moist remains. The two women looked at him with wide eyes. He kissed each one on her warm, willing lips and stepped away as the captain returned, looking grumpy.

"Hurry, lass. Get out of here, as the lord general is bound to make his rounds with all this fuss. Cursed women! Either scolding or wailing."

One last glance was all he was permitted as the captain hustled him to the servants' gate and thrust him out into the cold night. The captain shut the gate.

Rory stood on the cobblestone street, savoring the adventure. That had felt good! And he had learned something important about himself, just as Cat would have urged him to do: by understanding what it meant to flow and change, he could now shift from cat to man and back again whenever he wished! Sadly, he knew he would never be able to tell Cat about all the best parts of the night; she would no doubt be affronted and embarrassed.

A curious watchman paused to eye him and, when Rory snarled, hurried on. He stripped off the gown and shawl and folded them up to carry. He took in a draught of air. Beneath the many heated smells of the city, he sought his sister's distinctive scent, blended of both worlds.

Dressed in his man's clothes, with his soft woman's drawers beneath, he sauntered off in search of her. Sometimes things did work out. He had righted a tiny wrong, done some good in the world, maintained his honor, and been well-petted in reward.

It was good to be a man.

The Secret
Journal
of Beatrice
Hassi Barahal

The Secret Journal of Beatrice Hassi Barahal

~~The romantic escapades of~~
~~The amatory adventures of~~
~~The seven significant kisses of~~
needs more sword-fighting and fewer kisses

For years as she grew out of innocent childhood and into ~~budding~~ womanhood, Beatrice Hassi Barahal had imagined a kiss.

budding? like a delicate flower? what about axe-wielding?

Beatrice and her dearest cousin Cat attended the academy college in the city of Adurnam where they ~~prospered amid~~ the ranks of industrious pupils.
sowed mischief among

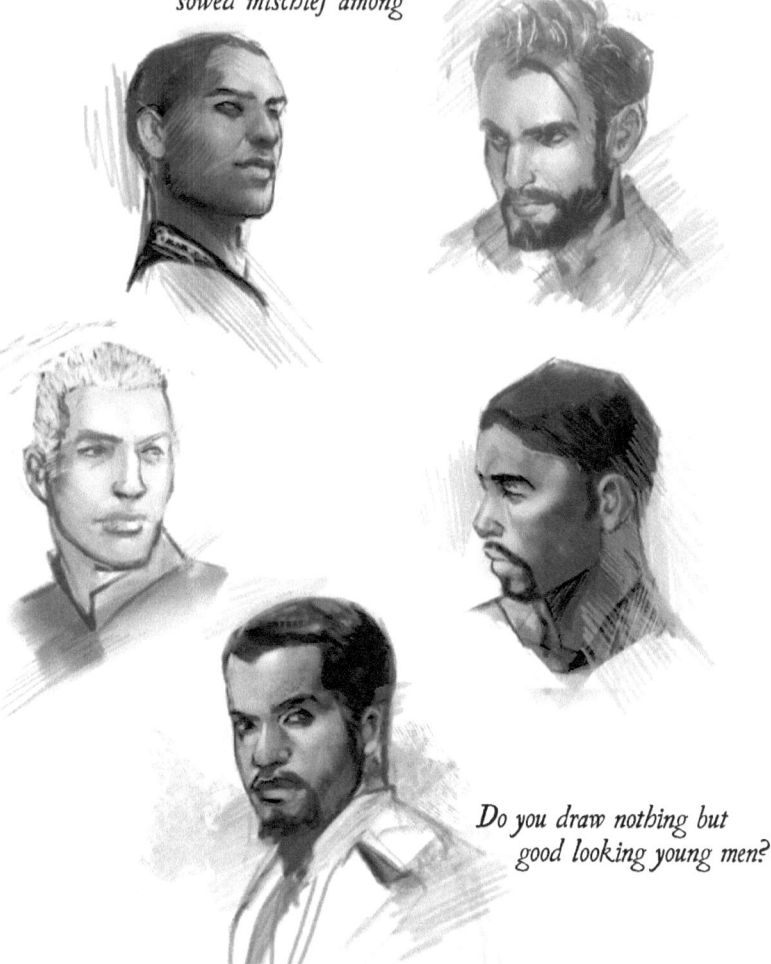

Do you draw nothing but good looking young men?

Because they were scholarship students it was incumbent upon the two loyal cousins to behave themselves, so they never got into trouble or at the very least were never caught even when they sneaked into places they weren't meant to go. It wasn't that they were mischievous or trouble-makers very often, it was just that the grind of daily life in their humble household where there was never quite enough to eat needed some spice they could not otherwise afford except by pretending to spy.

Yet one day a handsome, rich, and young man of high rank would arrive at the academy as a student and be received by the distinguished headmaster in a manner befitting his high station.

Of course he would have excellent manners and well connected relatives. The male students at the academy would position themselves to be accepted as his companions. The young women would befriend his younger sisters and smile at him, but in the end he would have eyes for only one because her beauty and her modest charm would ~~overwhelm~~ him *like a pig* *slaughter* **I'm ignoring you.**
Then, in her time of trial, he would rescue her.
I'm yawning. Why does he have to rescue her? Can't she rescue herself?
The rescue would be achieved despite perilous travails and in the face of such dangers as would leave most men quaking and paralyzed. It would include either an exploding airship from which hapless passengers plunged to their deaths or a desperate balloon ascent while slavering dire wolves howled in pursuit and snapped at the dangling ropes as at flying snakes. Or possibly savage northern Celts stampeding on mammoth-back amid trumpets and a blizzard.

But he would show no fear. His resolve would never slacken. He would pursue her enemies far beyond the city in which she lived to the very limits of the earth, and all at risk of his own life, and he would laugh – Ha! Ha! – in the face of death. *"Ha! Ha!" You cannot seriously write "Ha! Ha!" into a story.*

This is my dearest cousin Cat. ~~She snores.~~

I do not!

In the end, Beatrice and her rescuer would be reunited in the elegant, well appointed halls of his family's townhouse in the very best part of the city of Adurnam. In this refuge of painted walls and brocade sofas, he would realize their love was meant to be despite the gulf between their stations.

In the lush confines of the conservatory with its glass roof and forest of delicate orchids and cheerful chrysanthemums, he would forget everything except his need to declare himself.

"Beatrice! My beloved flower! You are in my thoughts day and night!"

Beneath a trellis of sweet-scented jasmine, he would take her hands into his and gaze deeply and longingly into her eyes. With a tremulous smile, she would touch her lips to his.

The kiss might be tender and gentle, or it might be fierce and passionate, or it might be bold and possessive, or it might even be shy and sweet. *Now I am snoring. Snoring. SNORING.*

The kiss would be more interesting preceded or followed by sword fighting. Or stampeding mammoths. Or perhaps a raid by soldiers trying to find radicals. Then there could be a sword fight.

But never ever ever ever had she imagined it would be followed by an insulting proposal that she become his mistress.

"Am I not worthy to be your wife?" Beatrice expostulated.

By the way he glanced away from her, she could tell his first instinct was to say, "No, of course you are not! How could you possibly believe you might be?" But he did not say it. His melting eyes fixed an amorous look on her rather, she reflected with a sudden hardening of the heart, as a seamstress in an impoverished household may fix ribbons to an old gown to give it the false appearance of something new.

"Of course you are, my lovely Beatrice. It is I who am not worthy of your sweet, accommodating nature and your beauteous raven tresses and your lusciously ample . . . form."

She wavered. The young prince and legate, Amadou Barry, was a handsome man with an impeccable noble lineage and a huge fortune. When he and his sisters had arrived at the academy college in Adurnam, many a girl had fixed her arrows on him. A young woman could not help but wish to show all those conceited, stuck up, snobbish rich girls that an impoverished girl of Phoenician ancestry could best them in love as well as in mathematics and the scientific puzzles of natural history.

Anyway he did smile so charmingly and grasp her so masterfully.

"I cannot allow you to slip away, my delicate and shy Beatrice. You are startled and so innocent. It is no wonder you do not quite know your mind. But be assured that you will be an apt pupil when you let me take control of your heart and your more intimate treasury. It is I who can instruct you in the music of sweet pleasure."

"Delicate and shy? Know my own mind? I fear you have mistaken this scene for one in the cheaper sort of theatrical entertainments."

He smiled, the very illustration of masculine condescension. "You drive a hard bargain, oh cunning Beatrice, but I am willing to pay any price to taste the tart dinner you will serve me."

In truth her dreams did not die a hard death.

They snapped out as quickly as a candle is snuffed.

*or as **quickly** I would have punched him!*

Although he held her against him, she insinuated her hands between their bodies and shoved him back so hard that he staggered several steps before he caught himself.

"I think that is quite enough! Blind Astarte! I am not a bargain to be purchased or a meal to be eaten. Nor will I stand here and be subjected to such nauseating phrases as 'intimate treasury' or 'apt pupil!' As for poetry, you have not the Celtic ear. I recommend civil engineering as more suited to those of your ancestors who are Roman."

His lips trembled, an expression she briefly hoped might be regret or shame. But as his brows drew down and his hands clenched, she recognized it as indignation.

As if she had insulted him!

His momentary speechlessness gave her the opportunity to escape out past the potted geraniums and the waterfalls of weeping wisteria and thus out the door of the greenhouse.

Chin high, cheeks flushed, she struggled to glide unconcernedly down the corridors past unsuspecting servants and up the stairs to the small guest room. There, she shut and barred the door and collapsed on the bed with gulping sobs. What a fool she had been! The shame of it battered her in waves. *If I had been there I really would have punched him! Or thrown him out of an airship!*

She wept for hours but then she fell asleep and had the most urgent of dreams, that her dearest cousin Cat was being pursued by implacable cold mages commanded by their master to kill her. They would catch Cat and slit her throat mercilessly if there was no one to defy them, for Cat was a vulnerable fugitive entirely alone out in the lonely countryside with no loving cousin to help her. Not unless Beatrice could scrape her shame from off the soles of her shoes and go back to the man who had so crudely insulted her and ask him to take soldiers to the ancient ruin of Cold Fort and there rescue Cat.

Because she loved her dearest Cat more than anyone else in the whole wide world, she swallowed her pride and did just that.

Saved and reunited, Beatrice and Catherine escaped from the vile prison of disenchantment. But they were unable to hide even among the most wretched and forgotten inhabitants of the city.

Fortunately they found refuge at the law offices of Godwik and Clutch.

Welcomed by like-minded colleagues, they determined to devote their lives to good works among the downtrodden, to learning the printing trade, and to assisting revolutionaries in overthrowing the ancient privileges that allow the rich and powerful to arbitrarily distribute wealth and favor to themselves.

while freeing unjustly-imprisoned radicals from impenetrable dungeons by means of daring raids

END OF BOOK ONE

Now Rory is sulking because you did not mention him or include a sketch of him.

Roderic Barr arriving in the mortal world
That was not what I had in mind. Blessed
Tanit! Put clothes on him!

Rory says he doesn't like to wear clothes.
You find this amusing, don't you?

Ha! Ha!

Even a young woman whose dreams illuminate snatches of the future cannot possibly interpret all that she sees nor can she state with certainty what miserably dreadful or blissfully delightful trials are yet to come. That morning how could she have known that her life would change forever because of the unexpected arrival of a man at the door?

If you, Perspicacious Reader, assume that she speaks of the most notorious man in Europa, General Camjiata, called also the Iberian Monster, you would be right. *But because Bee and Cat were far too intelligent to have anything to do with the Iberian Monster, they immediately and prudently fell down a well into the spirit world.*

It was here that Beatrice learned a salutary lesson: *Stay out of places where*
    A pawn that survives through cunning and disciplined game play has the *everything*
opportunity to become a powerful queen, if she only realizes that the very *wants to*
dreams people want her for give her a weapon she can possess and wield.   *kill you.*

    Therefore, when Beatrice found herself dripping wet, shivering, and
alone on the wintry shore of the Temes River, she commandeered a humble
carter and his wagon. On the road to Adurnam, she viewed her options as
dispassionately as a general considers strategy on the eve of battle.

    Hand herself over to the cruel mercies of the cold mages? *Never!*

    Join the tempting radicals, with their noble aspirations?

    and their handsome, whisky-drinking, fist-fighting rabble rousers?

    Or court the man who already almost conquered Europa when married
to a dragon dreamer and was poised to do so again? A man who had
already hinted that he knew secrets he could teach to a young woman who
desperately needed tutoring. A man she had seen more than once in her
dreams. *You never told me that!*

                                                        I don't tell you everything.

It is a sad truth, but one acknowledged by any person who can bother to read the law, that the inferior legal status of a woman in Europa means she is best protected by having a powerful family or, lacking that, by finding the strongest protector and marrying him.

A woman in Beatrice's perilous situation might not like this unpleasant truth but could not ignore it. Yet a man of Camjiata's worldly experience and ambitious temperament could not possibly be tempted by a callow young woman, no matter how beautiful she might be.

So she devised a cunning plan.

First, she became so seasick on the voyage from Adurnam west across the Atlantic Ocean to the mysterious Antilles that Camjiata was obliged to attend on her day and night lest she expire. This task he took on with patience and good humor.

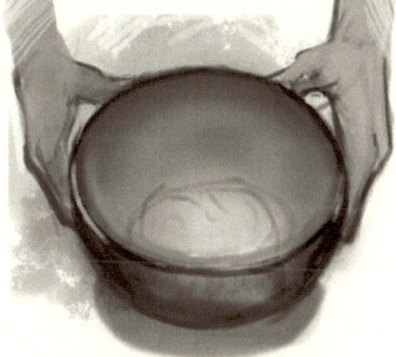

This is what I looked at for most of the voyage

How a person nurses you when you are appallingly ill is a sure test of their character. *Yes.*

It was during this dire period that Beatrice came to realize that however handsome and attractive she may have thought Legate Amadou Barry, *I thought* howsomever his kisses pleased her, had he been faced with a young woman *there was* nauseated and weak, he would have left the chore of nursing her to a servant. *only one* So it came about that upon taking up residence in a spacious and strikingly decorated townhouse in the hot and humid city of Expedition on the island of Kiskeya in the Antilles, Beatrice proposed marriage to the general one balmy morning while they were at their breakfast.

Marriage! Bee! You really were in love with him!

Yes. *But he's so old!*

Sometimes you are remarkably obtuse and annoying.

"So you see, General, that with my dreams and your knowledge of dragon dreaming and your superior military genius, we are eminently well suited. A perfect alliance."

He considered his cup, brimful of coffee, sweetened with four heaping spoons of cane sugar as was his habit although honestly it made the coffee sickly sweet.

"My dear Beatrice," he said in a kind tone that crashed against her tenderly fluttering heart like brutal hurricane winds. *Waves crash. Winds tear.*

As she looked up into his gaze, she realized he saw her as a child. He cared for her–she did not doubt that–and certainly he valued and even coveted her dreaming as a means to further his imperial ambitions, but he did not see her as his amatory equal, as a woman he would take to bed.

I will never be able to scour this horrible image from my mind

"My dear Beatrice, you are young still, and with all your life ahead of you–"

"Do not condescend to me," she cried, brandishing anger to conceal the tears that flooded her eyes. "I know what I am asking!"

"I am sure you do not, Beatrice. You have become infatuated with the idea of who I am. And I am flattered, truly."

"You think I am a callow girl! Too young for you! Not worldly enough!"

"I think I have caught you stealing kisses from Juba. The man is smitten with you, Beatrice. Do you not think it disrespectful to kiss him and then propose to me?"

"I informed Juba that he and I have no future together despite our mutual attraction."

"Have you no future with him? Of course he is an exile and thus not in a position to marry, nor can he welcome you into the shelter of his powerful family since they are the ones who exiled him. But you might become lovers, as you wish and as I am sure he greatly desires."

At this plain speaking Beatrice blinked so many times that at length the general said,

"Have you got something in your eye?"

Ha! Ha! Just when I want to hate him he makes me laugh.

"Oh," Beatrice said, still blinking *like the intelligent girl she so cunningly pretended to be.*

The general sipped thoughtfully at his coffee before going on. "Nothing but custom confines you to sexual congress within marriage. People defy custom all the time."

This is my story. You may phrase things otherwise in yours!

"You cannot possibly sit there as a man with noble connections and claim that my situation is the same as yours in this regard!"

"True enough. Women are judged more harshly on that score although I do not see why they should be. Meanwhile your particular situation is indeed full of hazards. But in this regard you will hear no censure from me if you choose to enter into a relationship with Juba. He is a good man. I believe you can trust him with your heart, or with an offer of intimacy."

Although she reflected that it was startlingly radical of him to say so, Beatrice could not but fume at how lightly he dismissed her heartfelt proposal and how quickly he suggested she ease her broken heart with thoughts of another man.

Not that Juba's kisses hadn't been passionate and exciting!

"Whatever I chose in that regard, General," she adjured tartly, "I am still left legally vulnerable. The Barahal clan has already betrayed both me and Cat to the cold mages, so I cannot expect help from my own natal family. Perhaps I should have stayed with the radicals!"

Having drained his cup, he rose and poured himself more coffee, then brought the pot over to pour for her. He studied her with a pleasant smile meant, she supposed sourly, to be heartening. Her heart beat a little harder and bit more sadly and wisely for knowing now that he would never see her in the same light as she saw him.

I was becoming afraid he was going to be one of the seven significant kisses.

"But if a high place in the world is what you seek, Beatrice, then I believe I can help you. If you are willing to involve yourself in my schemes."

"Haven't I already made it clear I am willing to involve myself in your schemes?" she demanded, vexed by his casual reply. *No casual reply! He is further reeling you onto his hook. It's how he works!*

"The Taino Empire is an ally worth cultivating. They have soldiers, weapons, and airships. I have something they both value and need: A dragon dreamer. I see no reason we cannot marry you to the man likely to become the next ruler. Juba's brother, Caonabo."

And thus we are forced to admire a master manipulator in his element!

To be sure, Beatrice's first meeting with Prince Caonabo was awkward due to the complicated pageantry of the court ceremony whose gestures and patterns she feared to get wrong because it would make her look like the veriest barbarian in their sophisticated eyes. Her anxieties were augmented by her concern that her stumbling attempts to speak his language would sound ridiculous, and by his astonishing resemblance to his twin brother, a man she had so recently kissed in regretful farewell. *Bee, were you INTIMATE with Juba?*

But the prince was a measured, rational, sensible man sensitive to the difficulties inherent in the unusual circumstances of their arranged marriage. Unlike some. *Vai was aware!* **It's sweet when you make excuses for him. Or sad. I'm not sure which.**

He served her food familiar to her palate before introducing her to the culinary specialities of his own people. He wore clothing that would remind her of home before showing her how to dress in the local style.

More importantly they soon discovered a shared passion for natural history and the study of scientific principles. He had the most sophisticated brass telescope with a refracting lens as well as an astronomer's inclinometer together with one suitable for marine use, as well as numerous surveying tools.

By reason of his exalted position as nephew of the ruler of the Taino Empire, he kept a small airship suitable for reconnaissance of the island and the greater sea, the realm he soon hoped to rule in part by means of having a dragon dreamer allied to him through marriage, and in this airship they toured the island of Kiskeya.

And he introduced her to the most interesting trolls, an entire academy (or Shiny-Ideas-Clutch, as the trolls call it) of trolls and humans devoted to the pursuit and promulgation of discovery and scientific principles. *I'm sorry I missed that!*

Their shared sympathies made the days pass serenely for it was at this time
that Beatrice came to comprehend the important lesson:
Sometimes kisses are sweeter than sword-fighting. Sometimes kisses ARE the adventure.
You're nauseating when you get that look on your face. You know that, do you not?
But I'm right.   *Why do you have no sketch of Vai?*
I knew you would ask that. *Well, why don't you?*
Because he is not part of my story. *Not even one?*
You're so annoying. *Please?*

No one likes cold mages. This is a portrait of Andevai Diarisso Haranwy, of Four Moons House, who so rudely and arrogantly took Cat away from the people who love her and then kept showing up at the most inopportune times despite that he was not wanted. However, it would be a lie not to admit that his clothes are splendidly magnificent.

How odd that Cat has nothing to say but I see it is because she is staring dumbfoundedly at the sketch with all the intelligence of mindlessly adoring overwarmed pudding. If pudding could adore.

You got the collar wrong.

Their shared sympathies made the days pass serenely for it was at this time that Beatrice came to comprehend the important lesson:

How can one guess that everything that is going so right is about to go so very very very wrong?

Her dearest cousin Cat betrayed yet again!   *and this time by the man you* Cat's husband kidnapped by a dreadful power!   *proposed marriage to!*
  at least you weren't torn to pieces by the Wild Hunt
  with your head thrown down a well! **I am indeed grateful for that.**
And when her cousin was arrested for the murder of the Taino queen, mother of Prince Caonabo, Beatrice was forced to make a choice between the shelter afforded her by newly acquired status and rank and the desperate situation her dearest Cat found herself in.

Of course it was no choice, despite the humiliation that happened afterward and the separation from a person she had greatly cared for.

Yet it taught her what she should have understood long since:

You cannot be protected from within the system no matter how highly placed you may think yourself, not if it is the inequities of the system that have made you vulnerable in the first place.

END OF BOOK TWO

Book Three: In Which Our Heroine
Discovers the Task She Is Best Suited For

Once upon a time there was a young woman named Beatrice Hassi Barahal who quite against her will walked the dreams of dragons. Because of her prescient ability to glimpse snatches of the future, she was relentlessly pursued by all manner of powerful people who wished to use her dreaming to bolster their own authority and power.

In the course of her adventures, she learned an important lesson:

Skip over all the other mistaken paths with their false promises, and start by immediately

The romantic notions she once held so close could not protect her.   *joining the radicals.*

But if a young woman could find the ~~tools~~ and the allies, she could learn
to protect herself.   *weapons*

What transpired in the Great Smoke and the many secrets Beatrice learned there will be presented as a lecture and an illustrated monograph under the auspices of the Shiny-Ideas-Clutch.

Meanwhile, her dearest cousin Cat was obliged to undertake a rescue mission, *and add more sword-fighting to this journal!*

Beatrice and her annoying companion Rory had perforce to make their arduous way alone to Havery and the radicals.

If only Amadou Barry had taken hold of my hand, but I suppose that was the measure of him in the end.

The city of Havery was a haven and a hotbed of radical philosophizing and debate because Havery's prince was sympathetic to the radical cause.

Trepidatiously *You have never done anything trepidatiously in your life. I don't even think you know what the word means.* **It means I have not stabbed you yet.**

TREPIDATIOUSLY she introduced herself to the august prince and naturally he was taken with her ~~modest charm~~ *lusciously ample* **Stop it!**

Here. Will this satisfy you so you will stop poking me?

Beatrice took advantage of her respectful acquaintance with the august prince to describe to him and his courtiers, and to the learned scholars, eager radicals, and interested guild members of the area, how the people of Expedition had thrown off the yoke of the hereditary Council that had for generations oppressed them and replaced it with an Assembly. This Assembly was made of up representatives selected by means of each adult who was a "citizen" of Expedition Territory casting a lot. These representatives then govern on behalf of all. *Not unlike the government of ancient Qart Hadast, however much the Romans like to say they were the ones who once had a republic!*

The men's surprise when she informed them that women cast lots and could serve in the Expedition Assembly exactly like men cannot be overstated. Many of the women present were astonished and skeptical, too, but clamored to hear more. Chartji and other Expedition trolls confirmed her account. As well, the many letters, pamphlets, and monographs written by the esteemed scholar Kehinde Nayo Kuti bolstered her argument.

The prince grew quite interested in this radical notion, that of allowing women and not just men to take part in governance, just as had been done in ancient days in Qart Hadast and other cities of Phoenicia, and as was commonplace in the Taino Empire and other societies in the Amerikes.

Having formed a plan to spread the word of liberty and assembly, the radicals split into small groups and dispersed into the cities and towns of Europa to do their work. Because of Beatrice's ability to dream of consequential meetings, she was sent with the famous and thus much pursued *Ha! Ha! pursued by the authorities or pursued by admirers lovestruck by his handsome face?*

If I were you, I would not be so free in laughing at people lovestruck by handsome faces.

Brennan Touré Du, the better to protect him by means of her dreaming.

So it happened that one night in a city I shall not name that I dreamed of swords and hammers knocking down a door painted with the image of a whistling pig ringing a bell.

Not a week later, escaping from a riot in another city I shall not name, we took refuge in a tavern called The Pig's Whistle. We had barely caught our breath and shared a few sips of an exceedingly smoky whiskey from a bottle proffered by the dazzled barkeep upon realizing that his guest was none other than the infamous Black-haired Brennan, when I heard the city bells ringing the hour. All at once I recalled my dream. I grabbed the poker from the fireside and cried out a warning just as the door of the tavern crashed open. Drinkers scattered as four city guardsmen shouldered in with swords drawn.

A stout iron fire poker may have no blade, but it serves well enough to parry steel, and so I fended off one man while Brennan slammed a chair over the head of a second. Fortunately the barkeeper was able to creep up behind the third and hit him with the heavy pewter pitcher from which he served cider. By this time I had struck unconscious my foe, for he had no expectation that a petite and smiling young woman of my remarkable beauty could in fact beat him senseless if given the opening, which I naturally took. Catching the last man's blade with the hook of the poker, I twisted the hilt out of his grasp with a maneuver that would have impressed even my cousin Cat.

Brennan finished him off with a right punch and left hook, or perhaps it was a left punch and right hook, but nevertheless a swiftly efficient dispatch. We dragged the men out onto the street and left them in an alley to believe they had been overtaken by criminals.

The last of our coin Brennan gave to the barkeep as recompense for his aid and his silence, and after this we escaped undetected out the guarded city gates by hanging on below a cart filled with dung.

Taking our leave of the carter some ways out into the country, we found shelter in a hayloft when rain began to fall. Having by this time only the clothes on our backs and the unbroken bottle of whiskey, we celebrated our narrow escape by admitting a mutual attraction. It was on this occasion that we became more attentive companions than we had been before.

An artfully deployed euphemism.

Did you not notice the swordplay?

I did notice it. It was splendid.

Also, you forgot to refer to yourself in the third person. **Oh. So I did.**

But a radical married to the cause and a dragon dreamer unable to escape her dreams can make no life together because other responsibilities and loyalties will always take precedence. Also, as attractive and attentive as Brennan Du could be, Beatrice found that she did not in fact wish to be married to

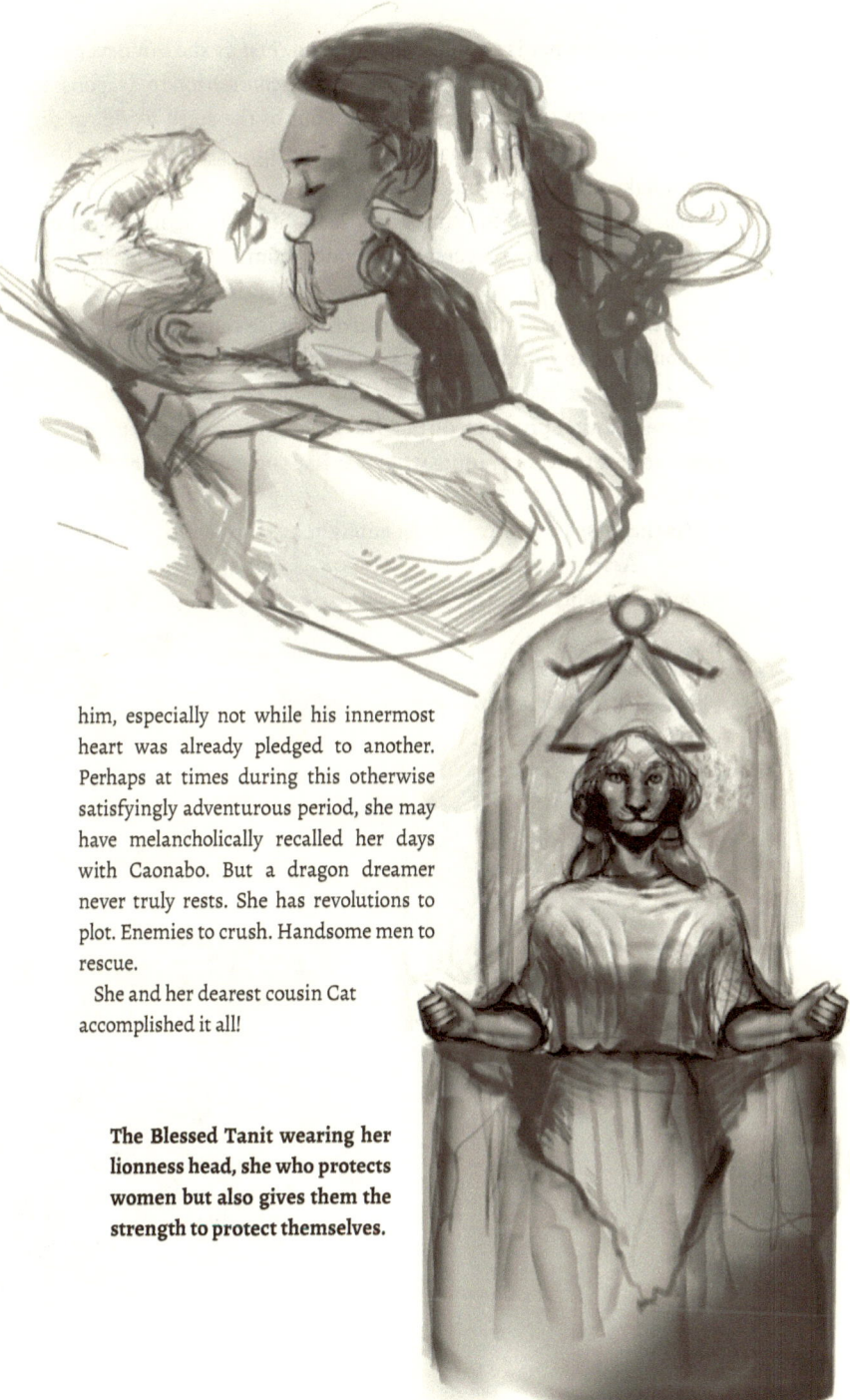

him, especially not while his innermost heart was already pledged to another. Perhaps at times during this otherwise satisfyingly adventurous period, she may have melancholically recalled her days with Caonabo. But a dragon dreamer never truly rests. She has revolutions to plot. Enemies to crush. Handsome men to rescue.

She and her dearest cousin Cat accomplished it all!

The Blessed Tanit wearing her lioness head, she who protects women but also gives them the strength to protect themselves.

A dragon dreamer is not like other women. Just as she can never stop dreaming, she can never fully be shed of her connection to dragons: to their dreams, to the hatchlings she dug out of the spirit world, to the scent of dragonkind which has the taste of burning cinders and the heat of sun-baked rocks in summer.

Perhaps that is why the fire mage Caonabo lit a warm glow in her heart. In this same way, a person descended from a creature of the spirit world might find the lure and taste of cold magic irresistable

for I can think of no other reason an otherwise sensible person like Cat could put up with that man's arrogance and vanity.

Do I need to go into detail?

Blessed Tanit! I pray you, do not, lest I feel obliged to stab out my eyes in order to avoid reading whatever it is you would feel obliged to write.

Was that kiss I drew for you not enough?

Never enough.

You were right. This story needs more sword fighting.

...for after all was said and done,
Beatrice had to essay a dangerous expedition
to the lair of the dragon.

There, in the headmaster's study, she confronted him, the man she had once–sad to say–ridiculed for his dog-like devotion to his master, the personage who was the closest thing to a father he would ever know.

"I have come as I promised I would, Kemal," she said with more bravado than she felt. Indeed, her legs were quivering and her chest was tight and her face was flushed with nervous excitement and the well-honed blade of apprehension.

As if the outcome of this scene was ever in doubt.

You may laugh! I could not.

Strange (but refreshing) it was that a man of such majesty yet carried himself with humility and gentleness and reserve. He felt no need to impress. Although he could doubtless have eaten up an entire army of cold mages, his chief venture was to nurture and protect the hatchlings for whom he was now responsible. For beneath that unassuming exterior dwelt a power so vast it is not understood by humankind.

Indeed, having considered all she had witnessed that day by the river when Prince Napata defeated his five challengers for the right to become a dragon queen, when Kemal had at last learned to become what he truly is, Beatrice could not but speculate on what manner of energy would be required to transform a smaller mass into a larger one at the same time as re-forming itself from one aspect into another. Kemal had actually seemed to ingest the substance of the iron gates to grow himself from man to dragon. By what mechanism was he able to accomplished this startling feat?

This is the most unromantical courtship scene I have ever read. Are you in love with Kemal or with the puzzle that is Kemal? **Can it not be both? Is there not always some secret we will never truly comprehend even about those to whom we are closest?**

I am an open book!

Besides you, dearest. Even if you had hidden depths you would eventually feel compelled to tell us all about them. At length.

"Beatrice!" he exclaimed

wishing his hopeful lover would stop analyzing substance and mass and get on with the kissing

"Beatrice!" he exclaimed WITHOUT INTERRUPTION. "I had no expectation you would truly return my sentiments, although it has long been the most secret wish of my heart *at which point I must suppose you were wondering if his heart is shaped in the same manner as a human heart or if perhaps he has two or more hearts?*

I could ignore you better if you did not keep snatching the pencil out of my hand.

that one day I might declare my feelings with the hope that you would reciprocate. Among my people any dragon who finds a dragon dreamer shall offer her the protection of our people so she will not suffer for the fate the Mothers of all Dragons sealed into her flesh millennia since."

When he extended his hands, he left them open, like an offering for her to take. The richness of his eyes had a gleam like the sunlit sea.

"Let me offer you the protection of my hand, my magic, my heart, dearest Beatrice. We can marry according to the laws of your people, if that suits you, as it would suit me."

The merest hint of a frown darkened her brow, for although her heart beat hard and her joy soared, she was unsure how he would react to the proposal she was about to make. She took hold of his hands.

"Do not doubt my feelings, Kemal. They have brought me this distance in the hope we would declare our mutual esteem. Yet after all my adventures I have determined that the business of marriage is tremendously dangerous for young women. I need only consider the sad example of my dearest cousin Cat. Of course you cannot abandon your responsibilities in order to orbit as a satellite around my busy life. Please understand that in the same vein I cannot become wife to the headmaster of your academy, for I have my own work."

He released her and stepped back as at a blow. Manfully he struggled to compose his expression. *dragonfully?*

"Do you not wish to marry me, Beatrice? Of course I would never desire to force any such arrangement upon you."

spoken like a true man and not an arrogant cold mage

Vai had no choice! **We always have a choice in how we act toward others.**

Made wise by experience, she chose her words carefully. *You should talk!*

"Of course I desire to marry you. But I must be honest. You are not the only one I love. According to the custom of my people a woman may take more than one husband if the connection brings benefit to her house. Can you and I maintain a loving and intimate relationship and each keep our independence?"

He answered her with a kiss.

So was it determined that the secret dragon academy in Noviomagus could be sold and a new property easily enough purchased (for Kemal's people display an affinity for amassing gold). Therefore he and his dragon colony settled in a peaceful town a morning's ride from Havery, far enough away so as not to disturb Havery's industrious troll population with dragon scent and dragon appetites.

Europa remained in upheaval *with the promise of more sword fighting! And spying! And daring adventure!* while in Havery and its environs a quiet if fragile peace prospered by means of burgeoning trade contacts, cunning diplomacy, and the institution of Havery's new Governing Assembly.

Beatrice Hassi Barahal was herself given the honor of declaiming the dedicatory address at the opening assembly.

A rising light marks the dawn of a new world.

END OF BOOK THREE

I thought there were seven kisses. Amadou. Juba. Caonabo. Brennan. Kemal. Vai (thank you). Who was the seventh? WHO WAS IT?

The Secret Journal of Beatrice Hassi Barahal

A supplement to the
Spiritwalker Trilogy

Words by Kate Elliott
(kateelliott.com)

Illustrations by Julie Dillon
(juliedillonart.com)

Layout and cover design by Joseph Eichstaedt
(josepheichstaedt.com)

Editing by Rhiannon Rasmussen-Silverstein
(rhiannonrs.com)

Originally published by Shiny-Ideas-Clutch

Distributed by Crab Tank Press (crabtankink.com)

Printing by ColorHausPDX
First Edition, August 2013

The Courtship

art by Lee Moyer

T HE HANDSOME YOUNG MANSA OF FOUR MOONS HOUSE WAS NO LONGER accustomed to sleeping alone, nor did he have the least desire to do so. For a man who was the most powerful cold mage in, and thus head of, a prestigious mage House to find himself solitary in a luxurious bed after the unpleasant shock he had just suffered merely added insult to the injury. He tossed and turned through a restless night and woke quite out of sorts with the world.

The day before, Five Mirrors House had turned out its best welcome for Andevai Diarisso Haranwy. He had been installed in a well-appointed guest suite with two rooms and a courtyard, quite fitting for his exalted station. His companion and friend Kofi Osafo, the young ambassador from the Republic of Expedition, was installed in a neighboring suite. Supper in the men's hall was magnificent. The elderly mansa of Five Mirrors House treated him and his guest with respect, as did the other magisters and notables. Over honey wine, they engaged in a long and fruitful conversation about the current upheaval in Europa and the prospects for peace if, as everyone feared, a new emperor was raised in Rome through military means. He was able to speak forcefully of the need to change the antiquated and unjust customs on which the mage Houses had for too long maintained their power. Kofi described the recent revolution in Expedition, in which the old hereditary council was replaced by an elected assembly. Hospitality demanded that their hosts listen politely, even if they did not agree.

But after the discussion wound down, the House djeli had sung the stirring and noble tale of how Sumaworo Kante's sister had voluntarily sacrificed herself to the spirits in exchange for the spirits conferring great sorcerous power upon her brother.

All night, he tossed and turned with nightmares of a young woman dying to save those she loved.

At dawn, he gave up on trying to sleep. Instead, he sat on the edge of the bed, staring at the wall, trying not to think about how angry he was at his absent wife. When he heard servants enter the adjoining parlor, he quickly pulled on his dressing gown. Servants processed in with pitchers of hot and cold water and towels that had been heated on racks in the furnace house. His boots had been polished, and his clothing cleaned and pressed.

As a courtesy, the mansa of Five Mirrors House had personally assigned his youngest son, Judoc, to oversee Andevai's care. Magic-less sons of the mage Houses fulfilled other duties, and this man, with his height and soldier's training and easy sense of importance, did not find the young mansa of Four Moons House one bit intimidating. As a mansa's son, Judoc had every right to consider himself Andevai's equal, and he obviously took seriously a House's obligation to offer hospitality.

"Mansa, please let me know at once if your boots have been polished properly and your clothing cleaned and pressed to your liking."

Nothing was to Andevai's liking, not this morning, but he bit his tongue instead of speaking. It would be ill-mannered to take out his bad humor on whatever hapless servants had no doubt done their best on a day when he could not help but find fault with everything. A nod sufficed.

"You have no servants in attendance, mansa? Shall I leave a suitable man to assist you in getting ready for the day?"

"I prefer to wash and dress on my own," said Vai, hoping the man would take the hint.

Maester Judoc waved a hand, and the servants gratefully processed out. Yet the cursed man did not depart. Indeed, his precisely polite smile leaked a thin knife, whose sharpened edges were mockery and challenge.

"Mansa, I hope the bed was adequate to your needs since, as I most vividly recall, you made it clear it was definitely not acceptable the last time you enjoyed the hospitality of Five Mirrors House. Please be sure, I would not wish any magister to find the accommodations of our House lacking."

"As I recall, the last time we met, you mistook me for a servant."

"Did I? On first setting eyes on you on the portico that day, I admit your lack of any retinue or baggage did confound me. But as you are now mansa, I think it unlikely your full magnificence would not be recognized at once."

A sardonic spark of amusement lit his face, souring Andevai's mood further. Few things pricked at him more than feeling he was being laughed at by someone who disrespected him. Worse, Judoc had the air of a man who knows he belongs where he is standing. It reminded Andevai all too cruelly of how he had arrived at Four Moons House as a confident but painfully naïve sixteen-year-old village boy, only to be rejected and brutally tormented by the very youth he had reached out to, in the hope they could become comrades and friends.

Yet those days were in the past, surely.

Meanwhile, a friendly, trusted face would go a long way to making the day bearable. "Perhaps Ambassador Osafo can be summoned to join me in the breakfast hall."

"I believe the ambassador arranged last night for a tour of the city, as he knew you had other House business this morning. The sightseeing party has already left for the day. Let us hope no one will run away from this expedition, not as happened last time." He gave a false cough in the most irritating manner. "Now that I think to remark on it, I am sorry not to see your wife, since the business of family alliances and courtship is usually best handled by women. Her meek demeanor quite struck me when you were last here. Perhaps her constitution is too frail and her nerves too delicate for the journey from Havery to Noviomagus?"

Andevai rose. The other man was taller and almost certainly far more proficient with sword and bow than he would ever be, but what did he care for mere physical prowess? It was possible there was a stronger cold mage in Europa than he was, but he doubted it. "Yes, I remember your solicitous manner toward my wife, Maester Judoc. Very considerate of you, I am sure."

"It is my measured opinion that women deserve respect and consideration. I humbly ask for permission to say that I hope your wife bides well at home, in comfort and at peace."

So quickly the dagger of words struck. The man was making it plain that he thought Andevai mistreated his wife and meant his disapproval of such behavior to be starkly clear! Annoyance surged, and with it, a flicker of cold magic. The temperature in the room dropped. A crackle of frost veined the windows. Yet these signs caused Judoc no hesitation, although surely he knew a powerful cold mage could smash him to the ground with magic alone.

If anyone had been mistreated, it was he! Abandoned by the woman he loved, without a single word of explanation, in her hour of greatest need! She hadn't even asked for his help! But Andevai was not going to pour out his troubles to a man he barely knew, and especially not one staring down his nose, in wait for a reason to sneer at him.

"She is about her own business," he snapped. Fists clenched, he breathed himself down to something resembling calm before he made a fool of himself with a quite discourteous blast of magic. "As I am mine. When I decided to introduce Ambassador Osafo around, I thought it best to combine the task with that of interviewing your magisters Kavan and Diarra, in case one might be appropriate as a husband for our widowed diviner, Serena."

Judoc glanced at Andevai's fashionable dash jacket and trousers laid out for dressing. He himself wore the traditional boubou and looked splendid in a starched, indigo fabric, meant to remind all and sundry that he was a mansa's son and, even without magic, a man not to be trifled with.

"I wish you best of luck with the interviews," he said in a dry tone. "I sincerely hope you take one of the magisters in question away with you as soon as may be possible. Both, if you can manage it."

With that parting shot, he at last departed. Andevai dressed in a stew of indignation. The other man's deliberate provocation chafed, churning his thoughts back to his sleepless night. His wife had herself engineered this trip as a diversion, hoping he and her cousin, Beatrice, would not question her too closely about the particulars of her peculiar Hallows' Night disappearance. All over again, he was struck by the full force of how unfairly she had treated him.

When he stalked down to the breakfast room, several of the women fawned over him in a way that made him want to say all kinds of cutting things, if only to get them to stop simpering and flirting.

"I hope you find our accommodations both adequate and comfortable, mansa. Do let me know what you might be lacking."

"If you need any assistance in your stay here, mansa, please do apply to me, for I have a particular responsibility to make sure our guests feel entirely at their ease."

"Your dash jacket is quite the most striking I have seen. Where do you have your tailoring done? I am sure my brother would be interested in procuring one like it, if you are not averse to being measured."

The servants had evidently let it be known he was sleeping alone.

To avoid their flagrant compliments and inane questions, he busied himself heaping far more food on a platter than he would ever eat. The food was edible, but he could barely bring himself to pick through it. He drank two cups of coffee to wake up, and when he could no longer bear the fulsome attention, he asked to tour the Five Mirrors' schoolrooms.

Listening to young children recite their lessons always pleased him, especially when he was able to gloat silently to himself over the thought of the schoolrooms being built and furnished at his own Four Moons House. There, every child in the House and increasingly children from the surrounding district could learn, not just the exalted few. Gently but sternly supervising hopeful young mages as they struggled to extinguish candle flames or pull tremulous bulbs of cold fire into existence occupied him agreeably for the rest of the morning.

Nevertheless, he was tremendously relieved when Kofi returned for the midday meal at almost the same time as his friend, Viridor. As mansa of White Bow House in the city of Sala, Viridor had also been invited to join the conference.

"I beg you, let us find some humble tavern and get out of this place," he said to Viridor and Kofi, the moment they were able to take their leave from the formal splendor of the dining hall.

"I know a place to drink," said Kofi.

"I thought you just arrived here yesterday," said Viridor. "That was quick work."

Kofi grinned. "I am a man who like to know exactly where he can quaff an ale. I had pointed out to me this morning a respectable sort of tavern, well enough garbed for yee high and mighty magisters." He paused, giving Vai a long look. "Perchance did yee not sleep well? Another time, yee would have laughed at my wit."

Andevai could think of no clever rejoinder, and he did not want to say the curt retorts that were all that came to mind, so he said nothing.

"I reckon yee is still fretting yee own self about that tale we heard told on the road here."

"What tale is that?" asked Viridor. "What did I miss?"

"Nothing," said Andevai.

Kofi added, "A tale his wife told that took many days in the telling. Of how she came to be married to Vai, and all that happened afterward, according to her way of seeing it. A few rare surprises, if yee take my meaning."

Viridor glanced curiously at Andevai, who studiously glowered at the ceiling. "What sort of surprises?"

"I cannot relate it to yee with my tongue so dry from lack of a drink."

The tavern proved to be the sort of place where important men from important families took their leisure. Because it was heated by hypocaust, it was an establishment in which magisters could mingle with lords, rich merchants, and officers, with whom they might have business or wish to socialize outside the mage House. A table in the corner gave the two young mansas and the ambassador privacy but allowed the buzz of conversation in the establishment to wash over them as they talked.

"You said there was another reason you are here, not just to meet me and discuss politics and pedagogy with the assembled mansas and magisters," said Viridor. "Has that something to do with this mysterious tale told by your wife?"

"No. Nothing to do with it." Andevai studied his glass of red wine, reflecting that it reminded him far too much of blood. "I'm also here about a marriage contract."

Viridor set down his glass with a jesting smile. "It hadn't occurred to me you might be on the lookout for a second wife, or I would have suggested my sister."

"Of course I'm not taking a second wife," said Andevai peevishly.

"I think the one he have is enough work, even for a magister of such unusual potency as he," said Kofi with a laugh.

Andevai shot him a glare that had absolutely no effect on the other man's good cheer and, indeed, seemed likely to heighten it, so he hastily returned his attention to Viridor.

"My predecessor's young widow, Serena, has chosen to stay at Four Moons House rather than return to her own people. However, she seeks a new husband, which means we are looking for a magister willing to take up residence in Four Moons House. The mansa here at Five Mirrors has two possible heirs, and he wants to rid himself of one so there is no conflict within the House after he passes."

"Ah, I see." Viridor nodded. "You are saying the two men are closely matched in power and more rivals than allies."

"Yes, that is what I have been given to understand. The only way to settle the succession is to move one out. I am willing to take one on, if he is willing to come to us."

Kofi smiled. "Had they seen the gal, they would be more willing. She is a fine woman and an excellent cook."

"And a powerful diviner," said Andevai in a stern voice. "A good match in all ways for a magister with ambition." He rubbed at his forehead. "No offense meant to your sister, who is in all ways a fine woman, Viridor. My apologies if it seemed I insulted her by speaking so sharply before. I did not sleep well last night."

"Ah." Viridor glanced at Kofi, who merely smiled in a way that betrayed he was amused by his friend's belabored attempts to be polite. "Under the circumstances, I thought your wife would be with you."

"She is not." Andevai drained half his glass in one slug.

Viridor studied him a moment. "It was obvious by the looks and whispers cast your way in the dining hall that several of the House women would be happy to fill your bed, if it is lack of feminine company that makes it hard for you to sleep. I heard the mansa's own granddaughter speak of you in a most flattering way."

Andevai swallowed the rest of the wine, its harsh bouquet hitting right behind his eyes. He set down the glass with a thump. "If any mage House woman tries to fill my bed, you can be sure she will hear exactly what I have to say about such a trespass, and furthermore, she will be promptly kicked out in whatever state of dress she may be in—and right onto her bare ass, if it must be. I don't care if she is the mansa's own granddaughter. I will not have it."

Kofi caught Viridor's eye and shook his head, which annoyed Andevai even more.

"Ah. Well." Viridor poured more wine to punctuate the change of subject. "Tell me more about this Professora Alhamrai from the university in Expedition. You said she has written a monograph on how shrinkage in the ice shelfs correlates with the advance of vegetation into the Barrens."

The three men grazed across this safe topic through a second bottle of wine.

"I brought along the monograph," said Andevai, at length, for the wine and the conversation had bolstered his enthusiasm. "I suppose we ought to go back to make ready for supper and whatever evening entertainment . . . Lord of All, I fear we are to be subjected to some tiresome singing or recitations . . ."

"I thought yee was joking about the Grand Tour, Vai," said Kofi, "but I have rarely seen a more determined assault than those women hopeful to catch yee eye."

"Never mind." Andevai rose. "But come along with me first, and I'll get the book. I mean for you to take it, Viridor. I have another copy at home."

Servants escorted them back to Five Mirrors House, since it was deemed necessary for cold mages of their rank and importance never to go anywhere alone.

"Blessed Mother," joked Viridor, "these guards and nursemaids do not follow us into our bedchamber and sleep around the bed at night, do they? For in a small and impoverished mage House like my own, I am not at all accustomed to this manner of formality. I feel I am suddenly become the ghana who rules Sala, in all his state."

Andevai gave a look back at their attendants. "I have no trouble ridding myself of their presence."

Viridor laughed. "No, I suppose you do not. But they are only obeying their master's orders. Far be it for you and me to countermand our elderly host's traditional way of doing things."

"Yet I wonder," said Kofi, "what servingmen such as these know of assemblies and voting and a new legal code."

Viridor glanced at Andevai, as for support, and then back at Kofi. "Radical views like yours are causing trouble all over Europa."

"It gladdens me to hear it is so," said Kofi with one his shark's smiles, both cheerful and aggressive.

A faint strand of mirth stirred in Andevai's tense thoughts, for he knew that the discussions he and Kofi were having with the other mage Houses were but the tip of a far larger revolution that would take time, trouble, sweat, and blood to implement. He was also fairly sure that the servants who attended the dining hall and salon, where talk raged, were listening attentively. However mighty the sword, words cut more deeply in the long run.

When they reached the parlor of his suite, he dismissed the entourage and went in alone with Kofi and Viridor to fetch the book.

"Ah, I remember," he said as he glanced around at the polished surfaces and plush sofas, all quite empty of the promised volume. "I asked them to set my valise of books on the table in the bedchamber."

He crossed the room, the other two men a few steps behind.

"It's a provoking piece of scholarship," he added, pushing down the latch and pushing open the door. "You'll be quite astonished to see the illustrations especially—"

The door swung open on well-oiled hinges to reveal a stark-naked woman lying on her stomach atop the plush feather bed.

Her nakedness really startled him, partly because it was daytime and partly because he was so astonished to see her there without a stitch of clothing on, nor any sort of dressing gown draped strategically nearby, just in case she needed to quickly cover herself. Her attractive thighs and shapely ass could not be ignored. She was propped up on her elbows, reading a book, the angle of her arms offering a pleasing view of her breasts. As he tugged the opening door to a halt, blinking, she calmly turned a page, not bothering to look over to see who had just walked in.

The other two men were right behind him—with a full view of the bed.

"Lord of All," Andevai said sharply as he slammed shut the door in their faces.

"What?" Viridor halted.

Clearly, Viridor had not seen the woman. Nor had Kofi.

"I just remembered something," said Andevai, sure that the stumbling stupidity of the remark gave everything away. "It's just that I . . . I didn't sleep well last night."

Kofi looked sharply at him. "So we already know."

"I'd best rest before supper. Can we . . . Can I . . . the book . . . later?"

"It don' seem like yee drank that much, but yee surely sound addled, maku."

Viridor examined him with concern. "Do you need me to ask one of the stewards to send in a servant to assist you?"

He could just imagine Judoc's reaction!

"No! I just . . . will gladly . . . later."

Viridor slapped Andevai on the shoulder in a comradely way, but it was Kofi who gave him and then the closed door a thoughtful look before the two men took themselves off. They were already talking of going out to see the famous amphitheater in the interval before the evening's grand supper.

As soon as they were gone, Andevai grabbed a chair from the parlor and carried it into the bedchamber. This time when he closed the door, he remained inside the room. Shoving the chair's back up under the latch to jam it, he sat on it, facing the bed, then crossed his arms and waited.

The naked woman turned a page.

He waited.

She lifted a foot, let it sway back and forth a little, then, with its toes, scratched gently at her other ankle. After this comely performance, she lowered the foot and turned another page.

"I can only assume this display is for my benefit," he said.

She twitched her rump but said nothing.

The familiar swell of arousal vexed him. "You women seem to have a low opinion of my self-discipline."

Still, she said nothing, and he could not help but notice she was reading the very book he intended to give to Viridor.

"Whatever would you have done had a servant walked in on you in this . . . this . . . state?"

With a heavenward glance of her eyes, she turned another page.

He exhaled sharply. "Very well, the question answers itself. I withdraw it. Obviously, you comprehend that I am outraged at your callous treatment of me. You seem to think you need only flaunt yourself for me to be . . . distracted into forgetting my grievance."

"Grievance? What grievance can you possibly mean?"

"You deliberately concealed from me your desperate expedition on Hallows' Night. You crept away without telling me, or Beatrice, where you were going. And you left knowing full well you might die in the spirit world."

She stopped pretending to read the book and looked at him. "I thought that might be what was making you so unreasonable when you dropped Bee and I off at the dragon academy."

"Unreasonable?! Did you think of me at all when you rushed off on that wild suicide mission into the spirit world?"

She rolled just enough onto her side that he was forced to watch her fingers trace an exploratory path along the folds of her cleft. Voice a little hoarse, she said, "I've been thinking of you all night and all day today. I've been missing your touch. Haven't you been missing mine?"

She let out a few short, sighing breaths. What had been an interested arousal stiffened to a full-fledged erection, pressing hard against his trousers. He jumped up so fast, he jostled the chair sideways.

"Catherine! Stop that! I am not coming over there!" Halfway to the bed, he halted and beat himself several times on the forehead with a hand, in the vain hope he could blind himself and not have to watch any more. "Do you think you can simply show up naked in my bed and I will succumb to your allurements and—without any scrap of explanation—forgive you?"

"If you're not interested, then I'll just please myself."

Lord of All. The spark of arousal, the smell of her, the way her eyelids fluttered slightly as she caught a nub of pleasure. The next thing he knew, he was on the bed, with her on her back beneath him, his mouth on her mouth, kissing her hard as her hands splayed over his buttocks and worked his flesh. She got one leg out from under him and, with her heel, rubbed the back of his leg.

He broke off the kiss, panting. He was so cursedly angry that it made his arousal all the more aggravating.

Her hands gathered the fabric of his dash jacket tight. "What I don't understand is why you still have clothes on," she murmured, her voice like honey.

He drew in a harsh breath to master himself. "Because it is daytime. People wear clothes in the daytime. At night, they may properly go into their beds without clothing, but in the daytime they remain dressed like proper people, who tell the people who love them exactly what manner of insane, dangerous, impossible plans they have in mind, rather than leaving them behind in utter and oblivious ignorance."

"Goodness, Andevai, you are ranting." She slipped a hand along the band of his trousers and probed until her fingers brushed the tip of his very hard penis. "I should just rip these clothes off you."

He could control his lust. It was his wounded pride—and the angry fear he did not want to admit to—that made him act rashly.

He pushed himself up and sat on the edge of the bed, just where he had at dawn. "We are not going to have this conversation while distracted by arousal."

She seemed about to touch his arm, but when he gave her a sidelong glare, she thought better of the gesture and withdrew the hand. "How are we going to have this conversation?" she asked, not at all intimidated by his tone.

Alone with him, she had not the least self-consciousness about displaying her body. He had been over every kissable place on her skin regardless. His gaze roamed along her beautiful body—and he realized she was distracting him again by lying there for him to ogle.

With a grimace, he rose, grabbed his dressing gown, and threw it into her lap before sitting back down on the edge of the bed. "Best if we have the rest of this conversation while you are covered."

She relaxed into a far-too-comely smile as she drew the silk over her shoulders and shook out the gown behind her back. The way she arched her back to slip her arms into the sleeves coaxed his gaze from her mouth . . . to her neck . . . to her breasts . . . to the slope of her belly and the dark hair at her cleft.

He forced himself to look away.

"Had you died, not only would I never have seen you again . . . but I would never have known how and why you disappeared. Nor what had happened to you." He had always had trouble untangling the surge of his emotions from the pulse of magic that throbbed everywhere around him. The chamber got distinctly colder before he choked off the threads of magic that wove power between the spirit world and this one. "Is that what you intended for me? To grieve all my days, never knowing?"

"I wrote you a letter and gave it to Rory to deliver. You never saw it because I came back."

The thought of discovering she was dead at the point of a pen made him crush his hands together, lest he otherwise flatten the entire mage House. He took in and released several slow breaths, as he was learning to do to control his pride and temper and frustration. "The point is that you chose for me."

"You couldn't come with me into the spirit world—"

"I could have been allowed to make such a decision for myself."

Anger darkened her expression. "It wasn't your decision to make," she said in a wintry tone, quite unlike her usual warmly teasing voice.

She was beautiful and funny and sweet and naïve and stubborn and strong, but moments like this reminded him that she had also the heart of a killer, which was not that of a wicked person who revels in pain and cruelty but that of a predator, for whom hunting and killing is a necessary part of its nature. Most people never saw it. They might overlook her because she preferred to bide half in the shadows, almost invisible behind the glamorous sun of her vivacious cousin. They might think her frivolous and light-minded because of the way she talked on and on, spinning stories as if they were entertainment, when in fact, they might be perfectly true and the more horrifying for being so. They might be fooled by the way she laughed so easily, quick to see the delight and the absurdity in things. She was all those things, but give her cold steel and enough reason, and she would reveal a side so ruthless, he was sure she wasn't able to admit its full power to her own self.

Or so he had gathered from the story she had told him, Beatrice, and Kofi over the days they had spent traveling from Havery to Noviomagus within the confines of the coach: the story of how she had left behind all the people she loved and allowed the Master of the Wild Hunt to carry her off into the spirit world, to be sacrificed by the spirit courts.

Pushing his anger against hers, as in a duel, was not the best argument he had to make. But the anger slipped out anyway. "A woman should let her beloved know beforehand that she intends to sacrifice herself and thus blight his happiness forever!"

Her upper lip curled back almost scornfully, as if she were about to transform into a snarling beast, in truth.

"If I had told you, what then, Andevai? You would have insisted on coming with me, for I cannot imagine your pride would have allowed you to let me make the journey alone. Had you climbed into the coach with me, you would have ruined everything. The courts would have taken your blood, and there would have been nothing I could have done to stop them." There was nothing provocative about her now; all he could see was the shadow in her eyes. "I was protecting you and Bee. But I was also protecting myself."

Another man might have shrunk back from the edge on her. Seeing her like this, no one could ever doubt that she could slit a man's throat. But he did not fear that side of her. Instead, he spun a glimmer of cold magic through the room to remind her that he was powerful enough in his own right to match her.

Since backing down was not her way, or his, he waited.

After a long pause, she went on.

"The truth is, I wasn't sure I could go through with it if you and Bee had known. I wasn't sure I could have done it if you two had been as miserable and frightened as I was. Not telling you two was the only way I had to hang on to my courage."

She challenged him with honesty, a glimpse of the abyss inside her where she hid her deepest fears.

Almost, he embraced her, kissed her, caressed her. But he held back. "I understand it was an exceptional situation. But your habit of keeping secrets must end if we are to have peace and harmony between us."

"You have just as many secrets as I do! I recollect a certain conversation held between you and a village blacksmith in the temple dedicated to Three-Headed Lugus, the one you call Shining Komo. I know nothing about that meeting."

"That is not what I mean. Obviously, I would never demand you reveal to me whatever mysteries of Barahal magic you learned as a child. Just as I cannot reveal certain sacred mysteries to you or to anyone. Nor have I any intention of trying to stop you from doing what you will. I am well aware I could not, even if I wanted to. I just ask you to trust me by trusting that I can be sensible about your . . . intentions. Do not make decisions for me!"

Just like that, she slid across the bed and deposited herself in his lap. Wrapping her arms around him, she whispered into his ear, her breath like heat poured into his body, "I am going to the city of Colonia to rescue a condemned printer from the prince's jail."

"Lord of All," he muttered. "When will you be undertaking this adventurous task?"

"Maybe right now, if you reject me, as you seem inclined to do." She wriggled her buttocks against his thighs.

He pulled her closer, always quick to relish the feeling of her breasts pressed against his chest. "I do not like to feel I am being seduced into forgiving you, as if you think I cannot be trusted to resolve this in any other way. I hope I have proven my feelings often enough!"

"Never often enough," she murmured.

He chuckled, then recalled himself to his purpose. "You knew I would be angry that you did not tell me you meant to offer yourself as the Hallows' Night sacrifice, to spare me and your cousin and every other soul in the world. I suppose you convinced yourself that if you did not return, you would never have to face our rebuke. But here you are. So let me be plain."

It was the first time he really considered how much courage it must have taken her that night, to walk straight into the arms of what she had known could be her death.

All the words he meant to scold her with seemed suddenly pointless.

She had broken the hold of her sire and the courts over herself, and over any children she and he would have, and had naturally managed to include untold other personages and creatures in the bargain when she unchained herself.

So he sighed and let it go.

"Well, it's done and over with. You and I have agreed you will henceforth inform me what you mean to do and we can argue over whether I am to be involved. I am a busy man, Catherine. As mansa of Four Moons House, I cannot just be running off all over, so you need not worry that I will be dogging your steps at every least provocation."

She was quiet for so long that, at first, he thought she did not mean to reply.

When she did, it was in a whisper. "I was a little afraid you could not forgive me for it. Not that I think there is anything to forgive, mind you, for I did what I had to do. But I knew that you and Bee would take my silence very ill."

"Did Beatrice take it ill?"

"Yes. Gracious Melqart! She must have said, 'Cat, how could you not have told me?' at least one hundred times, and in quite the most accusing voice."

He choked down a laugh, and fortunately, she did not notice his caught breath and trembling shoulders, as she was already going on.

"Kemal was shamefully eager to commiserate with her over my perfidy."

"I trust you left her in good hands."

She rolled her eyes quite magnificently. "I believe so. Last night over supper, the two of them were so formal and anxious that I would have laughed if I hadn't been fretting over you being angry with me when we parted. Then Bee tossed and turned all night in the bed she and I shared, so I couldn't sleep anyway. But the two of them went walking along the river after breakfast, and after that, I was no longer needed to keep Bee company. That is why I left and came here. I am happy for her, but I was lonely there."

"I am relieved all went according to plan with Bee's assignation. Not that I doubted it would, since Maester Kemal is so obviously smitten with her. Still, it is quite astounding that all along dragons have been living among us in human garb. Had I not seen it with my own eyes, I am sure I would not have believed it."

She settled comfortably against him, resting her head against his shoulder. "I can't believe all this time you didn't believe every word I told you, Vai.

That you thought I was telling outrageous tales to amuse you."

"My apologies. Of course there is nothing I think you cannot do, my love, but you always told your stories as if you were mostly bent on entertaining us and making us laugh. I thought you had perhaps . . . embroidered on the truth sometimes, to make it a little more decorative."

"I never do! Well." Her lips brushed his skin in a way that made him shiver. "There was one thing I told as part of the story that didn't really happen that way. I added it in because it made for a better story. But everything else happened exactly as I told it. Well. There was one thing I did that I didn't mention."

"I am not sure which I more fear to know, what was false that you told as true or what you left out for not wanting us—even Beatrice!—to know."

"It's why you love me, Vai."

It seemed simplest to agree by kissing her, slow and sweet. Afterward, she again rested her head on his shoulder, making no move to do more.

For the longest time, they just sat like that. Eyes closed, he drifted, so at ease that he almost dozed off, and then realized she had fallen asleep. He carefully lay down so as not to wake her, unbuttoned his dash jacket with one hand, made sure the dressing gown covered her, and, with her in his arms, surrendered to the sleep he had lost the night before.

A soft click woke him. Catherine still slept in his arms, just as she ought. As his eyes opened, he registered that the door was opening very slowly, for the chair had shifted off enough that it no longer blocked the latch. A lovely woman dressed in a flattering gown took a step into the chamber, peering about as her eyes adjusted, for the curtains were drawn. She took a step toward the bed. Her gasp betrayed the instant she realized he already had a woman in bed with him. Her startled gaze met his. He said nothing, letting the situation speak for itself. The worst of it was that he recognized her as the mansa's granddaughter, a lively and intelligent woman who, in some other life he was never destined to lead, he would certainly have encouraged closer with a smile.

Catherine did not move, nor did she open her eyes, but by a slight change in her breathing and a shift in the tension in her body, he could tell she had woken up.

"My pardon, mansa," whispered the young woman, and she fled, shutting the door a little loudly in her haste.

"Gracious Melqart," said Catherine, popping up to look toward the closed door. "You poor man. Do they never let you alone?"

"Your presence in this bed is certainly proof that they do not." He rolled off the bed, walked over to the door, and fixed the chair firmly under the latch.

"Goodness, Andevai, have you some plans that oblige you to block the door?"

He turned to see her stretched out, the dressing robe concealing her from neck to feet and thus all the more inviting.

"Since the news will be all over this House in an hour, I may as well enjoy the repast they will all be sure I am feasting on, do you not think?"

She smiled. "It would be a shame to waste all that rumor for nothing."

He walked back to the bed, shedding his clothes. She watched appreciatively, for she did enjoy watching him undress. He loved her naked, of course, but he particularly loved undressing her, so he knelt on the bed beside her and ran his hand along the length of the silk. The feel of her body beneath the slippery cloth, hidden from him yet right there, was a thing he liked to savor for as long as possible, the anticipation of uncovering her, the way she wriggled as he traced his way up her body, along her most sensitive spots: the crease of her thigh, the nub just above her cleft, her ribs, the hollow of her throat, her earlobes. Last of all, he parted the cloth so he could kiss her dark areolas, lingering on each one before sitting back up.

"Lie down beside me," she said, looking decidedly intent.

When he did, she rolled him onto his side and stretched out against him, so their bodies touched all the way down. She slipped a leg between his, pressing her sex against his erection. She was in a quiet, affectionate mood, and he was content to nuzzle and caress her for the longest time, whatever suited her. She was alive. She was here. Having her in his arms gave his heart so much ease that all the raw and ragged thoughts, which had for so many years chased him, fell quiet. In the last few months, some had even begun to fade.

Eventually, the slow burn ignited. And, sadly, in the back of his mind, he was all too aware that he was mansa now: to not appear in the salon before the evening's supper would be a tremendous act of disrespect toward his hosts. He rolled her up on top of him, and his gently cuddling Catherine smiled in a fierce way that promised a vigorous finish.

Which, indeed, it was.

Made rather sweaty, they availed themselves of the water pitchers and brass washtub to wash off. Then he sat her at the dressing table and combed out her hair.

"I would prefer it if you came with me to the family salon and supper and reception afterward, love. You can see what you think of the two magisters, and if you think either of them may be suitable to marry Serena."

"I suppose it is too late in the day for me to really think of setting out for Colonia."

"Do you think the matter so urgent?"

"I should hate to arrive there only to discover the printer has been put to death, all while I was carousing here." She watched him in the mirror. "It's not that I don't wish to meet all these fine people, Vai, but are they as unpleasant as the people at Two Gourds House were? For it is very tiring to be treated with such thinly veiled discourtesy."

He thought of Judoc, but the man's attempt to scold him for being a bad husband now made him smile in retrospect. "They will not be unpleasant or disrespectful to a mansa's wife, I promise."

"I can scarcely approve of people who would be pleasant to the mansa's wife but unpleasant if they thought me to be merely the unwanted wife of an ordinary cold mage." She glanced up as his hand paused in its combing. "Not that I mean to imply you have ever been ordinary, my love."

He resumed combing. "They all remember our last visit here."

"You were certainly memorably awful."

Really, he was in quite the best mood. "Their sympathies were firmly on your side at the time, that is sure. I expect they will be wildly curious to discover why you're still with me and what sort of tyrant I truly am."

Her smile dimpled. A look like that could portend any sort of unexpected mischief. "They will be sadly disappointed on that score, unless I make up a story, which could be very entertaining."

"Please do not. The truth is, I really should value your observations on the two magisters. They may show a different side to you than the deference they show to me."

He handed her the comb, and she parted her hair into three and began braiding it with the brisk confidence of long practice. "Is marriage to Serena what either man wishes for? No woman wants a husband who resents her because she reminds him of the thing he could not have."

"It is certain that one must leave Five Mirrors House. That is not an uncommon outcome at mage Houses, when two mages are so equally powerful that one cannot be unequivocally named as mansa. Therefore, they are looking out for the best situation possible should they not be named as mansa."

"They will not think to challenge you once they are at Four Moons House?"

He looked at her blankly. "Why would they attempt to challenge me?"

She covered her face with a hand, gave a snort of amusement, and went back to braiding her hair. "My pardon. I can't imagine what led me even to think there might be the slightest possibility any magister could believe himself equal to such an undertaking. Is there one of the men you like better? One you think would carry on better within Four Moons House? More importantly, is there one who seems likely to carry on well with Serena herself?"

"I would be very surprised if either man did not approve of Serena. But you may be better suited to determine which you think Serena might prefer."

Her gaze flashed up to touch his. She even blushed a little. "I consoled myself by thinking that when I was gone, you would eventually find solace in marrying Serena."

"Did you, Catherine? How kind and generous of you!" It was odd to think that not an hour before, he had been boiling with frustrated anger. All that had vanished as mist dissolves under the bright sun. He raised an eyebrow. "Perhaps we need make no marriage alliance here. As mansa, I can certainly take a second wife."

Her sidelong look flew like a poisoned dart, and he laughed.

She recovered herself. "Alas, our marriage contract forbids such a pleasing arrangement. And so do I."

"As do I. It would not be appropriate for me to marry the widow of the man who adopted me as a son. Furthermore, I learned from my father's bad example that if a man cannot give equally of his time and attention to each of his wives, then he ought not have more than one. I have an ambitious plan of action in mind, many things to accomplish as mansa of Four Moons House, and you are enough work as it is."

"Am I?" She met his gaze in the mirror.

He was flooded with an urge to make love with her all over again, but he was mansa and had responsibilities that took precedence. "Not that I mean to suggest I would have you change, for I would not, not for all the worlds."

Her smile gratified him, for he loved it when she preened because of his compliments.

"Well, then, I shall go along with you this evening to all these drearily formal festivities. What is your opinion of the two magisters?"

"That they are very different and would each bring advantages and difficulties with them. I wish Rory were here. He could take one sniff and tell me everything I needed to know."

"Yes, no doubt he could. And all sorts of other things you didn't want to know besides! I find it a bit strange to be interviewing possible husbands for Serena when, meanwhile, back in Havery, Rory is trying to seduce her. The more I think about it, the more surprised I am you did not command him to come along so he could get up to no mischief at home."

"I am not in the habit of ordering people to obey my commands when they do not wish to."

She regarded him as she tied off the end of her braid with a ribbon. "No, for all your vanity and pride, you are not a tyrant."

"I am relieved to hear you say so," he replied with mock seriousness as he began to dress.

The servants had brushed and pressed his best dash jacket and laid his clothing over a rack. His linen had been warmed by an actual fire, somewhere else in the compound, and a ghost of warmth lingered in the fabric.

"Rory will not succeed. Serena has very strict ideas about conduct. She asked me to undertake this commission for her, to look over the men. I can assure you, she would not ask one man into her bed while she is in the process of arranging for a husband with another."

"You may be correct. Although Rory can be very persuasive." Catherine had carefully folded her clothes and laid them atop the dressing table, next to her sword. She picked through the garments she had worn when she had walked across the city—to him. "My apologies. I left my baggage at the academy, for I could not haul it myself. Perhaps it could be fetched in the morning. I am sure these garments, however well-tailored, are too sober and creased to be appropriate for a magisterial hall. I should not want to embarrass you." She paused, drawers and bodice in hand, as she realized he was not looking at the garments but rather admiring her. "Perhaps you think I would be more suitable if I went naked!"

The longer he looked at her, the more she melted; he loved watching her struggle to hide the passion she felt for him, when he knew perfectly well how much she both loved and desired him. The world was a fine place, was it not, with Catherine in it? And made all the better because she was exceedingly likely to be back in the bed with him later tonight.

"I have something for you," he said, trying hard not to crow. The guest chamber had a dressing closet attached, but he had an aversion to closed spaces. He unlatched its lock and went in. When he brought out the gown draped over his arm, the way her mouth dropped open in surprise was all the thanks he needed.

"Vai! Is that silk?" She had by now put on her underclothes.

He held out the gown, and she actually petted the cloth before she allowed him to help her into the dress. She admired herself in the mirror. The gown had an ample skirt—he could not imagine her in anything that did not allow her to stride—and a fitted bodice, all in a creamy off-white that set off her complexion and her black hair. A second layer of green stripes was fitted in a cutaway with sleeves, and a half skirt opened in the front and cut to brush all the way to the floor in the back. The gown fit well, of course, for he had chosen the style and ordered it himself and probably visited the dressmaker more times than he ought to have done, and certainly more than the women at the shop had wanted him to.

"Where does it come from?"

"The bag of coin you brought back from the spirit world."

"That was for the kitchen and the carpentry yard!"

"Most of it did go there. I thought it acceptable to set aside a little. I believe it is you who reminded me that, as mansa, I must dress properly when I visit other dignitaries. It occurred to me that as the mansa's wife, you must—of necessity—also be attired in a manner fitting to my consequence."

He waited for her to tease him—he had deliberately given her an opening—but she was too stupefied by the elegance of the gown to manage a retort. It abruptly occurred to him that the gown was probably the finest garment she had ever worn, for she was not accustomed to luxury. With her braid pinned up on her head in a practical but elegant spiral, she looked exactly like herself: delectable, strong, and so shamelessly delighted by the gown that he had to kiss her.

"You'll rumple me!" She pushed him away so she could button him into a dark-gold damask dash jacket, dyed with a spider's web of brown filigree. The way she concentrated on each button, her fingers precise and efficient, made him gently bite her earlobe.

"So I intend to, later tonight," he murmured.

She laughed, almost delirious with excitement. With a half turn, she shifted him around so they stood side by side, reflected in the mirror.

"Gracious Melqart, Vai. We look very well together!"

So they did, for he observed it on every face when he and Catherine entered the salon. Women saw him and began to smile, then saw her and bent their heads to whisper together. Maester Judoc's eyes opened very wide indeed as he took in Catherine and, in particular, her radiant smile and beauteous aspect. Andevai offered him a condescending nod, just to drive the spike deeper.

"Love, I must present you to the mansa and the other notables."

"Which is the woman who came into the bedchamber? I shall have to make her like me, so she is not too disappointed."

"The mansa's granddaughter, in the red and orange," he replied with a tip of his chin.

She did not look that way, but she did smile across the salon at Maester Judoc, as at an old friend. Judoc's answering smile had the surprised brightness of a man smote by a hammer. Another man might have felt a tremor of jealousy, but Andevai saw no point. If it ever came to pass in some day yet to come that she chose to walk away from him, there would be nothing he could do to stop her, and any attempt to stop her would mark the end regardless. As long as he kept her happy, all would be well, and what man better to keep her happy than he was? All the world seemed made of sun.

Kofi strolled up to take Catherine's hand and kiss her on the cheek with a kinsman's privilege. "So, here yee are, Cat. Have Bee and her intended victim driven yee out of the academy?"

"More like their cooing and warbling caused me to flee."

Kofi's glance at Vai contained a wealth of unvoiced laughter. "Yee husband is glad of it, I can see, for he had a vexed look upon him this morning. Yet here he stands, all smiles now."

Catherine's blush had an unexpected sweetness because it was so rare to see her at a loss for words.

"Let us see for how long she can go without speaking, now I have silenced her with me rare wit," said Kofi to Andevai.

She lifted her chin belligerently. "Andevai, I believe you were just saying you must formally present me to the notables of the House," she said as she stepped on Kofi's foot, a punishment he took with not a sound, although he limped a few steps before he trod out the pain.

Andevai took her around the salon to present her to the mansa, the mansa's wives, and the older woman who, although not mansa, was the most powerful magister in Five Mirrors House, and who therefore was due a similar respect to that shown to the mansa. Catherine greeted them with her witty chatter, which could usually thaw the stoniest demeanor.

He retreated with Kofi to give her space to fight her own campaign. Viridor arrived and greeted them both, then did a double take. "Is that Catherine? I thought she was not with you. She's going to have a hard road with the mansa. He does not soften easily."

"Give her time," said Andevai.

"Next, she shall be serving them drinks," said Kofi, as she deftly roped in Judoc and also the two magisters being considered for Serena. "Yee have suffered a prodigiously altered change of mood, Vai. I thought it might be Cat's story that she told us on the journey that was fretting yee. That part about her running off on that wild and dangerous journey all on her own, without ever a word to yee that she meant to put she own self in so much danger. Shall I reckon yee and she have sorted out whatever was troubling yee before?"

"I'm not troubled," said Andevai and was simply unable to stop himself from smiling. "Doesn't she look beautiful?"

"Still that way with you, is it, Vai?" Viridor asked.

"What way?" He pulled his gaze away from how the line of Catherine's back curved into the swell of her overskirt to remind him of all that waited beneath, only to find Kofi and Viridor sharing amused looks that he was pretty sure came at his expense. "What do you mean?"

Kofi tapped him on the arm. "Yee's staring, Vai. Tisn't dignified. Every person in this fine chamber know what the two of yee have been up to by the expression yee have on yee face. At least Cat have the manners to pretend not to—"

At that moment, Catherine glanced over her shoulder to see where he was, and the look she gave him was as good as a lingering kiss.

Kofi sighed. "Never mind. I's proven wrong."

Viridor chuckled, taking Andevai's arm. "Let us go circulate, for while you may not be in the market for a second wife, I am. I should like to test the waters to see if any of these fine young women from this proud old House may be interested in joining a humble mansa who lives in the wilderness."

"Usually such things go through an intermediary first," said Andevai reprovingly. "Which is why I came on Serena's behalf. Not that she won't have the final choice, of course, but it is proper for others from the House to look into the matter first. Although we ought to have brought one of the aunts."

Kofi shook his head as they crossed the salon toward a promising cluster of women, some quite young and some rather older. "Now and again, maku, I's reminded that for all yee radical sentiments, yee have a very old-fashioned heart about yee."

"I just think things ought to be done in the proper way, the one least disruptive to the harmonious peace of the community. You properly came to me to ask my permission to court my sister."

"That's what I love about yee, maku. That yee can say so in that way yee have, as if the tides come and go at the command yee give them. I asked out of respect for yee, and because Kayleigh told me it was the way it ought to be done to make sure yee gave us no trouble over it. But don' think if yee had said no that I would have allowed yee refusal to end matters there."

Viridor tensed, glancing around to see if anyone was listening, and looked from the one man to the other, gaze flickering a little anxiously.

But Andevai merely gave Kofi a measured look. "I expect we underestimate how well Kayleigh knew how to manage both of us."

"'Tis certain she have a cannier way with people than do yee, me brother."

Andevai's gaze strayed back to his wife, although he knew he ought not to look at her so much. Just this one last time, and then he would stop. Several strands of hair had worked loose from the elaborate spiral knot she had made of her braid. The wisps brushed along her neck. He wanted to curl them around his finger. Kofi nudged him.

"Yes, yes," Andevai said hastily, not sure if he had missed some further portion of the conversation. "Kayleigh and Catherine did not make such a good going of it at first, but I think they are settling in."

"Vai, yee know Kayleigh was jealous of the attention yee paid Cat. But me gal have the one baby now and another on the way, which no doubt accounts for her softening toward Cat. Yee might consider the matter of children yee own self. 'Twould perchance somewhat leash that wild streak she have."

"I am certain it would not. But if you wish to suggest it to her before she is ready to venture into those waters of her own choice, just allow me to watch from a distance."

"Yee have a great deal more patience than many folk give yee credit for, Vai."

"I am an exceedingly patient man, as long as I am not tried by incompetence, inanity, and inconsequential men who think they are better than me."

"Spoken in all modesty," replied Kofi with a grin.

The women parted to allow them in and closed around them like so many curious wolves. Everyone had already been introduced. The mansa's granddaughter sailed right up to Andevai and tapped him on the arm with her folded fan.

"That is your wife. I remember her now, from when you were here so briefly last Martius. She ate an astounding deal of food, straight off the breakfast board. I do not recall her arriving with you yesterday, mansa."

Andevai had discovered that one of the best things about being mansa was that you never had to explain yourself. A nod was all the answer he had to give.

But he had forgotten to accommodate her pride, for no woman likes to bring herself to the point of sneaking into a potential lover's bedchamber, only to find that person already in bed with someone else.

Her eyelids fluttered and her lips crimped down, then up into a falsely sweet smile. "Have you fed her today, mansa? As I recall that last time you were here, you felt you could not allow her to partake of inferior comestibles—a striking phrase!—and begrudged her a scrap of beef. She had to steal food off the table while you were informing us of the rest of your discontents. It did not surprise me at the time that she ran away. It seems she has been fetched back."

Kofi whistled softly.

Had the mansa's granddaughter been an older woman, Andevai would have suffered the scolding meekly. But she was not. And he did not like to be spoken to in that way.

"By all means, please accompany me, for I believe you have not formally met my wife. You can ask her if she bides with me by choice or through some manner of coercion."

With a crooked smile, she accepted his retort. "Mansa, please believe me that no one who saw the two of you come in together just now need ask that question. If she is not content, then she is a better actress than any I have seen on the stage. Understand that I am not interested in playing second kora to another woman. Nor do I begrudge you whatever satisfaction you have achieved."

Andevai liked the gracious but barbed way she accepted that she had misjudged his situation. With better humor than he had expected, she crossed the room with him. Catherine had by now begun gesticulating with enthusiastic gestures no trained actor would ever have considered appropriate.

Lord of All. What tale was she telling them? The women were looking entertained, the mansa thoughtful, and the two magisters disconcerted. Meanwhile, Judoc was melting in the way men had used to do when she waited tables at the boardinghouse and teased the customers with her jesting tales and quick comebacks.

"A thread slithered down from the sky to slap the water. It was a rope ladder, lowered as by Ba'al's heavenly messengers! Its sway and bounce hypnotized me like a serpent waiting to strike. And then . . . *then* I saw two figures scrambling down, as from the heavens. The first gripped a lamp's hook in strong, white teeth. When he spotted me below, he drew a very long and very impressive knife from a harness crossed on his chest. I brandished my sword to show I would not go down without a fight! I could take out most men wielding a knife, but I wasn't so sure about taking him. He had the posture of a man who not only knew how to kill but had done so many times, without regret or hesitation. Although I grant you, his willingness to raid a plague island invested with salters did not inspire confidence in his intelligence."

The women chuckled, obviously enjoying the tale. The mansa sat with hands folded in his lap, watching the others.

Magister Kavan caught Andevai's eye and offered an inclination of his head, as in acknowledgment of a shared opinion. "These are the sort of tales that impressionable minds may read in uncultured pamphlets available on the streets. I am not at all sure they are fit for the ears of young people."

Magister Diarra glanced around to see who was listening. "When I was a boy, I sailed to North Amerike. To the port of Stapaha in the nation of Escampaha. A very clean and lively place, as I recall. In fact, I wrote an account of my travels some years later, if you should like to read a serious examination of the difficulties inherent in sea travel and the unusual customs of a far realm."

Judoc said, "And did the man with the knife and the lamp prove to be wise or foolish?"

"As well you should ask!" replied Catherine with a flourish of the arms that allowed her to mimic climbing a ladder. "Desperate to escape the salters, I scrambled up the ladder, only to find myself in the smallest airship imaginable! In the clutch of notorious pirates! This crew was known throughout the Antilles for any number of criminal ventures, daring escapades, and certain infamous dealings, in which they robbed wealthy merchants and distributed the treasure among the impoverished. They were called Nick Blade and the Hyena Queen. Quite the most fearsome people I have ever encountered. So perhaps the question would be better asked: was I wise or foolish to believe I had come to a place of safety?"

"Salters cannot enter water," said Magister Diarra. "Once you had waded into the ocean, you were safe from them. I have studied the history of the salt plague and the peculiar behavior of the disease at some length."

"It is better to seek tranquility of the mind than to excite the imagination," said Magister Kavan. "When the djeliw sing the stories of the past, they endeavor to teach us about where we came from, the worthiest manner of speech. Sensationalism is a trap for unwary minds."

Judoc smiled so slightly it was easy to miss. With a shuttering of one eye that was almost but not quite a wink, he turned back to Catherine. "Surely what we consider to be safe may change according to the circumstance. What would be foolish in one instance might be wise in another. Life and understanding is so changeable, is it not? What a person thought he saw—for instance, when you were last at this House, Maestra—may be interpreted quite differently when new light shines upon it."

Catherine offered him a conspirator's smile. "Please accept my belated praise and compliments to those who work in your kitchen. I recall those delicious jellied berries; I couldn't eat enough of them! The women of Five Mirrors House are to be honored for their excellent cooking and generous hospitality. Perhaps your own wife is one of those whose cooking feeds us."

"She was a fine cook, indeed, as well as many other things, but alas, she has passed from this world, together with our only child, two years ago, in the cholera epidemic."

Catherine pressed a hand to her chest. She had no need of insincere platitudes; her compassion was written on her face. "May her memory be a blessing."

"My thanks for your kind words, Maestra," he replied gravely, then looked past her to meet Andevai's gaze, as if to remind him how easily a man could lose the one he loved.

So had he almost lost Catherine.

The mansa's granddaughter looked from Judoc to Andevai and then to Catherine, sorting through these shifts of expression and unexpected silences. Clearly, she was not a woman to hold a grudge, as she glided forward to Catherine with a friendly smile as her offering.

"We have not formally met, Maestra. I am Aminata."

The old mansa leaned forward with the keenest interest. The women quieted, and even the two magisters waited.

Catherine clasped the woman's hands. "As you will have heard, I am Catherine. I hope you will not consider me impolite if I tell you that is a most stunning gown. The cut and color look simply lovely on you. May I ask where you have your clothing made? Or perhaps you are yourself a seamstress?"

Was it all an act? Not on Catherine's part, for what she felt flowed right off her. She had the gift of throwing herself wholeheartedly into meeting people, no closed gate between her smile and their presence. Andevai lacked utterly that ease and openness, and thus he always marveled at it. She and the mansa's granddaughter fell into conversation about fabric and thence slid sideways into a discussion of how it was possible to grow flax in more northerly regions than ever before. She must actually have been reading the professora's monograph and not just turning pages while naked in order to confound and irritate him. That was the beauty of Catherine: she took pleasure in so many varied activities.

Five Mirrors House was still old-fashioned enough that the men and women ate in different halls. As the company separated, he found himself beside Judoc. The man was looking cursedly diverted and not a little like a wasp waiting to sting.

"If I may ask, mansa, how did she get into the house? For I know she was not here yesterday, nor this morning. You must imagine that as I am tasked both as a steward and as a guardian of the House, I would take an interest in such a matter."

"The secret is not mine to share."

"I do recall being warned of her peculiar abilities." He clasped his hands behind his back, an action which made his back straighter and thus his height advantage a trifle more obvious. "But I also heard a tale of a supper party in Lutetia, at Two Gourds House, at which she vanished from sight in the blink of an eye. Which would explain a great many things I have been troubling myself over since your last visit, such as how she escaped our vigilance. Which I assume was your purpose all along in distracting our attention through your memorable behavior at that time."

Was the man's smile one of condescension or amity?

Andevai decided to take a risk.

"Desperate circumstances called for desperate measures," he replied stiffly. "My apologies for any offense I caused."

The man's smile peeped, then vanished, and Andevai could see why a woman would respond to its blend of intelligence and sardonic charm. "Mansa, the truth is, we laughed over it for months afterward. I'm sorry to say that a few of your more precise phrases are now commonly used among the young people of the House but, alas, not in an entirely flattering way."

"Not so sorry that you won't say it." But when he thought about how Catherine would laugh upon hearing this, he had to go on. "Which ones?"

"A particular favorite has been 'inferior comestibles,' which you must admit has a great deal to recommend it. Also, 'one scrap of beef, out of pity' has become popular because, as it turns out, it can be used to punctuate many more situations and conversations than one might at first realize . . . Is that a smile, mansa?"

"I beg you, please do not tell my wife, or I will never hear the end of it."

When Judoc laughed, Andevai felt as smugly pleased as if he had won a small victory. "Yes, I am come to suspect she is not the delicate creature we were meant to believe she was."

"Let me assure you that quiet, placid, cautious, frail, and meek are also words that do not describe her at all. But I hope we can set the episode in the past, Maester Judoc."

"Do you?"

The man's challenging gaze was not an easy one to endure. A year ago, Andevai would have hit back with sarcasm or biting criticism rather than feel he was being judged. But he was learning to let the jagged places smooth out so the anger would pour away rather than fill up until it flooded. Carefully, he chose prudent and neutral words.

"I do."

"Very well," said Judoc with that flicker of the eye that looked remarkably like a wink. "I'll give you this one scrap, out of pity."

Andevai laughed because it actually was humorous. Then Judoc laughed, too, and while the sharp lines drawn between them did not vanish, perhaps their edges softened a little.

He had a much more pleasant evening than he could possibly have anticipated when he had woken up that morning. So he informed Catherine when he undressed her that night by the light of four globes of cold fire.

"Yes, you were in quite your surliest mood," she agreed as she smoothed out her dress upon the bed and began folding it. "I am sorry to say that few things entertain me as much as you all caught up in your manly pride."

He glanced up from the side table where he was making his evening ablutions. "Then I shall endeavor to entertain you with my manly pride a bit more before we sleep."

Her gaze flashed up to flirt with his. "A scrap of beef, out of pity?"

"Catherine! How did you hear that?"

"Oh, Aminata and I are quite the best of friends now."

"Are you?" he asked suspiciously, for he was suddenly quite certain it involved shared amusement over his memorable behavior from their last visit. "How did you manage that?"

"That is a secret we women have."

Probably it was best not to inquire too closely. "Then I am pleased for you and her both."

Attention back on her task, she smiled in the mischievous way that made people wish to stand close to the radiance that was her delight in the world. "I have been thinking, Andevai."

"Have you?" He pretended astonishment.

"I have!" She packed the neatly folded dress into paper. "I am sorry if this disappoints you, but I cannot like either of the magisters. Since you wish for my opinion, I think you should invite Maester Judoc to come to Four Moons House."

"He isn't even a cold mage."

"No, but he is a much more interesting man than the other two."

"You say that because he admires you!"

"Goodness, Andevai, is that a flash of jealousy?"

He had to stop and think about it. She crossed to the dressing closet and stowed the dress within as he finished drying his face and hands. When she came back out, he altered course.

"What will Five Mirrors House do with the extra mage?"

"Let them sort that out. If you mean to make Four Moons House survive without clientage to support it, you need someone who can run the household business in a skilled, efficient, and forward-looking manner."

"He may not wish to involve himself in such a radical experiment."

"It is worth asking." She hitched a hip up onto the table, one foot dangling to swing back and forth. "He's an intelligent man who may relish a challenge. Anyway, an administrator with experience running a household is what you need more than anything. You wake at dawn and go to bed very late, and you work all day. I can't help but think that in another few years of overworking yourself, you will wear yourself out. I would hate for you to lose your looks."

He leaned against the table's edge beside her, crossing his arms and tapping his fingers thoughtfully on his elbow. "Yes, I suppose you might be swayed by such trivial considerations. Although perhaps not so trivial, since I am convinced that if it weren't for my good looks, you would have gotten rid of me long before you could properly get to know me."

"You might want to carefully consider that possibility when you make your decision."

"Be sure that I will. But you haven't yet convinced me, Catherine."

She ran a finger down his sleeve. She simply could never resist touching the silk of his dressing gown, which was one of the three reasons he liked to wear it. "He laughs at my jokes. That ought to tell you what a sensible man he is! From everything the women said, he is a competent, responsible person who is respected by all and who respects women. He was devoted to his wife and baby and devastated by their passing. Apparently, he is not envious of those who have cold magic, when he might have wished to have magic of his own. He has military training and acquitted himself creditably in the recent war. The kind of man you want to bring into Four Moons House is a man who isn't overawed by you and won't flatter you. A good administrator with military experience, who does not fear to disagree with you to your face, would be a far better addition than yet another swollen-headed magister."

"Swollen-headed? Who is swell-headed at Four Moons House? I thought all the difficult mages left with the mansa's nephew."

"Of course they did, my love."

He laughed, then kissed her for rather longer than he intended as he got caught up in the rich feast of caressing her while she slipped her hands underneath his dressing gown. When they broke off, he extinguished three of the shining globes. One bulb of cold fire gave just enough light to see her in her shift and with her hair down, but in a gauzy haze that veiled the proceedings with a pleasing glamor.

"I see you have something in mind, Vai," she remarked with a coaxing look that encouraged him to keep on as he had been. "As I recall, last time we were here, we used this table, did we not?"

When he picked her up, she squirmed in his arms, just enough to make it even more arousing as he carried her to the bed. "I fear we did not give the bed enough of a chance to prove whether it is adequate to your needs."

Much later, she declared herself entirely satisfied with the bed, but by then he was too drowsy and contented to bother thinking up a clever retort. He slept through the night deeply and restfully.

She woke him at dawn by opening the curtains to let in light and then sprawling across the bed to kiss him. She was already dressed in the traveling clothes she had arrived in. "I'll take the coach. You won't need it with all your meetings and discussions here. I'm sure Judoc can arrange for transportation if you wish to tour anywhere nearby."

"You are sure you don't want me to come?"

"If you truly wish to or think you can't rest easy if I go without you, then you may, Vai. But obviously, I will have the coachman and the footman with me to guard my back, should there be trouble. In truth, it will go more quickly if I just slip in and out without anyone knowing I was ever there, as I can do. I have the names of people into whose care I can convey the printer once I've freed him. Then I need have nothing further to do with the matter. I'll return here, and we'll go home together." She hesitated, searching his expression for any sign of disappointment or frustration.

But he knew what she was. He loved her for it. "I shall remain here and continue my work at remaking the mage Houses from within."

Her shoulders relaxed as she flicked a finger along his cheek. "Don't neglect the courtship!"

"The courtship? Ah, for me to persuade Judoc to visit Four Moons

House." He brushed a wisp of hair off her forehead, studying her closely as he did so. She arched an eyebrow as she waited for him to continue. "You're right about the other two magisters. Now that I think about it, even Judoc warned me off them in his own sarcastic way."

"He will make Four Moons House stronger, Vai. I'm sure of it."

She kissed him again before grabbing her sword and her winter cloak. So eager was she to get on the road that, when she paused at the bedchamber door to give him a parting smile, she did not even return to the bed for one final kiss.

He moped for a bit, feeling a little sorry for himself, and yet he also smiled to think of the story she would have to tell when she returned. When he heard servants enter the outer chamber, he quickly rose and pulled on his dressing gown.

To his surprise, upon knocking, only Maester Judoc entered the bedchamber. He set a full pitcher of water and fresh towels by the brass washbasin. After the usual greetings—drawn out rather long as each man waited for the other to broach the day's business—Judoc went to the window. He frowned at the clouds as if wishing to scold them for having the bad manners to spoil his hope of sun, then fixed his hands behind his back in a soldier's stance.

"It seems your wife has made an unexpected and abrupt departure."

"Yes. She will be returning in ten days or thereabouts. By that time, our deliberations should be complete, so my party will then make our way home."

Andevai walked over to the side table but paused before he poured water into the basin. The chamber was so quiet that he could hear a crow cawing outside. He rubbed a hand over his hair, as he did when he was nervous, sorting through possible phrases. Lord of All! He was mansa of Four Moons House. No need to feel this awkward! Truth be told, he was coming to respect the man and feared Judoc did not respect him in the same manner.

"Perhaps . . ." He sighed, turning over words until they got so twisted, he could make no sense of them. He tried again. "Perhaps you have some suggestions for sightseeing, for when we have an afternoon free and the weather is not too cold or wet to venture out."

Judoc did not stir, although he glanced out the window again as if seeking that noisy crow. "I do not get the impression you entertain yourself much, mansa. You seem like a man who is very fixed on his responsibilities."

"I have a great deal of work to do. Also, as mansa, I feel it my duty to set a good example."

"Of course."

He considered the pitcher, which Judoc had himself conveyed into the chamber when he might have left the task to a servant. As Andevai had learned from his extensive and intimate study of Catherine, there are ways to communicate that do not necessarily include speech.

"Maester Judoc, I have a proposition for you."

There! It was said. He swallowed, surprised at how anxiously he suppressed any sign of nerves by speaking in a cold, proud voice and with a posture that made him look unapproachable and arrogant.

"Do you?" replied Judoc with a derisive twitch of his lips.

He knew he could not emulate Catherine's effortless manners, so he accepted that this once, he would just have to plod gracelessly into the fray.

"You know that my main purpose is to advance new pedagogical reforms in the schoolroom. I've also been speaking of the need for the mage Houses to restructure our very legal and economic foundations."

"Revolutionary notions, indeed," agreed Judoc, without giving by tone or expression any hint of what he thought of such matters.

"But I also came here because Four Moons House is seeking a candidate for a marriage."

The other man nodded curtly.

Annoyance bled a sharp taste onto Andevai's tongue. Was the man uninterested? Bored? "You warned me about Kavan and Diarra. I find I agree with your assessment."

"Had you not, I confess I would have thought less of you," remarked Judoc.

"Less of me than you already do?" Andevai snapped.

"I think you do not really know my mind, mansa. So I would appreciate it if you did not pretend that you do."

To keep his hands busy and his magic in check, Andevai poured water into the basin. Then he left it alone, ripples stilling until it was a calm surface. One of the things his tormenters in the House had stolen from him was his ability to have faith or confidence in other people, men especially. He did not want to live that way. So he had to just get it out and let the consequences fall where they may.

"Perhaps you might consider returning with us to Four Moons House to meet Magister Serena. She is a powerful diviner. She is an intelligent person and a hard worker. She has a great deal of common sense and an exquisite sense of proper manners. To be honest, she is also a woman of exceptional beauty and dignity. She was my predecessor's wife, as you know, his third wife, and thus a woman he married purely because he respected and admired her, not for any political reason. She has one young daughter by him and, I have reason to believe, a hope for more children."

"As mansa, you could surely take such a paragon as your second wife."

Andevai frowned. "My predecessor was not my father, but legally, when he adopted me as his heir, he became to me in the nature of a father. Therefore, it would be completely inappropriate for me to marry his widow."

"Very traditional of you, mansa. But both you and I know that you could, if you wanted."

"I think the one wife I have is enough work as it is."

Judoc's chuckle made Andevai tense. "I would find it tremendously disconcerting to have a wife who came and went in such an abrupt fashion. On her way out, she dashed through the kitchen and flattered the cook into packing quite the largest basket of comestibles I have ever seen laid in. Is she meeting someone?"

"No, I expect she can eat it all herself."

"So that, at least, was no theatrical act. Does she always carry a sword?"

"Always. She is a more dangerous person than you may assume upon first acquaintance. Imagine what havoc a person might wreak, she who can walk about unseen in the world." Andevai almost laughed to see Judoc's startled expression, as if suddenly the man had run up against an aspect of Catherine that troubled him at last. "Which brings me to my point, Maester. Given all that you know of us and our situation, are you interested?"

Instead of answering, Judoc paced a circuit of the room, tracing a pattern only he saw. He cut around Andevai at the table and halted by the window that overlooked an interior garden, with its evergreen hedges and leafless shrubs awaiting spring's promise.

"This was once the apartment I lived in with my wife. I left it after her passing because the memories were too hard."

Andevai touched a hand to his chest, where his heart beat. He could not help but think of how Catherine had written him a letter that would have been all he'd have had left of her. "Grief is a fearsome companion. One who never truly leaves your side once you step onto that road."

Judoc inclined his head in acknowledgement. "I thought she and I were just beginning our journey together, but instead, we had far too little time. Yet her generous heart would not have wanted me to remain as I am now, caught in winter's grip. So I will travel with you, mansa. But I make no promises."

"I need no promises. If you and Serena choose to make a match of it, that is entirely your decision. By inviting you, I am merely letting you know that I believe Four Moons House would benefit by your presence. I would hope to have your assurance that you would always speak honestly and bluntly, even to me."

"Even to you, mansa! A challenge, indeed, but in the event, one I would courageously attempt."

Was Andevai willing to live with this acerbic manner for years, even decades, perhaps the rest of his life? Yet how dull a meek or obsequious man would be. He and Kofi had not become fast friends because Kofi was minded to guard his wit. Could this man become a trusted companion, even perhaps, in time, a friend and brother?

Judoc met his gaze proudly. They were not either of them men likely to back down when it came to what they believed right and proper. Yet like most people, Judoc had his own secret shadows that chased at him. However caustically he spoke, he had opened the door just enough to let Andevai catch a glimpse of the complicated architecture of his thoughts.

Andevai ventured a trifle farther out on the limb of vulnerability. "If you will give me time to wash and dress, we might go down to the breakfast room together."

Judoc's brows lifted. Andevai could see him consider a mocking retort and then the decision to let it lie. Instead, he fished around the chamber with his gaze and fetched up on the monograph set on top of the closed chest, where Catherine had placed it earlier.

"If I may," he said, indicating the book. When Andevai gestured for him to go ahead, he picked it up and went to the door. "I comprehend you are not a man who readies himself quickly in the mornings. I shall await you in the outer chamber. I hope the book will hold my interest."

As the door shut behind him, Andevai smiled. He went to the window and looked out onto the winter garden. Just then, a rent parted the clouds, and the sun glowed through. Light poured over the walls and hedges, turning shadows into gold. An unforeseen emotion stirred in his heart. It took him a moment to absorb it.

Maybe this was what serenity felt like.

With such a promising start to the day, he really expected he could accomplish anything.

"I Am a Handsome Man," said Apollo Crow

art by Jemma Salume

I AM A HANDSOME MAN," SAID APOLLO CROW, FIXING THE EMPEROR of Rome with a look that dared that august ruler to disagree. "If your desire is to have a woman kidnapped without alerting her confederates until it is too late to rescue her, look no farther. My skills are subterfuge, tracking down people who don't wish to be found, and an ability to lie with a straight face. I am also an exceptionally skilled swordsman."

The emperor set chin upon hand with thoughtful consideration, a pose suited to the stage, as he was well aware. "I was warned you always lie about something."

"Alas, so I do. It is a curse." His charming smile made a witticism of the remark.

"I am sure that to a ruffian like you, such a claim seems an amusing challenge. However, your situation is easy enough for a man such as me to expose. We'll start by process of elimination. Are you truly an exceptionally skilled swordsman?"

"I will duel any among your soldiers, or two or three at once. Bring them forth."

The emperor flicked up his fingers, straightening. "Will you duel me?"

One eyebrow only did Apollo Crow raise, a neat trick many an opponent had admired, to their cost. "It seems dishonorable, considering your age."

The emperor extended his right hand. An attendant guardsman settled a steel blade into the imperial fingers. He rose, took three steps down from the dais and onto the marble floor of the audience chamber, and indicated that he was ready to begin.

Naturally, Apollo Crow wore a hip-length, black cape, of the sort that swirls dashingly with any swift movement. He spun a full circle, the fabric floating like a whirl of shadow. When he again faced the emperor, he held his blade in his right hand, as if it had appeared there by magic rather than sleight of hand.

The emperor shifted stance, taking his sword into his left hand. Apollo Crow smiled and did the same.

Light pouring from high-arched windows framed their shapes to dazzling effect as uniformed soldiers and gaudily robed officials admired the show.

"What is your fee?" A probing flurry by the emperor, easily parried by Apollo Crow.

"That depends upon the distance to be traveled and the circumstances under which I must put myself at risk."

They circled.

"The woman is a beauty, so that part of the job is no risk."

"What one man calls beauty, another may find trifling. But that *you* call her a beauty tells me a good deal. Is she a woman who spurned you, the very emperor of shrunken Rome?"

The emperor laughed. "Quite the opposite, if you must know."

"Or at least, so you feel obliged to claim." Crow assayed a thrust, and the emperor of all Rome and its few remaining provinces turned it aside.

"I need affect no lies, Mr. Crow. I am hiring you to do a job and ascertaining whether you can succeed. The woman is secondary to my interest. I need her sketchbook, which she carries with her everywhere. She is herself exceptionally well guarded, and her movements well concealed by her many allies."

The emperor feinted left, then rapidly attacked right. Apollo Crow replied with a vicious riposte.

"Of what possible use can a sketchbook be to you? Are there compromising images that you seek to recover and burn?"

A flurry of parries and thrusts rang through the hall. Both stymied, they broke apart.

"These are tedious attempts at provocation," said the emperor, scarcely out of breathe. "Can you manage it?"

"It seems a simple enough job. Where do I start?"

"My agents report there will be a secret meeting in the town of Nikaia, a gathering of criminals and malcontents who harbor revolutionary sentiments. We don't know in which disreputable tavern it will take place. They change their meeting places every week. In any case, even if we did know, were my soldiers to appear in force, it would scare her off. Any violence done at the gathering will merely strengthen their querulous voices. So this is where you come in, Mr. Crow."

"Why, a seditious gathering with one foot into the empire itself! No wonder you are eager to crush this assembly before it can seed its roots into Roman soil. Yet what has a beautiful woman to do with such a masculine pursuit as revolution?"

The emperor flashed an annoyed look toward a tapestry on the wall, whose bright colors and bold design depicted his famous Amazon regiment striding into battle. As with the strike of an agitated viper, he pressed a bold attack straight at the other man. The ring of their blades striking and sliding, the scuff and stamp of their feet, and the movements of their bodies as they sought each to gain the upper hand were, for a time, the only dance in the chamber. The emperor pressed with his greater height and weight, while Apollo Crow answered with a speed and precision that made him seem almost to float above the ground.

At length, they disengaged, and the emperor stepped back to indicate the bout had ended.

"You disappoint me with your conventional thinking," he said.

"That you are a rejected lover, anxious to avenge yourself on an arrogant woman by stealing from her a personal item that is precious to her?"

A smile fluttered and faded. "That women cannot foment revolution. Indeed, they are the more dangerous, once roused. I had thought one such as you would not indulge in too much of convention."

"One such as me? What sort of one is that?"

"Among other things, a person who makes a living outside of the law." The emperor shook his head. "But I am finished dueling with you. Perhaps I can find a better person for the work."

"You cannot. If you have come to me, it means you have failed in your previous attempts to obtain the sketchbook."

"True enough," agreed the emperor with a gracious nod.

At a gesture from the ruler, an official walked forward and handed a substantial pouch of coins to Apollo Crow.

The man weighed them without opening the pouch.

"I know what you are lying about," added the emperor.

"Do you, indeed?"

"So we shall discover." With a decisive nod, the emperor indicated the doors, which were promptly opened by waiting attendants.

Apollo Crow smiled. He had a winning smile, a seductive smile, a handsome smile, and he knew it. With a flourish made into a mocking bob of a bow, he took his leave of the imperial palace.

Nikaia was a port town, seething with travelers, sailors, and merchants: a volatile and lucrative brew spiced with rumor, poverty, and discontented plebeians, whose ears itched the more fiercely as more promises of suffrage were whispered into them. The haunts where radical sentiments pooled like wraiths awaiting release on Hallow's Eve were many, and Apollo Crow was only one man, with one pair of legs. Yet he had other means of gathering intelligence.

A week after he arrived, a crow fluttered to land on the open windowsill of the room at the inn where he was staying. Since he hated being alone, he always found a way to have company. The woman in his bed raised herself up on an elbow, her beautiful eyes opening wide as the crow bobbed a greeting.

"What dreadful omen is this?" she gasped.

"You think like a Celt," he said as he slipped from under the covers. He grabbed a bit of bread off a platter on the sideboard and went to the window to offer it to the bird. "The crow is sacred to my namesake, the Hellene god."

The bird snapped up the bread, then cawed for so long a stretch that the woman laughed.

"Is it thanking you for the meal? Or boring you with a complaint?"

"Not at all. Just giving me a welcome scrap of information in exchange."

"What an amusing tale-teller you are! Crows would make magnificent conspirators and agents, if only they could talk and spy." Her voice turned coaxing. "You standing there naked has quite obliterated all thoughts of omens, battlefields, and carrion crows from my mind. I would take another welcome scrap, if you have a mind to come back to bed, for I certainly have no complaints."

"I am compliant in all things that harmonize with my wishes," he assured her truthfully, turning away from the window. "Are you acquainted with a tavern called The Four Abreast?"

"By rumor only, not from setting foot in it myself. You wouldn't want to go there."

"Why not?"

"It's in a very poor part of town, frequented by sailors, washerwomen, and cutthroats." She beckoned him closer with a pretty frown. "But I see from your expression you are determined to get yourself killed in that dreadful district. So be it. Come over here, so I don't waste this chance while you are still among the living."

Later, he made his way amid the dregs of twilight, down a dismal avenue lined with shuttered shops, on the trail of The Four Abreast. Dark, empty streets made him melancholy, pining for the open land he had once called home. Ahead, a man pushed a cart of refuse while whistling a cheerful melody that lightened the lonely night. He quickened his pace to catch up, and just as he was about to make a friendly remark, the carter halted next to a dank alley. A pair of ragged children crept out of the darkness.

"Go ahead, but be quick," murmured the carter.

The children pawed through the stench-ridden garbage for anything they might use, eat, or sell.

"There's a coin in it for each of you if you can lead me to the Four Abreast," Apollo Crow said to the children.

The carter slapped away their reaching hands. "Don't go walking with strange men."

"I meant no harm. Can you tell me, Maester? I know I'm bound for the streets below Castle Hill, but by what means may I recognize the tavern?"

"Why do you want to know?"

"I've served a cruel master, and I've escaped. It seems right to see what I can do to help others who may wish for a different way of life."

The carter grunted, not entirely convinced.

"For your trouble, then." Apollo Crow tossed a coin to each child, pressed a third into the man's hand, and walked away.

"Juniper wards the entrance," the carter called after him. "That's all I'll say."

The neighborhood crowded up against the flanks of Castle Hill, straight streets collapsing into a confusing web of cramped lanes. The night lamps that illuminated the harbor walk and main avenues were absent. Gloom spilled like an incoming tide, turning every doorway and alley into a pool of shadows. A figure detached itself from a wall, swinging a club. Apollo Crow made a great drama of drawing his sword, and the cutthroat thought better of attacking him and slid away into the night.

The harsh laughter of women drew him to a dilapidated gate framed by wreaths of strong-smelling juniper beneath candle lanterns, two on each side. Because it was set ajar, he pushed on it, then realized it was stuck. Anyone going in would have to squeeze through, making them easy prey to an ambush.

He cocked his head to one side, listening, and identified two heartbeats waiting beyond. Sheathing the sword, he stepped sideways through the opening and found himself in a hazy courtyard, redolent of fish being smoked. A pair of burly guards shone a light on him. They hadn't even gotten out their swords.

"You're a looker, and that's for sure," said one. He looked at his companion as if they were both about to burst out laughing. "But there isn't no one hereabouts who can afford the likes of you, if it's yourself you're selling. No fancy personages up to your scratch, of the type you must be accustomed to."

He tossed them each a coin. "I've a fancy to try the brew, that's all. I hear that, late at night, the tap flows with speeches and songs of a sort that interest me."

"At your own risk." They waved him on.

Beyond the reek of the smokehouses lay the more pleasant aroma of a stable and, beyond it, another courtyard overlooked by a portico in the Roman style, supported by old stone pillars. The building that rose up against the ancient columns was modern, built of wood. Lamps shone within to illuminate people seated in a spacious common room, their figures distorted by thick window glass. A pair of fiddlers unfurled a dancing tune into the air, two voices weaving around each other as people stamped along to the rhythm.

He made a cautious entrance to find himself in the cheerful clamor of a tavern common room, divided in the Kena'ani fashion with a rope fence down the middle so men and women sat separately. He took a step toward the right, corrected himself, and went to sit on the men's side.

A blond lad of Celtic fairness and stern Roman disposition brought him a mug of the house beer, so golden it might have been brewed from sunlight. He struck up a conversation with a group of local men whose calloused hands and sun-weathered faces proclaimed them dockhands.

"Where do you hail from?" they asked him. "What ship did you come in on? Perhaps you came overland from the east, for you have a bit of that eastern look about you."

He entertained them with fanciful tales, all of which were true but sounded false to their ears: that he was born in a place where every fresh tide altered the contours of the land; that a dragon ate his father; that his mother was a crow. All the while, he surreptitiously studied the women crowded at their ease on the other side of the fence, as at a cheerful roost. They were all females of the laboring class: washerwomen with lye-scarred hands; street sellers whose baskets of walnuts and onions sat at their feet; street sweepers dozing against their brooms. It had long been his observation that women labored from before sunrise to long after sunset. Sitting in a tavern late at night to hear the pronouncements of a radical who wielded words like the deadliest of swords might well be the most restful patch of their year.

His gaze caught on a young woman with a lively face, who seemed unable to sit still. She had brought a bit of mending to do, as women were wont, there always being some tear or fray that needed repair, as a bird must endlessly tend to its feathers. Sewing kept her hands busy. But it was her long, thick braid of hair, as glossy and black as his own, that made him twitch, as if he'd been pricked by a needle wielded by an invisible hand.

"What do you think of our fine harbor, and the countryside hereabout?" his comrades asked, for he had fallen inexplicably silent.

"The provinces of Rome I call a fair and lovely land, for all that its skies and earth are so very different from my homeland," he answered. "Yet this is the first time here in Roman territory that I've seen women seated in a tavern as if they are accustomed to take their ease where men usually perch. Usually Roman women stay home."

"We're a port town, not a staid Roman oppidum. Anyway, women as much as men flock to any meeting where there's a chance the Honeyed Voice will speak. Men for her beauty, and women for her exhortations and her knife."

"The Honeyed Voice?" He sat up straighter. "What knife does she wield?"

"The knife of persuasion."

The fiddles ran down a cadence and ceased. One man elbowed another as a table was cleared at the far end of the room.

"Here she comes," cried one of his interlocutors with an eager smile.

The crowd made way for three figures: a short, curvaceous woman flanked on either side by a tall individual of the people known as the feathered ones. These two had narrow jaws, vicious claws, and the slightly bobbing walk of a people who seemed a blend of human, bird, and lizard. Although soberly dressed as respectable lawyers, the feathered ones betrayed their true nature in having the toothy grins of dangerous beasts. In a chamber so filled with the strong scent of humanity, their dry, summer-burnt smell faded away almost to nothing, but Apollo Crow took in a deep breath to make his chest bigger and himself thus more threatening, lest they look his way and think they must attack. Then, recalling prudence, he hunched instead, so neither would mark him with their roving gazes. Not that the feathered ones had any reason to recognize him for what he was. Like humans, they were creatures of this world. He was truly alone, the only murder of his kind he had ever found in all his long and lonely years living in exile.

A shout arose from the company all around as the feathered ones helped the petite woman up to stand on the tabletop.

Taken utterly by surprise by her exquisite features and magnificent poise, Apollo Crow jumped to his feet to get a better look. With delighted remonstrations, his companions tugged him back down to the bench.

"Did we not say she would astound you?" they laughed as the vision raised her arms with a gesture that invited the chattering audience to be quiet. "Listen, and you will hear."

"My comrades. My friends. *My sisters*."

The women in the room ululated, then hushed expectantly.

"I am come into a hostile land bearing a message for those of you who seek freedom: the yoke of tyranny harnesses you, yet it can be thrown off here as it has been elsewhere in Europa."

She spoke in a compelling tone that, without apparent effort, filled the large room so no listener need strain to hear. With effortless eloquence, she lectured on the means by which the rich and powerful arrogate wealth and favor for themselves and exploit those who toil under their lash. She described in convincing detail the creation of a governing Assembly in the city of Havery, presided over by the prince of that territory but subject to no master except itself. Half the room leaned forward as she detailed how the elections for representatives to this Assembly included women, while the other half exchanged troubled looks. Yet all listened, for she had the gift of speech that made every word bloom from her mouth into a flower, so that every sentence became a fragrant bouquet.

"It is true that by ancient Roman law, women are forbidden from holding magistracies, priesthoods, triumphs, badges of office, or spoils of war. But what is law if not words written by hands?" she went on, as if the men's surly glances and hot murmurs impelled her to harden her phrases. "What the hand works can be made or unmade, as times change and philosophies take new paths. This is our new path, if we wish to walk it."

"Is she an actress?" Apollo Crow demanded of his new friends.

The men hushed him with slaps on the arm, for however appalled they might be by her rhetoric, they were also entranced by her person and her voice.

"No actress! She has roused the hearts of people all across Europa. They say the emperor would imprison her, if only he could catch her."

A dangerous woman, indeed, if you were emperor over all the Romans and feared the discontent that simmered beneath the surface of the normally silent plebeians. She was the fire coaxing the water to boil, and a fine, fierce blaze she was. But whatever else he might think, he had a job to do and a curse that bound him.

When at length she finished her speech to thunderous applause, he winkled a gold chain from one of the many pockets secreted about his clothing, where he kept the bits and bobs he collected on his travels. He caught the collar of a passing child, young enough to be allowed to wander both sides of the fence.

"There is a denarius in it for you if you take this gold chain to the Honeyed Voice and let her know what man sent it."

"What if I just steal the chain and run away and never come back?" the child asked, perplexed by such a naïve offer, while also staring greedily at the glittering links.

"Let me assure you, I never forget a face." Apollo Crow's smile made the child shudder. "If you disoblige me, then I promise that one day you will find yourself set upon by crows and pecked to death, with no one the wiser."

The child pretended to laugh to save face, but at the same time, cast a frightened look to either side, seeking escape. Yet the possibility of earning a denarius was no trivial inducement. After less of a hesitation than Apollo Crow had expected, the child fished both chain and coin out of his hand and ducked under the rope.

As he had known they would, the women pressing forward to speak to the Honeyed Voice allowed the child to slip through their ranks, for women always made room for hatchlings. She dipped to listen as the child spoke. Her shoulders tensed in surprise, and she looked up to scan the chamber.

Her gaze met his. The light was a little too dim and she a little too far away for him to read the subtleties of her reaction, but he could guess by her shifts in posture that she was displeased—and yet also tickled by an incurable swell of curiosity. Hard not to notice that she took in several bosom-heaving breaths. He lifted his mug to salute her. The men around him, captured by the gesture, applauded and laughed, praising him for his steely nerve. Everyone knew, they said, that the Honeyed Voice had no patience for men who tried to bribe her with gifts; she chose as she wished for interest, not for gain.

She handed the gold chain to a woman who stood beside her and indicated that the other woman should return the rejected bauble to him. Then, with an empty hand pretending to hold a nonexistent cup, she saluted him back.

He was abruptly head over tail in love with the challenge.

Oddly enough, the woman entrusted with the necklace was the very same seamstress he had noticed before. He hadn't, however, noticed her leaving her bench, and therefore studied her more closely as she approached. Her clothes were sturdy, not fancy, her boots worn by much walking.

"Maester, I've been asked by the maestra to return this to you."

"No, no, I insist you keep it for your trouble."

"A generous offer." She swung the chain between her fingers. "I'd best not, for that would put me in your debt in a way you might misinterpret."

"Not at all. It is a mere bauble, a token of appreciation for the fine speech by the Honeyed Voice that so entertained me. Since she rejects me so cruelly, my sole request is that you would be so kind as to exchange a few words with me, a gentle balm to my aching heart. What is your name?"

"Catherine, Maester. And yours?"

"I am Apollo Crow, a traveller. Please sit."

The seamstress seated herself on an empty bench beside the rope and smiled expectantly. She was attractive, with the grace of a fighter about her long limbs and easy physical confidence. He might find a way to the other woman through this one: jealousy and competition sometimes fired women's interest when a handsome man became involved.

He called for a round of drinks and seated himself close enough to talk to the seamstress across the fence. He essayed teasing banter, but she wanted only to discuss the coming revolution.

"Many speak against the radical proposal to allow women to vote. You must have a thought on this topic, Maester."

"What is your opinion, Maestra?" he parried.

"Why, do you really wish to hear my opinion? I'm often told I talk too much. Many men say women are formed for bread and butter and not for philosophical debate. What do you think, Mr. Crow?"

"I come from a people where everyone talks a great deal, women and men equal in their vociferousness. As for what I think, I am new to this town and thus prefer to discover what the locals may think. How else may I come to an understanding of how people get on here? Your compatriot speaks compellingly. I would wish nothing more than an evening of innocent conversation with such a persuasive voice. Perhaps in your company?"

He had a smile that melted women, and when he used it now, she leaned closer, and even closer still, gaze alight with interest. Over her shoulder, he noticed the Honeyed Voice moving toward the exit, then pulled his gaze back to the seamstress.

Her lips parted as if in delight at his advances. In a low, husky, sensuous voice, she said, "She's well guarded, Mr. Crow. Don't believe otherwise. It's best if you leave us alone."

She rose and cut her way smoothly through the crowded common room and out the door to the courtyard, through which the Honeyed Voice had departed.

His new friends laughed. "Well, well, you've been put in your place *and* lost your coin besides!"

"I shall need a drink to drown my sorrow!" He gestured to the server. "Fill my friends' cups again."

As the youth moved forward, Apollo Crow surreptitiously tipped the bench so as to knock the server in the legs and send him sprawling. A great splash from the pitcher—and a mighty shout from everyone around as they got wet—distracted his male companions. In the ensuing commotion, he slipped the chain into the server's pocket, then left as quickly as possible, elbowing through the crowd in his haste to get out the door. Outside, he had to pause and set an elderly man to rights, who had lost hold of his cane and stumbled in the crush. Then he strode on the path of his target, who was even now slipping out the gate.

As he hurried past the reeking smokehouses, a slender young man fell into step beside him. He had hair as long and black as the seamstress's and, indeed, there were other signs of a family resemblance in the coloring and the shape of their eyes.

"A word of advice," said the young fellow with a smile that was more a baring of teeth. "If the Honeyed Voice has rejected your offer, as she has, then do not press your suit."

"My thanks," replied Apollo Crow, with the sardonic eyebrow lift he had perfected as a means to intimidate people who thought to spar with him. "What business is it of yours?"

"I am her kinsman. Therefore, her wellbeing is my responsibility." His new companion eyed him as a cat would a bird. "Just a warning, Maester. Personally, I find the Honeyed Voice bossy and impatient, but I understand that, for men of your type, she presents an irresistible attraction. The need to prove that her beauty and her fierce confidence will yield to you, and you alone, where lesser men have failed."

"My type? What type do you believe that to be?"

The young man braced himself in the narrow opening of the gate so no one—and particularly not Apollo Crow—could pass. He sniffed the air, then frowned, just as if he could sift through the fug of the courtyard's air and tease out threads of information.

"Now I'm not so sure. Where did you say you come from?"

"I didn't say. What was your name?"

"I didn't say," said the young man, with another of those smiles filled with charm and menace. "If you have family, you'll understand we look out for each other."

"I understand the sentiment very well. I am, in every possible way, a family man."

The fellow kept standing there, meaning to block the gate until it was too late to follow. While Apollo Crow was never averse to a headlong attack, he judged the other man too much of a puzzle to assay with too little to go on. There was a coiled energy about him that reminded him of . . . himself, that sense of a body lodged in this world but with a spirit anchored in the world beyond. But he had learned the hard way not to speak to strangers and ordinary people about mortal worlds and spirit worlds; no one ever believed him. Instead, he had learned to turn truth into tales that people accepted as entertainment.

He bowed as if in gracious retreat, acknowledging the right of family to protect their own. But upon stepping away from the gate, he at once sought out the darkest and most isolated corner of the courtyard. Behind a smoke-house, amid the crunch of ashy scales and discarded refuse, he paused, looking around one last time to make sure he was entirely alone. The night was not kind to his eyesight, and he could never rely on his sense of smell. Cocking his head to one side, he listened. Fiddles and stamping feet, adrift in the air, made it hard to pick out any softer noise, but then the young man spoke over by the gate, addressing the guards.

"Where did he go? I didn't see him go back into the tavern."

With a sigh, he sloughed the self he wore. In a flurry of one hundred and thirty-four pairs of wings—because it takes many crows to make a man—they flew out over the night-drenched streets, in search of a woman.

The flock followed the woman and the two feathered ones to a respectable inn on the waterfront in a well-lit and prosperous district of the town.

In a dense cloud, they descended onto the rooftop of the inn as if coming to roost for the night. Individuals flapped down to spy. One even got into the common room and perched watchfully in a smoky corner as the Honeyed Voice sat down to a supper and drinks were sent to her table by hopeful suitors and shy admirers. A crow flew to every windowsill, looking into every room, awaiting her arrival in one of them. But it was the crow stationed at the kitchen yard who saw her leave by a back door and slip away into the night, joined by the seamstress and the young man, while the two much more conspicuous feathered ones remained behind to make it seem she hadn't left yet. A cunning scheme, indeed, to throw off the scent of people who would be following her. Cawing in excitement at this simple ruse, some of the younger crows had to be hushed, lest they draw attention.

Her route took her into the humbler streets along the riverbank, where lived folk of modest circumstance and law-abiding habit. She came to rest at last in a small two-story inn with a ramshackle, windowless exterior. Despite their unprepossessing appearance, the gate and walls presented a formidable challenge for a person on the street who wanted to get a look inside without being noticed. The crows merely settled all around the roof, overlooking an interior courtyard. No fire burned in the courtyard's hearth; the ashes were as cold as if they hadn't been lit in days.

Even this late at night, a solitary soul sat at a table, intent on reading by the illumination of a floating sphere of cool-white light. Several crows hopped forward to get a better look. He was a well-dressed and well-preened man, who might be said to be as handsome as a crow, not that that was possible. When the others hurried in through the gate, he rose to greet them. By the intimate kiss he gave the seamstress, it was evident that Apollo Crow's plan to seduce her, in order to instigate the envious attention of the Honeyed Voice, would probably not work. Indeed, by the way the four conversed with casual remarks and overlapping interruptions, they themselves had the manners of a flock.

After a short wait, the two feathered ones appeared. Once they were inside and the gate closed, the target crossed the courtyard and entered a gated stairwell, alone.

The inn was really two old buildings stitched together: a set of rooms facing inward around the courtyard and a separate wing stuck on at right angles. This extra wing protruded over the water, a relic from a now derelict ancient bridge that no longer reached the opposite shore. The repurposed bridge had no lower story, only the arched foundation, so the rooms atop were unreachable except by the guarded stairwell and an interior passage.

The windows of these rooms overlooked the river. Soon enough, a pair of shutters were opened from inside. The woman leaned out and took in a deep breath of night air, then winced at the smell of refuse and smoke. The moment she retreated into the room, two crows landed on the windowsill to watch. She lit a candle and, by its light, locked the door from the inside and tucked the key into her sleeve. Then she set the candle into a brass holder on a dressing table. Flame glimmered in the mirror as she opened a sketchbook and sat down to draw.

One crow flew to a perch atop the wardrobe.

Although flight and landing made no discernible noise, the woman's hand paused.

"Was there something more you needed to tell me?" she said to the air.

The air offered no reply.

Both the crow on the windowsill and the one on the wardrobe hopped out of sight as she closed the book and rose. After a puzzled glance around the chamber, she opened the door into the passage and went out. As soon as she shut the door, crows mobbed into the chamber.

He quickly stitched himself into a single shape, all but for three parts. First, he tested the door to the passage, but she had locked it from outside. No chance of escaping with the sketchbook out that way, not without the key. Taking a seat at the dressing table, he weighed the sketchbook in hand. Too heavy to fly with, even if he created a net for the crows to carry.

Therefore, he reluctantly had to accept the third option, although he liked it least and would have to play for time. He tore a scrap of blank paper out of the back of the book and filled it with exceedingly precise and tiny writing. This scrap, he slipped into a message tube, which he fixed to the leg of one of the crows. Thus dismissed, it flew, and the other two parts took up watch outside.

At last, he opened the sketchbook. With the greatest interest and delight, he examined the first drawing, which depicted a crowned young woman riding a bull—clearly meant to be the Phoenician queen, Europa—and a lion sneaking up behind them, dragging a length of chain. As a metaphor for the shrunken empire of Rome wishing to recapture the lands it had lost hundreds of years ago, it was, if anything, a little obvious.

A key tumbled the lock. Apollo Crow shut the book, set his elbows on the dressing table, and, in the mirror, examined his lean face, his glossy-black hair, his nimble fingers. Was there anything wrong with him? Something he could shape better? Why was there a man in this world handsomer than he was?

The hinges creaked. A figure loomed up behind him like a stain expanding in the mirror. Candlelight glinted on the edge of a slim sword, but it wasn't as sharp as the pique of the woman's smile. He met the reflection of her gaze and smiled in lazy reply.

The Honeyed Voice had an interrogative eyebrow, not unlike his own, and she used it now. "You are sitting in my chair."

"It is hard to resist admiring myself when I have the chance, for I am certainly a sleek and shiny fellow."

Her gaze had a measuring look. "Indeed, it is hard to resist wondering how such a sleek and shiny fellow as yourself could have gotten into this locked chamber."

"You are irresistible. Therefore, no barrier can keep me from you."

"Really?" Her posture had the angles and muscles of someone who knew how to fight. "The passage to these rooms is guarded day and night, which, as you may imagine, is why people who have enemies like to sleep here. The door from this chamber into the passage can be locked both from the inside and from the outside, and I have the key. So common sense suggests you came in through the window. Yet the roof is too steep to negotiate, and the wall too steep to climb. Even if you could climb it, you aren't wet, as you would have to be if you'd come up from the river."

"I might have arrived in a boat."

She went to the window and looked down, then turned back to him. "There's nowhere to tie it up. Do you care to explain this mystery?"

He rose carefully, held his hands palms out to show himself unarmed, and offered a courteous bow, hand to heart. "I am not the only mystery in this chamber. The greatest mystery is your allure."

"You should have tried that line earlier, before your back was to the wall. Why are you here?"

"Perhaps you and I may trade secrets. Why has the emperor of Rome hired me? That your revolutionary agitation troubles the Roman regime is one answer, but I sense it is not the only one. I fear I am afflicted with an implacable curiosity."

"I could placate your curiosity by running you through with my sword."

"Ah, but what about your own curiosity? Do you not wish to know by what cunning and skill I appeared in your chamber? Imagine those same attributes turned solely to the task of . . . pleasing you."

"Pleasing me?" She considered the whole of him, a twist of amusement playing about her lips. He took the opportunity to turn his head so she would see his best profile. With a rueful laugh, she shook her head. "Before or after you turn me over to the emperor of Rome?"

He considered this question with the seriousness it deserved. "Before would be a sure thing. After would be determined by his whim."

"I can see you are a strategist," she said, a scrape like swallowed laughter in her tone, which annoyed him. Was she mocking him? "But what if I don't want to be kidnapped and taken to the emperor of Rome?"

"Perhaps you could match his price and thus dissuade me."

"I do not have access to the same sort of funds. Or were you offering a different sort of trade?" Her gaze measured him from top to toe.

"Naturally, you like what you see, and I certainly am formed in all ways to please you, if you like how I am formed. But I fear money is the only coin I trade in."

"Naturally! Anyway, you don't want to make an enemy of the emperor of Rome, not if you are, as I am coming to suspect, some form of hired ruffian, who makes his living doing dirty work so the rich and powerful can keep their hands clean."

"Your peaceable acquiescence will make this all go so much more easily. I'll wait while you gather a cloak and such traveling niceties as you desire." He carefully did not pat the sketchbook, although it rested alongside his left hand. "I have a ship waiting to leave within the hour."

"You do not. Given the tides, no ships will be departing until dawn. So that, my mysterious miscreant, was your first lie."

"My first lie?"

"You've cleverly avoided a second lie, I note. I gave you several opportunities to agree that the emperor wants to kidnap me, and you never quite did. So I think he wants something else, and I know what it is."

Faster than he expected, she snatched the sketchbook from the table, leaped backward, and tapped the point of her sword to his chest.

"You may fight, or you may retire gracefully from the field. I'm not in a mood to hand over my sketchbook."

He leaned away from the point but thereby found himself backed up against the dressing table. This was proving much more exciting than he had hoped. So he crossed his arms and relaxed. Fearlessness in the face of blades always impressed people.

"Why does the emperor of Rome want your sketchbook? What have you drawn that he feels such a desperate need to possess?"

"Ah. That would be telling." She fished a key from her sleeve. "Because I am merciful and you have entertained me, however briefly, you may unlock the door and leave."

When she tossed the key, he allowed it to strike his thigh and fall to the floor with a quiet clunk. She cocked her head with corvid-like grace, a question without words.

"Just one," he said, because he still had to stall for time.

"Just one what?"

"Show me just one page from the sketchbook. If you would be so kind. He told me what treasures it holds and why he wants it."

"No, he didn't tell you. Why do you keep lying?"

"It's a curse." His insouciant smile was one of his greatest gifts, a little higher on one side than the other, so that it promised both pleasure and mischief. "I always lie about something."

"And if your lie is found out? What then?"

"Curses fall in threes. Three lies caught out, or three lies uncaught."

"And then?"

He shrugged.

"How interesting. Two lies caught so far. You'd best be careful."

He was a little disturbed that she probed no further but rather retreated to the bed, just far enough that if he lunged, she could sidestep and attempt to skewer him. She set down the sketchbook and flipped through it. He could see that the first half of the book was filled in, while the latter remained blank, pages as yet unfilled. From this angle, he could not discern what exactly she liked to draw except dense shadows and crisp lines. At one point, she studied a two-page spread, lifted her keen gaze to him, then back down to the page.

"Oh!" She smiled in an assessing way that puzzled him as greatly as it excited his inquisitive nature. "That explains it."

A crow landed on the windowsill and cawed thrice.

"Among the Hellenes, crows are considered divine messengers," she remarked as she slapped shut the sketchbook, slid it into a pouch, and slung it over her back with every appearance of making ready to depart.

Politeness had taken him as far as he could go. He expected her to grab for the key, but instead she flung open the door of the wardrobe, jumped inside, and slammed it shut. With a leap, he grabbed the wardrobe door and tugged. It was like dragging on weighted chains. With a croak of frustration, he yanked with all his strength. The door gave way as if she had let go. He fell back, thumping into the bed, then spun a full circle to unsheathe his sword out of the adamant shadows that wove together the world he was in and the spirit world he came from.

Besides a set of shelves, on which traveling gear was neatly folded and stacked, the wardrobe had a false back, which formed a passage into the adjoining bedchamber. This chamber's door stood wide open. The woman's footsteps slapped as she raced down the passage. He pursued on foot, although the dim light and the low ceiling hampered his speed, and he tripped once on a loose plank.

She halted at the top of the stairwell, just as the sound of clashing weapons broke out in the courtyard below. A voice shouted, "You are all under arrest, by order of the emperor of Rome!"

Her frown fell like a sledge blow upon him. "You led them to us. I do not call that a kindness."

She lunged, driving him back with a series of fierce, tight thrusts that he scarcely had time to turn aside. Just as he got his bearings and turned the force of his greater height and skill against her, he bumped the back of his head on the ceiling. As he flinched, she attacked, and he skipped back to gather himself—and again hit his head on a low beam. She suffered no such vicissitudes, being short and, more importantly, knowing her ground. Her blade flashed, but it was the force behind it that dismayed him, the relentless press he parried—once! Twice! And thrice! —as his head pounded in time to the slap of her feet on the floor.

Then, of course, he tripped on that cursed loose plank.

He went down hard on his backside. Sucking in a sharp breath, he took hold of the threads that stitched him together, making ready to release them. He was bound by the curse to never reveal to any inhabitant of this world what he truly was, and doing so would trap him in this world forever, but to survive a killing blow, he would have to scatter.

Yet no steel pierced him. The Honeyed Voice pelted back to the stairwell. By the time he picked himself up and ran after her, she and the mysterious sketchbook were halfway down the steps.

He plunged after, sure there must be a side gate through which she would escape. Instead, a stunning sight met his startled gaze: despite the disparity in numbers, the imperial soldiers had defensively backed together into an outward-facing circle. They were hampered by a lack of light, for none of the lanterns they carried flickered with even the weakest flame. Only a cold sphere of white light drifted above the head of the particularly handsome man, who stood over to one side, away from the altercation, leaning against a wall with his arms crossed like he was annoyed that his reading had been so rudely interrupted.

Round and around the imperial soldiers, the two feathered ones prowled. Their claws and teeth and height and speed proved a formidable barrier. One of the soldiers made a probing stab, only to have a claw slash the sword right out of his grip. It clattered away onto the pavement. As the soldier leaped boldly forward to retrieve it, the young man Apollo Crow had met at the tavern gate bolted out of the shadows. He melted in a smear and twist of shadow and became a large black saber-toothed cat.

Apollo Crow stared, almost losing control of his selves as a shock of recognition pulsed through him. Here was another creature like himself, a denizen of the spirit world who, like all the inhabitants of the spirit world, had the capacity and necessity to change.

The huge cat roared into the soldier's startled face. The man staggered back to the safety of his soldierly flock, drawing a knife. By now, all were quaking.

The Honeyed Voice marched forward to confront the hapless men. She looked very powerful with her flock all around her.

"Throw down your swords and you may go in peace, my friends. You labor for a power that will happily sacrifice you for its own selfish purposes."

"What strengthens Rome strengthens us all," said one of the soldiers, stoutly.

Her back was to Apollo Crow—and the bag slung there invitingly, gaping open. He crept forward on soft feet. She kept talking, perhaps a little too accustomed to hearing herself speak.

"They who rule give you just enough rope that you feel you can walk freely, while they keep all the advantage to themselves. They pay you a pittance, while they sit on a vast treasury . . ."

He slid the sketchbook out of the bag and took a step back.

". . . They allow you to till the land as long as you pay a tithe to them for the honor."

A flutter of air disturbed his senses, for he was adept at adapting to any slight change in the loft and direction of the winds. The currents of movement suggested something moving alongside him, and yet he saw no one. Not until the seamstress appeared as out of the air itself. Her edged blade pressed across his chest.

"Stop there," she said.

Apollo Crow laughed out of sheer surprise. Her sudden materialization where she had not been before caused the poor soldiers to lose their tenuous hold on courage. As one, they bolted for the street. The feathered ones stood politely aside to let them pass. The big cat chased them to the gate and lashed its tail with vigor.

"What manner of creature are you?" he asked the seamstress.

"I might ask the same of you," she said. "For you are wrapped in many threads, a skein of shadows, but I don't know what it means."

"Those are the threads of a curse, laid on me when I was exiled from my home."

"How interesting!" said the seamstress, looking as delighted as a child settling in for a thrilling tale. "Why were you exiled?"

"I took back something that belonged to me, but it was deemed theft by those with more power than me. So I was cursed into exile on the charge of being a thief."

The Honeyed Voice turned to meet his gaze, her attention as bold and solid as truth. Just for an instant, it seemed that within her eyes, he glimpsed a vast and silent vision of shapes and colors, tumbling like flashes of light and line.

"That is the most honest thing I've heard you say," she began, but broke off as a crow fluttered down to land on his shoulder.

The big cat hissed.

The seamstress vanished, like a thread pulled out of the fabric of the world.

The emperor of Rome and a company of his imperial soldiers marched through the gate, their ranks bristling with spears, swords, and crossbows. The cat retreated, teeth bared. The feathered ones lifted their crests threateningly, while the well-dressed and unfortunately handsome man remained standing quietly in the shadows, easy to overlook.

The Honeyed Voice faced down the emperor with the look of a person sure that her confederates would back her up, that as a flock, they were stronger together than alone.

"As much as this may come as a surprise to you, I confess I did not expect to meet you in Nikaia," she remarked, as if she and the emperor were well acquainted and accustomed to sparring.

"Foment revolution among the Celtic principalities if you must, my dear Beatrice." His avuncular tone made her lips pinch. "The turmoil you and your associates create among the border lords serves me well enough."

"You mean to expand the empire to its old borders. You will start by moving your troops into areas where you think the ruling princes are too weak to resist or will be grateful for imperial protection against radical agitators."

"Do you say that with certainty, or is it a guess?"

"What do you think?"

"I think I do not intend to share my plans with you. When you bring your radical ideas into my empire, then you become my business."

"Is it your intention to arrest me?"

The emperor of Rome looked past her. "Do you have it?"

Apollo Crow tucked the sketchbook under his arm. "Yes."

One luxuriant eyebrow raised, the Honeyed Voice quirked her lips in a silent laugh.

There came a pause, a sort of expectant silence, a drawing in as of breath.

The emperor of Rome suddenly caught sight of the man standing almost hidden against the wall. "Archers! Kill him!"

"Your mistake," uttered the Honeyed Voice.

Crossbows raised, the archers targeted the man—just as the temperature in the courtyard plunged from a summery balm to an eye-stinging freeze. The cold hit like a hammer, slamming the emperor and his troops to the ground.

The magic hit so hard, like an invisible downward slap, that Apollo Crow almost came undone. He held himself together by sheer will, kneeling on the ground as his thoughts swirled. In his time in this world, he had encountered magic rarely; he stayed away from mages, as a wise bird avoids sunning itself on a rock beside snakes: they might not wish to harm him but it was better not to find out.

By the time the emperor and his soldiers picked themselves up from the ground, the Honeyed Voice and her associates had fled into the darkened streets. The soldiers turned toward the gate, then paused, awaiting orders.

"Let me see," said the emperor, extending a hand.

Apollo Crow handed him the sketchbook.

A soldier lit a lamp, and by its light, the emperor flipped through the pages, at first with a self-congratulatory smile, and then with an increasingly furrowed frown.

"This isn't her sketchbook!" he roared. He flung the book so abruptly at Apollo Crow that he didn't have time to dodge. It thumped against his chest and thudded to the ground in a crush of paper.

"Curse it!" shouted the emperor, then, "Go after them! Search the premises. And arrest this useless thief."

Apollo Crow hastily picked up the sketchbook, but since he was immediately surrounded by bristling spears and angry soldiers, who acted as if this was all *his* fault, he had no chance to look at it. The puzzling question of what he had stolen and why it wasn't the right thing nipped at his heels all the long march to Castle Hill and down ill-lit steps to a corridor of prison cells dug into the rock. Rough hands shoved him into a narrow chamber, then slammed shut the door, leaving him alone with the smell of old urine. High up, right against the ceiling, some manner of opening allowed in a breath of salty sea air. It was too dark to see anything, so he groped around until he found a cot. There he sat.

Not long after, light gleamed beneath the cell door, amid the drum of footsteps and the jangle of keys. The door clanged open, and he hastily got to his feet as two soldiers entered, carrying lamps. The emperor appeared.

"You shouldn't promise what you can't deliver," said the great man, without preamble.

Apollo Crow let the book fall open into the glow of the lamplight. A blank page greeted him, and another, and another: all blank.

"She substituted this unused one for the other one."

"They played you." The emperor shook his head, jaw set with anger. "And to think I actually believed you could manage what you promised."

"From your description, I thought there was only the woman involved, a persuasive speaker hiding secrets from you in her journal. I thought she'd be accompanied by a few fellow radicals and malcontents. I didn't realize her comrades would be two feathered ones, a shape changing sabertooth, a woman who can vanish at will, and a powerful mage. Had you warned me, I would have changed my strategy."

"So you say, now you've failed." The emperor walked to the door and, pausing at the threshold, spoke to the guards. "Keep her locked in here until I return."

"*Her*?" said Apollo Crow.

After a generous pause, like an actor deciding whether to give the final flourish to a bow the audience is anticipating, the emperor turned back.

"I have my own spies. You are, in fact, Apollonia Crow, a notorious lady thief and smuggler, whose last known residence was the Illyrian city of Salona." The emperor eyed the fine, glossy-black garments Crow wore, then gave a grimace of disgust. "There is a simple way to reveal the truth about you, but I disdain violent and humiliating methods."

"But you are an emperor. Empires are always violent."

"Empires bring peace and order and justice, so long as an enlightened person rules."

"And that enlightened person is you?"

"This sparring is pointless. What I know is that when it suits your purpose, you use a male disguise, as now."

"In this world, I find my path is better smoothed when people believe I am a man."

"So you admit I have seen through your lie?"

Crow offered a polite bow and tried very hard not to make it mocking, although he wanted to laugh out loud. "I disguised myself as a man when I am really a woman. Allow me to introduce myself properly, Your Excellency. I am Apollonia Crow, espionage agent and recoverer of stolen objects, at your service."

"You are a thief and a swindler. You'll serve a year in Nikaia's prison for your crime."

He stepped out into the passage, followed by the guards.

To his back, Apollo Crow remarked, "Three lies uncaught."

"What?" said the emperor impatiently, over his shoulder.

"The curse forces me to accept any offer of employment made to me and compels me to finish the work to my employer's satisfaction, whatever I may think of the job. But three lies uncaught allow me to walk away from the contract, as long as I tell the truth about the curse to the employer I'm leaving. As I am leaving you now."

"I've heard enough of this farrago. Close the door!"

The cell door slammed shut. Bars dropped into place. Locks clicked. The sound of footsteps receded.

Apollo Crow tossed the blank sketchbook onto the cot and waited a little longer to make sure everyone had gone back to their expected routine. Then, he unstitched the threads that held him together and became a murder of crows, one hundred and thirty-four pair of wings. Each crow fit easily through the barred slits, built to be too narrow to admit a human body.

Most of the flock flew down to the harbor and roosted in the masts until the crack of dawn, as ships began to sail with the tide. Although they circled in their numbers, they saw no sign of the Honeyed Voice or her confederates on any deck, escaping by sea. At length, two of the farthest-flung scouts returned with news of a coach fleeing west on the coastal road. By the time the flock caught up with the coach, the vehicle had crossed out of Roman territory and into the bordering principality of the Arverni, beyond reach of any but the most foolhardy of imperial soldiers.

Crows were perfect scouts. They accompanied the travelers all day without being spotted. At dusk, the coachman and groom put into a well-guarded inn. Soon after, the woman opened the shutters to an upstairs room. She sat down at a small table, opened her sketchbook, and began to draw.

Apollonia Crow took shape in the carriage house and thus avoided the guards at the gate. Climbing the back steps, she knocked on the appropriate door and, when it was opened, stepped inside with a charming smile.

"You!" said the Honeyed Voice.

"You recognize me?"

"You're very striking. What are you doing here? And why, Mr. Crow, have you affected this disguise as a woman? Did you think to confuse me with a fashionable gown and your hair styled in the antique Hellene fashion?"

Apollonia Crow paused to look at her reflection in the dressing table mirror. Her black hair fell in pleasing ringlets past her shoulders, but perhaps her chin was a little too square for this face. What a wonder it always was, to know that a mere change of clothing and outward presentation altered so radically how people responded to you, whether they thought you too manly for beauty or too feminine for handsomeness.

"The emperor discovered my ruse." Apollonia Crow's gaze slid toward the sketchbook.

The woman closed it and sat on it. "Your ruse? What ruse is that?"

"That I disguised myself as a man, when really I am a woman."

She tilted her head to one side, examining him as if to untangle the threads of his being. "No, you aren't."

"I'm not?"

The Honeyed Voice seated herself prettily at the table, opened the sketchbook, and resumed her drawing with a speed and precision that made the images emerge as if by magic, although it was merely skill. Crows and yet more crows flowed out of her pencil and across the page, flocking, roosting, arguing, spying. They were handsome crows, too, not a single ugly caricature among them.

"Do you know, I was once infatuated with the emperor of Rome, before he became emperor. I offered to marry him, even though he is old enough to be my father, and yet he turned me down, even though he wanted my dreaming for his own uses. How strange that he rejected such a facile way to gain my undying loyalty."

"I should think it puzzling he did not choose you as his lifemate when he had the chance."

She pressed a hand against her bosom and fluttered her beguiling eyes. "Do you think so?"

"Yes, of course. You are loquacious and intelligent."

"Why, you flatter me."

"Why would I need to flatter you when you are already so fine a figure, almost as fine as me?"

"Why, indeed!" she said with a laugh. "Alas, for he had scruples and was loathe to take advantage of my infatuation in that particular way. Yet it was a fortunate escape on my part, for otherwise I might be a very different person, with a very different outlook on the world than I have now. Rather than calling for revolution, I would be standing among those trying to stamp it out. An irony, do you not think?"

"What are your dreams to him?"

She set down her pencil. "I can see the future, in a manner of speaking. My dreams give me glimpses of what is to come. Often, I cannot interpret the visions because they appear as details without context. A hat. A flowering branch. A broken tea set. So I draw the visions I see in my dreams in my sketchbook. If their details and context can be properly untangled—which is no simple task—my drawings may be said to predict the future."

"A lion—that would be the emperor—chaining Queen Europa."

"Ha! That was no dream. That was just a metaphorical sketch." She tapped the pencil against the page. "For example, last week I dreamed of crows. One hundred and thirty-four crows. Isn't that an unusual number?"

For once, Crow had no answer.

"Crows are messengers. Of all creatures, they can pass most easily from the spirit world to this world. If a saber-toothed cat can become a man, then why not a flock of crows become a man, or a woman, for that matter? Since a flock contains both male and female crows, why be limited to one or the other?"

Almost, the crows fell apart, so shocked by how casually the Honeyed Voice dropped the truth upon them.

"What brought you across from the spirit world to bide in this world?"

"None of your business." The words came out as more of a harsh caw.

"But you already told us, didn't you? You just thought we wouldn't believe you, that we'd think you were telling a tale. What did you steal?"

"I stole back part of myself," Crow snapped. "Two of my number, stolen by a power greater than mine to serve his needs, as kings and emperors do. That is why I was punished, and exiled to this world, cursed to serve anyone who offered to pay me, as if I am nothing more than a petty mercenary."

"And here you have landed. Are you back to make another attempt on my sketchbook?"

"No. I am no longer obligated to serve the emperor of Rome. Now I have come to make an offer to you."

"To me?"

"You caught me in three lies. Therefore, I must henceforth always tell you the truth."

She frowned consideringly and made no retort.

"You told me earlier that you are low on funds."

"We are not as well funded as we'd like to be, it's true. Revolution is an expensive business. Often, we spend what funds we have on charitable work. Also, we have an exceedingly large household to feed. None of this is a secret. Why do you care?"

"I don't like powerful people who punish me, which means, to start with, that I don't like the emperor of Rome. Crows hold grudges. You can help me."

"How is that?"

"A woman who can catch glimpses of the future, a vanishing seamstress, a saber-toothed cat, two fearsome feathered ones, and an annoyingly handsome mage. I've had the chance to take a good look around the imperial compound in Rome. I know where an extensive treasury is kept. With the right flock, we can steal it."

Dark eyes flashed up to meet Crow's gaze in the mirror. The Honeyed Voice smiled in a gratified and appreciative way that jolted all one hundred and thirty-four crow hearts.

"When do we start?"

A Lesson to You Young Ones

art by C.N. Rowen Shiotsuki

"TｈｅＴ reminds me," said Maester Godwik, "of the story my grandsire used to tell us young ones when I was no older than you rats and clutch-children are now."

The old troll tapped his cane on the ground and, with this aid to manage his weight, settled his arthritic limbs more comfortably on the bench. He sat at the front of the schoolroom. The pupils were mostly human children, but a number of young trolls sat among them in the twos and threes of clutch-siblings. The youth were a restless crowd today. Harsh winter weather had kept everyone indoors for five days, and even using the long corridors of the mage House as raceways could not contain quite so much vitality for so lengthy a period with not a single respite for outdoor play.

"What story is that?" prompted the teacher from where he stood at the back of the room.

"Why, as small and as great a story as how trolls came to walk in this world. In those long-ago days, you see, there were no rats, only trolls of all shapes and sizes, who strode upon Earth and flew over and swam amid its vast territories."

"If there were no rats, then where did humans come from?" asked the teacher.

"Do you rats not have your own explanations on this account?" replied Godwik with a grin that displayed his impressive teeth.

"Of course we do, although some strike me as more fanciful than plausible. I am besides that acquainted with all the most up-to-date theories through my correspondence with various natural philosophers and educators who concern themselves with scientific matters. But I am curious about your own reflections, for you are a personage of venerable age and eminent wisdom, Maester."

"Whatever theories I may have in this regard, they are not part of the story I tell today, for rats came but recently into contact with trolls. As the sages say, 'Share everything, but guard your clutching territory to the death.' So it is with us that in the long-ago days, which our scholars measure as epochs rather than years, a sudden cataclysm shattered the paradise of trolls. This catastrophe caused a great cloud to conceal the sun and kill all the plants. Snow

fell for years instead of months, and all the world became covered in particles of dust and ice. So many creatures died that their bones littered the ground like wheat scythed down at harvest."

By now, the restless children had quieted, eager to hear more about such a violent upheaval. A few glanced warily at the windows, wondering if the weak light of a cloudy day heavy with falling snow presaged a coming doom. In truth, the teacher's resplendently orange-and-green dash jacket brightened the room far more than did the occluded sun. Godwik's vivid blue feathers and black-and-green crest matched the fabric for visual eloquence.

"Within this devastation, this wilderness of fear and hunger, only the smallest could survive."

"So it always appears, that a few do survive, else Earth would be a barren wasteland," remarked the teacher.

"Yes, this we know for certain, even if the specifics of the truth remain in doubt. As Earth made countless revolutions around the sun, the ancestors of our people slowly expanded to fill the territories where once their greater brethren had shaken the very earth in their passing. They were as yet mindless, like the beasts, but the terrors and dangers of the world caused them to grow in cunning."

Godwik paused, puffing up his crest as trolls did when faced with danger, so as to appear as big as possible. The children stirred, murmuring with excitement at this rare demonstration on the part of the famously mild-mannered old lawyer.

The teacher said, with a smile, "What could possibly terrorize a fearsome troll, Maester? For your teeth, your claws, your intelligence, and your rebelliously inquisitive natures are surely a match for any creature on Earth."

"On Earth, indeed, they are. But I speak of the creatures who inhabit what you rats call the spirit world, the world beyond our mortal world, which lies intertwined with our own in ways even the wisest among trolls and rats do not comprehend. The worlds are a maze with many paths, and we but wanderers lost amid its twists and turnings. Now, next there came a time when an Age of Ice settled over Earth. This tremendous cold was the consequence of disordered energies, brought about by a war fought beyond the ken of mortal creatures. Vast ice shelves crept down from the north to cover our homelands. Our ancestors survived in valleys and pockets of land amid the ice. Those you rats call the courts began to seek power by culling energies from among the rats, and those you call the dragons did the same, only among trolls. By eating the bones and energy of our kinds, each side in the spirit world sought to gain advantage over their enemy. As we trolls struggled to save ourselves from the rapacity of our elder cousins, we became caught between the ice and those that hunted us. Thus, our minds grew sharp with need."

"The need not to be eaten is a powerful goad, is it not?"

Maester Godwik's grin grew wider, teeth gleaming. "Let this be a lesson to you young ones," he said, letting his gaze rest on each tender face as they waited in expectant silence for some lurid detail of savagery pitted against pluck. "Sharpen your minds as assiduously as cooks and butchers sharpen their knives. A well-honed mind is the only defense against the predators of sloth and indolence. If you wish to eat instead of being eaten, you will read all of the texts assigned you, complete your grammar and mathematics exercises, and work with eager intensity on the essay questions each class has been given."

Many of the children groaned outright, while others sighed in disappointment or rolled their eyes. Not bothering to hide his smile, the teacher dismissed them and was himself almost immediately called into the corridor to deal with a scuffle in the hallway.

As the last of the children hurried out, eager to get to their midday dinner, one small human child and a pair of troll youth politely approached the old troll.

"Yes, young ones, I see you. Have you something you wish to say?"

The troll clutch-siblings nudged the human child, who stepped from one foot to the other to gather up courage before speaking in a soft voice.

"Wasn't the magister rude to ask so many questions and interrupt so much while you were speaking?"

Godwik's crest flared, feathers rising with amusement. "No, no, child. He was being obedient to the most important rule of storytelling: Among us trolls, no tale is complete without numerous interruptions. Each question is a gateway to a new story, and to a fresh thought."

The three young ones looked at each other, and the young trolls showed a bit of teeth in anticipation while the rat nodded enthusiastically.

"In that case, how *did* trolls and rats first come to meet?"

"Ah, a refreshing question. That reminds me of a story . . ."

Finding the Doctor

or,

The Many Clever Ideas
of Andevai Diarisso Haranwy

art by John Picacio

T HE COLD MAGE WHO WAS MASTER OF FOUR MOONS HOUSE WAS content with his orderly existence. Although by custom and law, Andevai Diarisso Haranwy ruled the mage House, in fact, a council of elders governed the day-to-day workings of the House and its one hundred inhabitants. Tyranny held no interest for him. He preferred the new, radical ideas of suffrage, people casting lots to elect an assembly, which would then act on behalf of all. He had the power to rule as a prince, but if a man was going to be morally and philosophically opposed to the rule of princes, then he could not act as arbitrary master over others, not even in his own home.

Anyway, he had a great deal of work. Setting up a schoolroom and teaching at the new mage House had led him to consider educational reform. He had also a great deal of correspondence in progress with scientists eager to devise theories about the workings of cold magic and fire magic. Of course, he had to continue to hone and comprehend his own phenomenally potent magical skills. Meanwhile, he also worked some hours each day in the household's carpentry workshop to pay the bills.

So it was really the outside of enough when, one evening, as he was writing a complicated letter to a professor overseas, his wife sat on the edge of his desk and poked through his neat piles of correspondence and precisely ordered and sorted stacks of scientific and historical monographs in the manner of a person who pretends they do not wish to interrupt you but, in fact, are bent on doing exactly that.

He attempted to ignore her and keep writing, but she scooted closer. Given that she was dressed only in a linen shift that she had hitched up to reveal the length of her thighs, she had the look of a woman who either was desirous of his presence in their bed or had something urgent she wanted to talk to him about.

With a sigh, he set aside his quill pen. "Catherine, why are you bothering me now when you have had all day to ask me whatever is trembling on the tip of your tongue?"

"It wasn't trembling on the tip of my tongue or, indeed, on the tip of any

part of me until just now," she retorted. "I am excruciatingly worried about my cousin's pregnancy. She is five months gone and yet still has trouble keeping down food, though, meanwhile, she has grown as big as a horse."

Andevai took one of her hands between his own. "I know you are worried, love. It is not every day a woman gets pregnant by a dragon who walks in the shape of a man. How can any of us predict what will come of it?"

Leaning forward, she kissed his brow. The movement made the neckline of her shift gape open, and it occurred to him that he hadn't kissed and fondled her since yesterday. Perhaps his breathing shifted, or he stirred in other places; of course she noticed.

She sat back with a smirk of satisfaction. "Exactly my point. So you will understand why I feel obliged to travel east to find the only doctor I trust to supervise what might be a difficult birth."

He jumped to his feet, the chair squeaking noisily as the movement shoved it back. "You are not walking alone into a war-ravaged countryside where two armies are fighting!"

Her silence had a mulish familiarity. Arguing with her never got him anywhere once she had already made up her mind.

"Because I will go with you," he added. He punctuated the words with a grimace as he contemplated the neglect his correspondence and reading and teaching would suffer.

"I knew you would!"

Rather than endure his papers becoming more disordered than she had already made them, he picked her up and carried her to bed.

Thus it was that, one week later, they set off into the teeth of a late summer's blustery east wind, although at least it was not raining. Not yet. The rain came in their first afternoon on the road and plagued them for the next fifteen days as they traveled from Havery through the Republic of Lutetia and thence south, beyond the prosperous trade city of Liyonum.

A clear day dawned at last. They fetched up midday in a village within sight of the vast ice shelf that covered the Alps. The moment the coach came to a stop, Catherine leaped out and strode up a lane toward the village's hilltop temple, her face turned to the sun. Andevai climbed down and paused to inform the coachman and footman that he did not expect they would stay for long. Shopkeepers emerged from their shops to stare. Villagers about their errands halted to whisper to each other. A pair of brawny men arrived, one with a musket and one with a sword, and eyed him with clear intent to intimidate. A third fellow had spotted Catherine and begun to trail her, at a distance, but Catherine could take care of herself. If anyone was at risk, it was the man following her.

Andevai acknowledged the onlookers with a curt nod and, after straightening his disordered sleeves, walked to the double doors that gave entry to the local inn. Rather than going inside in the normal manner, he halted at the threshold.

The door opened immediately. A stout, gray-haired woman wearing an apron looked him up and down with an appraising gaze. "City fellow, are you? That's a dazzling coat. Shines like sun in my eyes."

The dash jacket he was wearing was one of his more muted garments, its fabric swirling gold stars against a shimmering-green silk, appropriate for travel to the countryside. "I was born and raised in a village not unlike this one, Maestra. In the northwest."

"You don't sound village-born. Mage-born, I reckon." She spoke with the sharp patois of the disputed border country that lay between the Gallic princedoms and the Empire of Rome. The folk here had good reason to be suspicious of strangers. "You're a cold mage," she deduced.

"So I am, Maestra," he said courteously.

"Then I thank you for staying outside and not coming in and putting out all my fires. I just got the evening's fare to cooking. It would have set me back an hour to have to start it all up again."

"I am glad to oblige, Maestra."

"Well-spoken and polite too," she added with the familiarity of an elderly woman accustomed to ordering about ill-mannered youth. "I like that in a young man. So I will offer you a piece of advice."

"My thanks."

"I saw you arrive along the western road. Hard not to notice a coach-and-four, not to mention your unusual coachman and footman. They're an interesting pair, aren't they? Are you perhaps en route to the new mage House? They'll have the conveniences to put you up for the night."

"Which mage House do you speak of?" They had overnighted at the mage House in Liyonum. No one there had informed him of a minor mage House along this route. The Empire of Rome had banned mage Houses from imperial territory, so once they entered the disputed territory, there would be no mage Houses at all. The innkeeper wouldn't be speaking of the mage House in Massilia because they'd turned east off the main road that ran south from Liyonum to the Middle Sea and the port city.

"It lies not far up the road from here, toward the ice," she said. "They've not been there long. They took shelter in an abandoned manor that has tiled baths and a hypocaust from the time of the old Romans. A pair of them have walked in a few times to buy supplies, a sassy lad and a strong-minded lass, who seems to be the one in charge. Their coin is as good as anyone's."

"Of course," he said in the haughty tone he had mastered long ago, which the woman might interpret as him having known about these mages all along. This was curious news, indeed, but he did not want the locals to know how much of a surprise it was for him to hear it.

"They're some of those who had to leave in haste when that monster Camjiata retook the imperial throne," she added, but this, at least, was a situation of which he was perfectly aware.

He did not trust himself to speak on the vexing subject of Camjiata, the man who had tried to claim Catherine as his daughter and thus heir to the imperial throne. So he merely inclined his head to show he had heard and understood. But still, he tensed, waiting for the trap to be sprung.

"I suppose you're headed there," the woman went on, taking his nod as an answer. "I must warn you, there've been skirmishes in the area. The trouble gets closer every day. Why, I sent my younger children and my grandchildren to my kin in Liyonum just last month, to keep them safe."

He realized now why the village seemed so quiet: he'd neither seen nor heard a single child.

"I suppose you've come to take the mages away. It would be best for us all. Maybe the imperial scouts will stop probing into our valley and killing our sheep for their night's meals." She paused, then said, "Rumor says they're all young, you know. The mages there, I mean."

"Are they?" This news alarmed him more than her mention of skirmishes. He'd known he and his party were traveling into war-torn country, at risk of running headlong into an unexpected battle, but they were adults, able to fend for themselves; not to mention that the coachman, footman, and coach-and-four were denizens of the spirit world and therefore impossible for mere mortals to damage. But refugees—children! And mage-born children at that—were another matter. "Just up the road, you say?"

"An hour or two, not more. There's an old oak, the horned oak, we call it. Cernunnos himself is said to rest beneath its boughs on Hallows' Night. A lane turns north. You can see the old pavement still. Folk tend to avoid it because of the oak and its ill associations."

"That would certainly give anyone pause," he agreed with a flash of anger, remembering how the Master of the Wild Hunt had so easily taken him prisoner. But Catherine had followed him into the spirit world, as he had known she would, and they had contrived to rescue themselves. They'd had no choice, then. Now, in truth, traveling into a war zone to find the enemy's most prized field doctor was a fool's errand, reckless beyond belief. Exactly the sort of expedition Catherine would undertake for one she loved the way she loved her cousin Beatrice. She saw it not as reckless, but as necessary as breathing.

He shaded his eyes against the sun and looked toward the temple hill with its Roman-style pillars and roofless shrine. Catherine had become a small figure; she was almost to the top. Of the man who had followed her, he saw no sign.

Seeing his gaze shift that way, the innkeeper gestured toward the hill. "Who might that young maestressa be, she who strides in such haste to our temple? A devotee of Our Lady of Plenty?"

"My wife," he said, unable to resist a proud smile.

She chuckled knowingly. "Still new to the marriage bed, eh? Yet you're not so very young, are you? It's said the mage Houses marry their mages quite young, so as to get more fruit on the vine. How many children do you have? A handsome fellow like you must have quite the flock of darling young ones!"

He could not stop a flicker of frustration tightening his mouth.

"Oh dear. No wonder she wishes to visit Our Lady's temple. Our Rosmerta is a generous patroness, I assure you. Any lass who leaves a suitable offering on the capstone can be sure of becoming pregnant within the year."

Andevai's hands tightened as he choked back a pulse of cold magic. This was a subject he had not broached with Catherine for three months, not since her dear cousin had announced her pregnancy and he had foolishly taken the announcement as a sign to suggest that they might consider starting a family right away too. Catherine had informed him quite plainly that she would let him know when she was ready—and then had immediately departed on one of her secret and dangerous missions to rescue yet another imprisoned unionist or dissident pamphleteer from some authoritarian prince's gaol.

"Ah! A handful, is she?" expostulated the innkeeper in an egregiously confiding fashion. "Young women these days are very stubborn, are they not? It's the fault of all those novels they read, instead of cleaning and cooking and mending and gardening and selling at market, as women ought to do. You should put your foot down, young man! She looks old enough to have birthed two or three children by now! I had, by her age!"

It took all his training in good manners—and the knowledge that his mother would disapprove—not to quench all the fires in the inn, although a flicker of magic did escape him. A person inside yelped out a startled question about the fires dimming and almost going out.

He pulled his magic back inside himself. "Maestressa, we will get on and not trouble you for any longer than we must with our presence. I will gladly pay for a picnic lunch, if you can put such a thing together quickly."

That she could. He haggled relentlessly over the price, as well as the expected amount of food, just as his mother would have done, because he was still irritated. He didn't have Catherine's ability to charm people, and at the moment, he wasn't inclined to try. In the end, the innkeeper handed over a full hamper of bread, cheese, sausage, and several acceptable apple tarts, then made a cool farewell, clearly glad to be rid of rude and unwanted passers-through. Or, at least, of him and his airs and impossibly gaudy jacket, as he heard her mutter under her breath.

He climbed into the coach, and they set off. As he expected, Catherine had spotted them. He caught sight of her descending the hill down a goat's trail, chatting merrily with the very man who had followed her up. Trail and road converged to the east of the village. At the roadside, she bade the local a friendly farewell, complete with a promise to come by the family farmstead, should the occasion arrive on the return trip, for a hearty meal and a taste of the fellow's sister's seasonal ale and the dill-flavored goat's cheese his wife sold at the market. She made sure to open the coach's door and introduce the man to Andevai, with a cheerful, "Yes, this is he."

The local greeted him politely, to which he replied in kind, and then the man said to Catherine, too heartily, "Do not forget the efficacy of leaving an offering of honey and cream at Rosmerta's temple."

She laughed as she swung up into the coach and shut the door behind her. As the vehicle started forward, she regarded Andevai with an arched eyebrow.

"Goodness, Andevai! You're broody and curt. What has set you off?"

He crossed his arms. He was not about to tell her about his vexatious conversation with the innkeeper and her comments about Rosmerta's "full purse," a commonplace euphemism for pregnancy. Nor did he intend to allude to the local man's talk of an offering of honey and cream. No, indeed, he had committed to not mentioning the matter again. Not unless Catherine mentioned it first.

"Don't say you're sorry you came! It's not too late to go back if you wish . . . " She broke off, studying him with a perspicacious eye, and changed tack with her usual deftness. "Although I confess, I am glad you are here."

"Why is that?" he said, aware of how ill-tempered he sounded.

"Why, because of all that I have learned by climbing up to that temple. And from Auberi. He's a font of local knowledge!"

"Auberi?"

"The farmer! He marched in the Arverni militia when he was a youth. Got wounded in the leg, as folk do. Anyway, that's not the point. The point is, there are mage House refugees nearby."

"So I heard." His bad humor sheeted from him. He leaned toward her. "What did you learn?"

"What did I learn? Better to ask, what did I see? These hilltop temples are superb viewing points for scouting, meanwhile folk think you are going up to pray for some godly blessing. I saw smoke! Auberi said there have been many skirmishes two or three leagues from here, but that the vanguard of the Roman army has begun pushing toward Old Goscelin. That's a different village, and a different branch of the valley. It leads south. I'd guess the Roman forces want to cut a path all the way to the sea and besiege Massilia. But I might be wrong. Anyway, this thread of smoke is nearby. The thing is, these refugees are children, and they're stuck out here. We can't just leave them."

"I have been given to understand there's a turnoff by an old oak that will lead us to the abandoned manor where they're staying."

"Excellent!" Now that the decision to search was settled, Catherine turned her attention to the hamper, folding back the lid. "Apple tarts! My favorite!"

For a while, she ate heartily, while he picked at the bread and cheese, never having much of an appetite when he was disrupted from his preferred routine. Once she had satisfied the high edge of her hunger, she described the temple and the offerings laid there.

"Honey and cream are Rosmerta's favored offerings. I couldn't resist taking a taste—"

"Catherine!"

"It's all right. Anyway, Auberi caught me. All he said was that women who seek to get pregnant will come up to the temple and drink the cream that's been left."

A kind of lightning struck through him, a bolt of hope and longing. He barely restrained a gasp, but either she did not notice because she was nibbling on the delicate crust of a second apple tart or she merely pretended not to see his reaction.

She licked the crumbs off her fingers. "I know I have said I am not quite ready to proceed with any new endeavors, but Bee getting closer to her time makes me think of how nice it would be for our eldest child to have little cousins, close in age. In that case, we would need to think about having a child sooner rather than later."

He swallowed, considered several emphatic replies, and then said in a tight voice, "You know my feelings on the matter."

"Yes, you are a village boy through and through, Vai. Quite the traditionalist, despite your flamboyant taste in city clothing and your distinguished and magnificent status as mansa of Four Moons House." She patted him on the knee, laughing soundlessly. But a moment later, she frowned. "I'm sorry for the villagers here, though."

"The villagers?" The abrupt change of subject took him off guard.

"They seem a kindly people."

They hadn't seemed so kindly to him, but Catherine moved through the world in a very different manner than he did, so he said nothing as she went on.

"I would hate for the war to reach them. I suppose that is out of my hands."

He sighed.

She gave him a scathing look. "I am not a diplomat, Vai!"

"Are you not? You seem to have charmed Auberi the farmer."

"I could not end the war, not even if I walked up to Camjiata and told him I had changed my mind and wanted to become his heir. I would hold no real power while he still lives. I'd be nothing more than his puppet. Once he died, I would have to fight all the factions inside the empire to hold on to power no one would want to give me anyway, for they would never accept me. And even if I could do all that, do you think for an instant that is what I have ever desired?"

"To be emperor of Rome? No, I do not."

She nodded. "Exactly so! What I saw from the temple suggests we are already close to the forward edge of the fighting. That means we are close to the imperial field hospitals, which means we are closing in sooner than I expected to finding Doctor Asante."

"If she is in the field at all."

"In the last letter I received from her, she spoke of taking an evening to relax in the baths of Nikaia."

"That was four months ago!"

"Four months is no time at all in a grinding campaign. The fighting has gone on back and forth in these territories for over a year. It intensified this summer because the Illyrian princes signed a peace treaty with Camjiata. That's why he could march more of his forces out of the east and into the west."

He knew the outlines of these political tides, as a mansa must, but he did not follow them closely, not as she did, nor, indeed, as she had to, in service of the undercover work she engaged in throughout the continent. He was mostly insulated from the strife in the center of the continent because the city of Havery, where Four Moons House had resettled, lay a fair way to the west, far from the troubled frontiers between Celtic princedoms and the resurgent empire and thus the ferment that roiled Europa's fractured lands.

The coachman rapped on the closed window between the driver's bench and the interior. Andevai slid it open.

"We have reached the old oak, mansa. It's horn-marked, should you care to investigate more closely."

Horn-marked. Indeed, it was; the massive oak's leafy canopy hung with antlers: ram and cattle horns, drinking horns and shoehorns, all dangling from leather cords and fraying rope as offerings to the Horned God of the Hunt.

Catherine glowered, no doubt thinking of her sire. She sniffed at the air and shook her head. "I don't like it here."

Andevai instructed the coachman hastily, "Let's continue on down the side lane. Catherine saw smoke."

"Indeed," the coachman replied in his phlegmatic way. "There does seem to be a disturbance up ahead."

Andevai sighed. He'd known this moment would come. He'd seen enough of war to last him a lifetime, as the saying went, and he also understood that Catherine was not one to rest while others suffered. He unbuttoned his dash jacket and peeled it off to leave himself in shirtsleeves. Without him asking, Catherine neatly folded the jacket and packed it at the top of the suitcase.

After this was done, she said sternly, "I'll scout. I'm most concerned about rifles among the imperial skirmishers, since generally fire mages are held back to the main line of advance. This would have been easier if I had come alone."

He had been waiting for her to scold him on this very matter, so he merely regarded her with his most aloof expression. "Whether this mission will be made easier or more difficult because of my presence is not yet determined, Catherine. Here I am, and here I shall stay."

"It's never any use arguing with you when you get in this fussy mood, Andevai."

Without waiting for a reply to this ridiculous statement, she clambered out of the coach and up to the roof. Once there, she drew her cold-steel sword. He felt its release from its scabbard as a shiver against the drowsy afternoon. She was in her element, and he knew better than to interfere. His magic was exceptional, of course, but he was astute enough to understand that his skills worked in complement to hers, not in competition.

They were a good team. None better, not that he would ever have said so aloud. No need to boast.

The lane through the woods did indeed prove to be an old paved track, likely built in the time of the first Roman Empire. Probably a rich landowner's villa had been built here, off a secondary road, only to be replaced by a manor house several hundred years later, when the Celtic princes reasserted their rule. The ride over the lane's ragged stonework was smoother than Andevai expected, but that was often the case with a coach that had come over to the mortal world from out of the spirit world.

The tang of smoke tickled his nose. He braced himself, scanning the trees ahead for any sign of movement. Magic came easily to him, but nevertheless, he'd learned to be prepared, to think about his options so he need not dither about which action to take: illusions to confuse and confound; fires to quench; heatless light to call in darkness; strong winds to blow down a blast of ice; or the brute hammer of cold, if it came to that. As well, the great ice sheet that covered the Alps lay so near that he could draw on the weight and presence of its majestic cold.

At length, the coach stopped about two hundred paces from the edge of the woodland. All was quiet. Catherine swung down from above. Andevai got out and walked with her to the edge of the trees. They halted behind the screen of a bush to survey the scene.

The wide clearing had a few scraggly fruit and nut trees and a crudely fenced garden plot, behind which rose a small, decrepit, and partly roofless stone manor. A very old construction, likely a Roman bathhouse, squatted beside it, linked to the manor by a stone portico, so people might walk back and forth under cover of a roof.

On the other side of the bathhouse stood a livestock shed and adjoining stockade. The shed had old stone walls but a recently thatched roof. It was this roof that was on fire, more smoldering than aflame, although one corner was spurting up in occasional fiery bursts. A group of children were running with buckets from the interior of the bathhouse and flinging water up onto the burning thatch. They all looked like adolescents still in the schoolroom, no longer little and yet not quite grown. The eldest was a young woman who shouted instructions at the others. She was slight, dressed in the sort of clothes a mage House girl might wear to a fete, entirely unsuitable for gardening or putting out fires.

The fire was bad enough to do worse damage, even flare up, if it were let to run. Even so, for Andevai, it would be a trifling matter to quench it. He needed only to get a few steps closer. As he moved, meaning to walk around the bush and enter the clearing, Catherine pressed a hand to his arm to halt him.

"There's something tugging at my nose," she murmured. "Let me go first."

She walked straight out into the open, across the clearing, toward the ruins of the shed. A whispery aura, like a shadow, shimmered about her body. Fire mages and the feathered people could see her when she veiled herself, but no one else could. No one except him, of course, but that was only because of the soul-bond forged between them.

As such, the children did not notice her as she eased past them and went inside the burning shed. Andevai waited impatiently, flexing a hand open and closed. The smolder atop the shed's roof was just out of his usual range, unless he used the ice sheet's presence to call down a much larger and far more noticeable pulse of cold magic, of the sort an adept fire mage, as close as several miles away, might feel as a disturbance in their bones. Best not to risk it. They didn't know how close the imperial troops might be.

Their plan was to infiltrate Nikaia without being caught—just another pair of random travelers seeking work—and see what they could learn in the taverns and inns about the location of field hospitals and medical staff on the main front lines. They knew the city reasonably well, having spied there before. The coach would drop them off some miles away. They would walk one of the country paths through the hills and slip into the bustling port with no one—no Roman emperor, anyway—the wiser.

It was a good plan, but he had a strong instinct that the presence of these children meant their plans were about to change.

Seen through the open doorway, a figure moved inside the shed. He tensed, closing his right hand, ready to slam down a pulse of cold magic, discretion be damned. But then Catherine emerged, halting in the doorway, where she could be sure that he could see her. She furled the veil that hid her from normal human sight.

The child nearest her shrieked, terrified by this sudden apparition. The others scrambled back toward the bathhouse while the eldest, covering their retreat, flung her bucket at Catherine. Not a bad choice for a girl in a frightening situation, Andevai reflected. That took some quick thinking. He knew he was trying to distract himself. His feet itched to run out into the clearing, but he had discipline—he prided himself on his discipline—so he waited for Catherine's signal.

It did not come. Instead, Catherine followed the children into the bathhouse. After a long pause, she appeared at the door with the eldest and gestured toward the lane, which ran in a straight line across the clearing, from the front portico of the old manor house and into the woods where Andevai and the coach-and-four waited out of sight. This was not the signal either, so, still, Andevai watched. The young woman shook her head. Catherine spoke again. This time, seeming to have an abrupt change of heart, the young woman gave a gesture of acquiescence and strode briskly along the lane that crossed the clearing.

Andevai did not venture to meet her because Catherine had not yet given him the signal, and he respected both her skill and her exceptional sensory acuity. However, he did venture out from behind the bushes to a shadowed spot on the lane, so he wouldn't seem to be lurking. It was here that the young woman spotted him. She hurried under the trees to greet him, then halted to look him up and down with a fierce grimace.

"You are meant to be the cold mage? You scarcely look the part!" she cried with a sneer of withering disdain. "Can you prove it?"

In another circumstance, he might have felt offended, but the girl trembled as she spoke, and she looked as exhausted as she was defiant. So he raised a hand, palm up, and easily called a globe of cold fire, glossy and bright, casting bizarre shadows beneath the canopy of trees. Then, because he was just a trifle piqued by her comment about his perfectly decent shirt and trousers, both suitable for traveling in disguise—sewn by Catherine herself!—he added a trifling display of his illusory prowess, spinning an icy vision of the shed and Catherine and the ruined manor out of the moisture in the air.

"Oh!" She clapped a hand to her mouth in astonishment, although his efforts were hasty and not as accurate and detailed as he could make them, when he had time to study the landscape properly, with no still-burning thatch fire and distant battle lines to take into account.

He closed his hand to quench the gauzy illusions and, belatedly, his annoyance. The girl didn't deserve his irritation. He glanced toward the bathhouse to see Catherine sheltering in its doorway, waiting for him to do his part in persuading the young people.

"Where are you from? And how are you come here?" he asked in the gentle tone he used when teaching, particularly with children who were struggling with their lessons.

She lifted her chin proudly. "Victory House, in Nikaia. Named after the city, of course. But then . . ." Her expression creased with fear and worry. "Then the Roman army came and arrested all the mages in the house. They took the children too."

"Are you not children, you and the others who are here?" he asked.

"I am nineteen, not a child!" Her bravado collapsed as she bit at her lip in remembered shame. "We are the ones with no magic, so they left us behind. The Roman army, I mean. They only take cold mages and young children, by the emperor's decree."

He wanted to ask why the mages had not fought back or tried to escape, but this was not the time.

She was going on anyway, words pouring out as if she had to speak, or else sob. "Once they were gone, our neighbors drove us out. They said we weren't wanted. Other folk needed to live in our compound. They stole our home from us. Our own neighbors, folk we had greeted every morning, children our own age, who we'd grown up with. The boy I kissed!" She sucked in a tremulous breath, controlling herself. "But what could we do?"

"What did you do?" he asked in his mildest voice.

"We walked," she said hoarsely. She sniffled, trying to swallow the fear she must surely be feeling for her parents, siblings, cousins, relatives, and friends, now lost to her, their fates unknown. And the shame of being left behind because she was without magic and had therefore been deemed useless. No one wanted her, or the ones left behind with her. "No one stopped us. Why would they?"

"You've been very brave," said Andevai. "We have a coach that will take you to Liyonum. There's a mage House there."

"Why would a mage House want us?" the girl asked bitterly. "No one wants us."

"I am Andevai Diarisso Haranwy, the mansa of Four Moons House," he said, noting the flare of surprise in her eyes. Of course she had heard of Four Moons House, one of the most important mage Houses in the world.

She dropped into a curtsy, as a well-trained mage House child certainly ought to do!

"May it please you, mansa, I am Eloysia Sy of Victory House. Although—" Her expression twisted with grief and anxiety. She tried again. "Although maybe it no longer exists, at the emperor's order."

The emperor of Rome was dissolving mage Houses and taking cold mages prisoner! This was crucial news, which not even Catherine's widespread network had heard, or if they had heard it, they'd not yet had a chance to convey the dreadful tidings as far as Havery. The wildfire of war burned fast on windswept flames. But he could only do one thing at a time.

"Maestressa, you and the other children will come to Havery, if it pleases you all. We at Four Moons House have a small academy and a need for more hands—not servants! Skilled people!" he added hastily, seeing doubt crease her expression. "The capable man who manages Four Moons House is a son of Five Mirrors House, who himself has no magic. However, he possesses many useful skills that an establishment with many people depend on for the smooth running of its administration and daily life. Would such a life and similar opportunities suit you and the others?"

"What choice do we have? We are your prisoners now," she said morosely.

"You are free to go," said Andevai with a sigh, for he understood how easily a young person might feel trapped by such an offer. "Yet I wonder how far you will get on foot. Or what provisions you have laid by for the journey. The war may yet overtake you and yours."

"It already has." She wrung her hands, distressed and shaking. "A squad of soldiers took over the shed last night while we hid in the manor. This morning, we heard shouting and shooting. Then it got quiet. Then the fire started. The men inside are dead." These last words died away as she shuddered, thinking of what she'd seen.

"Romans or Celts?" he asked sharply. "How long ago did the skirmish cease? Did the soldiers retreat from this area?"

"I don't know. Not long ago." The pressures and fears of her situation overwhelmed her, and she began to cry.

Alas, Andevai had no time for pity or soothing words. If the skirmish had happened not long ago, then soldiers of one or both factions most likely still skulked nearby in the woodland.

"We must get all you children out of here at once," Andevai said in his schoolmaster's voice, the one he used when he needed fractious children to line up and march to class without incident. "Come along. We'll go together and fetch everyone."

The girl wiped her eyes, sniffling back the tears, and straightened up obediently, as he'd known she would. She was mage House-raised, after all. To his surprise, she said, a bit tartly, "The Maestra said to tell you not to go out into the clearing. She knew you would want to do so."

Of course Catherine had said as much! Her caution annoyed him, but he had been shot before and preferred not to get shot again. That was the problem with the new rifles, as opposed to the old muskets. Rifles fired beyond the range with which his cold magic could kill their ignition.

Reacting to his expression, she added hastily, "I told the Maestra I would come first, to see if you were really a cold mage."

"I hope you were reassured," he said drily.

Eloysia offered an apologetic curtsy. "Mansa, I will go back and fetch the others and the Maestra. I'll bring them right to you."

She ran back along the lane, straight through the clearing, although a concealed rifleman might as easily have shot her as Andevai. Meanwhile, Catherine had clambered up onto the bathhouse's roof, scanning for trouble amid the trees and through the remaining smoke. Eloysia did not see her up there because Catherine had again veiled herself in shadow. She had also, evidently, made the decision to let the shed continue to burn. It was a good way to cover the children's retreat if the enemy thought everyone in the old manor was dead.

The girl hurried into the bathhouse in haste.

Not long after, the others emerged one by one. Besides Eloysia, there were six more, three boys and three girls, each carrying a bag. Andevai studied them as they hurried along the lane, with Eloysia shepherding them like so many lost sheep. Their clothes were fashionable if very rumpled, having not seen a press for weeks. Their cloth bags and suitcases were of a kind that well-to-do people carry when they set out on a journey they expect will entail comfort. Their faces and hair were as tidy as washing in that ruin of an old bathhouse could make them. Eloysia chivvied them along as if she were their captain, and without question, she had become so to them. A smart, determined, and decisive girl. Four Moons House could use such a doughty youth, he thought, suddenly pleased not just because they had a chance to save abandoned children but because he liked to think of ways the world could be shaped into a better place. What was the use of having any form of power, if not to use it to change what needed to be changed in order to create a world molded more to justice and mercy and less to greed and rapacity?

The children stared at him at first, but they marched in a disciplined line when he led them the three hundred paces to where the coach waited. To them, the equipage would look like an ordinary coach-and-four with a plain, black vehicle, stolid horses, a stocky, pale coachman, and a tall, dark footman with sparkling eyes and no trace of shadowy wings.

Andevai surveyed the children, addressing them sternly. "You will be conveyed to Liyonum. It's very important that, once you are there, you explain everything that happened to you in Victory House, so the other mage Houses will know we are all are under threat of imprisonment and worse should Rome press farther into these lands."

Being given an important task heartened them. The six youths crammed into the interior, while Eloysia demanded the right to sit beside the driver.

Andevai grabbed the suitcase Catherine had packed, as well as his tool case and Catherine's sewing bag. He considered the picnic hamper, and left it with the children.

"You are remaining here?" asked the coachman.

"I am. Take them to Liyonum. They shall bide at the mage House until the Maestra and I return. Then we shall go all together to Havery."

"So shall it be done," said the footman.

The children are in safe hands, he thought as the coach drove off down the shadowed lane. The coach and coachman had their own defenses, while the footman, an eru of the spirit world, possessed more magic than even Andevai himself did.

He waited until the vehicle vanished from both his sight and his hearing. Then, without turning, he said, "I thought of saving the hamper for you, Catherine."

"I should hope you gave it to those poor, bedraggled children! Though I ate most of it already."

While he was assisting the children, she had come up the lane, swathed in the veil that was part of her magical inheritance from her uncanny sire. He always knew where she was, her presence a constant pressure on his heart.

Now, she gazed after the coach, still frowning. "I wish you had gone with them."

He was not inclined to argue or to justify himself, so he said nothing.

She grinned in that charming way she had of laughing at him and his prickly pride. "Well, I suppose a powerful cold mage like you might yet prove useful to me."

"I daresay I might! Who were the dead? How many?"

"Three soldiers wearing the badge of one of the Arverni princes. A thistle. Do you know which that is?"

There were so many that even he—with his capacious knowledge of the various principalities and mage Houses and assemblies of western Europe—could not recall which prince it might be. "I do not."

"There are so many hereabouts that I cannot keep them apart. But anyway, what it means for us is there is likely a Roman scouting party wandering about. I do worry about rifles, mostly because—"

"Yes, we both prefer I not get shot," he agreed, feeling a tendentious urge to lecture her about how he worried every time she hared off on one of her many secret rescue operations. She might be able to sneak about unseen, but she was still mortal, even if her sire was not. But he refrained from saying all that lay in his heart. After all, he had not fallen in love with a woman just to mold her into some perceived ideal. He had fallen in love with the person she was. He would no more wish, nor attempt, to change her than he would wish, or attempt, to change the rise and fall of the tides, the phases of the moon, the rounding of the seasons, or any other natural phenomenon.

Catherine remained still for a while, head cocked to one side, listening with her ears and her other senses. Finally, she rose, hefting her sewing bag. "No one I can sense in the immediate vicinity. Whoever killed those Arverni soldiers isn't close by. Gracious Melqart smiles upon us, for it is a pleasant day for a walk, given that we shall now have rather more days to reach Nikaia than we expected," she added cheerfully. "I'm hungry!"

He hoisted the suitcase with its change of clothes and the suitcase-like toolbox that contained a selection of his second-best carpentry tools; his "disguise" for the trip was that of a down-on-his-luck carpenter seeking employment. They set out down the lane and toward the main road.

For some time, they strode amiably side by side, well matched. It was indeed a pleasant day, not too hot, not too sunny, not cold, and not raining either. Andevai had a great deal of work to do back home, certainly, but he could not help but relish this unexpected solitude with his beloved wife, for it made him think of what might come, and of the things Catherine had said earlier in the day.

He cleared his throat, trying to decide whether or not to broach the subject.

"Fiery Shemesh, Andevai! Just come out with it!"

She knew him too well. "I was thinking about what you said about cousins."

"Ah! Were you?" She slid him an amorous look, although she did not break stride. "I suppose in such a fine weather, we might make a cozy little nest for ourselves at nightfall, out among the trees. We could make a try of it."

"Catherine!" Her name was all he could say, too overwhelmed by the hope that she and he might, at last, as he had long hoped, begin a family of their own.

But before anything more could come of this promising conversation, her gait shifted, growing tense. She raised a hand in warning, although, still, she did not halt. They ventured forward cautiously and, by good fortune, found a spot where the lane wasn't visible, but from which they could see onto the main road.

Along the verge of the road, right where it met the end of the lane, a con-tubernium of soldiers had gathered in the shade to drink from their canteens and chew on bread. The bland-gray fabric, stiff collars, and narrow lapels of their direly unfashionable jackets immediately identified them as Roman in-fantry. Celtic and mage House soldiers, as a rule, dressed with more flair and an eye for bright colors and practical but elegant fit. Andevai glanced down at his well-made but not-at-all flamboyant shirt, for once glad he wasn't wearing an expensively fashionable dash jacket.

"I have an idea," he whispered.

"Do you?" she murmured archly, never more jauntily reckless than when there was danger in which to plunge. "Shall I like it?"

Unfortunately, once he explained the plan, she found the idea delightful, which meant it was a tremendously bad idea. He saw few alternatives, how-ever, since she would not give up until they found Doctor Asante for the sake of her beloved cousin. To do that, they needed to get through the skirmishing zone without being poached like deer in the woods. And this was a way that might allow them to do it with the least risk.

"Oh, I know what will make it even better," she said enthusiastically. She pulled his dash jacket—the very one!—from the suitcase, rolled it up, and stuffed it under her skirt and jacket to make herself look as if she were in the middle months of pregnancy. No getting the jacket back now. "Now they'll never doubt this ridiculous story."

"Perhaps a different plan . . ." he remarked, but she only grinned.

They made their way roundabout, down to the road, keeping out of the sight of the soldiers. Then, swinging her sewing bag, Catherine trod merrily out in front, singing a maudlin song in the southern patois about a girl who didn't know how to plant cabbage and thus was doomed to marry an old lecher. She had a clear voice, easily heard when she wanted it to be heard. Therefore, he—trailing behind her, carrying the suitcase and the toolbox—was not surprised to find the soldiers gathered around her, with laughter and smart remarks, as she stood at their center, doing what she did best: telling them an absurd story, so well woven that they all believed it.

She wore her usual traveling clothes, practical garb in dark, practical col-ors, jacket and walking skirt so well made that a person who didn't under-stand garments wouldn't realize that the fabric was of the highest quality and the tailoring fit to her slim figure was superb. Which was why his dash jacket, cleverly molded beneath, made her look pregnant, but not so pregnant that she should be lumbering.

She was chattering away as he trudged into view, pretending to be more tired than he was, given that he was, in truth, aflame with adrenaline, expecting the worst and ready to unleash magic.

As the soldiers spotted him with a flare of alarm, she exclaimed, "And so, rather than marry that vile old lecher—as wrinkled and stinky as a head of cabbage, I assure you—I decamped in the middle of the night with this carpenter. It isn't his fault he's down on his luck, surely! That's what he told me! He's just seeking employment!"

There came a silence as the soldiers stared at him. They were the usual Roman fellows, skilled enough to be scouts and mindless enough to be enamored of their new emperor, the fabled Camjiata, who was determined to restore Rome to its ancient glory.

Thankfully, the skilled but mindless soldiers laughed.

"A likely story," said the middle-aged decanus, looking Andevai up and down with a snort. "But, lass, who am I to tell you not to fall in love with a handsome face, when the man your elders told you to marry is an old fart like me! Still, might you kindly open that tool case, Maester? So I can take a look and make sure you're not smuggling pistols."

It was phrased as a question, but it was a command. Andevai set down the suitcase and opened the tool case, displaying handsaw, hammer, plane, chisels, files, braces and bits, and a framing square, all neatly secured.

"We could do with some carpentry back at camp," observed one of the soldiers.

"You could do with some mending too," added Catherine enthusiastically, "for half of you have torn sleeves and hems, and the other half missing buttons and ripped pockets. I'm surprised you haven't done it yourselves, as soldiers usually do. But never mind! For I'm a great dab at mending. It would be a relief to get an escort to Nikaia. That's where we're bound. I have a cousin there. I'm sure she'll take us in."

"You're a hopeful lass. Does the fellow speak for himself?"

Catherine smiled in a way that made half the men blush and the other half chortle. She rested a hand on the rounded lump made by the clothing stuffed under her jacket and walking skirt. "I daresay he does, when he chooses to, but in general, he's a taciturn fellow."

In the village where Andevai had grown up, they'd spoken a rustic melange of Mande and Celtic. He laid it on thickly now, as a performer might. "I did leave my yon birth village, back in the west, for to make my fortune in richer lands."

"That's some good boots and shirtsleeves for a poor village carpenter," said the decanus.

Catherine broke in. "I sewed the shirt myself, but I am sorry to say, I confess I stole the boots from the old lecher, for he didn't need a third pair, did he? And my dear Tacitus had no shoes at all!"

"You steal that sword too?" asked the meanest looking of the soldiers. "Do you even know how to use it?"

Her aspect took on the darkening threat of an incoming storm. She met the soldier's gaze squarely, and in her softest voice, she said, "Do you want to find out?"

The man looked away first, and not one of the other soldiers mocked him for it. Catherine had a way about her that made men warm to her, but now that she'd dropped that charm, the soldiers kept a pace back, for they could sense she was a predator even more than they were.

As for himself, Andevai was perfectly happy to stand and wait for the business to be concluded so they could approach the Roman battle line with less trouble and find the doctor as soon as possible, so they could go home as soon as possible, at which point, his thoughts stuck: A child! She wants a child! At last!

A shot rang out.

A hard shove on his left shoulder sent Andevai stumbling backward. He dropped the tool case, heard its clatter as it hit the ground, then tripped over the suitcase, which had somehow tangled in his legs. Next thing he knew, he was sprawled on his back on the ground, staring up at the cloudy sky. So he stayed for a long, breathless moment.

"Vai! Breathe!" Catherine's face loomed over him, her eyes wide, her expression wild.

"I'm fine," he said. "I just fell."

He pressed his left arm into the ground to brace himself as he pushed up. A hard, hot pain coursed through his left shoulder. When he looked down, he was surprised to see a red stain, just below his collarbone. He could feel it was wet as it seeped through the fabric.

Catherine gasped. "No, you aren't! You're hit!"

All around them, the soldiers had dropped, some to their knees, rifles raised back toward the forest, while others lunged back into the cover of the trees.

Only the decanus remained standing, surveying the woodland. "That was one of our rifles," the man said, then canted his voice to a shout that carried into the trees. "Why are you fools shooting at your own people?!"

An unintelligible shout rose in answer, followed by a whistled signal that made all the soldiers spring to attention.

Catherine snapped in such a rage of anger that every man there flinched, "Is there linen to press on this wound? A medic among you?"

Everything around Andevai had a clarity heightened by the pain, which he felt and yet did not feel, as if his shoulder were no longer part of him. His body felt cold, and he began shivering.

"Here, lass," said the decanus, crouching beside him. He cut at the shirt's fabric and peeled it back, his grizzled face as stern as that of a schoolmaster who has finally had enough of hearing wrong answers for the day. Which was an odd thought to have, Andevai supposed, and yet, for some reason, he found himself going over and over in his head the recent correspondence he'd been having with several mansas about the possibility of reform in mage House curricula, and whether mage House academies ought to open their doors to the local children, so as to expand the reach of education among all people, as well as connect themselves to their local communities rather than hold themselves apart in the traditional way of mage Houses . . .

"He'll need a surgeon to get that bullet out, and we can't leave it to fester there," said the decanus. "I'll wrap it up for now."

Catherine clutched Andevai's hand. "Speak to me!"

"I'm a taciturn fellow, you said so yourself," he remarked at random, then blinked as a fresh spasm of pain flooded through him. He gritted his teeth as the decanus deftly wrapped a field dressing around his shoulder, pressing hard enough that it really hurt. He broke out in a sweat, then felt clammy and unwell. A crackling noise throbbed in his ears—only the noise did not come from his body.

A squad of Roman soldiers came crashing through the underbrush, just now appearing as they sprinted onto the road.

"I got him!" exclaimed one of the riflemen, tipping back his shako with a cocky smile.

A pulse of strange, airy heat washed against Andevai's shield of cold magic. A young woman wearing an officer's uniform strode up, hands clenched, and planted herself in front of Andevai's felled body. If he hadn't felt her magic before, he recognized it now as a barely controlled fire, burning a hand's breadth from his already sweating face. She hadn't a particularly strong aura of magic, but she had an iron control over the intangible flames that lived inside her and could so easily kill her.

The fire mage's eyes shone with an uncanny gleam as she turned to the decanus and said, triumphantly, "He's a cold mage. The ice pours off him in waves, though I suppose you can't sense it. Good shooting, Drusus," she added, with a nod at the sharpshooter.

Catherine let go of Andevai's hand. She rose like the unfolding of a terrible weapon, setting a hand on her sword. Her lips curled back in a snarl.

The fire mage did not even look at her, oblivious to the threat as, instead, she looked around herself at the other soldiers. "There will be a rich reward for bringing him in alive. But if he gives any trouble, kill them both."

The pain was hot and fierce. But Andevai had discipline enough to breathe with it and enough presence of mind to see outside it. His instincts flared as he saw Catherine ready herself to strike. She was going to kill the fire mage. He knew it. No one there could stop her.

No one there but him.

And, anyway, he conceived in that instant of another very bad idea, desperate, reckless, and steeped in a sudden determination to get what he wanted. Catherine would probably approve of this idea too. Because he really wanted a family, his and Catherine's family, two boys and two girls at the very least, surely that was not too much to ask— although he would never demand it of her, but rather ask if it was what she, too, desired. At this point, fighting past the pain that his entire body curled around, the only thing he could think was that it all depended on finding the doctor.

So he grabbed for his power; he grabbed for the amplification the nearby ice sheet granted him. He reached—and he hammered the full force of his cold magic down upon the area in which they all stood. Every person there, even Catherine, was slammed onto the ground as if by the great, invisible hand of his astounding magical potency.

The effort shocked through his system. Fresh blood gushed from the bullet wound as his body tensed with the pressure of all that magic wielded, pulled from the spirit world and through his own flesh to manifest in the mortal world.

He grunted . . . then fell back helplessly, half-swooning.

Catherine leaped up first, kneeling over him with her sword drawn, daring the others to try to harm him.

A murmur was all he could muster. To speak took an effort as vast as the ice shelf itself. He whispered, "A cold mage is a great prize. A battle-wounded cold mage surely must be seen by only the best of the emperor's field doctors. This is our path in."

Catherine looked down at him, her aspect as sharp as an unsheathed blade, her anger as thick as a blizzard of knives. Her lips pinched together, and her shoulders heaved with emotion. "Blessed Tanit, protect us from your clever ideas."

But she set down her sword and turned her face to the others. "Now you know why we had to flee. He's a fugitive from his mage House. I'm just a poor seamstress with nowhere to go but my cousin's inn in Nikaia."

"What inn might that be, for you did not mention it before?" the decanus said suspiciously.

"It doesn't matter!" the fire mage broke in. She was in charge now, that was clear. "Will the cold mage live? I need the prize."

Catherine tensed as if ready to spring. Hastily, to get her attention, Andevai coughed, which was a mistake. A new stab of pulsing agony coursed through his shoulder. He had to shut his eyes to stop from spinning away into the darkness. A trickle of sweat, or blood, oozed along the curve of his neck. His hands were growing cold again, but not due to his magic.

"If we get him to a field hospital, I daresay he might live," said the decanus, although Andevai heard his voice as from away down a long distance.

"Your best field hospital! Your best doctor! Your senior doctor!" Catherine cried, and she meant it, she was genuinely distraught and enraged and terrified for him, but she was also an experienced operative and adventurer. She knew how to take advantage of even the worst disasters. He would have smiled, loving all that she was, unflappable in even the most distressing situations, but he didn't have the strength.

"Let's get moving!" commanded the fire mage. "Before those cursed Arverni come back."

The decanus barked to his men, "Get a litter put together. Double-time."

Catherine stayed crouching beside Andevai, ready to fight off the entire contubernium should the soldiers turn against the two of them, but no one approached until the litter was prepared. In the end, the jostling as they shifted him none-too-tenderly onto the stretcher was too much, even for his steely will. A cascade of pain, like an avalanche of ice, swallowed him up, and he lost consciousness.

Dizzily, Andevai woke. The sky swayed above him, torn by clouds. A jolt thumped his wounded shoulder against one of the stretcher's wooden poles. Pain engulfed his consciousness.

Why was there so much pain?

Dizzily, Andevai woke. The sky swayed above him, overcast by clouds. Drops of rain spattered on his cheeks and forehead. Catherine's dear face loomed above him. She wore her most thunderous frown.

"Are you awake?" she demanded angrily.

No, it wasn't anger. She was frightened. Catherine was never frightened, not of anything. Her sire was the Master of the Wild Hunt, he who rode as death through the world, every year on Hallows' Night. What had she to be frightened of, knit through as she was by blood both of the mortal world and the spirit world?

He tried to speak, but nothing came out. Maybe he wasn't awake. Maybe it would be easier to slide back into the darkness.

Why did it hurt so much?

*

Voices he did not recognize wove around his head. Stars wavered in and out of view up above.

"Is he feverish?"

"No, he's ice-cold."

"Why is he doing so poorly?"

"The bullet is lodged deep, Lieutenant. The likes of me can't fetch it out without making it worse."

"By the Blessed Fire, decanus, make sure he lives, or I'll see you stricken down the ranks."

"What matters it to you, Lieutenant? All this for the prize money?"

"Not the money, you fool. The status. Bringing him in alive will give me prestige within the ranks of the fire legion. This is a very powerful cold mage, as you would know if you knew anything." The fire mage scoffed and tramped off.

"I've more of that brew," said the decanus, in a kinder voice, speaking over his head. "It will keep him drowsy. That'll be for the best, until we reach the field hospital."

"My thanks," said Catherine. "I won't forget how you have aided him. Here, let me have the cup. I'll do it."

Andevai blinked, surprised, as his head was lifted by comforting hands and a cup set gently to his lips. He was so thirsty, and he sipped as well as he could, trying not to cough because coughing would explode the constant, throbbing ache in his shoulder into fresh pain. An overly sweet liquid eased down his parched throat, cloying and harsh. After some sips, the cup was taken away, and the dressing was peeled back. A damp, warm cloth, smelling of honey and sage, probed at the shoulder.

"He's lost a lot of blood," remarked the decanus, his salt-and-pepper hair and sun-weathered features fading in and out near Catherine's face as the old soldier watched her tend the wound.

Only it was Andevai fading in . . . and fading out.

He was jarred awake by a babble of voices and the bustle of movement swirling around him. After a few minutes of confusion, he realized he was being conveyed through a camp on a rolling cart pulled by a horse. Campaign tents rose on either side, in the fashion of a town set out along neat lanes and precise squares.

"No, not that tent, this one here," barked an authoritative voice, spoken by a man Andevai could not see because his shoulders and his head had been tied to the canvas stretcher to keep them fixed in one place; it made for less jostling as the cart bumped along. He could see the cloudy sky above, the sloped tops of canvas tents, and people moving up alongside the cart and then out of view. Also, the tip of his nose, somewhat blurred. He had a headache. His mouth was dry, tasting of bile, and there was a blanket over him, even though he wasn't cold. Or was he cold? Where was he?

He tracked back, grabbing at the flashes of smeary memory. The temple to Rosmerta. The children. The road. The too brief joy of their discussion! The Roman soldiers. A hazy journey, blurring in and out. From what he could gather by what he saw around him, they had reached an encampment of the Roman army.

But where was Catherine?

He shut his eyes to eliminate the distracting visual movements. He sank past the clamor. And—there! Her presence shimmered, close by, not next to him but somewhat ahead, as if she were scouting out the path. Muzzy and hurting, he hoped he wasn't going to die from this ridiculous calamity. Shot in the shoulder by a rifleman! And not just shot—shot again. He'd been careless. He'd succumbed to his weakness of overconfidence. Hubris, as the Hellenes would say. He'd been mansa of Four Moons House just long enough that perhaps he had begun to consider himself invulnerable. For good reason, on many counts, of course! It wasn't braggadocio to call himself the strongest cold mage of his generation. Truth wasn't boasting. But truth, and cold magic, was not impervious to bullets.

War was not his purview. Rome's enemies, which included many mage Houses, had used his magic and the magic of other cold mages to battle Camjiata's army in the great conflagration that had roared out of Iberia a few years ago. He'd done his part, but he hadn't relished it. He was a carpenter by training. Building was what he wanted to do, not tearing things apart . . . or, at least, not tearing them down unless he had the means to build out of the wreckage something stronger and better suited to sheltering a decent life for people.

The cart halted with jerk. Orderlies untied the ropes securing him and lifted the stretcher off the back of the cart. A shadow poured over him as they conveyed him into the interior of a tent and, more gently than he expected, shifted him onto a table. He panted softly as his body spasmed. The latest batch of sedating brew was beginning to wear off. Its slimy taste coated his tongue. The throb in his shoulder felt like an old companion kneading claw-sharpened hands into the meat of his body.

Outside, the fire mage's shrill voice raised yet again as she argued with another hapless victim; he had no idea who, nor did he care.

A petite young woman appeared at his bedside. She was dainty, almost doll-like in feature, if you overlooked the blood-splashed apron she wore over a drab, brown jacket and the cool, collected manner in which she assayed her new patient.

Catherine slid into view. "Who are you?" she demanded with unusual curtness. "I was told we were being brought to the senior surgeon, the best field doctor."

The woman turned her gaze calmly on Catherine. "I am she," she said without pride or hesitation. "You may address me as Doctor Ba, senior field surgeon. Who are you?"

"I thought we were being taken to Doctor Asante!"

"General Asante? She no longer operates in the front-line hospitals."

"Where is she?"

"You ask a lot of questions, yet have not answered mine. Move aside. This man needs immediate treatment if he is to survive. Can you not see that?"

"I can see nothing else!" expostulated his beloved wife, catching back a sob. "And it is all my fault."

"Very affecting, I am sure, and I can save him, if you will but move aside," continued the doctor with an impatient burst. "And, of course, if the gods will it, but I would put more confidence in my skill than their benevolence. Now. I need to get that bullet out. Do you intend to impede my operation?"

"No." Catherine bent to kiss Andevai's cheek with a soft brush of her lips. Still close, she glared at him fiercely. "Stay alive. Do you hear me?"

"I would dare do nothing different, if it displeased you," he whispered.

"I doubt that!" She roughly wiped the tears from her cheeks, then squeezed his right hand. "I'll find her," she promised, after which she moved away, out of his sight.

A crisp, martial voice spoke loudly from the door. "Maestra, you are not allowed to leave this tent. You and the cold mage are prisoners."

"Oh dear, I'm sorry to cause any trouble, Centurion." Her tone altered to honey. "I was just looking for a place to relieve myself. I would be much obliged."

"An orderly will bring a pot and a screen."

"Might I also have a cot, for I haven't slept a wink for days, I swear it. Perhaps a bite of food and something to drink? I'm famished."

A mumbled reply, words he didn't catch.

"My thanks!" Her bright answer did not fool Andevai, but he had no time for further observations as Doctor Ba's orderlies and assistants crowded around, bearing various trays and implements and a strong smell he could not identify, but from which his entire being recoiled.

Yet he had no strength to resist as they squeezed bitter drops between his parted lips. The surgeon and her team spoke to each other, right over his head, in a brisk conversation that might as well have been a continued discussion from the previous evening's supper conversation as they cut away his shirt and began to soak the area with moistened sponges. A stark, stinging pain flooded his shoulder.

Fortunately, he passed out.

Andevai roused with a cough, choking. Someone helped him roll onto his uninjured side and vomit into a basin, then cleaned his mouth and chin. Confused by the pain and the darkness, he said, "What happened?"

He could not see anything in the dark, but he knew intimately the feel of Catherine's hands as she clasped his in hers.

Her sweet voice was a merciful comfort as she murmured into his ear, "You were shot, Andevai. Doctor Ba got the bullet out. She sewed you up almost as neatly as I would have."

"Catherine," he said, all the world in that one word. It was enough.

He slept.

Woke, startled, to the pressure of a queasy stomach but nothing left to expel. Catherine washed his face and hands with a cloth while murmuring endearments that calmed him.

He slept.

He woke, and she coaxed a few sips of water down him.

He slept.

When next he woke, seams of light showed through the gaps in the tent's fabric and made of the canvas ceiling a pale sky. Catherine lay asleep on the cot. In her stead, an orderly sat watch over him, gave him a bitter potion to drink, studied his eyes, wrote a note on a slip of paper, and sent it off. This time, Andevai stayed awake for a while, watching her sleep, until Doctor Ba arrived. Catherine came awake like the report of a gun and leaped to her feet.

"Well?" Catherine demanded of the doctor.

"Stand aside! I need to examine him." Doctor Ba's tone was brusque.

Catherine's lips pressed together as her expression darkened. She did not tolerate being spoken to that way. His beloved was many things—fine things, splendid things—but her anger was a deadly weapon once loosed.

He coughed, all the noise he could manage. Catherine's gaze flashed to him as he gave a twitch of his chin and a flicker of his lips that, thank the All, she understood. She stepped back to allow the doctor to step forward.

The doctor looked in his eyes, opened his mouth, pressed fingers along his neck and, more gently, down to around the wound, probed his abdomen, and palpitated his calves and ankles.

"Nothing putrid," she announced to the waiting centurion. "I'll return in the afternoon."

He slept. He woke as it was getting dark, when the doctor returned.

She performed the same examination. "I'm satisfied," she announced to the centurion. Then she turned to her assistants, who trailed her like dogs eager for scraps. "We'll look in again in the morning, but I believe he will recover. He's doing better than I would have expected, given the condition he arrived in. I wonder how much that has to do with his cold magic . . ."

He lost track of her voice as she and the others left the tent. Catherine bathed him with a cool cloth, informing him in her tenderest voice that he was doing very well, all things considered, and that he was required to keep doing well. For the first time, he felt enough peace from the pain to realize his mouth felt crusted.

"Might I get more to drink?" he asked hoarsely.

The request made her smile brightly. He drank more than he had before, then rested in silence for a bit, relishing the touch of her hand on his cheek. Pain lay in a constant pressure within his shoulder, but something had shifted within him, maybe just the bullet having been removed from wherever it had been grinding away against bone. After a while, again, he slept.

And woke to find Catherine beside him. It was night. A single lamp burned by the tent entrance, illuminating the orderly, still seated on a chair, his head bobbing as he dozed off.

Catherine bent to whisper in Andevai's ear. "Can you bide here alone for a day or two? I got a lead on where Doctor Asante is, not far, a day's walk each way. I'm going to find her, if that's all right with you. But I don't want to leave you if you'd rather me stay here and nurse you for a bit."

Hoarsely, he said, "We haven't much time. They'll get a command to take me to the emperor with five fire mages in attendance. Even I may not be strong enough to stop them . . ." He coughed again, but the urge subsided. "We need an escape plan. Go."

She kissed him again. "Whatever you do, convince the surgeon you can't be moved."

Thus, it happened that at dawn, the guards were shocked to discover that the young woman had slipped out during the night, a dereliction of duty for which they were all stricken down a rank for carelessness.

Doctor Ba arrived soon after. She said merely, "I took her for a fickle one. Jumpy and demanding, all show and no loyalty. Now, let me examine the patient."

She removed the bandage and examined her handiwork with an approving nod. Like him, she had a high regard for her own skills. And why not, if it were true?

"You are a fortunate man," she went on. "In my experience, cold mages are less likely to develop an infestation in the flesh, gangrene and such. Something about cold magic protects its wielder. I believe it could be that the flesh is less prone to heating excitedly. The change of temperature often, in my experience, leads to a tendency to develop gangrene. We have laid in buckets of ice to keep the temperature in here as cool as possible, but not too cold, in the hope of giving your body what it needs to heal itself from here on out. You shall be weaned of the opium by stages. Now tell me, why did your faithless companion ask about General Asante?"

"Who?" he asked, distracted by the abrupt change from the firm tone of her lecture.

She said, a bit louder, "General Asante. The head of the field hospital division in the empire."

He did not think he was sharp enough, so drugged as he was, to answer in a clever way, so he asked himself: What would Catherine do? She would misdirect.

"What did you say about gangrene?" he ventured. As he had hoped, she repeated her lecture, only to veer off, enthusiastically launching into a detailed explanation of field medicine, the trials and experiments by which she and General Asante, and later just she herself, had observed what methods worked best, which worked least well, and what conditions led to what outcomes. All he needed to do was grunt and, once, when she paused as if she had come to a close, say, "And then?" to set her off again.

Eventually, someone came to fetch her away to deal with a difficult case.

The day passed rather more easily than he had hoped. Mostly, he slept. He took broth, then later porridge. Whichever orderly was on duty helped him to use a chamber pot. The doctor visited twice more, each time keen to see if there were any signs of infection in the wound, which there weren't, thankfully. He slept most of the night.

The next two days passed in a similarly uneventful way. Bit by bit, he began to stay awake for longer stretches, as the opium doses were steadily lowered, although he remained weak from the early blood loss and the exhausting overland journey to the field hospital. Soon, he was able to rise to use the chamber pot with the help of only one orderly, which was a relief to his pride. He discovered that, in his sick bed, he was almost as invisible to the others as Catherine could become. He listened to every exchange within his hearing so he might build up a sense of where he was and what was going on. More skirmishes had been fought, and more wounded arrived in a steady stream, but it seemed the Roman army and the Arverni confederation had hit a stalemate, as evidenced by the fact that this field hospital had remained in this location for almost a month.

The doctor continued to look in on him twice a day. She was fascinated by the pace of his recovery.

"He's not ready to travel yet," the doctor said to the ever-waiting centurion. When the soldier left to deliver this message to his superior, she turned to the orderly on duty and said, "Don't allow them to take him away, not until you clear it with me. This is a rare chance to follow the recovery of a cold mage. For the sake of my research, I can't let it pass! And keep those cursed fire mages outside. I hate them."

"General Asante is a fire mage," remarked an assistant.

"She is a physician," Doctor Ba objected, clearly offended. "She uses her magic to heal, not to harm."

Another assistant called from the door, "Doctor Ba! An amputation case!"

She swept out, leaving Andevai alone but for the orderly, the sentry, and his thoughts. For the first time in his recovery, he bent his attention outward, beyond the canvas walls. Ah! He was now strong enough to feel the tremor of fire magic close by—fire mages, set to guard the tent and thus him. The regular soldiers set on guard outside chatted about the chicken they were going to kill and eat for their supper. A friend came by to tell them that the mail coach had come from Nikaia, and that he'd gotten a letter from his mother, and that maybe they had letters waiting too. Meanwhile, the orderly sat at a tiny table beside the tent's open entry flap, humming to himself as he scribbled notes in a journal.

Thus, neither of them were expecting it when a shadow darkened the open entry. The orderly looked up indignantly, ready to scold the person who had so impertinently blocked his light. His eyes and lips opened in an expression of surprise, and he jumped to his feet as a stately figure moved into the tent, leaning on a cane.

It was a woman, her face obscured by the daylight outside that lit her form from behind. She wore a brown skirt and jacket, fitted with a second, cutaway sleeve on her left arm, sewn of green fabric and trimmed with silver braid, the mark of the Amazon Corps. Her black hair had mostly gone to silver, and as she moved into the tent, he saw her face was as dark as his own. She was a woman of about the same age as his own mother, though far more robust, yet weathered, as if she had seen many painful sights.

"So, this is the cold mage," she remarked, and the orderly said, at once, "Yes, General! The very one!"

She was not speaking to the orderly, though, not that the orderly knew that.

On the other side of the tent, a shadow crept in where the corners gapped—or had been slit, as if by someone sneaking out that way several days before. Someone who needed to not be seen by the fire mages out front.

"You must be Doctor Asante," Andevai said.

"You must be Andevai Diarisso Haranwy."

With a hitch in her step, Doctor Asante walked slowly to the table where he lay. Abruptly, she turned, as if remembering something. "Orderly! Get me a tray of decent food, at once! And burdock salve. And a basin of salts, so I may soak my foot. Let the flap down behind you."

"At once!" The man scurried off obediently, dropping the tent flap closed behind him.

Catherine appeared on Andevai's other side, but she did not look happy to see him, frowning fiercely at him as she wiped away a tear. "Goodness, Andevai, you look quite thin and strained. Are they not feeding you?"

"Hush, child," said the doctor. "Let me examine the wound."

"The other doctor was very rude and abrupt," Catherine remarked.

Doctor Asante's smile was reassuring, kindly, and also sharply amused. "Was she?"

"It made me wish you were here to repair the injury instead."

"That is very kind of you, little cat, but Doctor Ba was my best apprentice, and she's an excellent, if rather young, doctor. So I expect her work to be everything it needs to be. Now, I pray you, give me silence to examine the patient."

A glance passed between the two women, the old and the young, and in it was an understanding of the connection they shared, which bound them through the woman they had both loved, each in their different way: Tara Bell. Catherine held Andevai's hand and remained silent.

After a thorough investigation, Doctor Asante told Andevai to get up and use the chamber pot. "Don't be shy, young man. I have seen every patch of the human body, inside and out, and every bit of effluvia that a human can discharge. Catherine, you may look away, in respect for his modesty and dignity."

Catherine obeyed without comment.

He found he was grateful for Doctor Asante's consideration. He was able to walk without assistance over to behind the screen and do his business and return, and her attention to the mundane act did not feel intrusive to him. She had that knack, being a healer.

But he was relieved to sit back upon the table and cover himself with a sheet, although he did not lay down, as she went to look behind the screen at the contents of the chamber pot.

"Everything I see heartens me," she said, coming back and settling herself in the chair the orderly had been using. "You may turn back around, Cat. So, what is this business of your cousin Beatrice and a dragon who walks in the body of a man having gotten her pregnant? I confess, I struggle to believe such a wild tale."

"You believed Tara and Daniel when they told you the Master of the Wild Hunt had gotten her pregnant!" retorted Catherine.

"A fair point." Doctor Asante was one of those people who was impossible to rattle, which no doubt made her an excellent surgeon.

"The story is true," said Andevai. "I saw the man turn into a dragon and then back into a man, with my own eyes. What further assurance would convince you?"

"That the man in question can shift into a dragon and back, rather than that you saw merely clouds and shadows? Or that, if he were a dragon who can walk as a man, there is proof that Beatrice's pregnancy is incontrovertibly his get and not some other man's, since dogs and cats, just as horses and cattle, cannot interbreed?"

"That's a bit insulting to Bee." Catherine crossed her arms.

"It is not meant so, I assure you. But you must admit, it is possible she is mistaken, or that the mansa mistook what he saw of the supposed dragon, for that matter. I say it not to insult her, or him, but because it is often true that mistakes occur."

Catherine clenched her hands, a stormy expression of intense frustration settling on her brow. "Vai, I don't know how to convince her. I've tried everything."

"Yes, in the day and a half we have traveled together, you have waxed volubly upon the subject of your dear cousin and your worries for her," agreed the doctor in a tone so mild that Andevai knew at once that she found Catherine's insistence on going on and on both a little annoying and rather endearing—just as he did! "But that is not enough to make me leave my responsibilities in Nikaia."

Andevai wasn't always correct in his first impressions of people. Sometimes his prejudices and the heavy tread of his emotions made it hard for him to see what was truly there. But he felt no such barrier with Doctor Asante. He liked her. More than that, he was seized with a sudden and powerful belief that she belonged with them, not in Camjiata's army.

"We would welcome you to Four Moons House and treat you with all the respect you so clearly deserve," he said with the assured dignity of the mansa of an important mage House.

"It is quite an intriguing proposition, I admit. To midwife such a miraculous and unexpected creature must entice any person who finds the natural history of our mysterious world to be a vast and enticing puzzle. But I do not have the liberty of taking leave whenever I wish it, and certainly not to cross the battle lines into the principalities with which we are at war. I would be marked as a traitor and condemned to the firing squad. That would mean that were I to go, I could never return. However, I can direct you to a good hospital in Lutetia, whose head midwife should be able to recommend—"

"But I want you!" Catherine cried. "Because my mother loved you, and my father trusted you. Because you saved my mother's life. There's no one else I can truly trust with this!"

The doctor's gaze held the wise compassion of a person who has seen a great deal of death, and who has had a hand in dragging a fortunate few back from the brink, into life. "On that day, Daniel and I, together, saved Tara's life, and yours, too, little cat. I didn't act alone, as you well know. It was the most important day of my life. I have forgotten none of it."

"But you didn't leave with them when they fled Camjiata's army!"

She shrugged. "Theirs was not my path. I can both regret and not regret that I chose not to go with them. Tara and I made our peace with each other. Nevertheless, I miss her—and the life she and I might have had together—more deeply than I can express."

"But you came here, now, with Catherine," said Andevai.

The doctor turned to him then, cocking her head with a look that might have been exasperation or curiosity. "What mean you to say, mansa? You may be clear with me."

"You could have refused to come with her when she reached you in Ni-kaia, if Nikaia is where she found you."

"At the main military hospital, yes. As you say, I could have refused. I have a great deal of work there that needs doing, many patients, apprentices to teach, orderlies to supervise, my correspondence, and a little community work, although community work is discouraged, which I find to be short-sighted, as well as inhumane. A better organization of medical establishments, in a city the size of Nikaia, could do a great deal of good for all."

The litany sounded familiar! In that moment, he knew that not all hope was lost. With a burst of eager energy, he conceived of an idea. "That's my point. You did not refuse. You came here."

Footsteps sounded outside. The flap was thrown back, and Doctor Ba rushed in, all aflutter. "General! I did not know you were coming! No! I pray you, do not rise. I know your gout has been troubling you."

"It is good to see you, Livia. Describe to me your work here, if you will."

The brisk, confident Doctor Ba dissolved into nervous student Livia, eager to please her respected teacher. Andevai suffered himself to be examined, poked, and discussed by the two women, as meanwhile, his thoughts wound down two streams.

In one stream, he kept half an eye on Catherine in the corner, her hands clasped, stymied, upset. She had found the doctor, as a fisherman gets a bite, but she did not know how to land her prize. In truth, she would have had an easier time of it had her task been to free the doctor from an impenetrable, locked prison rather than from a lifetime of loyal service to a corps and an empire. But Andevai understood that conundrum well, since he was refashioning his own approach to magic, the mage Houses, and the world in which he had been raised, whose traditions and customs had, for many years, seemed to him as if they were the only possible way of living.

In the other stream, he noted how Asante listened more than she talked, and how when she did talk, it was mostly to ask questions of Livia Ba: what choices she had made, what had she observed, how did she mean to proceed. At a few points, very gently, she offered a correction or suggestion that the young doctor hadn't used or considered, yet in such a careful way that Doctor Ba walked herself through the teaching without realizing it she was being taught.

Asante was not just a healer but a teacher as well.

He could work with that.

At length, he sighed with as much pent-up insinuation as possible.

Asante gave him a keen, searching look. "Ah, the patient tires. Livia, go about your rounds. I'll meet you later."

Doctor Ba flushed, rubbed her hands together as if worried she'd forgotten something, made a great deal of anxious fuss, and finally departed.

Asante turned her perspicacious attention back to him. Andevai felt himself a glamorous butterfly skewered by a collector's assessing pin. "What have you to say, mansa? I can see it all over your face."

"Yes!" cried Catherine, appearing out of her shadows now that the others had left. "What have you to say, Andevai? I think the orderly will be back soon."

The doctor arched an eyebrow. "Not as soon as you'd think. They'll have to make the burdock salve from scratch, as it doesn't keep." Inquisitiveness animated her broad features. Her curiosity could get him a fair way to what he—and Catherine—wanted. "But do go on, mansa. I'm eager to hear what you have to say."

"I shall not wax further upon the interesting scientific opportunity that awaits you, should you agree to midwife a human woman giving birth to a dragon's child."

"Children," Catherine broke in. "She dreamed there are three!"

"Three!" Asante looked startled, then calmed herself. "More like a litter than children! And to conceive across lineages, human and dragon. That would be something to study, indeed. Yet I say again: I doubt it is possible."

"You knew Catherine was possible. Is possible."

"Ah! A hit. Very well, mansa. Go on."

"Of course, scientifically, the circumstance interests you. But I perceive it may not be enough to overcome the serious objections you raise. But let me say to you, doctor, that Four Moons House can protect you from the empire, and from Camjiata himself. His hand cannot reach you once you are under my protection. I am powerful enough, and we have allies in the prince of Havery and with a network of people who keep their ears open and pass on information."

"Do you mean to say, 'spies'?"

"That's one word," he said. "I would say . . . reformers."

"Radicals," added Catherine.

"Let us say it is plausible for you and Catherine to extricate me and, afterward, to protect me," she answered. "My life's work is medicine. Specifically, field medicine amid the military. How am I to abandon that?"

"You need not abandon medicine at all! There is no city hospital in Havery, but, as I said, Four Moons House has a good relationship with the prince of Havery. He is a reform-minded person, who will certainly listen and consider fresh ideas about the organization of medical care in his principality. And that's not all. We ourselves at Four Moons House have opened an academy that is available to all children in Havery . . . well, as many as we can accommodate. I and other like-minded people are in the process of discussing how to open more academies within the various principalities, so any child, whether born to a prince or a farmer, a cobbler or a shopkeeper, may learn to read and write—and more besides! Have you ever considered a teaching hospital? Your methods. Your oversight. Yours to do with what you wish, for the benefit of the generations to come."

The doctor pressed her lips together so tightly that, at first, he thought he had offended her.

In a measured tone, pausing now and again as she thought it through, she said, "Such an institution might be created and run in association with or alongside these academies for young pupils. People with different aptitudes might be encouraged into professions that would not have been open to them before, and that they would have been discouraged, if not outright forbidden, from pursuing. In my years in the army, I have seen how the Amazon Corps have a degree of discipline and cohesion which is often lacking in the regular legions. Any woman may join the corps, if she so chooses. The officer ranks are not filled entirely with people of high status and inherited rank, as they are in both Roman and Celtic militaries, but rather from people who show an aptitude for command, whatever their background. What if more of our lives functioned in this way?"

"It must start from seeds planted in the ground, then grown—nurtured—to maturity," he said.

"Spoken like a villager."

"We cannot place a roof upon air," he added. "There must be a framework first, and someone must build that scaffolding. I and some of my like-minded associates are engaged in an ongoing discussion of these issues and how solutions may be implemented. You could join us. Why not build a hospital to which all and sundry may come? A community hospital, as you say. Bring your expertise to bear on the matter of community health. I have connections in the Antilles. Taino healers have many advanced theories and treatments that outpace our own in these matters. Several of their scholars may well be encouraged to come for a year to share their knowledge and to see what you have to teach them, particularly based on your experience in field hospitals. I would encourage the prince of Havery to gift you a compound for these purposes. Or, with patience, an edifice can be constructed on an empty lot next to Four Moons House, built to your exact specifications!"

Catherine stirred, wanting to expostulate, but instead she pressed her clasped hands to her mouth as she turned her intent gaze to Doctor Asante.

"This is all very tempting, I admit," said the doctor, "yet it is a great deal to ask of me, as well as a great deal to offer in exchange for my presence at young Beatrice's labor and delivery. I am not sure what to say, or that I can find it in myself to overset all my life, especially for this one thing."

He smiled. Even the pain in his shoulder abruptly seemed lessened as he assayed his clever idea; it had fallen into his head not out of nothing but, rather, out of the events of the recent days.

"It so happens, doctor, that Catherine and I may have something else to offer you that is a great deal more tempting, even than this."

Abruptly, Catherine laughed and, with a brilliant grin, lowered her hands and offered Andevai a brief but intensely promising look.

"What might that possibly be?" Doctor Asante asked, now openly skeptical. "For I admit, half of my interest in this conversation is studying your astonishing weave of vanity and pragmatism. Do go on, for I am quite at a loss as to how you can possibly proceed from here."

"She told me the story of meeting you, doctor. It is apparent you think of her almost as your own child, that you are bound to her. I must suppose that you would have raised her as a third parent, had Tara and Daniel been able to reach you when they fled the second time. Instead, they died, and Catherine landed in the care of her aunt and uncle. I want Catherine to receive all the generous affection her loyal heart deserves. Should you accept our offer, you will live with us as our kinswoman. We will cherish you, as you, too, deserve."

Asante touched a finger to an eye, dabbing away a tear. "That is very affecting, I admit. But—"

"And I can sweeten the deal too." He rarely interrupted his elders, having been raised with the strictest village manners. "I have something more. Something that I believe will act as the greatest inducement of all."

She sighed as if he had finally pushed past all her mighty patience, yet she leaned a little forward as she said, drily, "And what, pray tell, might that be?"

"The honored title of grandmother."

"Grandmother!" She sat straight up, so quickly, it was almost a recoil.

He had surprised her. He went on. "All these ties between you and Tara and Daniel link you and Catherine most of all. She and I would be honored for you to stand as grandmother to our children."

"Naked Diana!" she swore. She stood, so energized that she took a turn around the room without resorting to her cane, then landed her foot wrong, winced, and limped back to the chair. She sat with a heavy thump, breathing as hard as if she'd been running. Leaning forward, she stared hard at Catherine, who sat as tidily and smugly as any cat who has gotten into the cream at last.

"Your *children*! Cat, are you pregnant?"

A sly smile lit Catherine's face. "Not as far as I know. *Yet*," she said, and cursed if she did not wink at him.

Andevai was suffused with such an intense feeling of well-being that nothing hurt at all. Or, at least, not for a breath or two, as his body held taut, waiting for the doctor's answer.

"Grandmother," Asante whispered, testing the word, shaking her head. "That's so formal. What about . . . *Grandmama*?"

"Goodness, Andevai," said Catherine smugly. "This is the first idea you've had on this journey that may actually work out."

"All of my ideas have brought us here, right where we hoped to be," he said with the absolute certainty of a man who knows he is the strongest cold mage of his generation. "Perhaps not in the manner we expected, and with far more trouble than we had hoped for, but I, for one, am content."

When I Grow Up

art by Kelsey Liggett

M Y PAPA STILL LETS ME SIT ON HIS LAP EVEN THOUGH I THREW UP on his favorite dash jacket.

Now when I sit on his lap he wears an old jacket that is red and gold. I like it because the cloth is so soft and old. Also I like it because I can touch all the tiny stitches where Mama mended it. She says she must have mended it a hundred times, which is a lot of times. Mama says each stitch is a thread of love.

I am the best lap-sitter because my brother Daniel is too big now. He says when I am ALMOST THIRTEEN I will not want to sit on laps. That is how he says it, ALMOST THIRTEEN, like he thinks someone has forgotten. He just wants to run off and set fires with our cousins, the triplets, Hannibal, Tarquin, and Suren. He doesn't have time for me anymore, but I don't want to play with them anyway. I don't like fire.

I haven't told anyone yet, but I can quench a candle flame, even though I am not quite six. I know it doesn't count if you lick your fingers and pinch the flame dead, but I pretend I am a cold mage when I do it.

When I grow up, I am going to be a cold mage like Papa.

My big sister Fati says that sitting in laps is for babies, but I don't care. She is mean, and she pulls my hair, and I hate her because she always tells me to "just go away, you big baby, why don't you just throw a tantrum?" Then I go and sit on Papa's lap. He lets me sit on his lap while he is working at his desk, writing letters. He says I am the stillest sitter he has ever known.

I sit so still I get to listen while the grownups are talking. They don't notice I am there. Fati can't ever sit still. She bounces all the time. She is up and down and running after the boys. They don't mind her, even though she is only nine, because she can climb better than they can, so they send her to get things they can't reach. Yesterday she climbed onto the roof. All the grownups came out and got very quiet. Papa ran to get a ladder. By the time he came back, Mama already climbed up and helped her back down.

Papa told Fati he thought maybe she had invisible wings because she is such a fearless climber. She said maybe she does and maybe she keeps her wings hidden. Then he looked very interested and very concerned. Afterward all the grownups had a talk together around the big table, with the door shut. They said things I didn't understand like *wings would suggest a troubling manifestation of the spirit world and perhaps a rip in the veil.*

I don't believe Fati has wings. I think she says so to get attention. But she could never stay still like I did, hiding under Papa's desk, and not get caught listening. She didn't hear Mama say, "What are we going to do about her?" and Papa say, "Let her be. No harm in it. You have to admire her patience."

I don't see why lying about wings is admirable, and Fati isn't patient. She can't grow up to be a spy like Mama, like I am going to do. But I am also going to be a cold mage like Papa. So I am going to be a cold spy.

Sometimes I have to sit at the big table in Papa's study because Papa is holding my little baby brother, Sumaworo. He is not quite two, and he is very small, considering what a big name he has. Everyone calls him Sunny for his sweet little smile. Sunny should be walking by now. Grandmama says he is slow to walk because he rushed early to the world, before he was ready. Ready for what, I don't know.

For a long time, he slept in a box by Grandmama's stove. She and Mama and Papa and Aunt Bee and Uncle Rory fed him with a dropper. Now he is bigger, someone is always holding him. Except me. They say I am too small to hold him, but Fati says they won't let me hold him because they are afraid I will throw a tantrum and drop him.

I would never drop him! He doesn't say Daniel or Fati's names yet. He only says mine. He can't say Tara so he calls me Ta-wa. He loves me best because one time, when he was very tiny like a wrinkled little raisin bug, I sat beside his box singing to him, and he turned a funny color. So I ran and fetched Grandmama because she is a doctor. She rubbed him with oil and blew kisses into his mouth until he turned to a normal color. Grandmama says I saved his life and that is why he loves me.

When I grow up, I am going to be a doctor. I will be a cold spy doctor.

Because I am very fortunate, I have three grandmothers.

One is passed.

One is Nana. She sewed Bunny for me out of scraps of cloth. That was before she went over the seas to stay with Aunt Kayleigh and Uncle Kofi and their children. She said I can come visit when I am bigger.

The other grandmother is Grandmama, the doctor.

The morning after The Incident with Fati and the roof, I could not find my Bunny. I searched high and low for Bunny in the bedroom nook I share with Fati. I searched under my bed and around my bed and in the wardrobe and behind the chair. Bunny was nowhere to be found.

After breakfast in the big hall, the bell rang for school. All the big children got in their lines and marched away. Aunt Serena came like she does every morning to escort the youngests to the nursery for the day. The little children are noisy, and they run around, and they push me. I am too old to play with them. So I hid under the table until they were gone. I hide there every morning, and no one ever finds me.

Most mornings, I go and sit in Grandmama's office. As long as I am quiet, she lets me play with Bunny in a corner while she examines sick people. Maybe I forgot Bunny in the office. But when I got to her office, Bunny wasn't there.

Grandmama told me I couldn't stay.

"But I can't find Bunny!"

Grandmama has a kind voice, but when she says no, even Fati cannot wheedle her. "Now, Tara, I have a surgery that I have to do immediately. You're a big girl. You can find a solution." She paused, then added with a strong eye, "A solution that doesn't harm things that belong to other people."

"I said I was sorry!"

"Yes, you did. Now, go on, little soldier." She kissed me and sent me on my way.

Grandmama's office is at the back of the house, beside the kitchen. As I walked past the kitchen door, I heard Uncle Rory and Aunt Bee arguing, like they always do. They were in the pantry packing supplies.

"We shouldn't bring along this cheese," Uncle Rory was saying. "It will give away our position to any passing patrol."

"Only to people who smell like you do," said Aunt Bee.

I clapped a hand over my mouth, but they heard me giggle.

"Uncle Rory doesn't smell," I said when they looked out the door at me.

"I have an exceptional sense of smell." Uncle Rory held a cheese wheel at arm's length, with his face all squinted up. "Your Aunt Beatrice, on the other hand, is well known to be insensitive to nuance."

Aunt Bee snatched the cheese wheel out of his hand and stuck it in a travel bag. "You'll be glad of this humble cheese by the third night we're tramping through the forest."

She closed the bag to make the cheese safe. Then she knelt and put out a hand toward me, in case I wanted her to touch me.

"What is it, Tara? You have such a look on your face. Your mama won't be gone for more than eight or ten days this time. We are going to rescue some unjustly jailed prisoners, like we always do. There's nothing to worry about."

I don't like it when the grownups say there is nothing to worry about. I stuck my two fingers in my mouth to suck on. Then I remembered Fati calls it a baby thing to do, so I took them out and pretended it was a mistake.

"I can't find Bunny. Can you help me?"

"Oh, dear one." I let her give me a hug because she gives big warm hugs. "I would, but we have to go at midday, and your Uncle Rory didn't pack the travel gear he was supposed to . . ." She looked at Uncle Rory for a long time and gave a big huff of a breath like a dragon. "So I don't have time. Maybe the boys can help you. They have carpentry in the workshop today."

"You'll scout out your Bunny, my little soldier," said Uncle Rory. He grabbed me up and twirled me around the way he does, like I am a whirligig. That made me laugh and feel better, so they kissed me and sent me on my way.

The house I live in is very big, and it has two floors and an attic and many rooms. It has a long front to face the street and two wings like an eru's wings that fold back. After I left the kitchen, I walked down the corridor toward the front. The corridor is wide enough to play piggy-in-the-middle, bowling, and hopscotch when it is winter. I saw Daniel and the triplets ahead of me. They were carrying a pot and holding a lid on it like there was something inside they did not want to get out. I even heard scritching.

I ran to them. "Can you help me find Bunny?"

The triplets looked at Daniel and then at the pot.

Daniel said, "You have to go, Tara. We're doing something important. You'll just get in the way."

"I won't get in the way!"

"I mean it," he said. "And if I have to drag you to Aunt Serena, I will."

Aunt Serena will hug me and fuss over me and make me stay with the little children, so I let Daniel and the triplets go. For a while I stood in the corridor staring at the wood floor that I swept yesterday evening. I did not know what to do with myself or where to go without Bunny.

Then I remembered that once a week Papa teaches the youngest students. They are the ones too young to become cold mages yet. He likes to see how everyone is going on and how well they can recite the lessons they will need if they bloom.

Cold mages bloom like flowers. They are closed buds, and one day they open. When I grow up, I will bloom.

But today I was just missing Bunny, so I sneaked into the back of the schoolroom. Sometimes, if I sit at the back bench very quietly with the seven-year-olds, no one notices me.

When I tiptoed in, Papa saw me sit down, but he didn't say "Tara, you are too young to be here" like the other teachers do, so that meant I could stay.

I like to watch Papa teach. He wears colorful dash jackets, even though his friends tease him about his clothes. He only smiles when they tease him. When I grow up, I am going to be like Papa and learn to only smile when people tease me, instead of screaming and trying to hit them.

Mama says Papa has a *persuasive* voice. I think that means it is not too high and not too low but just right. He walks along the benches listening to the young students recite from the primer on cold magic. He encourages the soft voices to speak up and the loud voices to leave room for the others. If everyone has done well, he lets students recite from the old epics like when the snake comes out of the well.

Because I am not old enough to start school, I speak the words without saying them out loud. When Papa passed me he gave me a little wink, so I sat up straighter and pretended I was a real student. It is so hard to have to wait until I am seven before I can start school.

Papa left, and Maester Godwik arrived to teach geography. He set everyone to a writing exercise with their stylus. While they did that, he started to draw a big map on the chalkboard.

I did not have a stylus or a wax tablet for writing, so I traced on the desktop with my finger. I know all my letters.

Fati sat at the row of desks right in front of me. She did not turn around, but I heard her whisper to her friends on either side, just loud enough for me to hear, "Mama finds her so *exasperating*. Not that she knows what that means."

"It means you smell," I whispered to her back.

She snorted under her breath. "I do not smell. That is such a baby thing to say to someone." Then she nudged her friends, and they all giggled behind their hands.

My ears burned. "You do too smell!"

She bent over her tablet, writing out words so if Maester Godwik looked he would see her working. He did not look around, but his tail twitched.

She kept talking in a low voice only those around her could hear. "You used to be fun when you were a real baby like Sunny. Now you're just annoying. You annoy everyone with your tantrums and your screaming and your hitting."

My throat felt like a hornet was stuck in it. I blinked because hot tears got in my eyes.

One of her friends whispered, "Didn't she cut up your birthday jacket?"

Fati's shoulders heaved with anger. Something fluttered at her back, like gauzy wings opening. But maybe that was just the light coming through the windows.

"Yes. Yes, she did. The one Mama sewed for me special, from the fabric that matched Papa's new dash jacket. She was just jealous. What a big baby."

Her friends turned to look at me like I was a dirty insect. When Maester Godwik made a coughing noise, they all turned back and bent over their tablets.

Fati didn't stop talking. Her voice was as mean as poison. "Papa made her do my chores for a week. Mama is making her do extra mending to teach her what it means to repair things that get torn. But my birthday jacket was ruined. I'm turning it into doll clothes. And even though Mama is sewing me a new one, a *better one*, it's not enough. It will never be enough for that little brat."

The hornets burst out of me. "I am not a brat!"

She turned to look at me. There was a beast in her eyes and a snarl on her lips. "Do you know why you don't have any friends? Because no one likes you. Because you are a pest. Just go away and stop pestering me. You will never find your smelly ugly old Bunny."

"Bunny doesn't smell! You're the one who smells! You are. *You are! YOU ARE!*"

I jumped up and crawled over the desk and I hit her on the back with my fist, and I hit her again because she laughed at me, and again because her friends shrieked and jumped away, and then Maester Godwik appeared with all his teeth showing.

He said in a calm voice, "Tara, the classroom is for children seven and older who can act with discipline and focus. You are not yet among their number. It's time for you to leave. As for you girls, back to work, but understand that I will speak with you all later about your behavior."

I stumbled out to the corridor and curled up against the wall. Each time I took a breath, a big sob came out. There were so many and they were pressing so hard against my chest that I could not stop them. I didn't have Bunny to help me stop them. I can tell Bunny anything and Bunny listens, never screams or throws tantrums.

Footsteps clip-clopped down the corridor. I was still crying but I peeked up through my hands. Uncle Judoc walked past with an important-looking visitor. The visitor tried not to stare at me.

In a low voice he said to Uncle Judoc, "Should we not ask if the child is well?"

Uncle Judoc used his indoor voice. "Let her be. The doctor says she is going through a sticky patch and we should give her space."

They kept walking because no one cares about me. I sat in the empty corridor and cried and cried and cried.

After a while soft padding steps approached me. Felina settled next to me and started to purr. We don't really know Felina's name, and maybe she doesn't know her name or even have a name. She only came to live with us not long ago, when a pretty young woman came to the door and yelled at Uncle Rory about how angry she was because she thought she was going to have a baby but she had a big kitten instead. Why would anyone be mad about that? Kittens are much more fun to play with than big sisters.

Everyone says maybe someday Felina will be able to turn into a person and back into a saber-toothed cat like Uncle Rory can. I hope so too. Then I would have a friend.

I rested my hand on her back and let her purrs talk through my skin like someone telling me it will be all right. The purrs chased away the hornets. I wiped my cheeks and sucked in a breath and wished I had Bunny to hug.

Then I remembered that maybe I left Bunny behind in Papa's study yesterday when I was spying on the grownups when they talked about Fati.

So I gave Felina a pat and jumped up and ran to Papa's study in the other wing.

The door was *locked.*

Because my hair is UNRULY like me, there is always a hairpin in my braids. A hairpin is like a weapon. It can be a sword for a little soldier. I am a little soldier. I was named after my Grandmother Tara, and she was a soldier, so her spirit resides in me. If a person is very patient, even if she is not quite six, she can jiggle a hairpin in a lock until the lock opens.

Carefully, I pushed down the latch. Slowly, I pushed open the door a crack because I thought I heard a noise inside and I have very good hearing. Peeking in, I saw Mama was sitting on Papa's lap, and they were kissing!

"Goodness, Andevai," she said, pulling away. "We will only be gone a few days."

He smiled like he does when he is with Mama.

She said, "Will you be all right with the girls? They are both in quite the state these days. They were so sweet together for so long, and now they fight all the time."

"It will pass," he said. "Fati got accustomed to Tara being her loyal little shadow. But now Tara is ready for more independence. We have to let them sort out a new relationship without too much interference from us. Sometimes people have to fight before they can learn to get along, Catherine."

"Do they?" she asked in her teasing voice, which is a nice teasing voice and not a mean teasing voice like Fati's.

He laughed like he does when he is with Mama. They went back to kissing, so I snicked the door closed.

Coming to the study made me think. I thought and thought about when I was in the study, squeezed under the desk and listening to the grownups talk at the table about Fati climbing up to the roof. I did not have Bunny when I was hiding under the desk. I was all alone.

You will never find your smelly ugly old Bunny.

How would Fati know I will never find Bunny? Unless she knows where Bunny is. Unless she put Bunny somewhere she thinks I can't get to and where no one will notice.

That's when I knew what a terrible thing Fati had done, just to be mean to me.

I ran outside to the big courtyard behind the front of the house and between the wings. I remembered exactly where Fati climbed the wall, where there are window ledges and a drain spout and an overhang. And there was Bunny on the roof, all alone, ears flopping over the side. If it rained, Bunny would get wet. If it snowed, Bunny would get cold. If the wind blew, Bunny would blow into a far country and never find her way home. I had to rescue Bunny.

So I pulled myself up to the window ledge, and I wedged my feet between the drain spout and the wall, and I climbed until my hands hurt, and I got to the top of the tall window where there was another little ledge because the window has an arch on top with more glass.

I grabbed and held on. I heard people shouting from inside. My fingers were aching, and my feet were slipping. It was so far to the ground because the windows were very very high, as high as the ceiling inside the rooms. And it was even higher to the roof, another whole set of tall windows. But Bunny was waiting for me, so I had to be brave and strong like my Grandmother Tara.

I heard a lot of shouting. People came running into the courtyard. Fati ran in front of them all.

She was yelling at me like she does, in her bossy voice. "Don't move, Tara. Don't move. Papa is getting a ladder. Just don't move or you'll fall. I'll get Bunny back for you."

"I won't fall! I won't! You think I'm a baby and can't do anything but I'm not a baby anymore and I can!"

My shout was so loud it made my hands slip and my feet slip. I screamed, and I fell. I grabbed for the drain spout but I couldn't keep hold of it. My forehead scraped against the metal like it was a knife cutting me open. I fell again and hit the ground on my elbows and knees with the biggest bump. My head was on fire. Blood poured into my eyes, and it tasted nasty, and I screamed, and Fati screamed, and everyone was screaming.

Except Papa and Mama. He set down a ladder, and Mama rolled me onto my back and told me to look at her and tell her my name, as if I didn't know my name!

"I'm not a baby!" I yelled at her. "I don't want to be a baby anymore."

"She might have a concussion," said Mama concernedly. "We'd better get her inside."

Papa picked me up, and my head hurt so badly I felt really sick, and I threw up on him. He carried me all the way to Grandmama's office and laid me on a table. Mama closed the window shades so it was dim. That was better but it still hurt. It hurt especially when she brought a cloth and dabbed blood from my face, but even that didn't hurt as much as the thought of Bunny alone on the roof.

"Hush, hush," said Papa. "You'll be all right."

"Hush, hush," said Mama. "You'll be all right."

The door opened, and Grandmama came in. Her hands touched my skinned knees, my skinned arms, my skinned shoulder, and my scalp. She stared into my eyes and made me look at her finger when she moved it back and forth. Then her fingers pressed a little circle above my right eye, where the spout had cut me. I made a whimper and then I wished I hadn't because I wanted to be brave.

"I don't think she has a concussion, but I will keep a close eye on her," Grandmama said to Papa and Mama. "As for the blood, it is just a cut. Scalp wounds bleed copiously, but it's not serious. I will have to stitch it up."

"No! No! No!" I started to kick.

Mama bent over me. "It's just mending, Tara. Like I mend your papa's jackets. I'll stay here with you."

Grandmama has a brisk voice she uses when people don't want to take the medicine she gives them. "Cat, given what we know, you must go because you are the only one who has a chance to rescue them. I have seen many a wound, and I can tell you that Tara will be fine. We can handle her for a few days."

No one argues with Grandmama about medicine. Not even me.

"Let me get my suture kit while you give her a kiss for courage." Grandmama went out.

Papa said to Mama in his *persuasive* voice, "It doesn't hurt to let her sit in on the class. Godwik said she was fine until Fati and her friends started teasing her. I know she is younger than the other children, but she can sit so still. If she can learn to cause no trouble, then what harm in it? She's bored. And she likes the routine of the classroom. Which is more than I can say for some."

Mama laughed in the low, secret way she does when she is with Papa. I could tell she wanted to kiss him and began to lean toward him but wrinkled up her nose. "I'll tell Fati to wash your jacket." She turned back to look at me. "As for you, sweetling, I'll be back in a few days."

She kissed me on the head and left. Papa stood by the table, holding my hand and humming a lullaby. I tried not to cry but the cries kept coming because my head hurt and my knees hurt and my arms hurt and my heart hurt.

Grandmama came back. She opened the shades. She was armed with a needle, and it had a very sharp point.

"No. No, no," I said, trying not to cry, and just as I was trying so hard not to cry and kick, the door opened and Fati the mean beast burst in.

"Fati, haven't you done enough for today?" said Papa, sounding *exasperated* for once.

His stern voice made her stop right there by the door. She had snot and tears all over her face like she'd been crying, and she looked so funny and so stupid that I stopped crying.

"I didn't mean for Tara to get hurt." She crept forward trembling, and she held out her hands because she was carrying a lump of cloth.

"Bunny!" And it was! It was really Bunny!

Papa smiled just a tiny bit. "Give that poor abused creature to Tara and wait outside."

"Yes, Papa," she said in the tiniest voice ever heard. She pressed Bunny onto my chest and ran for the door and then she was gone.

Grandmama held the needle, and I held Bunny tight. Even if Bunny smelled like rain and mildew I didn't care.

Grandmama moved to where I couldn't quite see her. She dabbed at my forehead with a wet cloth that stung and made me blink lots of tears.

Papa placed his hands on either side of my head, and he looked me in the eyes with his big warm eyes. "Now hold very still like I know you can. Close your eyes and press this side of your face into my arm. I'm going to hold you so you don't move."

Grandmama said, "You are a brave little soldier, Tara. Your Bunny is a brave little soldier too. Can you both be brave for me right now? Then you'll be mended and good as new."

I could be brave. When I grow up, I am going to be a cold spy doctor soldier.

The prick of the needle hurt, but it wasn't so bad after all, because each stitch is a thread of love.

THE
ESSAYS

Why I Wrote the World of *Cold Magic*

F OR THE SPIRITWALKER PROJECT, I WANTED TO WRITE A MULTICULTUR-
al world in which a mixing of cultures and people was the expected,
the norm. I happen to think that when cultural change is considered across
time, mixing is the norm. It went on all the time throughout history. It continues to happen to this day. Interaction and influence are what keep cultures
dynamic. A closed, static culture is a dying culture. In addition, these processes
are not one-way. Cultural change happens in many directions, some of them
exploitative and coerced and others subtle, subversive, and unexpected.

Certainly, living in Hawai'i since 2002 has influenced my choices in this regard. My earlier Crossroads Trilogy is influenced by, although not specifically
based on, the Asian-Pacific Islander cultural mix of Hawai'i. While *Cold Magic*
and the other Spiritwalker books do not use any specific local-to-Hawai'i cultural influences, they do incorporate ways in which I perceive that local culture
has found to keep the cultural integrity of varying cultural groups (not always
easily; certainly, Native Hawaiians have fought a tremendous battle against
colonization and erasure), while at the same time being inclusive in a way that
allowed a unique, syncretic local culture to arise that incorporates elements
from all the different ethnic and cultural groups that coexist here.

In Spiritwalker, cultural mixing plays out this way: an immigrant Malian
culture meets and mingles with northwestern Celtic European culture, while
old imperial Rome and merchant Phoenicia retain a strong influence, just to
name the four most prominent cultural groups in the book (the second novel
in the trilogy, *Cold Fire*, adds the Taino culture of the Caribbean to the mix).
I wanted to highlight the immense and too-often overlooked power and richness of the West African Mande traditions and civilizations, specifically the
Malian Empire. Western media and narratives too often and too easily deliberately dismiss sub-Saharan Africa (as if it is all one thing) with a few words:
famine, civil war, guns, blood diamonds, slavery, trauma, and so on. In doing
so, they miss, denigrate, and outright erase the significant history and culture
that was present historically, not to mention the actual life and culture and
history-in-the-making that is there right now. The history and culture of Mali
is not my story to tell, but I did feel I had a story to write about how we *tell*
history, with all its manifold interrelationships.

I grew up in the USA, on the continent, in a school system that taught history as if it was almost exclusively about the Western world and specifically the European and American experience. This history took brief detours into the "ancient glory" of China and India (because the British Empire was there), with a glimpse of samurai-era Japan because of the cool armor and Admiral Perry. At the time I was in school, we were also treated to a bit of quaint mention of the sad fate of so many indigenous peoples, not least of whom was the doomed and tragic figure of the proud and noble (but sometimes savage! so we were assured) American Indian, exemplified in the famous and possibly apocryphal "I will fight no more forever" speech of (the very real) Chief Joseph of the Nez Pearce.

Yet the history I was taught in school, and in most of the books I was able to read at that time, was an extremely narrow and blinkered view of the far vaster and more complex history actually lived by human beings, even though it was treated, at that time, and in my school system and the American mainstream culture, as if the centrality of the West were the only possible view, the only possible outcome in the teleology of history.

When I began writing *Cold Magic* and thus the Spiritwalker Trilogy, my primary goal was to tell a story that would be exciting and rich, a page-turner that was difficult to put down. I wanted to tell a story in which the central emotional relationship was a female friendship (sisterhood), and one in which the concerns of a young woman finding her way in the world could include sword fighting, sewing, finding enough to eat, sex, science, revolution, spying, and fashion. I wanted her voice to carry the tale. I wanted to write a fantasy novel in which the neutral universal stance—the one that expresses the story's highest level of privilege, which no one thinks about in this world because it is the default expectation—is embodied in a man of African ancestry. And I wanted to write about lawyer dinosaurs.

One of the other things I wanted to do was to try to move outside common assumptions about the weight of "the West" in world history—by which I specifically mean the early modern and modern era colonial powers. I wanted to create a world in which a mix of cultural traditions have created a dynamic, changing world that looks similar in many ways to our own but different as well. In other words, I hoped to make the point, under the surface story, that modernity is not dependent on the existence of "the West" as we know it. Technology and science and industry, individual rights and political revolution: these things are ways (although not the only ways) to define modernity, and they belong not to any one regional place but to the human condition.

I wanted to write about what I always seem to write about: the change and evolution of cultures. Because cultural change has been going on since the dawn of humanity. And it is going on, right now, around us all.

On the Efficacy of Cold Magic, With an Aside to Cold Mages & their Antipathy to Technology

by Habibah ibnah Alhamrai

*natural philosopher and lecturer at
the University of Expedition*

I T IS WELL-KNOWN THAT THE GREAT MAGE HOUSES ARE ANATHEMA TO the technologies developed and developing in the Amerikes, especially those so abundantly useful in Expedition and other areas where the technologies have been employed. One might assume that the cause of this antipathy might be that much of these technologies are the handiwork of the Trolls, and that the mage Houses have, in general, an inborn hatred or even natural dislike for their species. One would be totally mistaken.

The mages do not care about the Trolls except that they create and perpetrate many new technologies that the mages find repulsive, or rather that they find unusable and from which they are repulsed. Part of this is undoubtedly physical, but some may be psychological in the sheer inescapability of their being cold mages. A common example of this physical repulsion can be seen in nearly any locale where gas light has been installed and is currently enhancing the environs of most normal citizens. We know that gas light is produced in lamps designed specifically to allow small amounts of gas to expand inside the globe and ignite and burn, thereby providing light and a bit of heat. The heat in this case is useless as the globes are high above the street, but because of that height, the light is able to shine down upon the ground and illuminate the surrounding area.

But watch a carriage carrying a cold mage through the streets and it is easy to see the problem. As the carriage approaches the light, the light dims. When the carriage is beneath the lamp, the light within becomes nearly invisible. And when the carriage passes, only then does the light begin to brighten and eventually return to burning in its natural state.

It is widely known that cold mage Houses are heated by an indirect method originally invented and employed by the Romans. It might be thought that they use this old style through some propensity toward ancient knowledge. That thought would be wrong. While it is unclear if the cold mages themselves would actually suffer much from the cold itself, their spouses and children, if not possessed of their abilities, certainly will. Therefore, cold mage manors must be heated in some way. This indirect method, though in some ways less efficient than direct heating by stove or fireplace, is nonetheless the only method available in any abode where cold mages reside. These Roman heat pipes are just that: pipes beneath the floors of the rooms, that carry hot water or air. The heat source must be located somewhere away from the main house so that the cold magic cannot reach it, as not only will a cold mage put out a fire in near proximity, but it will also be impossible to light the fire until the cold mage has departed. Generally, the mage Houses place the fire building uphill from the house, at a spring location, so that water can be heated and then flow naturally down to the manor house itself. As far as can be understood, cold mages have had difficulty with fire for their entire existence, but, since little is known about the early days of the cold mages, little can be said as to how they adapted to their difficulties before adopting the Roman methods.

On the essence of cold magic, its spontaneous generation and use

Cold magic is not an old ability. It did not exist during the height of the Roman hegemony. During that time, while various magics undoubtedly existed, cold magic did not. It is only due to the Salt Plague that cold magic could come into existence. One need not repeat here the history of the Salt Plague or the ghouls that emerged and destroyed entire civilizations. Nor the subsequent migrations and resettlements. The history may be read in any one of many treatises, but a simple explanation may be found in the workmanlike discourse found in *"Concerning the Mande Peoples of Western Africa Who Were Forced by Necessity to Abandon Their Homeland and Settle in Europe, Just South of the Ice Shelf"* by Catharine Hassi Barahal of the famous Hassi Barahal Kena'ani lineage.

Let it be said that one fortuitous result of the plague, or rather the migration caused by the plague, is that the Mande from Africa met the Celtic druids of the north. Obviously, not all Mande were equal in either wealth or magic. The wealthy of the Mande married into the princely Celtic houses of the north, while those possessing magic found the Celtic druids to be of a kind and joined together with their societies and their houses. This combination led to the emergence of strong mages who had the ability to wield the powers of ice. This merging of two disparate elements formed the mage Houses.

However, not all or every merging of Mande with Celt produced or, to this day, produces cold mages, and not all cold mages are equal. Because cold magic does not show up at birth, and because all joining does not produce a cold mage, the current mages have taken to occasionally plowing somewhat far from home and only reaping the outcome if it seems favorable. At this point, the lineages of the Celtic druids and the Mande run throughout many of the villages and towns within their realms, so where a cold mage will appear is unknown. The biology of this phenomenon is undoubtedly fascinating but is not yet understood.

It is widely known that scholars believe that magic *could* be explicated on scientific principle, if only those who handle magic were not so secretive. It is my thesis that much of cold magic can be explicated using only the principles of natural history and the sciences without the aid of the mages. In fact, help from the mages would probably serve only to further confuse.

For example, it is widely held by the mages and others that the source of cold magic is in the spirit world. That is, that the source of the vast energies available to the mages is somewhere hidden in that world. The path to that energy may be in the spirit world, but the source of the power is the ice that covers the entire northern portion of our planet, and on whose edge we settle. It is doubtful that if the Celtic druids had been the ones forced from their homes to settle in the Mande area of Africa that cold mages would today exist. Perhaps in that environ, the essence and control of fire magic might have become dominant. However, the vagaries of the gods forced the Mande to the north to sit on the edge of the source of their great power.

"The history of the world begins in ice, and it will end in ice."

The Celtic bards and Mande djeliw of the north say this, but they do not know how correct they are. The Romans may have believed the world began in fire, but now, ice rules, as do the cold mages. The power of cold is extraordinary. Anyone in the proximity of a cold mage releasing his power will attest to this. Area-wide storms of wind, ice and snow rain down upon those in the path of a cold mage's ire. Liquids freeze and solid objects become so cold they brittlize and shatter. Through the spirit world and into the ice the mages reach, releasing the power. The ice is the ultimate source.

This is why one of the few things that a powerful cold mage fears is the Wild Hunt. The Wild Hunt will identify mages who overstep their bonds, who use their power too much, too often, or too impulsively, and sweep down and remove that mage from the mix. We cannot know the machination of those in the Wild Hunt, nor the rest of their ilk, but they monitor and punish not just simple mortals but the cold mages, too, for those of the Wild Hunt own the ice.

While I cannot explain to you how the mages channel their power from the ice, nor whether that power is limited or limitless, I can explain their use of that power and why they themselves have a repulsion to fire and technology. We all know how fire can change metals in the forge or pottery in the kiln, but cold can do the same if wielded by a skilled mage. Take glass for example. For most of us, a broken pane of glass can only be repaired by re-melting and pouring a new pane, but a cold mage can take those shards and knit them into a whole. How can this be done with cold rather than heat? We know that glass is amorphous, if the two edges are held together, the mage can make the components at the edges move and intertwine, thereby fusing them together with intense cold. In this case, there are no crystals to reunite or layers to re-adhere. Just as the masses of ice on the glaciers move, melt and reform under the great mass of the ice, so a mage's touch can cold press the glass into reforming.

One does not often see a mage re-forming glass, but one does see the effects of a mage's presence on fire and technology. The principles of fire are well understood, but a short explanation is appropriate here. In general, heat, from a fire, friction of rubbing, concentrated sunlight or striking of flint on steel, warms the material to be burned, and when the temperature rises sufficiently for the substance to become gaseous, the material ignites. The material remains lit and burns because the burning itself provides more gaseous fuel for the fire. An easy example to see is a candle. An ember transferred from the fireplace ignites the wick, which burns rapidly until it approaches the wax. The wax melts, moves up the wick, evaporates and ignites, and the process continues until there is no wax left.

When mages enter areas where there is fire of any kind, the intense cold presence around them sucks all the warmth from the area. The flame can no longer consume the material, be it wood, candle wax or gas, because the heat is drawn into the mage. Subsequently, the fire dies. Fires cannot be lit in the presence of a mage because their cold aura prevents any of the materials from igniting. Even if a spark from flint *can* be created, the materials themselves will not burn.

The effect of this sucking of energy on a fireplace fire or candle are transient, and while the mages dislike them, they are merely annoying. The presence of large furnaces, like the ones created in Expedition to run the boilers that power the factories, contain much more energy, and while the mages have a similar effect on a factory as they do on a candle, the great heat absorbed by the mages is no longer simply annoying, but can begin to eat into their very essence. This, I believe, is why the mage Houses are so opposed to the new technologies. They fear first, that the presence of so much technology producing so much heat will interfere with their magic, but they fear foremost that the technology will become all pervasive and interfere with their well-being, melting them and eroding them from inside.

Science writer A'ndrea Elyse Messer wrote this piece "in the style of" an early 19th century paper or lecture. The character Habibah ibnah Alhamrai appears in Cold Fire and is referenced in Cold Steel and in "The Courtship" and "Finding the Doctor."

Doggerland, the Ice Age, and the Landscape of the Spiritwalker Universe

T WENTY THOUSAND YEARS AGO, EARTH WAS IN THE GRIP OF AN ICE Age (technically we are still in an Ice Age, in one of the interglacial warming periods). Massive sheets of ice covered much of North America, northern Europe, and parts of north Asia. These ice sheets locked up so much water that the contours of the continents were different from what we see today because the sea levels were lower. As temperatures began to rise, the ice began to melt and the oceans to rise.

Back in that day, the island we today call Britain was not an island but part of Europe. The English Channel did not exist, the Rhine River flowed a lot farther south before it reached the Atlantic Ocean, and people lived and probably often thrived on what was then an expanse of land that now lies beneath the North Sea.

When I "built" the landscape of Spiritwalker, I wanted enough ice that Britain would be attached to the continent, but not so much that most of Europe would be too cold for extensive human habitation. I settled on the shoreline in Spiritwalker falling somewhat close to the year 8000 B.C.E (Before the Common Era), although, of course, all of this mapping is educated guesswork.

Europe's Lost World: The Rediscovery of Doggerland by V. Gaffney, S. Fitch and D. Smith (CBA Research Report 160, 2009) provided a great deal of information by some of the scientists at the forefront of this research. Doggerland got its name from the Dogger Banks, a shallow area in the North Sea well-known to fishermen.

Europe's Lost World also provided a crucial set of figures depicting "Iso-pollen maps showing changes in vegetation over the postglacial" (in Europe). I needed to know how a late glacial landscape would differ from today's European landscape in terms of climate zones and vegetation, not just shorelines. For instance, how far north could people farm? Would there be other geographic variations in vegetation zones? What could farmers grow? Some grains can grow in harsher conditions with shorter growing seasons, while others need warmer, longer seasons. I never go into detail about issues like this, although they are alluded to, and specifically if briefly mentioned in *Cold Steel*.

The city of Adurnam lies in what is now the English Channel, south of Portsmouth, more or less on the old paleolithic watercourse of the Solent River, although the city itself is named after Portus Adurni, the Roman fort at what is now Portchester, a suburb of Portsmouth.

The land controlled by Four Moons House lies east of London and Canterbury, in what is now the southern part of the North Sea, but which in *Spiritwalker* is all land. For these landscapes, I consulted references like the *Journal of Quaternary Science*, which has an entire volume dedicated to the Quaternary history of the English Channel (Volume 18, Issue 3-4, March-May 2003).

I also wanted to know how melting would occur, how quickly vegetation could "migrate" north, and by what "mechanism" the trolls (the feathered people, that is, the intelligent descendants of troodons) might have survived into the "present day" of the novel, while at the same time allowing for human migration into the Americas.

The land bridge between Asia and the Americas was generally ice-free during the Ice Age due to climate variables. Called Beringia, this land bridge had a significant population of mammoths and other now-extinct mammals. Meanwhile, however, the massive North American ice sheet cut off Beringia from the ice-free southern part of the North American continent for a long time.

E.C. Pielou's excellent *After the Ice Age: The Return of Life to Glaciated North America* (The University of Chicago Press, 1991) is a superb resource for fantasy writers. It taught me about Beringia's ice-free corridor, conditions in newly deglaciated landscapes, and how plants return to those zones, which they can do remarkably quickly under the right circumstances.

It also taught me about refugia, which are ice-free areas, including large ones like Beringia and then also small ones: nunataks are ice-free zones at high elevations like mountaintops, while coastal refugia are small ice-free sections of "coastal plain in the lee of high mountains" (Pielou). Some plant and animal species survived in refugia, surrounded by ice and thus cut off from other populations for long periods.

Refugia and nunataks gave me a rationale for the survival of my intelligent descendants of troodons. Also, the existence of coastal refugia made it possible to suggest that humans, after crossing ice-free Berengia either on foot or by boat along the coast, had coast-hopped down a string of coastal refugia to the ice-free lower portion of North America (as they likely did in our own history). Meanwhile, the ice would have kept the two populations—

the small but expanding feathered people population in the north and east and the small but expanding human population in the west and south—from meeting until rather late in this prehistory, at which point contact between outlying groups would have brought caution, conflict, cooperation, trade, and eventually yet more complex interactions.

It was easy to find information on Europe and North America—the above referenced books and articles are not the only resources I used—and far more difficult to find information on how the Ice Age affected, for instance, the climate of the Caribbean, something I needed to know for *Cold Fire*. I did what I could with maps of the seafloor in the Caribbean to consider how the ocean currents would work, since the islands of the Caribbean Basin are larger in this alternate landscape. As well, I posited that the hurricane season would be shorter due to water temperature changes, and I winged it a bit.

I dredged around to find what I could about world regional climate variation. For instance, although my map of the Eastern Hemisphere doesn't extend that far south, I posit that Lake Chad in the West and Central Sahel is huge because of the climate itself making west and central Africa wetter. Mostly, though, I focused on areas I knew I was going to visit in the story.

Names in the World
of *Cold Magic*

THE MOST DIFFICULT GEOGRAPHIC CHALLENGE I FACED IN WRITING the world of *Cold Magic* is that, according to the fantasy alternate history I have constructed, there are no Germanic-descended languages and thus no Germanic place names on the continent of Europe.

Because of the extended Ice Age and the large ice caps and shelves covering much of far northern Europe, there is no Scandinavia, no England as we know it, no Germany. Thus, no Germanic-speaking tribes develop the Germanic branch of the Indo-European language tree. Instead, Europa offers up a mélange of Celtic, Roman, Mande (Malian), and Phoenician cultures and languages, with a tangled history that bears both similarities to and differences from our own.

Now, I grant you that I deliberately borrowed elements of Anglo history and Anglo novelistic tropes as stage settings and devices for the Spiritwalker books. I have reasons for that, which I won't go into here.

But when it came to geography, I tried to be strict. Insofar as I was able to manage it, Germanic-derived place names are never used because those names never existed.

Obviously, it is impossible to get across that there are no Germanic-descended languages in this world because I am writing in English. Nor can I declare outright that I'm not using Germanic place names because my heroine Cat would never stop to think about the lack of Germanic place names which, after all, do not exist in her world or her consciousness.

What this meant for writing *Cold Magic* (and its sequels) is that I had to examine every place name I used to see if I could determine its etymology.

Fortunately, many modern place names are already of Celtic or Latin or Greek or Punic/Phoenician derivation. Rome remains Rome. London was Londinium, which became Londun. Carthage still exists, although I use Qart Hadast because it is closer to the original language. Marseille turns back to Massilia, the name used in the classical era.

In other cases, I had to seek out the earlier name of a place that now carries a Germanic-derived name. For example, Colchester's earliest name was the Celtic, Camulodunum. I compressed that to Camlun.

A particularly good discussion of how the map in *Cold Magic* gives the reader additional information that is not in the book can be found in a review of the book by Edward James on the Strange Horizons online website (http://strangehorizons.com).

In many cases, I sought out the oldest name I could find for a place, usually recorded in Roman or Greek records. Orleans in France evolved from its Roman name of Aurelianum, but it was originally called Cenabum when it was a principal town/fort of the Carnutes tribe; I shortened that to Cena. Some of the towns and cities in Iberia (what we now call Spain) are Phoenican: Gadir is now known as Cadiz, but it started life as a Carthaginian colonial port. Because of the expansive nature of the Roman Empire and their record-keeping, I was able to track down older Celto-Iberian place names in Spain, many of which we know because they were recorded by the conquering Romans. General Camjiata, for example, hails from Numantia, near modern Soria; Numantia was an important political center in the Iberia of that time, and the Romans laid siege to it and eventually razed it, although it remained inhabited for some time afterward in a diminished form.

It is quite fascinating to see how names shift, which change, and which retain their original roots. Physical features show great resilience in terms of name permanence. Many rivers in Europe retain ancient names or appellations, even if the form of the name has changed over time. The Thames is a good example. So are the Alps, even if, in the world of Cold Magic, they are covered by a massive ice cap.

When writing an epic fantasy meant to include a depth of history, it is worth considering which places and features change names, and why, and which become so deeply embedded that they do not change, even if the spoken language changes around them.

Cat's Voice & Deciding What Point of View to Use

I ONCE FLIPPANTLY DECLARED THAT I WOULD NEVER EVER WRITE A novel in first person.

As a narrative style, first person is heavily and primarily dependent on voice. The narrator is right there, talking to the reader directly, and it has always seemed to me that there must be something distinctive in the voice which necessitates it being told in first person rather than third. That distinctiveness is there in addition to whatever unique circumstances within the narrative make it a story best told in first person.

*

I interrupt this discussion to give a quick and simplistic definition of different types of point of view:

- First person: I walked down the street. When I turned around, I saw a tiger walking behind me.
- Second person: You walk down the street, and when you turn, you see the tiger walking behind you.
- Third-person limited: She walked down the street. When she turned to look behind, she saw a tiger following her.
- Third-person omniscient: She walked down the street, and a tiger was walking behind her. (She hasn't turned to see it yet, but the narrator can see it.)

In first person, the "I" is the narrator. In second, the narrator is speaking to the "you." In third-person limited there is a (usually hidden) narrator, but the story is being told solely through the eyes of the point-of-view character, who can only see and observe what she would naturally see and observe. In third-person omniscient, the narrator can see all.

*

When I wrote the very first pieces of narrative that would eventually become the Spiritwalker Trilogy, I had trouble finding a voice that worked. My first attempts, all in third person, didn't catch; they did not feel right.

I finally tried first person. The narrative voice flowed far more smoothly in first than it had in third.

Here is the original first page of the novel. This is from the earliest draft, unrevised and (you'll note) a different opening point than the novel has now. Also, notably, I later changed Bee's name from Bianca to Beatrice.

*

Bee and I sat in the window-seat with a blanket tucked over us to keep off the chill and the heavy curtains closed over our backs to hide us from anyone who might wander into the sitting room. Our breath made steam flowers on the windowpanes. Winter's cold had come early; it was still a week away from year's end. Outside, snow glittered in the square and on the crowns of trees, although the streets had been swept clean.

"What did he say?" Bee whispered. By the light of the streetlamps lining the square outside, I could see her bat her eyelashes in that truly obnoxious way she had, the one that never failed to demolish the objections and reproaches of any adult caught in the beat of those dark wings. "Cat," she added breathlessly, "you have to tell me."

"I swore I wouldn't tell."

She punched me on the shoulder. Though she might look like a dainty little thing, Bee was a bruiser, really mean when she got roused.

"Ouch!"

"You earned it! I've been in love with him forever—"

"Two weeks!"

"Two months!" She pressed a hand to her ample bosom, which was heaving under her tightly laced, high-collared dress. "I kept the truth of my desperate feelings to myself for fear—"

"For fear we'd wonder why you'd so suddenly left off being in love with and destined to wed Maester Lukas of the lovely, dark, curly hair and turned your stalwart heart to the beauty of Maester David of the handsome, black eyes."

"Which you yourself admit are handsome."

"Yes, he's almost as pretty as you are, and well aware of it. He's the vainest boy I've ever met."

"How can you say so? The story of how his family escaped from the assault on Sawili by murderous ghouls is heartbreaking."

"If it's true. Anyone can say what they like when there are no witnesses."

"You just have no heart, Cat. You're heartless."

"Thank the Lady! The family is well-to-do, that's certain. A point in his favor."

"You're going to tell me what he said because otherwise I will pour a handful of salt into your breakfast porridge for the next month—"

"Hush."

I have good hearing. I could hear footsteps coming from a mile away, or at least from the landing. Bee froze with the hand to her chest and face raised—she was still glowering at me—posed unmoving like one of the living re-creations of the honored ancestors in a tableaux at the New Year's Festival.

"Bianca? Catherine?" The voice of Servestra Artistina rose in volume as she entered the room behind us. We had carefully turned down all the lamps to make it gloomy. "Darlings? It's time to leave for the lecture."

*

Although first person felt like a better fit for the story, nevertheless I worried that first person wouldn't be effective, that I couldn't keep it up for an entire novel, much less a trilogy, that the "voice" would become tired. I hadn't yet learned that Cat, in fact, never gets tired of talking.

So I rewrote the scene in third-person limited past tense because all my novels until then had been in third-person limited past tense, and thus it is the point of view I'm most comfortable with. Here is that same section in third-person limited:

*

Cat and Bee sat in the window-seat with a blanket tucked over their skirts to keep off the chill and the heavy curtains closed over their backs to hide them from anyone who might wander into the sitting room. Cat's breath made steam flowers on the windowpanes. Winter's cold had come early; it was still a week away from year's end. Outside, snow glittered in the square and on the crowns of trees, although the streets had been swept clean.

"What did he say?" Bee whispered.

By the light of the streetlamps lining the square outside, Cat could see her cousin flutter her eyelashes in that truly obnoxious way she had, the one that never failed to demolish the objections and reproaches of any adult caught in the beat of those dark wings. "Cat," she added breathlessly, "you have to tell me."

"I swore I wouldn't tell."

Bee punched Cat on the shoulder.

"Ouch!"

Though she might look like a dainty little thing, Bee was a bruiser, really mean when she got roused. "You earned it! I've been in love with him forever—"

"Two weeks!"

"Two months! Ever since I had that dream of walking with him through the golden palace undersea—" She pressed a hand to her ample bosom, which was heaving under her tightly laced, high-collared dress. "—I have kept the truth of my desperate feelings to myself for fear—"

"For fear we'd wonder why you'd so suddenly left off being in love with and destined to wed Maester Lukas of the lovely, dark hair and turned your stalwart heart to the beauty of Maester David of the handsome, black eyes."

"Which you yourself admit are handsome."

"Yes, he's prettier than you are, and well aware of it. He's the vainest boy I ever met."

"How can you say so? The story of how his family escaped from the assault on Sawili by murderous ghouls is heartbreaking."

"If it's true. Anyone can say what they like when there are no witnesses."

"You just have no heart, Cat. You're heartless."

"Thank the Lady! The family is well-to-do, that's certain. And his sisters are known to be very clever and maybe touched with a breath of magery. All points in his favor."

"You're going to tell me what he said because otherwise I will pour a hand- ful of salt into your breakfast porridge every morning for the next month—"

"Hush."

Cat had good hearing. She could hear footsteps coming from a mile away, or at least from the landing. Bee froze with the hand to her chest and face raised— still glowering at Cat —posed unmoving like one of the living re-creations of the honored ancestors in a tableaux at the New Year's Festival.

"Bianca? Catherine?" The voice of Servestra Artistina rose in volume as she entered the dark room. "Darlings? It's time to leave for the lecture."

*

Two things jumped out at me when I switched point of view.

First, third person had no "pop." For me, it read flat.

Second, and more importantly, my attempt to write in third-person lim- ited felt and read (to me) as if I was instead writing in third-person omni- scient. I couldn't get the voice into third-person limited because, as I realized, the story had a narrator who was speaking, and that narrator was Cat. So I had to switch back to first person and trust that I would be able to fully "get" her voice right and hold on to it for three volumes.

In the end, writing a trilogy in Cat's voice proved easy, especially as I discovered the "sound" of her voice. The rhythm of her speech is distinctive; she observes and speaks with a flavor all her own, and she is funny, often on purpose, though sometimes inadvertently. That she loves to talk matters to the plot. Better yet, I enjoyed the challenge of filtering the story through her eyes and her words while leaving a little space for the reader to maybe see some things and some characters a little differently than Cat does.

The other thing I learned? Never say never.

Writing a Woman Who Eats What She Wants Without Being Shamed

T HIS ESSAY WAS WRITTEN IN RESPONSE TO A READER'S QUESTION, quoted here: *Why did you choose to elaborate on Cat's love of food? I thought it was interesting that we have a heroine who actually appreciates food. Was this in response to society's view on female bodies, or did you just write it as part of her character?*

*

Have a story:

When I was a sophomore in high school, I was asked out by a senior.

You have to understand that I was a geeky girl before the word was in common use. I had spent my childhood playing outdoors, climbing trees, mowing my family's vast lawn (we lived in the country), moving irrigation pipe in the pasture, swimming in the river, making up maps of places that didn't exist, and so on. I desperately wanted to walk through a portal into another world, one where I could be an adventurer. I was not "date" material. In fact, I have to tell you quite honestly that this was (I believe) the only date I went on in high school. I don't even remember the guy's name, but—wow!—a date! Back in the day, when I was in high school, a girl's worth could be measured in whether or not she was considered "date-able."

So understand this context.

It was a double date. He had a friend, and his friend's girlfriend (also a senior) was on the dance team with me. The four of us went to see a movie.

But first, we got pizza.

There we sat in the pizza parlor (I can still see the scene in my mind's eye, even though I can't remember any of their names). The pizza arrived.

I know American pizza is considered an abomination by some, but I remain fond of it. We each took a piece of pizza and ate it, and then the guys took a second piece of pizza—and so did I.

They all stared at me. Truly stared; they were shocked. Genuinely shocked.

One of them said, "Wow! *You really eat a lot!*"

I thought (but did not say), "A second piece of pizza is not eating a lot. Eating a lot is four pieces of pizza, which I could certainly manage on a good day."

There I sat, fifteen years old, an active young person being shamed into not eating as much as I wanted to, simply because having a hearty appetite wasn't considered *feminine*.

I understood exactly what was happening, and I didn't like it that girls' appetites were being policed, that my companions thoughtlessly believed in and, by their actions, supported this cultural narrative about femininity, which I was meant to also adhere to. They weren't being malicious. They just had never thought to examine the narrative. The guy and I never went on another date. As much as I hated being the girl no one wanted to go out with, I hated more having to cut out my own heart and deny my own stomach.

This stuff is pernicious. And it's wrong.

This is all to say that I actually walked backward into the business with Cat and food.

In *Cold Magic* when Andevai takes Cat away from her home, they travel partway through the city and halt at a mage House inn for the night. There, they are offered a sumptuous supper, but he (in a scene cribbed from Shakespeare's *The Taming of the Shrew*) rejects almost all the food as unfit. As it happens, he is rejecting it not to be an asshole to Cat but because he is involved in a status competition with the people who run the inn, and Cat is collateral damage (so to speak) to his need to put those other people in their place.

Cat hadn't yet had her supper when she was taken away from her home earlier that evening, and she gets barely anything to eat at the inn, which means she goes to bed hungry and thinking about food. That was how the scene played out as I wrote it.

Cat stays hungry for much of *Cold Magic*, and she thinks about food frequently, and when she does get food, she eats it with relish and appreciation. Somehow, Cat's hunger triggered my own memory of the disastrous pizza parlor evening, the anger I felt then that I was meant to feel shame for loving to eat, that I would have to choose between social acceptance and enjoying food.

In other societies and eras, eating and weight will have different cultural meanings than they do in modern American culture. I don't want to go into that here except to note that I did not do any research into the history of eating as a social phenomenon.

However, somehow, in the middle of writing *Cold Magic*, the thing with Cat and food became settled in her character: Cat loves food. She is often (always!) hungry and can eat an impressive amount. She never apologizes for or feels shame about how much she likes to eat. Never.

In fact, Andevai never remarks on how much she eats either, though later, in *Cold Fire*, he deliberately uses food to court her because he is observant enough to realize that she loves food—and because he is trying to make up a little for what he now recognizes as his awful behavior when they first met.

There are also a number of asides in *Cold Fire* that equate appetite for food with appetite for sex, and it is no coincidence that sex is another way in which women are policed and shamed, and that I am also making the point that, just as there is nothing shameful about loving food, there is nothing shameful about loving sex.

So, yes: partly Cat loves to eat because it became part of her character as I wrote the first draft. But I very much deliberately elaborated on her love for food as a response to the way women can be shamed about food and eating. For Cat, food is a joyful and happy thing. It matters to me that she be an example of a female character who loves to eat, who eats a lot, and who is never shamed or policed for it.

Why Cat Sews

I<small>N</small> C<small>HAPTER</small> O<small>NE</small> <small>OF</small> *C<small>OLD</small> M<small>AGIC</small>,* <small>OUR HEROINE,</small> C<small>AT</small> B<small>ARAHAL</small>, sneaks downstairs at dawn to return a book she's not been given permission to remove from her uncle's library. It's clear she is well educated and from a family with a high degree of education for girls as well as boys.

While in the parlor, Cat notes that:

"(A)ll eight mending baskets were set neatly in a row on the narrow side table, for the women of the house—Aunt Tilly, me, Beatrice, her little sisters, our governess, Cook, and Callie—would sit in the parlor in the evening and sew while Uncle or Evved read aloud from a book and Pompey trimmed the candle wicks."

This sentence is meant mostly to describe the poverty of the household. I don't go into detail about the arrangements, but the reader may guess that the family does not have enough money to heat and light more than one room in the evening.

Another way to show their straitened circumstances was to show that they sew almost all of their own clothing because they can't afford to have their clothes made by others (the book is set before the era of inexpensive, ready-to-wear clothing that can be bought off the rack in clothing stores). Mending is a crucial part of economy, as well as refurbishing older clothes, repurposing worn garments, and refitting them for a different person.

This mention of sewing and how the family mostly makes their own clothes also tells us something about their world, in a time in which sewing, knitting, weaving, and other fabric crafts were not a luxury or a hobby but a necessity. People who could not afford bespoke clothing (i.e. made-to-measure by a tailor or dressmaker) had either to sew their own, buy used clothing at markets, or hope to obtain cast-off or stolen items by other means.

Sewing is mentioned in a second context as well:

"Our governness, Shiffa, had been imported all the way from the Barahal motherhouse in Gadir to teach us girls deportment, fencing, dancing, sewing, and how to memorize large blocks of text so we could write them down or repeat them later."

Cat is portrayed as a sensible, practical girl who has learned a number of skills, some of which are specifically tailored to the role all children of the extended Hassi Barahal clan are expected to take up in service of the clan's business, which is that of mercenaries, spies, and couriers. Fencing and memorizing texts are skills clearly useful for spies and couriers. Fighting and spying are also skills that many adventure novels highlight.

In Book Two, *Cold Fire*, Cat is thrown out into the wide world, alone and far afield from the place she grew up. Basically, she finds herself with the clothes on her back and her sword as her only possessions. It would have been easy for me, at this point, to focus on Cat's sword-craft.

Being confident with a sword is a useful competency for a young woman unexpectedly out on her own in an insecure and often dangerous world. Her ability to use the sword could have become the most important and most visible of her skills as she continued her adventures.

But I did not want to imply that the skills most important to her ability to adapt to her new circumstances were solely or chiefly the skills that have long been culturally identified as "masculine," such as fencing (fighting). I wanted to depict skills identified (in Western society but by no means in all societies) as "feminine" to be equally important to her survival.

Why? Because as a society, we often tend to value the "masculine" over the "feminine." "Masculine" is public and strong, "feminine" is private and (often) sexual, and frequently "feminine" concerns are defined as trivial and unimportant. Such definitions are cultural constructs, as is the relative value assigned to various skills and experiences.

For instance, is *reading* a "masculine" skill? In places and times when the literacy rate of men far outpaced that of women, or when boys were far more likely to be given an education than girls, reading was considered a masculine pursuit. It's easy to forget that today, when one of the common assumptions in the USA (again, this will be different in different places) is that girls somehow naturally tend to be better at reading than boys. This idea is pervasive now, but in other times and places would have been considered radical or ridiculous.

Thus, what is Cat's most important "possession?" What does she see it as? When Cat washes up in the city of Expedition in the Antilles (in *Cold Fire*), she acts to secure the goodwill of the woman who has shown her hospitality by describing the skills she thinks would interest her host:

"Can I help in some way? I'm a good worker. I know how to sew, cook, read, and write. I must tell you, I have nothing, no coin, no possessions, nothing but my labor to offer you."

Competency and willingness to work matter when it comes time for a character to adapt to new situations. Competent characters are more likely to adapt successfully regardless of whether their skills are culturally identified as masculine or feminine, of course, but as a society we tend to depict stereotypically "masculine" skills as more valuable, or just tend to depict those skills at all, as if they are the only ones "people" will be interested in reading about.

In fact, a wide range of skills are necessary for societies to hold together. In a fully realized world, it is important to acknowledge more than a limited few.

In *Cold Fire*, Cat's skill at sewing gives her a way to make a place for herself in her new circumstances. It gives her a bit of status and respect and creates an interesting contrast to her old life because in the city of Expedition, sewing (as well as tailoring for both men and women) is a predominantly male profession. Additionally, she mends while conversing with other women—because hand-work like sewing is a job that can be done while listening and talking—and the ties she builds with other people are crucial to her success in being accepted in a new place.

Sewing helps her to survive.

As a character, Cat sews because, in the cultural landscape and time she grew up, she would have learned how to sew. She sews well because sewing well is a challenge she relishes. Because she likes fashionable clothes that flatter her figure, sewing is the only way she has to fit herself in such clothing.

As a writer, I emphasized Cat's sewing because it was true to the character and the time and because it worked well within the plot.

I emphasized her sewing because it allowed me to give life to the world through details of daily life that intersected with the character and the plot, rather than simply using discrete details pinned on like photos or backdrops. Sewing is a detail that helps to illuminate Cat: she is a very physical character, very active, and, of course, very talkative, but her facility at sewing also reveals that she is painstaking, likes to do things well, and that, despite her talkative nature, she is also a good listener.

Finally, I emphasized her sewing because I wanted to make a statement about the importance of all the different kinds of work that underpin human society, especially those that, in my experience, are too often brushed aside in the science and fantasy fiction that I love to both read and write.

The Creole of Expedition
Part One: Setting the Stage and Asking the Question

WHEN I BEGAN WRITING BOOK TWO IN THE SPIRITWALKER TRIL-
ogy, *Cold Fire*, I knew the plot would take my protagonist, Cat
Barahal, to the Caribbean. Because the Spiritwalker books are a version of alternate history, I also knew that the 19th-century Caribbean in this universe
would have a different power dynamic from the 19th-century Caribbean in
our own world.

For one thing, in the Spiritwalker world, the Americas were not colo-
nized by the European powers. (As it happens, the European powers as we
know them do not exist.) Among many other consequences, this meant that
the Taino and other peoples who populated the Greater Antilles were *not*
devastated by disease, forced labor, slavery, and various attempts to erase and
subsume their cultures. Thus, they continued to expand and thrive.

I had already established (if not explicitly in Book One, then in my own
notes) that a fleet from the beleaguered Empire of Mali had reached the Caribbean two centuries before the main story begins and founded a settlement.
With these refugees from Mali came also Phoenician sailors and merchants,
and later they were joined by Roman sailors and merchants and immigrants,
as well as by Celtic immigrants, Iberian immigrants, and other people who
had left Europa, for one reason or another, to make a new life elsewhere.
Clutches of trolls, also known as the feathered people, had also migrated
south from their ancestral homelands in North America.

Together, these settlers had established Expedition Territory as a small,
autonomous territory within (and with the permission of and through a
treaty with) the greater Taino empire, which I decided had, by this time, absorbed all the islands, greater and lesser, of the Caribbean.

In the Spiritwalker world, Europans refer to the area as the Antilles rather
than the Caribbean. I used Antilles in preference to Caribbean because I felt
it would be clearer to readers that the cultures they would meet here would
not be the same as the cultures many in the USA and elsewhere most often
refer to as "the Caribbean." The word "Antilles" has its own long history, with
a Latin- (Romance language-) based etymology and what is possibly an origi-

nation in old Iberia, which fit well enough the altered history.

However, it also made sense to me that—given the several centuries' separation, and with the slow sea travel of the time, and with a different blend of languages present within Expedition—the speech of the people in Expedition would be noticeably different than the speech Cat had grown up with in her own home city of Adurnam.

I don't talk about this in the text (and I realize that it is a contradiction regardless because I am writing in English), but in Adurnam *theoretically* the basic Latin foundation of the common language is heavily influenced by local Celtic and Bambara dialects, with elements of Phoenician blended in. Cat also speaks a modern version of the Punic dialect that would have developed in Qart Hadast (Carthage) and later adapted to Gadir (Cadiz) where the Hassi Barahal family has made its base for many generations, but I never had time to deal with her multilingual capabilities because it never really came up in the story. Cat would also have studied a "schoolbook" form of Latin, which would be known among all literate people in her society, and which would be in general use for correspondence. This "formal Latin" is the foundation for the common trade language.

My assumption had to be that many people who lived in cities spoke more than one language and understood multiple dialects as a matter of course, and that villages who were governed by legal clientage to a mage House or princely clan would have at least some members of the village who could speak their masters' language, as well as the ability to communicate with outsiders and people passing through in a local pidgin version of the trade language. Only in the most isolated villages would you find monolingual people, and even then, there would surely be peddlers who came through periodically, bringing with them goods, stories, and bits and pieces of the outside world in the form of scraps of a more cosmopolitan language.

Regardless, once Cat reached Expedition, it was clear she would hear a language that she could partly understand but which would sound very different to her ear. Even if I presupposed (as I did) that Latin had retained its place in the Antilles as the basis for the common trade language, with a strong Phoenician secondary influence, the other secondary influencing languages would be present in different proportions. In Expedition, Celtic dialects would be weak, while a variant of what is Bambara in our world would be strong. Additionally, because the dominant culture in the region is the Taino Empire, the language of the Taino would certainly have made its mark on the language that developed in Expedition, even if it did not replace it, and many people would speak both the creole and "standard Taino" as a matter of necessity.

As I worked on *Cold Fire*, I had to face this crucial question: do I use a creole to represent the local language of Expedition, or do I write people's speech to be indistinguishable from Cat's own?

Using a creole would create several significant problems:

One, of course, is simply the extra effort for a reader who is not familiar with the creole to read and parse. For example, "Dat is di way dem chat" as opposed to "That is the way they talk." There is a certain learning curve for readers unfamiliar with creoles (blended languages) to get comfortable with the vocabulary, grammar, and rhythm of a creole, and that is a lot to ask of a reader who is already parsing multiple fantastical elements as well.

Second, writing dialogue in a dialect or creole that one is not intimately familiar with is difficult to pull off well and easy to do poorly. It may come across as insulting and appropriative, or as awkward or demeaning. It may seem to some readers that the speakers of the creole are being made to look ignorant and ill-educated because they are not using grammar "correctly" (although they are, in fact, using a streamlined grammar rather than standard grammar because a creole has a functional grammar of its own, and none of its features are a marker of ignorance or stupidity regardless).

For these reasons, I was extremely hesitant to try to use a creole for the local speech in Expedition. Given that I am not a native speaker of nor intimately familiar with any of the actual Caribbean creoles spoken today or in historical times, how could I possibly write a creole that would feel authentic within the text and would not be disrespectful to indigenous speakers of creoles?

Set against those objections there rose answering responses:

Cat is a visitor to Expedition, not a local. What she hears will sound different to her ear than to a native speaker of the creole. If I simply wrote people talking the same way she did, the story and her experience would lose much of the sense of being in a truly different place from where she grew up. Instead of a foreign city, it would just be her city with a different backdrop. While that would be the safe choice, it would also be the blandest and weakest choice. And it would be disrespectful in a different way.

The actual historical presence of the many Caribbean creoles and their importance to literature, music, culture, religion, and history must not be ignored. The Caribbean is a vibrant and vital cultural sea. To not even give a nod to the reality of the Caribbean we know in our world, simply because it would be hard to do so, seemed wrong to me. As disrespectful and appropriative as it can be to ham-handedly write clunky, bad dialogue with precious dialect-isms, it seemed more disrespectful to me to erase the existence of creole altogether.

I knew that, regardless, Cat's experiences in Expedition would be filtered through her point of view, her limited knowledge, and her presence there as a foreigner. That gave me a little leeway.

In the end, I decided I had to use *a* creole.

My answer was to use not an extant creole—which I could not pull off—but to create a creole for the Antilles of the Spiritwalker world that would echo and draw from the English-dominant creoles of our Caribbean, but which would have its own blend of borrowed words, rhythms, and grammar and, furthermore, would be influenced by the Taino language and empire that surrounds Expedition Territory.

Does the creole in *Cold Fire* work? I don't believe that is my question to answer. For some readers, it will work; others will find it problematic or annoying. I did my best, that's all I can say for sure.

In retrospect, looking back, I would do it again the same way. Not because I think I did it well (or not well) or even necessarily right, but because I did what I felt I had to do to make the culture of Expedition feel like a real place, with its own history and set of traditions, a culture that has developed over time because of the particular circumstances of its founding, setting, and development.

The Creole of Expedition
Part Two: Creating the Creole

A s I WORKED ON *COLD FIRE*, I ASKED MYSELF THIS QUESTION: DO I use a creole to represent the local language of Expedition, or do I write people's speech to be indistinguishable from Cat's own?

Ultimately, I decided to use a creole to represent the speech of Expedition, a place which is the alt-fantasy equivalent of our world's Caribbean. At this point, I had to ask myself a second question: given that I am not a native speaker of nor intimately familiar with any of the actual Caribbean creoles spoken today or in historical times, how do I write a creole that will seem authentic within the text without being a clumsy imitation or offensive parody of actual creoles?

Let me first give a couple of quick definitions.

Oxford Dictionaries defines a pidgin as "a grammatically simplified form of a language, used for communication between people not sharing a common language. Pidgins have a limited vocabulary, some elements of which are taken from local languages, and are not native languages, but arise out of language contact between speakers of other languages."

A creole, on the other hand, is "a mother tongue formed from the contact of two languages through an earlier pidgin stage." (I would add "two or more" because that was certainly the case in Hawai'i. Lest you wonder, Hawaiian Pidgin is a creole.)

A dominant culture: Taino

My friend and fellow writer Katharine Kerr has done a great deal of research in linguistics (her Deverry epic fantasy series is a superb example of what you can do with language in a fantasy sequence that spans hundreds of years), so I asked for her advice. We both knew I could not possibly replicate any of the existing or historical Caribbean creoles and, in any case, given that the Spiritwalker Trilogy posits an extremely alternate history, the actual historical creoles would not fit regardless.

She suggested that I devise a creole unique to Expedition.

Kerr wrote, *"The dominant language in any creole is that of the dominant culture. What is your dominant culture?"*

The city of Expedition was founded by a Malian fleet supplemented by Phoenician navigators and sailors. The fleet's chief language would be a variant of modern-day Bambara with Punic loan words woven in. But any trans-Atlantic trade and intercourse with Europa would be heavily influenced by the presence of Latin as the lingua franca (trade language) of continental Europa. However, because Expedition is a small territory on the island of Kiskeya (Hispaniola in our world), the regional dominant culture in which it exists would be that of the Taino because the Antilles (Caribbean) in this alternate universe is ruled by the Taino.

Therefore, the first thing I decided was that a number of Taino words and phrases would be present as part of the everyday language. These would be reinforced (insofar as I could) with elements of Taino culture that would have become part of the society of Expedition in the way cultures adapt, adopt, and blend to become something unique to a specific place. I could only pick a couple of things to give Taino names, lest the plethora of new words become overwhelming for the reader, so besides words we already use in English that are of Taino derivation (such as hurricane, hammock, and papaya), I highlighted Taino elements which would matter to the plot.

Taino words that are part of Expedition's creole include:

> *maku* (foreigner)
> *opia* (spirit of an ancestor)
> *areito* (dance, song, or festival)
> *batey* (a ceremonial plaza often associated with a local version of the ball game that was known throughout the Caribbean and Central American region. As an historical note I should mention that in the Dominican Republic, the word "batey" came to mean the company towns associated with sugar cane fields and processing.)
> *cemi* (a sacred object)
> *behique/behica* (shaman; also used to mean a fire mage in Spiritwalker)
> *cacique/cacica* (chief; ruler; king/female king)
> *cobo* (queen conch)

Additionally, fish vocabulary in the creole include: *pargo, cachicata, cajaya, anolis, carite, guinchos, barracudas*

As for place names, Bahama itself is a Taino place name. So, possibly (likely), is Cuba (a shortened form of an older name), Habana, Boriken (Puerto Rico), and Kiskeya itself (the island we know as Hispaniola divided now into Haiti—from the Taino *Ayiti*—and the Dominican Republic).

The creole continuum

However, the creole of Expedition could not just be a peppering of words foreign to the English I was writing in. The creole as Cat heard it would have not just differences in vocabulary but differences in grammar, in word choice, and in the rhythms of its speech.

Fortunately, through the miracle of the internet, I had previously made the acquaintance of Dr. Fragano Ledgister, a professor at Clark Atlanta University and who is himself Anglo-Jamaican. In a similar way to how Dr. Kurtis Nishimura allowed me to pick his brains about the physics of cold magic and fire magic to help devise a "plausible" explanation for cold magic, Dr. Ledgister was exceedingly generous in answering my questions, offering insight both into the Caribbean language and into the Caribbean culture as he knows it. It is really through his offices that I was able to develop the creole as it appears on the page.

As well, many details of our world's Caribbean are present because of things he shared with me. I will briefly mention that he introduced me to the many varieties of fruit commonly enjoyed on the islands that are not as well-known elsewhere and which play such an important role in Andevai's courtship of Cat.

Dr. Ledgister also discussed with me the work of Mervyn Alleyne, which became very important in how I began to understand structuring a creole on more than just a superficial level.

Alleyne's classification of Jamaican English is that it operates at three levels: the hierolect, Standard Jamaican English, that differs from the international (British or American) standard primarily in terms of minor differences of vocabulary and usage. The mesolect, or generally understood creole, spoken by most people and heavily influenced by the standard language. Lastly, the basilect, or "'di real raw-chaw Patwa,' as my friend Hugh Martin put it," which is spoken by rural people and the less-educated. Each level of language is used in different social contexts.

Therefore, there are three versions of the creole in Expedition: an acrolect (the term that has replaced Alleyne's hierolect), a mesolect, and a basilect.

For example, Abby, on Salt Island, is a country gal. She speaks the basilect. She (and her brother, who we meet on the airship) are the only people Cat encounters who speak the basilect. It is characterized by having a simpler grammar and more archaic elements. Besides including all the features of the mesolect, it drops linking verbs (except "shall") and drops the "th-" sound to "dat" and "di" and so on. Also, basilect speakers do not use past tense, only present tense (more on verb use below).

Almost all the people of Expedition speak the mesolect, the most common form of dialect that Cat hears. I'll elaborate on its development below.

The acrolect is spoken by the most high-status families in the old city of Expedition; technically, the Taino nobles speak the acrolect since they speak what might be termed "formal Latin"—that is, Taino who are not Expeditioners never speak in the creole. For instance, at the dinner party at the townhouse in Expedition where General Camjiata is staying, the son of a Keita merchant house speaks mostly with "correct English" but words like "yee" and "shall" are still present in his speech.

People of Taino ancestry who are Expeditioners speak the creole the same as any other Expeditioners. "Maku" (foreigners), however, are usually distinguished by not speaking the creole, although I allowed a few usages to creep into the speech of foreign-born residents of Expedition, most commonly the use of "gal" for "girl" or "woman," the use of "yee" for "you," and the generic use of "shall" as an all-purpose verb (more on those below).

The building blocks

I wanted to write a simplified creole that would not be too difficult or distracting for readers to parse.

> Dr. Ledgister pointed out that:
> "A creole has a streamlined grammar because it starts out as a pidgin or lingua franca before becoming a birth tongue. (Pidgins combining a language of rule and vocabulary and grammar elements from several subordinate languages encourages simplicity.) It's also liable to contain archaisms because it will retain terms from when it was first formed (e.g. Jamaican speech still has words last used in standard English in the 17th century, like peradventure)."

With his help, I focused on four elements (besides the presence of Taino words) to highlight which features would thus distinguish the Expedition creole (in its mesolect form) from the language Cat speaks:

1. Verbs and verb tenses
2. Pronouns
3. Word choice (e.g. substitute words and archaisms)
4. Speech rhythms

Verbs

Simplifying grammar meant simplifying verb tenses. I needed to emphasize that a simplified grammar used in a creole did not mean that the speakers of creole were ignorant, stupid, ill-educated, or demeaned; it was merely an element of the creole.

Dr. Ledgister said:

"One example of this is that verbs don't decline. You have Abby say [in an early draft], "I does not like it that this man Drake, this maku, decides so quickly to make yee his sweet," where a Jamaican would say, "Me doh like it dat dis man Drake decide so fas to make you his gyal," and a Trinidadian would say, "Ah don' like it dat dis man Drake decide so quick dat you his sweet girl." My point here is that the verbs don't decline."

In the final published draft, Abby says, "I don' like dat dis man Drake decide so quick to make yee he sweet gal."

I came up with a simplified set of rules for myself to follow as I wrote:

1. Present tense should use the infinitive in all cases (i.e. without the "to," unless the "to" is called for. So, for example: "we have," "he have," "you have.")
2. While technically it should be "we be" and "you be," I use "is" (because it is easier for speakers of standard English to read). Similarly:
    "I am" becomes "I's." "You are" becomes "you's."
    We and they "is" depends on the context but is often "We's" or "they's."
    "It is" and "It was" are contracted into "'tis" and "'twas"
3. Simple past tense works pretty much as in standard English.

I could have done more with the verbs, but I figured that was enough.

Pronouns

Originally, I had this challenging and exciting idea that the basilect (as spoken by Abby) would use Bambara pronouns to reflect the Malian ancestry of the majority of the early settlers in Expedition. But when I tried to write it, it just became impenetrable, especially from a reader's standpoint.

Instead, I adapted the Bambara "you"—rendered as "i" (ee) in English transcription—by turning "you" into "yee." Yee is used throughout all forms of the creole, my one hat tip to Bambara pronouns. I left all other subject pronouns the same as they are in American English.

Object pronouns, meanwhile, I left generally the same, although on a case-by-case basis and depending on the rhythm of the sentence, the object pronoun could be replaced with the subject pronoun.

The possessive is generally replaced by the subject pronoun—"his book" becomes "he book," except in the case of "I," in which the object pronoun "me book" is used.

Word choice, replacement words, and archaisms

Here are some replacement words I utilized in Expedition's creole, or words commonly used differently than we might use them in standard English:

GAL: "girl" (as in old enough to have sex) or "young woman" is always replaced by "gal," which became the local equivalent of an all-purpose term for girls/women in the general ages of 15–late 20s.

Older people would usually refer to young adult males (ages circa 15–25, depending on the age of the older person referring to them) as "lad." Young men refer to other young men as "men" and to young women their own age as "gals." Similarly, young women apply this rule the other way around for young men.

SHALL: this is an all-purpose verb used where appropriate and often in place of verbs like "would," "ought," and so on.

DON' : replaces "don't" or "do not."
In general, I tried to avoid "do" (and Abby, using the basilect, never uses "do"), but sometimes I left it in because it got too convoluted or hard to understand or choppy to take it out.

RECKON: used instead of "think."

In regards to archaisms, people use some older locutions and/or regional words like "peradventure" and "arseness."(In case you are wondering where "arseness" comes from, here is a quote from Dr. Ledgister's correspondence:

"I just grabbed my copy of (Richard) Allsopp and was struck as I opened it by the Trinidadian term "arseness" for "stupidity" (or as most West Indians would say "stupidness"), that's worth using!"

And, indeed, it was!

Rhythm

When I had all these things in place, the rhythm took care of itself.

The grammatical patterns, the pronouns, and the adapted words themselves began to structure how people spoke. Once that happened, the rhythm of their speech took on a distinctive flavor and inflection. By the time I had finished writing *Cold Fire*, the people of Expedition had a way of speaking that sounded "natural" to my ear and that, more importantly, did not have the same rhythm as the speech used by Cat and other Europans.

Conclusions

There is a lot more detail I could go into, but this post is already quite long. One of the best parts about corresponding with Dr. Fragano Ledgister was getting to read his anecdotes. (If you ever get a chance, ask him about meeting C. L. R. James.)

Not everyone will agree that the creole in *Cold Fire* works, nor need they do so. But for my part, considering it as an experiment and as a challenge for me as a writer, I felt good about the final result. Whatever else, and no matter how it holds up, I am glad to have pushed myself past what I was comfortable attempting to write. In certain ways, making the effort was its own reward.

Character Study: Catherine Barahal

H ERE'S MY ANSWER TO THE READER QUESTION: *WHAT WAS YOUR thought process for the creation of Cat?*
First, I wanted Cat to be physically confident, someone who knows when to run and when to stand her ground, and who isn't afraid of a physical challenge. At the same time, I wanted her to *not* be a person whose feelings are bottled up; Cat is very free with her feelings; she laughs and cries easily and does not judge herself for having strong feelings.

That is the initial contrast I was going for: She is both physically confident *and* emotionally confident in the sense that she doesn't try to hide, disguise, or be embarrassed by her emotions, nor does she see being emotional as something inherently weak. She wears her heart on her sleeve, and she is not afraid of a challenge.

I did not want her to be a girl who needs to be rescued; I wanted her to be a young woman able to rescue herself (and others). I did not want her anger to be debilitating or shameful; I wanted her anger (when it manifests) to be clean and pure. I did not want her to be coy or retiring; I wanted her to be forthright, curious, and fully engaged in exploring all the aspects of herself that commonly unfold as people come into adulthood, like her sexual feelings, her growing understanding of how politics and the world works and her place within the world, and her concern for and loyalty toward others. I wanted her to judge injustice harshly but to feel compassion even for people who may have hurt her. I wanted her to display a sense of the absurd and to have the capacity to see joy in the world. Most of all, I wanted her to speak for herself because I wanted readers to read about a character who believes in her own voice, as I hope we all can learn to believe in our own voices.

That last aspect turned out to be easy because the book is written in Cat's first-person narration. All I had to do was move my own "voice" aside and let the book emerge in her voice. One of the most interesting things about writing in Cat's voice is that she's funny. My usual serious-business, epic-fantasy-writing voice is not funny, so it has been an illuminating experience writing books that people tell me make them laugh out loud at moments.

The other thing I wanted to do with Cat was to show her flaws in action and to allow her to make mistakes, even stupid mistakes, like people do; for example, she makes a couple of bad choices in *Cold Fire*, particularly with regard to James Drake, that merit further examination. Cat is levelheaded and practical, but she can also be naive without truly realizing it. She's compassionate but can be judgmental. Her rashness gets her into trouble, and she is a classic example of a person who leaps before she looks, although fortunately for her, her instincts are good and her reaction times excellent.

For all that she talks, Cat can also be very secretive, and this very trait gets her in trouble in *Cold Fire*. However, if I have done my job correctly as a writer in setting up her history of and reasons for secretiveness, it will be understandable to the reader why she acts as she does.

Cat is accustomed to a close-knit family life. Not only is she an extrovert, but she genuinely desires and prefers to be around people. That's how she feels most at rest in her heart. In *Cold Magic* Cat is actually never fully alone, in terms of being without actual or "political" familial relations with other people. She is with Bee and her aunt and uncle at the beginning. Then she is married to and travels with Andevai (however unpleasant that experience may be for her). Fleeing the mage House, she is rescued by the coachman and the eru, and, of course, the eru calls her "cousin." The villagers treat her both as a relation (Andevai's wife) and as a person with customary guest rights (i.e. not to be turned over to the mansa because it would result in her death). Additionally, she trusts Kayleigh because Kayleigh presents herself to Cat in the relation of a sister (even if she is actually working for Vai). Lastly, after Cat and Andevai have their brief adventure in the spirit world, Cat returns to the mortal world with Rory—her half brother—and reunites with Bee.

It is not until Cat is cast out of the spirit world by the Master of the Wild Hunt that she truly finds herself alone (in the ocean, which has metaphorical resonance to her because of her fear of water and because of her parents' death by drowning).

The reckless decisions Cat makes come under pressure of being alone. Her instinct is to try to create relationships with people, as she does with both Abby and Drake on Salt Island and as she perceives she will not be allowed to do with the Taino (the question of whether she has misjudged her initial interaction with the cacica is left for the reader to judge). Her curiosity and her tendency to leap before she examines things closely also play a part in her relationship to Drake—and, of course Drake takes advantage of her naïveté and her ignorance about his true purpose in being there.

In my experience of the world, people make smart decisions, bad decisions, hasty decisions, hesitant decisions, lucky decisions, and stupid decisions, and so on. With Cat, I wanted to portray a person who makes a variety of decisions, some good and some bad. She figures out on her own that her relationship with Drake was a mistake, but she does not let making a mistake rule her psyche, just as she did not let the mansa's command for her death rule her life.

Treated as a whole, one of the crucial traits Cat displays across the entire trilogy (no spoilers here) is that she learns. In any life, that is one of the most important qualities of all.

Character Study: Andevai's Character Development

I N THE ORIGINAL CONCEPTION OF *COLD MAGIC*, A MAGE COMES TO THE protagonist's house with a legal claim to marry the young woman who is the protagonist. The story always had the "forced marriage" trope as part of the plot. A "forced marriage" is any story in which two people *must* get married because of outside forces. For example, one partner might have to marry to secure an inheritance, while the other partner might need to marry because she or he is destitute. An accidental encounter might impel them to marry because of societal strictures or for convenience's sake. A fraud marriage might turn into a real marriage. Or they might both be required to accept a marriage arranged by others for reasons of political or economic or family alliance. And so on.

That is to say, in *Cold Magic*, Cat was always going to have to marry a strange man who walked into her house with a seemingly unshakeable claim to her.

And the man was always going to be of a higher social status than Cat and her household.

When I first had him walk into the house, in the very earliest version, as I was writing the scene for the first time, this man was older, about thirty, a sophisticated and knowledgeable man of privilege at the height of his powers and well aware of his status. But as I wrote that initial encounter, I realized I was reluctant to write the trope of the Experienced Masterful Man meets the Naive and Innocent Girl plot.

More importantly, Andevai himself kept falling out of focus as I wrote this version of him. If I tried to slot him into the older, sophisticated man role, he got blurred; he didn't work. As I wrote the dialogue, his replies and responses remained arrogant and proud, but increasingly, I sensed they were touched with something else. That something else is what I eventually identified as insecurity. He was an asshole in part because he was genuinely overly proud and vain and a jerk, but more so because he was covering for something. I just didn't know what he was insecure about. In writing the first draft of *Cold Magic*, as I unfolded Cat's journey, I discovered Andevai's character too.

First, he was younger than I had thought, twenty-three going on twenty-four. He had therefore some of the faults of youth: He lacked perspective and the ability to step back and use experience to measure his situation. He had a young man's hyperawareness of and defensiveness about how he may appear to others. He also knew less than he claimed, but tried to cover it up.

Additionally, once I stepped back and let his reactions come from my gut rather than my head, I discovered that he was prickly about matters of status, in a way that people who are steeped in their own privilege aren't. Indeed, he didn't get along with the high-status stewards and officials of the mage Houses—or it might be better to say that they could barely deign to respect him, and he reacted to that with defensiveness. When the characters reached the Griffin Inn in South Londun, he treated the innkeeper with disdain in a way that was out of proportion to the situation, a classic mark of youthful insecurity, but when old men of humble birth asked him to sit with them, his manners changed entirely to a tone of respect and deference. Why the difference?

In this first draft, it was not until Cat and Andevai reached the lands under the rule of Four Moons House that, out of the blue, the secret of his background opened up, literally, as I wrote:

> He was not born "in the House" but in one of its client villages. He was in fact born into a legal status somewhere between indentured servitude and slavery, beholden by law (with the rest of his village) to serve the House because of an ancient contractual arrangement.

The scene in which he gets out of the carriage and goes over to greet a field worker, a young woman, who he then confesses to Cat is his sister, was the first time I began to fully understand the complicated emotional landscape which he was trying (and mostly failing) to negotiate. Born into the humblest rank, he had been elevated to a high station and now no longer fit into either place.

In the world of *Cold Magic* and its sequels, the highest level of societally acknowledged and embedded privilege and status is embodied in a man of African ancestry. (A man because this is still a society ruled in a patriarchal manner, although as it turns out—more on this in Book Three—the mage Houses are more of what I would call a "soft patriarchy," by which I mean one in which men are the public rulers but women's skills and strengths are considered crucial to the success of the clan in a way that includes but is not limited to childbearing.)

I did this not to reverse roles or to place people of European ancestry in an underprivileged position (as if to prove that white people can be oppressed too). There are plenty of high-status men (and women) of Celtic, Roman, Iberian, and other European ancestry in the story, exemplified by Brennan Du, Lord Marius, and even General Camjiata (who, like most people the reader meets, is mixed-race).

I had originally intended that Andevai would be that embodiment of privilege and status, and in many ways, he is. To Cat's eyes, at the beginning of their acquaintance, he certainly seems to be and acts as a man of the highest status and power, and he definitely makes sure everyone knows who and what he is. In most ways, outside of the mage House, he is that man. But in their journey together, she discovers that his story is far more complicated, and that his status, like hers, is provisional where it matters most.

As it happens, the person in the Spiritwalker books in whom the highest level of privilege and status is embodied is the mansa of Four Moons House. He is a man who was born and raised knowing that he can speak without being spoken to first, that he is the equal of any man and the superior to all except the emperor of Rome, the other mansas of the highest-status mage Houses, and the most powerful of the Celtic princes. He is a man who can casually use the first name of any man or woman he meets, if he wishes to, while being addressed solely by his title by all but a handful of people.

It is not until I, as the writer, met the mansa in the text that I could fully understand how Andevai was caught out on this difficult terrain between his humble place of birth and his assumed place of power.

Andevai's character unfolded even more in Book Two, in Expedition, where his status as a cold mage was disdained and his skill as a carpenter—skills seen as low-born in the mage House—were respected and valued. In Expedition, Andevai turned out to be far more comfortable and at ease than he had ever been in Europa. This other and more appealing side of his character could then be revealed, although I had to rewrite a lot of scenes as I figured out exactly how that deepest and most essential and instinctive level of his personality would manifest in these new circumstances. Coming to understanding him in both venues—the arrogant cold mage and the still vain and proud but far more personable carpenter—made his character finally, wholly fall into place.

If there is one thing I've learned over writing my many books, it is that if I am patient, and if I leave myself open to change, even my most difficult and secretive characters will reveal themselves to me in time. Some, like Cat, fall pretty much fully formed into my lap: Her voice was strong and distinctive from the start, and she really did mostly wear her emotions on her sleeve. But others, I need patience to find. In the end, both sorts of characters are a delight to bring to life.

Love and Infatuation in the Spiritwalker Trilogy

To my mind, and in the approach I take when writing, love and infatuation are related but different things.

Love has so many variations; it is infinite; nothing bounds it. Infatuation is often defined within the bounds of sexual attraction (e.g. infatuated with someone you are sexually attracted to) but there are multiple ways to be infatuated that have nothing to do with sexual attraction. One can be infatuated with people intellectually; one can be infatuated with a new friendship; one can also be infatuated with an idea or a song or a new activity, and so on.

All my novels deal in part with loving relationships. Some are romantic relationships, while others are friendships and/or family relationships. How people build and sustain bonds of trust and love remains a central element of everything I write.

Reading across my body of work, one might notice that almost all my novels include romantic love stories. These romances are woven into the larger plot as part of individual characters' stories, part of their life experiences. These love stories, whether primary or secondary, may also reflect or comment on other elements in the overall story or may be important to the larger plot in related ways. So far, many of these "love stories" have been sexual in nature, but not all of them are.

I wanted to talk about love versus infatuation in the Spiritwalker Trilogy because the trilogy involves two love stories: one a romance and the other not.

The obvious romantic love story in Spiritwalker is that between Cat and Andevai.

I worked hard on the character of Andevai. He was difficult to write because he is a difficult man, meant to be layered and contradictory. He is purposefully introduced in a manner that signals to most readers that he is the inevitable love interest.

I wanted to mention here, again, that he is not meant as an exemplar: He isn't meant to represent an ideal man or a perfect love interest. I wrote him as a character who has strengths and weaknesses, who struggles to find himself, who has his own journey (just as Cat has hers), much of which involves reconciling his (humble) village birth and upbringing with the immense prestige and authority his cold magic allows him. He is a man Cat falls in love with even though she knows it is probably a bad idea, even recognizing his flaws.

Here is how I see their relationship, and I hasten to add that readers don't have to agree with me. A reader will develop their own insights into the characters, ones that might be similar to or different from mine. That is the magic of reading.

Cat has grown up in the shadow of her beautiful and vivacious cousin, Bee. As many people have noted, Cat is, in a way, the expected sidekick character, not the heroine. Rather than resenting Bee, she loves her in part because it is in Cat's nature to be loyal and loving, and in part because Bee reciprocates that love. They squabble and tease, but the love between them is solid. They accept the other's faults and weaknesses, find them amusing or irritating, but at its root, their acceptance and trust in each other is unconditional. Theirs is the central story of love in the trilogy: their love for each other never wavers, and they support each other no matter what.

Cat's relationship to Andevai is a love story, of course, but I would argue that by the end of Spiritwalker, Cat is only beginning to learn to love him. For most of the "love story" of the trilogy, through the second half of Book Two and almost all of Book Three, she is infatuated with him and, to an extent, infatuated with his love for and courtship of her. This infatuation manifests in many of the typical symptoms of the heady first months of new love. She thinks about him constantly. His presence makes her giddy and joyful. She doesn't notice or she patiently puts up with (and in some cases, finds charming or amusing) behavior that others do not see at all in the same light.

She is also very much sexually infatuated with Andevai in a way fairly typical of new relationships. I did not want to downplay this sexual intensity because, for me (as the writer), I felt it an important part of the well-trodden course of early love, but also a natural component of Cat's personality and approach to life.

Cat has strongly physical interactions with life and the world (as does Andevai, I should note); she is not a person who lives in her head, who analyzes at length, who stands at a remove from what she is experiencing, who abstracts what she is going through. She immerses in life. Specific to her character, her infatuation and growing love for Andevai play out as much physically—of the body—as emotionally. Her physicality is her emotion.

My feeling is that it is dangerous to assume that a woman's strong sexual feelings lessen her or mean she is effacing herself in a relationship. They might simply be an expressive sexuality that Cat herself openly embraces. I see nothing wrong with that, and while I understand that there can be concern about portrayals of young women obliterating themselves in pursuit of a young man's admiration, I myself do not believe Cat obliterates herself in Andevai, nor is he her ultimate goal. A relationship with him is *one* of the things she achieves in the trilogy, not the only or the main thing. I do not mean to trivialize their relationship either. During the story that relationship has—and in their post-story it will continue to have (if we may, for a moment, consider their lives as a full trajectory)—immense influence on the course of their lives and development and the choices they made and will make.

Andevai is infatuated with Cat as well, but I perceive him as less infatuated and more in love. He does not trust easily; to him, love equals trust equals love because infatuation is not trustworthy. He has more reason to distrust people because his complicated and, at times, abusive circumstances at the mage House, combined with his exceptional magical potency, have boxed him into numerous situations where his trust was betrayed. His initial infatuation with Cat ("love at first sight") is deepened throughout Book One as he witnesses her loyalty to her cousin and her refusal to give up.

However, having said all that, structural clues within the trilogy point directly to the central relationship in Cat's life:

The first person Cat "meets" in the story is Bee (because she is already with her).

The resolution of each individual volume involves Bee's well-being.

If the romance were the central spine of the story, then the sexual tension would not be fully resolved until the end of Book Three. Rather, the sexual tension between Cat and Andevai is resolved in Book Two, while Book Three deals with the young couple wrestling with problems inherent in their situation (i.e. being caught between the mage House, General Camjiata, and the nascent revolution) and with the necessity of learning how to be together when they both are such powerful personalities with differing goals.

While Cat and Andevai meet and learn to know each, Cat and Bee already know each other. While Cat and Andevai have to come to terms with each other's fiery personalities and complicated circumstances, Cat and Bee never waver in their trust and loyalty and love. At the end of Book Three, Cat and Bee are (again) living together in the same household (even if it is founded within the re-built mage House with Andevai as mansa); they are in the process of developing a shared spy/investigative business in consortium with Chartji; and they each have their own personal objectives, Bee's being politics and Cat's to introduce a batey league to Europa. It is clear they will continue to live together within this extended household, raising children together, remaining confidants, and being always the support the other one can lean on.

This, the heart of the trilogy, is stated at the beginning of Book One, in Chapter Three: *Cat and Bee, together forever.*

Acknowledgements

BECAUSE I AM SO GRATEFUL TO ALL THE MANY PEOPLE OVER THE years who have helped with and encouraged the Spiritwalker Trilogy and its ongoing in-universe stories, I collate here, in one place, all of my previous acknowledgement lists, with my most heartfelt thanks. These are the people whose assistance brought the novels, stories, and essays about (and if I've missed anyone, my most sincere apologies; I owe you a drink).

To Rhiannon, Alexander, and David Rasmussen-Silverstein and their friends Jamie Blair and Stephen Blocker, who asked if I wanted to world-build with them. This project would not exist without them.

Agents extraordinaire, Russell Galen and Danny Baror, who got *Cold Magic* where it needed to go.

My most excellent editor Devi Pillai, for midwifing this project into the world.

A long (alphabetical) list of crucially awesome and amazingly knowledgeable beta readers, research consultants, editorial assistants and assistant editors, bookmakers, and advice givers (don't blame them for any mistakes; those are all on me): Constance Ash, Susan Barnes, Aliette de Bodard, Karen Brenchley, Marie Brennan, David B. Coe, Vida Cruz-Borja, Cheri Ebisu, Jennifer Flax, Rebecca Houliston, N.K. Jemisin, Cora Kaichen, Katharine Kerr, Laura Kinnaman, Darcy Kramer, Christopher Kribs, Cynthia LaCount Samaké, Fragano Ledgister, Robert and Bernice Littman, Alyssa Louie, Edana Mackenzie, Kari Maund, Victoria McManus, A'ndrea Elyse Messer, Shweta Narayan, Kurtis Nishimura, Ann Marie Rasmussen, Gerald Rasmussen, Rhiannon Rasmussen, Jeanne Reames, Barou Samaké, Michelle Sagara, Jay Silverstein, Nathaniel Smith, Sherwood Smith, Raina Storer, Naamen G. Tilahun, Mark Timmony, Melanie Ujimori, Anneke Van Couvering, Andrew Vitro, Theodore Vitro, Amanda Weinstein, Catherine Wood, Alberto Yáñez.

All the reviewers who have talked up the Spiritwalker world over the years, with a special shout-out to those who did so in the early days of *Cold Magic* as it first found its footing in a cold, indifferent world. I would be remiss if I did not mention the publicity boost *Cold Magic* got when it was included in the 2011 Dear Author Bitchery Writing Award for Hella Authors (DBWAHA) March Madness book tournament, held on Twitter and jointly sponsored by the websites of Dear Author and Smart Bitches, Trashy Books.

The incomparable illustrators who tackled the universe: Tom Canty, Julie Dillon, Jody Lee, Allaine B. Leoncio, Kelsey Liggett, Todd Lockwood, Nilah Magruder, Lee Moyer, John Picacio, C. N. Rowen Shiotsuki, Jemma Salume, Charles Tan, Jeffrey L. Ward, Wendy Xu.

The ever-patient and eagle-eyed line- and copy editor for this collection, Cheri Ebisu.

Fairwood Press publisher, Patrick Swenson, for courageously agreeing to publish my long-dreamt-of project of bringing out an edition of all the in-universe short stories and essays.

Finally, to you, the readers, who have let me know how much you love this story and these characters. That means everything to me because I love them too. I appreciate each and every one of you more than I can say—except to say that this collection truly is for all of you.

About the Author

Kate Elliott has been publishing science fiction and fantasy for over thirty years with a particular focus in immersive world building and epic stories of adventure & transformative cultural change. She's written epic fantasy, space opera, science fiction, Young Adult fantasy, and the Afro-Celtic post-Roman alternate-history fantasy with lawyer dinosaurs, *Cold Magic*, as well as two novellas set in the Magic: The Gathering multiverse. Her work has been nominated for the Nebula, World Fantasy, Norton, and Locus Awards. Her novel *Black Wolves* won the RT Reviewers' Choice Award for Best Epic Fantasy 2015. She lives in Hawaii, where she paddles outrigger canoes and spoils her schnauzer.

Artist Biographies

Tom Canty was born and educated in Boston, and is a graduate of the Massachusetts College of Art and Design. He is a book designer, interior illustrator, book cover artist, and a founding member of The Newbury Studio.

Julie Dillon is a Hugo Award winning artist living in the Pacific Northwest.

Jody Lee is an artist who does commissioned art for fantasy and science fiction books and creates works in imaginative realism. She holds a degree in Illustration from the Academy of Art College and has been working in this field for over 40 years. Her art has been shown at the Society of Illustrators Museum and been published in *Spectrum* and *Infected by Art*. Website: www.jodylee.org Email: astudiobythesea@gmail.com

Allaine B. Leoncio is a freelance illustrator who loves using vibrant colors and textures to bring stories to life. Her work is inspired by fashion, fantasy, and iridescence. She has contributed to several projects by Metal Weave Games, Die Hard Dice, and Hit Point Press. In her idle time she's a full time cat mom, gym gremlin and sweet tooth.

Kelsey Liggett is an illustrator and background designer living and working in North Texas, alongside her elderly dog and a reasonable amount of books.

Todd Lockwood is an illustrator and author, whose work has appeared on NY Times best-selling novels, magazines, video games, collectible card games, and fantasy role-playing games. It has been honored with multiple appearances in Spectrum and the Communication Arts Illustration Annual, and with numerous industry awards. Always known for the narrative power of his paintings, Todd's debut novel, "The Summer Dragon" was released by DAW Books to rave reviews, named by B&N and Amazon both on their shortlist of "Best Sci-Fi/Fantasy Novels of the Year." View his art at http://www.toddlockwood.com or get chummy at https://www.facebook.com/artoftoddlockwood

Nilah Magruder is the author of M.F.K., a middle-grade graphic novel and winner of the Dwayne McDuffie Award for Diversity, *How to Find a Fox*, and *Wutaryoo*. She has published short stories in *Fireside Magazine* and the *All Out: The No-Longer-Secret Stories of Queer Teens throughout the Ages* anthology. Nilah has also written for Marvel Comics, illustrated children's books for Disney-Hyperion, Scholastic, and Penguin, and illustrated covers for *Uncanny Magazine*. She is currently working on graphic novels for middle-grade and young adult readers.

Lee Moyer is a two-time Hugo Award Winning artist (for the *Small Gods* series with Seanan McGuire), designer and writer; Lee created world-premiere posters for Stephen Sondheim and Andrew Lloyd Webber, Tori Amos and Andy Prieboy, many Laurel & Hardy films and 'The Call of Cthulhu'. An art director for EA, lead artist for D&D, and co-creator of13th Age, Lee also served as a docent at the Smithsonian's Natural History Museum for a decade. He's currently collaborating with Italian artist Melissa Spandri on *The Trident of Aurelia: Book III Corazon*.

John Picacio has created best-selling art for George R. R. Martin's *A Song of Ice and Fire* series, as well as over 150 major science fiction / fantasy book covers by authors such as Michael Moorcock, Leigh Bardugo, Rebecca Roanhorse, Harlan Ellison, James Dashner, Lauren Beukes, Jeffrey Ford, Joe R. Lansdale, and many, many more. He's a three-time Hugo Award Winner for Best Professional Artist, as well as the winner of nine Chesley Awards, four Locus Awards, the World Fantasy Award, and the Inkpot Award. Visit johnpicacio.com for more.

Jemma Salume is an illustrator based in the Pacific Northwest, where she makes art for games and comics. She works as a senior artist on *Among Us* at Innersloth, and her art has been featured in *Mouse Guard*, *Rolled & Told*, and more. When not drawing, she can usually be found reading, cooking, obsessing over stationery supplies, and preparing for some voyage or another.

C.N. Rowen Shiotsuki, who also goes by Engetsu Nao in the wilds of the internet, grew up drawing and making up stories since they were a wee child and doesn't remember a time when either was not a part of their life. They currently live in the oak strewn valleys of Northern California and sometimes can be found wandering the countryside, taking photographs of the local watershed and its denizens, still to this day drawing, and making up stories.

Charles Tan is a digital illustrator and designer from Vancouver, BC, currently working for Skybound Entertainment on the *Invincible* animated TV series. He has been working in the TV animation industry since 2016, and has had the wonderful pleasure to work on shows like *Sonic Prime* and *Strawberry Shortcake*. Today, he enjoys drawing fashionable and warrior ladies, and when he isn't drawing, he takes to the critically acclaimed MMORPG, *Final Fantasy XIV* (have you heard about it?).

Jeffrey L. Ward created the maps, originally appearing in Kate Elliot's *Cold Fire* and *Cold Steel* books. His work has appeared in best-selling books of fiction by Joseph Kanon, George R. R. Martin, John Jakes, and Tom Clancy, best-selling books of non-fiction by S. C. Gwynne, Nathanial Philbrick, Pat Buchanan, David Grann, Andrew Lawler, Bill O'Reilly, Doris Kearns Goodwin, and Hampton Sides, along with Pulitzer Prize winning books by David Hackett Fischer, David M. Kennedy, Joseph Ellis, and Alan Taylor.

Wendy Xu is a bestselling, award-nominated Brooklyn-based illustrator and comics artist. She is the creator of *Infinity Particle* (2023, HarperCollins/Quilltree), *Tidesong* (2021 HarperCollins/Quilltree) and co-creator of *Mooncakes*, a young adult fantasy graphic novel published in 2019 from Oni Press. Her work has been featured on Catapult, Barnes & Noble Sci-fi/Fantasy Blog, and Tor.com, among other places. You can find more art on her instagram: @artofwendyxu; on twitter: @angrygirLcomics; or bluesky: @wendyxu

Dates of Original Publication of Spiritwalker Universe Stories

Novels

Cold Magic (Spiritwalker Book One, Orbit Books, 2010) | *Cold Fire* (Spiritwalker Book Two, Orbit Books, 2011) | *Cold Steel* (Spiritwalker Book Three, Orbit Books, 2013)

Stories

"The River-Born Child" (Original to this collection, 2023) | "Bloom" (*The Book of Magic*, ed. Gardner Dozois, 2018) | "A Compendium of Architecture and the Science of Building" (*Lightspeed Magazine*, 2018) | "The Beatriceid" (Originally published by The Book Smugglers, with an illustration by Julie Dillon, 2015) | "To Be a Man" (Published on Kate Elliott's website as a free extra, 2011; in *The Very Best of Kate Elliott*, Tachyon Publications, 2015) | *The Secret Journal of Beatrice Hassi Barahal* (Published as a chapbook and an ebook with illustrations by Julie Dillon, 2013) | "The Courtship" (Originally published on Kate Elliott's website as a free extra, 2014) | "'I Am a Handsome Man,' said Apollo Crow" (*The Book of Swords*, ed. by George R. R. Martin and Gardner Dozois, 2017) | "A Lesson to You Young Ones "(Sent as a free extra on Kate Elliott's newsletter; not published elsewhere, 2020) | "Finding the Doctor" (Original to this collection, 2023) | "When I Grow Up" (Originally posted on Book Smugglers and in a newsletter with an illustration by Kelsey Liggett, 2020; then published in *Don't Touch That!* anthology, 2023)

Essays

"Why I Wrote the world of *Cold Magic*" (2011) | "On the Efficacy of *Cold Magic*" (written by A'ndrea Elyse Messer, 2010) | "Doggerland, the Ice Age, and the Landscape of the Spiritwalker Universe" (2013) | "Names in the World of *Cold Magic*" (2013) | "Cat's Voice and Deciding What Point of View to Use" (2012) | "Writing A Woman Who Eats What She Wants Without Being Shamed" (2013) | "Why Cat Sews" (2012) | "The Creole of Expedition (In Two Parts)" (2013) | "Character Study: Catherine Barahal" (2013) | "Character Study: Andevai's Character Development" (2012) | "Love and Infatuation in the Spiritwalker Trilogy" (2013)

www.ingramcontent.com/pod-product-compliance
Lightning Source LLC
Chambersburg PA
CBHW020840020726
47497CB00005B/1186